The Notch

by

L.W. Hawksby

**Grosvenor House
Publishing Limited**

The right of L.W. Hawksby to be identified as the author of this
work has been asserted in accordance with Section 78
of the Copyright, Designs and Patents Act 1988

This book is published by
Grosvenor House Publishing Ltd
Link House
140 The Broadway, Tolworth, Surrey, KT6 7HT.
www.grosvenorhousepublishing.co.uk

This book is a work of fiction. Any resemblance to
people or events, past or present, is purely coincidental.

A CIP record for this book
is available from the British Library

ISBN 978-1-83975-226-1

For my ever-supportive LinkedIn friends (especially T!)
My three fabulous sons, my angel baby Nacho and the
prettiest Parisian I know, Webby.

Disclaimer

This novel finally found its way to the treacherous peak of my list of writing projects in July 2019. Any similarity to anyone living or dead, is entirely coincidental.

The Notch will be the 1st in a series of novels, featuring the characters (dead and alive!) in this book. I'm using the Notch, particularly the first quarter of it, to introduce in detail a series of, *very different*, people. Once you've got to know them, there are some real....twisty turny surprises coming your way! Settle back, buckle in and enjoy the ride up to **The Notch.**

In my writing, I explore mental health quite deeply and I specialise in exposing the neglected details and pathologies of relationship-based abuse. That said, I want to make it absolutely clear, this book **does not** in any way endorse or encourage the act of stopping taking any medication without a GP's say so.

List of Chapters

Prologue

It's dark. Really dark. I don't know where Michael's gone. Perhaps he was never here at all. Stumbling on slippery scree, snatching at slimy bracken and catching my face on heather, I'm trying to see but peering into dark grey gloom, I feel suffocated by the silence. I can smell green, brown and dark red. Feel a wide expanse of space around me and hear virtually nothing bar my own breaths.

Mossy rocks, mud and sticky bloody cuts on my hands and knees seem to signal where I am but I still don't understand. My mouth's thick with saliva and my face feels numb. I can't move but know I must get away from here, wherever I am.

Now, the coconut scent of torn gorse flowers is taunting me. The smell so comforting yet frightening. I'm not baking a cake in my kitchen; I'm on a steep, dark hillside. There's a throbbing, pulsing between my ears and my nose is blocked with the salty, sweetened musk of my own fear.

Panting and crying now and stopping to turn left then right, I'm desperately trying to work out how I got here. All I can hear is this strange ticking sound. My own heartbeat? Or time falling away, towards something terrible. Something bad. I'm horrendously scared. Ok, Alice...be calm. It's just The Dream. Don't worry. It's just The Dream.

In the distance a stag roars; a haunting stretched out bark of power and loneliness. It echoes round and round inside my head like a Viking warning horn. Twisting then slipping to sit on the ground suddenly, I realise with a sickening thud, exactly where I am. It's the Notch. I'm on the Notch. Why am I here?

I don't like this peak. Michael knows it! All of our walking friends know it.

No, it's the same nightmare again. Trapped in the night terror and desperately trying to open my eyes, I'm gritting my teeth and whimpering. But still stuck here, on the damn mountain, rigid with fear. A pressure on top of me pins me to the ground; The Devil himself pushes down on my chest and I start to hyperventilate as things on the mountain slow down to a sickening sludgy slide-reel. I feel his breath on my face and hear his laughter echoing around me. I don't know who he is. I never know. It makes it all the worse; a space where there should be facial features, it's just a black hole. Lacking eyes, a nose and a mouth; he terrifies me. He is but a shadow.

There's a sound behind me; maybe it's the stag? I've always loved them. I stop bucking with the comforting thoughts trying to creep in; the night-terror has layers, each time it takes over me. I see the stag arrogantly strutting through harsh mountain-ranges and unforgiving seasons, developing such beautiful rusted fur. That pulsing body-language that they own the land and we're interrupting their space. Then I sink into the black again. The stag is gone and night has fallen. Everything is back to gloomy, misty monochrome. It's all my fault. I should never have come here. *Why did I come here?*

The instinct that someone is nearby, makes me want to turn but I can't. Not yet. My heart's racing so fast, I know I'm going to die. The pressure on my legs and chest intensifies. Writhing and grunting amongst damp sheets, I start to buck. This is the worst bit. A soft voice; the words are muffled. Then the fall. Screaming and flailing now, there's a release like the opening of an air-locked door; a hatch to sunlight and then, blessedly, I'm suddenly free to move.

"Shush Alice. It's just a nightmare. Shush my darling." Michael's here. The relief makes my face tingle with unused adrenalin. My Husband gently untangles me from the bedding and wipes damp hair from my forehead. "I'm here. You're fine" he whispers in the dark.

"The Notch. The Notch. It's the Notch". Repeating it over and over, I mutter the name of the place that haunts my nights, until my heart stills and I fall asleep to the sounds of Michael's deep slumber, in the bed next to mine.

Chapter 1. When the Black Water Comes

Serena

My name means "Star", apparently. Nothing star-like about me that's for sure. Dylan means sea god, son of the waves but my Husband's off-shore more than he's on land. Life's funny. Yet, so often it really isn't funny. Well not for me.

Wrapping my cardigan tighter, I pull lank red hair from Its trap of thick black wool; the scarf I almost always seem to have stretched round my neck and shoulders these days. It's mid-May, but my bones just can't get warm. Embracing solitude, I like to stand and watch the distant waves at night. This fills the time better than anything that would need true concentration like a book or television programme.

Dylan's due back tomorrow, he's been gone for 6 weeks this time. One of his longer stints on the rig this year. I used to dread him leaving, before.... before *it* started happening to us. We'd spend his shore-leave, making love and laughing about how we missed each other like salt misses' vinegar on chips. Now, almost over 10 years on from meeting, we barely laugh at all. Too many babies lost to the waves. Tiny bodies flushed away. Our hearts broken each time the little soul decided it didn't want us to be its parents.

My breasts are stretch-marked, each papery silver line a lie. I'm NOT a mother. I'm not a parent. I didn't proudly breastfeed on the beach or chase chubby legs on rough, shell-stubbled sand. I don't have crumpled school shirts on an arm-chair by the dining table and I've never baked a sliding, slanting birthday cake. My heart's admitted defeat and I've accepted being a useless vessel with the stubborn set of my jaw and stoic refusal to make love to my Husband any more. He has an uncanny knack for making babies; I have an uncanny knack for losing them.

A small pipping sound startles me. It takes 10 seconds for me to register the buzzing in my pocket. It's the alarm Dylan sets for me in my mobile phone; a twice daily reminder to take my pills.

Apparently, it's the pills that keep me right. So day after day I take all 8. It's not an unpleasant feeling to float through life on a strange tide of nothingness. Getting really thirsty and having bad dreams where I'm falling is common, but it's far better than crying all the time, planning how to end my life and shouting at God for his lightning bolts of cruelty. So, instead of being inside a storm, the pills ensure it's just an ongoing hint of thunder behind my eyes. It's ok, I guess.

Sliding the veranda doors open, I step back inside the home that sometimes feels like it listens to me. Weeks and sometimes months on end, the roof and walls are my only company. When my sister died a few years ago, I lost my soul-mate. Don't gasp. Just because I'm married to him doesn't make Dylan my soul-mate.

Ceris and I weren't like typical sisters. Born two years apart and siblings of the same sex, we loathed each other when it suited. She a raven-haired mermaid all junk in the trunk bomb-shell, with an astonishing motor-boat friendly cleavage. Me? Taller, slimmer, described as "academic and wispy". Freckles scattered over my far-too-big nose like a super-nova just passed by. My wide full lips often pursed in concentration over a magazine or newspaper. Ceris on the opposite sofa, doing her nails for the 10th time that day or taking bad selfies, muttering to herself and trying again for a better one.

As we entered our mid teen's we found our common ground; coping with bullying, painful periods and being mortified by our ball-room dancing, karaoke singing parents. Then Ceris and I were forced to be soul-mate-close. Pushed into it. Bullied by something worse than jealous, acne riddled school mates; along came Ovarian Cancer.

Yes it was injustice, loss and anger, that made us closer than ever, just before she died. People call it "The Big C" like it's something impressive, a place to visit or even a badge of honour. It's not big, not at all. It's not honourable either, especially in those last few months before death arrives. Hearing it shortened from the frightening, dreaded "Cancer" to one simple capital letter, makes me want to pull my hair out. Yes, my sister and I loved each other way more than I love my Husband. But now she's gone. I have no one to love now. Not even myself.

Alice

Making a deep-fill quiche and watching my Husband doze in a ray of sunlight in the conservatory, I realise, even after all his recent efforts, Michael and I don't love each other like normal people.

Yes, Sometimes things aren't what they seem. When we met it was smarts at first sight, do you know what I mean? When you meet someone and it's not physical attraction but this odd, mental link that you share, drawing you together?

Well, anyway, Michael and I we just stuck together and stayed together. Like a limpet would stick to a boat. With a glass of wine in me, I'd say Michael is the limpet though. Often, I wonder how I came to be brave enough to have an affair. Women like me, we don't do that.

I'm not a confident person. Not remotely sparky, fun or sensual. Those lovely phrases that sexy and empowered women wear like coats of arms. No, I'm just Alice. Perhaps, I've a nice face. *No*, hang on. People *say* I have a lovely face! Chin length, thick curtains of silken chestnut hair and brown eyes, often sparkling, behind a thick fringe.

See! Maybe I do have a confident turn of phrase after-all. When smiling, my chin lifts up like I'm proud to be me. My eyes crinkle at the sides and I think I'm ok to have around. Michael often tells me I need to stop talking about myself this way. In an *"arrogant"* way. That's how he describes it, *"vain and arrogant"*. Nearly 50, I think I look quite a lot younger than my age. That's mostly due to a life half lived.

Though, I understand, it's best to not mention it again. It annoys Michael, as he's the vain one of the two of us. I probably shouldn't even think about it; it's like he can read me, like a book. I'm glad that our time together is coming to an end, even though it's slower than I would prefer.

For the last few years my Husband's been distant. But not in a physical sense; In a strange observing way. Uncomfortable, I feel akin to the small lone green-pecker in our garden. Like Michaels' little binoculars are trained on me. On my nest, or what you could call my favourite part of the lawn, near the pond, I am watched. At first, I quite liked his attention. Now.... after all this time, I feel unsettled....in fact, I need to be honest with you. I'm unhappy, very. Perhaps this is why I am having so many bad dreams? Anxiety, depression or the need to escape.

Serena

Dylan's sleeping. I'm only half surprised. He almost staggered in the door this morning and after wolfing down a cheese omelette, 3 slices of brown toast and 2 (very strong) black coffee, he fell into bed. Sliding past my face with a messy kiss to my lips, he disappeared but left his mark. A lazy paint brush of rain stain along the wall in our hall.

Do I miss him? My Dylan? Or do I miss another body in the bed and another sound in the house? His twice a day showers, noisy singing and stompy feet on the decking are drum beats that at the time, make me grit my teeth and supress the urge to shout "Leave me alone! Be quiet!". Then when it's just me, I want those noises to echo around the house we live in. Dylan say's I need to "cheer up" and "keep busy". He has no idea how busy my head really is, although agreed, it's not cheerful.

We have a beautiful home; glassy, metallic and modern. We use drift wood like ornaments, while candles of white chocolate wax drip over slate and onto carpets like we don't care. And really, we don't care.

The house to me is a cage. It is ribs and bone and an empty pelvis crowned over nothing. Sofas and tv's and beds all maddeningly empty of snoring, dozing little bodies. The hall missing rows of stubby wellington-boots and sandals. The garden lacking plastic trucks, one armed barbie-dolls and rusty bikes. Yes, I obsess over what is missing and not what I have.

Is it ok to be ungrateful? I'm really ungrateful. I have no monetary need to work, but my head isn't well enough even if I wanted to really. We overlook the sea on a long green finger of headland. The house sits as alone as I feel and I have to walk almost a mile before another house greets me.

We used to socialise with the neighbours, but as the years stretched on and seasons circled us over and over again with no spring pregnancy announcement or Christmas births, we grew ashamed of our lack of success in mating. People stopped inviting us over, tired of the stilted conversations and our wincing at sticky topics of family holidays, graduations and naughty-funny children.

A solid thump from upstairs. that's Dylan. He does this thing where he stomps on the floor after a nap or at the start of a new day. A manly announcement; I'm up, I'm here, let's do stuff.

Looking out of the living-room window, I can see a little cornflower-blue sky, shyly edging along the headland ready to join us for lunch. In half an hour the early May sun will be at its height. With so little breeze today it should be warm enough to lunch outside. We haven't done something so gentle and touching as eat together outside since last summer. No, two summers ago. Yes, I really need to make more of an effort with Dylan. I know I do. It just feels like it would take so much energy and I don't have much these days.

Opening some wine and taking my tablets with a swig from the bottle, I almost smile. I like to do little reckless things like this. It makes me feel just a little more alive. The pills help dumb down my wild streak. They pour sensibility and calm over me which Dylan welcomes even if I don't. It's best this way because I need him even if I don't madly love him anymore. I'm unashamedly in need of his anchorage bound of muscle, steel and grit.

Alice

Michael wants to head to Wales for a trip today. A nice crisp day with "no bad weather on the horizon", he said. Just throwing the idea at me like a penny! Indeed! We were eating lunch and companionably reading the papers, then out of the blue "Let's go a good walk! Not quite a hike, but a nice strong walk. Head to Wales again. You liked it last time darling!".

I almost choked on my quiche! Honestly, he really is full of surprises these days! I didn't remind him, that actually I'm not a fan of hiking at all. A jolly little walk and perhaps a pic-nic and yes, I'm there! But, confused unsteady stepping upwards on an unforgiving incline into the sky, is not really for me! Unwilling to ruin the relatively pleasant hiatus from discussions about our retirement, I smile at him, nod, and start to clear the dishes away.

Friends laugh at my lack of homing instinct. "You could get lost in the veg aisle in Asda!", they giggled last week over coffee and cake. I shouldn't really eat cake mind you. God blessed me with ample thighs and a cuddle girth that has spread wider on my journey to middle age. Can't even blame it on the infamous Baby-Weight. Michael and I've never been blessed by any expensive little cherubs!

I'm fairly successful in my work and he's always rather indulged in his man-child play-boy lifestyle; playing 5-Aside Football every week, enjoying plenty of trendy clothes, a perky little car regularly and annual lads' holidays. These have been his way of enjoying life without the joys of parenthood. In fact, it's almost like he parents himself with his own birthday gifts and impulsive flights of fancy!

On a good day, I liken him to a big spoiled child. On a bad day, his immaturity and lack of responsibility troubles me. A lot.

I've made efforts to get over his attitude to finances. I really have. In the past, when I attempted to apply a gentle thumb of prudence to the soft flesh of his costly plans, Michael would scowl and pout with such vigour I'd back down anyway in the end. I can't bear his grumpy reactions and tantrums, so at the slightest hint of one on the horizon, I say no more and slide the bank card out of my little purse, place it in his hand and leave the room to read, or pot seeds in the greenhouse.

✳ ✳ ✳ ✳ ✳

Trees, plump hedgerows and bracken, blur past as we drive towards the slick stony muscles of the Welsh mountain range before us. We left home and shot with enthusiasm started out driving quite fast, although now we have slowed. Michael is certainly enjoying the anticipation of the surprise and has gone unusually quiet. He said earlier that he prefers this walk, the one we are headed to, above all others.

The long ribbon of melded green to my left's almost hypnotic and as a passenger, I can't help but feel just a tad sleepy after that substantial lunch we devoured 2 hours ago. All the excited planning and joviality about our "surprise day out" has probably tired him Michael out. It was a bit chaotic getting organised to leave! I'm a touch tired so I might let myself nod off for forty winks.

* * * * *

"Why don't we go tomorrow" I suggest tentatively as my Husband stomps around the house, room to room, looking for my boots. "The day's getting on now and we won't even be in Wales until mid-afternoon". I'm rooting around in the wardrobe for my rain-coat but turn to make eye-contact, hoping Michael will see I'm not as excited as he is.

"Oh Alice! I've got my heart set on it now", he wheedles digging about under my bed first, then his. "It's a Spring surprise! All part of our fresh start! I'm a poet and I didn't know it!" he declares, dangling my pink and yellow walking shoes in front of me. Star-dust dirt and sand scatters the carpet and his frantic organising has me on edge. I'm sure now, that I just want to stay at home. Maybe have a snooze in front of the fire, before washing up. Michael looks a little manic to be honest. But I sweep my worries away easily, like the sand from the carpet. I'm just glad he's happy to be doing something for me, rather than himself for a change.

* * * * *

Now, looking out of the car window and trying not to nod off again, I'm wondering if our constant chats about my mistake last year, haven't just inflamed in him a sense of fear that I might leave, but rather an understanding that we need to do more things *together* and with more sparkling sequined joy, than tweedy marital responsibility! I think perhaps, if he does truly show a commitment to a genuine new marriage together, I might not leave him. It's time I was patient and let him show the way.

As the car starts to ascend, I sense we are nearly there, but Michael still hasn't told me where we're headed. Impatient with his vagueness but admittedly, now a little excited, I posted a twitter update a few minutes ago. I just put up a skyline pic of the mountains ahead of us through the wind-screen and the words, "This looks super high! Wish us luck!".

Satisfied with the brief but factual post, I tap my phone shut, let out a small sigh and put it on my lap. "Put the bloody phone away Alice. Stop attention seeking", Michael snaps. Stunned, I watch him throw the phone in the glove-box and slam it shut. The car swerves a little because of his lack of attention to the road and I look sharply at him. "Today's all about me and you and this, the *great* outdoors!" he cries and grips the wheel tighter.

We've brought my car; Michael said his sounded "clanky and jumpy" yesterday and I'm actually rather reassured we're using my faithful little orange Corsa. I secretly call her Cassie the Corsa. Why Secretly? Michael thinks I'm foolish for naming things that are (to anyone else) inanimate objects.

When we first met, giddy with school-girl excitement at winning such a wonderful charismatic man as he, I eagerly introduced him to all 30 of my bears and dolls. Each furry friend, a paw-shake and each doll a stroke of the head. "This is Costas. He sleeps with me. This is Melanie she likes to wait while I have a bath. This is Jacob he likes to come to gigs...."

In my eagerness, I missed Michaels eye's darkening and the clouds of disgust as they passed across his furrowed brow. Years passed, then during a debate on holiday, about where to eat dinner, he spat: "I'm choosing where we dine. You're not right in the head. Who names cuddly toys? Well apart from sad little girls Alice. Little girls eat where they're told!"

His spluttering chuckles felt like syringes scratching my sun-scorched skin. Smiling tightly, I'd defended my cuddle companions, "Its harmless. Just fun darling. Don't be *mean*" "I'm not being mean", he said and laughed even harder, spilling his drink on the veranda. "I'm being honest", and another of his high cackle's, frosted then shattered the last of the warmth between us that day.

I didn't persist in explaining my comforting little habit to him. My Husband had embarrassed me and filled me with shame, and that was enough.

"Michael, can you tell me yet where we're going for the Surprise Trip now". My voice is small in the car and as he makes a tutting sound, it feels like my car speeds up again.

Vast mountains loom above the road; stony giants bending down to meet us. Green, grey and yellow decorating their slate and marble chests. The wind, their whispering warnings that they are the guardians here and we are entering their kingdom now.

A small fly hits the window and I wince at the sound. A rain-drop follows and I'm glad I brought the thicker rain coat, even though Michael suggested the lighter "prettier" one before we left.

"Looks like real, proper rain coming", I whisper under my breath and sneak a look at my Husband. I'm hoping he's going to suggest we go home via Waitrose and light the fire.

Feeling my eyes on him, Michael glances sharply at me then winks. If he could take his hand off the steering wheel, I think he would put a finger to his lips and *"shush"* me.

The view is starting to look familiar and I think I know the range we're headed to. We've visited here a few times over the years, but because I prefer the more walkery excursions over the hikey ones, some of this looks a bit threatening today.

It's probably a walk spanning the foot of one the smaller mountains. I vaguely remember one from a few years ago. Flat, green and lush it was! Yes, hand in hand we trotted through a lovely big savanna type valley with lots of pretty insects. I did like it very much indeed! Yes, a wander in the sunshine enjoying marshland and some wild-life. That, for sure, would be a nice afternoon well spent!

Since My Mistake last year, Michael's made a lot more effort to spend time with me; a lot more time talking about our impending retirement in particular.

Maybe today he has another idea for a location for our holiday home, or perhaps will agree to my suggestion of renting the spare rooms out and travelling more? If he starts to warm to my ideas of the future, I will almost certainly re-consider my own secret plans.

Leaning my face out of the window, I close my eyes and can feel a mild, but moist, breeze. "Are you sure the website said that the weather up here is ok? *Fine and dry* you said?". Reluctantly, I pull my head back inside the car and settle back in my seat. Michael doesn't look at me and now I can see how fast we are going again. He is fixated on the road. His eyes are shining. Terrific! he really *is* thrilled we are out together today.

"Lovely day darling! Lovely day! Look up and see those blue-sky-bits. There, just there!" he's leaning forward over the wheel and nudging his nose upwards to encourage me to look too. There is indeed a blanket of patchy blue, grey and white above us. The clouds look swollen and sour; like gone off milk. The weather was better this morning. We've left home too late in the day I think.

My Husband is too revved up and eager to please me to care. "It's only just after half 1 my precious Wife! Time a plenty, to enjoy a little walk in the hills!" he smiles and pats my knee closest to his. Relieved, I decide to hold his hand in place; I like this new caring, and forward-thinking Michael.

Serena

"Hun. I'm on mountain-rescue shift tonight remember?" comes Dylan's gravelly shout from the hall. I look at the wine rack and wonder if I can get away with another quick swig, before he walks into the kitchen.

"Are you!? But you only just came home this morning!" I call back. My body sags, at the thought of another night alone, so soon. But ever the lone-wolf, I'm already working my way through my mental rolodex of where to go for my night-time walk and what flask of alcohol to take.

"Hugh's texted me twice already, saying Tom's not able to be on. Mind the new kid they had? The one they had last summer? It isn't well. It is still that awful, determined, dose of chicken pox on that *poor baby!*" Sparks sting my chest; a coal fire piled too high. Grief, fuelled by anger burns me at any mention of a child these days.

"Well.... I suppose that's fair enough. A difficult time for him and Rhona. Contagious too....", I reply then tail off, as Dylan finally appears in the room. God- he really is handsome. Is it the sneaky Shiraz or the fact he's been away?

Dylan is undoubtedly a man to attract a second and maybe a third look; at 6ft 4 and broad built, he has no need for the gym. Untidy, dirty-blonde hair and the stubborn jaw of a man used to being told "no", yet never taking it as *no*. He wears the Viking-look, beautifully. Yes, my Husband is to many people, handsome as Hell.

"I don't leave 'til 3. I can maybe do some jobs in the shed before I Go? Tell me what you need doing". He's facing away from me and folding the familiar red and blue water-proof the English and Welsh Mountain Rescue Team use. I can hear the crinkling waxy fabric and soft whispers of tissues in the pocket; items specially reserved for snotty, tear-streaked walkers who think hiking in bad weather or on unfamiliar paths, with just a jumper and trainers on, is perfectly safe.

I don't repeat my unsavoury thoughts to Dylan; he absolutely loves his time with the team and is committed to them 100%. More committed to them than me, perhaps. Ooooft! I really am in a bad mood today!

"Ok well, I've made you a coffee. Give me two minutes and I can chuck together a kit-kat and some soup for you to take with you". In trying to cover up my nasty thoughts, I sound almost happy. He might suss I'm secret-sipping again.

"But, in all seriousness Dyl.... please don't book yourself on shift again when you're just back home". I add some anger to my tone to make it authentic. I've forgotten what real emotions feel like. All I do is pretend.

"Yes...You're right. Sorry. Thought I'd be back last night but the weather was awful so I lost 8 hours!" He runs his hands through his hair and I feel a tug of what might be lust.

No we don't feel that; It's dangerous. Reaching high up I stretch to the top of the kitchen cupboard to get the largest flask out. From the corner of my eye, I catch Dylan slide his phone out of his pocket and leave the room.

Alice

Crikey. This is hard going! Michael's skipping ahead of me like a hare. Gleeful and hungry for height, he keeps leaving me several metres below him. I'm huffing and puffing behind him, but not in lack of fitness. God no! In anxiety! It's really, really steep this path.

We've passed a few other walkers on their way down. Well, not walkers, I could tell by their clothing they were hikers! They've cheerfully waved mostly, but in two so far, I've seen the moist, pale faces, of our shared fear.

One lady smiled at me and grasped my wrist as she went past. Truly jealous at her descent, I sucked in my cheeks and powered on. I even shouted "well done!" at her and the other walker with her, as she slowly staggered downwards away from us. "Enjoy the view!" she shouted back at me without turning, and I smiled when Michael stopped to salute them.

He's so steady on his feet! I've never been that good on things requiring balance. I love the outdoors; flora, fauna and anything involving nature though. This walk isn't enjoyable at all! Stopping to rest one foot on an erratic, and smiling at the memory of learning that word, I can't help but remember in glorious technicolour, our constant giggling and kissing. Especially in the early days of the affair.

* * * * *

Simon and I have driven to a park in a nearby town, having slipped away from work at lunch-time. Eager to touch and talk in equal measure, our words slip over each other; bare feet on wet pebbles scattering a sunlit beach.

"Erratic! Not Erotic!", you whisper, gently shoving me then pulling me back into your embrace.

"No? so not Erotic then, hmmmm.....Are you *sure*, that you are *sure*?", I whisper back. But loudly because I'm suppressing giggles. We are lying together on a tartan blanket you brought in your car. I'm resisting the pull of your long arms and pretending to not want to be drawn in to your body.

"No!" You pretend to huff then kiss me hard, silencing me playfully. "So, Erratic's aren't erotic?! Who says!?" I laughed louder now, giving up to the passion and fun. You throw your head-back and laugh with me. Giving in to your strength, we kiss properly close together; One body, no resistance. Then the rain starts, and scrabbling for the blanket we race to the car, already planning how to explain that we both got rained on in separate offices.

*****

Eyes filling with tears suddenly, I take a few seconds to close them and wipe a tissue across my brow; trying to wipe away the memory of Simon and I. It's only right, especially, on this special day, here with my Husband.

That's the first time in a while I've thought of you Simon, and the quick sharp pain in the details of what I remember, startles me. Stifling a sob, I look up again hoping to see Michael so I can more easily forget "us" again. I indulge myself too often as it is, by talking to you in my head. Exploring memories, as though they were yesterday or tomorrow even, instead of last year.

Simon, we can't go back now. I know this. It's far, far too *late*. No matter how much I wish it, I know too much time has passed. Michael knowing about us, is one reason and you choosing to leave me is the second. Even if I could find out where you went. It's important, Michael says, to remain quiet in my misery and get on in a life without you.

You didn't *want* me and he clearly *does*. Michael has said this many times. He's made such a lot of effort since Christmas and I'm considering if I should really just dig in and make things better in our relationship *myself*. Perhaps, I'm too old now for doing anything different? Lot's to consider.

It was lovely though wasn't it my darling Simon? That discovery of who we really were inside? What a beautiful summer we had! Gosh Simon! Why am I strangely nostalgic today? No, this afternoon! It must be anxiety and the lovely scenery combined; they have me thinking too much and not walking enough!

The wind's started to pick up now we're so high. I've walked, no hiked, for ages now.

Occasionally, I spot Michael but he isn't in my eye-line for long. I'm losing conviction that this walk is about the both of us going somewhere together!

Sweating, but feeling the cold, I grasp onto a sharp brontosaurus blade of rock. Positioning myself, with my head down, I make my legs lock, to stop me falling forward or backwards. It's easy enough to succumb to either fate! Hah!

My walking shoes aren't made for *this*. Michael chose them and irritatingly, not my heavy-duty walking boots. God knows where *they* are! I always keep them under the bed with these ones. Another silly thing to worry about once home. I'll need to set about looking for them. They were expensive, are old and trustworthy *and* I just re-laced them!.........

My thought's start to wander again, but looking up, I see a thick mist has settled in across the path ahead. It's like we're climbing a ladder up into the sky.

"Michael! Do you think we should turn back?! It's getting a bit funny up here now!" I shout loudly and wince as my own voice comes back to encircle me. Tensing to listen for his reply, I wait. Expecting him to show himself again and start coming down the path towards me, I remove then wipe my glasses and wait. There's nothing.

Slowly putting them back on, I can see my hands are trembling. Then looking up through cleaner glass, my heart thuds when all I see is his backside and boots disappear over a ledge above me again. "No darling! Not much longer! The view is so worth it! My gift to you. This view! Oh! I'm a poet and now *you* know it!" I catch his manic giggle on the breeze and try to smile as the echo of it tips and turns, spinning past me like a feather.

Serena

It's a lovely big deep green velvet sofa we have. You know when you go on holidays and lie face up in the warm salty water, close your eyes and smile up at the sun? That sense of weightlessness and peace? I should feel that right now, all cosy and tipsy on my beautiful sofa, but I don't.

Something's nagging at me; Dylan due home yesterday lunchtime but wandering in exhausted this morning. The way his face went all ferrety when his phone buzzed earlier. His napping and contentment even though we aren't having sex. Yes- sex; not making love. See, I'm bitter again.

The drugs to calm my depressions are ok...... but they barely take the edge off when the paranoia and fears kick in. Bad instincts, intrusive thought's and sometimes voices, have always been a part of who I am. They change in tone, depending on my own moods. Nana-Jones always said I had The Night-Eyes. No one else calls them that, just my Nana. Other people use the word "Psychic" or "Seer" if they are really into it.

There's something about the lack of sunlight and long, dark cold nights that draws me downwards into pits of despair, and other potentially dangerous emotions. If only for my own sanity, I've waited impatiently this year for Spring to come. Although still low in mood, my head settles down each time the May buttercups bloom. That shiny, almost painted on yellow. To me it is a signal, that we have several months of warmer longer days coming. For some reason now though, I'm not remotely settled.

The voices are not letting me relax. They have me going over and over Dylan's movements earlier.....they say it's happening again.

Persistent and loud, they've gone on and on, bullying me into glass after glass of wine and keeping me from sleep. I don't think he would do it to us again? *Surely not*. But I can't deny that the signs are there. In sharp focus, almost as though I'm zooming in on moments that jarred with me since he came home this time. The pictures are chasing each other round my head and just won't stop.

"Fuck it!" I shout, throwing the blanket off and grabbing my wine-glass. I'm going to challenge the voices. "He wouldn't do it again. I know he wouldn't!" I rant to no one at all. Staggering out into the hall, I almost skid and spill red wine on the slippery slate floor.

Holding onto the drift-wood railings curling round our stairs, like an old dying man would hold onto a young, pretty lover, I wait a few seconds and don't climb yet. Within the minute, I'm back on dry land again and the floor steadies. My Dylan wouldn't do it to me again. He knows I can't go to the edge of that cliff again. He knows!

Step by step, I creep up the stairs like he's in the house and not sat bored to death in the mountain rescue station, miles away.

Slowly swinging his office door open like a shy cow-boy, I rub my eyes to adjust to the sudden harsh brightness; he's forgotten to turn his desk-lamp off again. Sitting down on his office chair, the grumpy old seat makes an angry sound at my bony arse deciding to invade its privacy.

I'm not even sure where to start looking to be honest. It's been years since he ended it with her. At the sudden surge of images, my heart clenches. A sea anemone touched by an unwelcome finger; the little hidden creature twitching itself inwards, preferring to be left alone.

Bronwyn's big round smiling face pressed up against a fluffy grey grumpy looking cat. Selfie after selfie in his phone. Her breasts on show. Her huge satisfied smile. Dylan's long-winded fairy-tale texts to her. His distorted face pressed up to the stippled glass, of our front door. Him yelling that it meant nothing and she was just a comfort. My, now dead, sister holding me as I sobbed and sobbed.

The images are painful, and so stark, I wonder if I really should dare to yet again, go looking. Is it worth it? Maybe I should be one of those Wives who simply turns the other cheek? Is it a Stepford Wives'? Or is that something else? Gosh, I'm a bit drunk actually.

Holding on to the chair arms I let my head drop forward, my chin almost touching my chest. A silent prayer to the fidelity Gods that again, as I check up on him, I find nothing. Maybe you wouldn't understand, but finding nothing every few weeks is a treacle dark comfort that sticks to my ribs. A devilish nourishment that I feel guilty about, yet feast on again and again. Obsession or addiction? Who care's? It helps me, I think.

There's no point in checking his computer; he changes the password every 7 days. We've battled over and over about it of course but in all honesty, his accounts work offshore and volunteering with the Mountain Rescue is delicate. So last year I had to backdown and drop my bloody sword in defeat.

I'm so tired and sad most of the time, I prefer to reserve my energy for late night crying and lonely walks on the shore, when sleep drifts from my grasp. In a strange way, the pills have smothered the pain of his affair. Maybe that's why he likes me to take them? This thought isn't new but it is unwelcome.

Tipping back in the chair, it tells me off again so I tut in reply. Swivelling left, then right, a smile forms. Perhaps I'm the one who should have a big fluffy cat, a gun with a silencer and even a silver toothed bad-guy to do my bidding. In fact, I could take that bitches cat! We already know she's happy to share her moth-ball riddled pussy, with any Tom, Dick and Harry.

Barking a short laugh, I play at swivelling the chair round and round again and kicking my legs out. Hmmmm, I probably shouldn't have taken my evening pills and drunk so much wine!

Reluctantly coming to a stand-still and half-heartedly sliding paper-work this way and that, I flick through Dylan's journal. Bored and needing to re-fill my glass, I realise this is rather silly now. Turning the chair to face the door, ready to go back downstairs, I accidentally catch some post-it-notes with the sleeve of my dressing-gown. They flutter to the carpet like feathers from a pillow-fight and for a few seconds I just stare at them.

Dylan and I once had a pillow fight in a fancy spa hotel in Cardiff. It was our 1st wedding anniversary. We didn't leave the room for the whole weekend and it resulted in my first pregnancy. We were *so* in love once. Connected on every level. Our biggest connection was hope and now all is lost. But this, my snooping and fear of yet another affair, is all his fault.

Bending to pick up the mess, I spot something poking out from under the filing cabinet. Dylan always was messy, and a hoarder! Tugging at what looks like black cartoon ears, my first blurry thought is how odd!

Lifting the small Mickey Mouse shaped frame out, I can see the tiny writing on the back says Disney-land Paris. The picture shows a blonde man, with a child seated on his shoulders. Frowning and still not quite getting it, I squint closely at the slightly greasy glass. Spitting on to it, I polish it with the palm of my hand. My fingers are shaking; they're faster on the pick-up than my brain.

The picture's Dylan. Yes, that's my Husband. Ok. But the child? I have no idea who he is. He looks like Dylan. That's funny! No, it's not funny. That child looks like my Husband. But we don't have any children. Dylan is smiling his special-happy-smile. Big and wide, I can see the gap between his top front teeth. The child's about 5, no at least 6 years old. He has wavy, light, red hair and a prominent gap between his two front teeth. Just like Dylan and his mum.

A family trait they laugh about every Christmas. "You could post the mail through it!" my father-in-law jokes every year, pouring the Sherry and handing out cheese straws.

Black, blue, deafening and murderous the agony and rage sweeps me up and I start to drown. No fight in me left I just let the horror sweep over me again and again dashing me against rocks as I scream in agony. From the road outside our house, all you can hear is a woman in pain and the smashing of what used to be, a reasonably tidy home office.

Alice

Pebbles tumble towards my feet; dozens of little stony children chasing a tide. Stumbling again, I reach out automatically to grasp at the tails of Michaels' walking jacket. But look up to see he's goating up and away ahead of me again. His balance seems perfect. It's like he's taunting me with his skills.

Clenching my jaw, I'm going to let my teeth grind and squeak. He can't hear me up here! "For god sakes, Alice! Stop making that god-awful sound!" he says when I accidentally gurn in frustration at an elusive crossword clue in the Guardian or try to find the right funny phrase for an important Tweet or Facebook post.

Dear God, I wish I was down at the pub along the road that spans the mountain. Slowly sipping a glass of white wine and getting red in the face from the candles that adorn a pock-marked and scratched old table. Yes, I want to be anywhere than on this ridiculous hike! Michael said it was easy but it's not! "Michael, how much further to the surprise bit! I'm struggling here!" I call, trying to sound perky but failing.

"Not far darling! Only a little while yet! You can go past me and be the leader... in only a few minutes in fact!" That's good. It's nearly over. Once we've been to his surprise bit, we're half way home. Well, at least half way to a nice drink and a bite to eat!

Standing up, brushing my hands on my knees and wiping my cheeks with my sleeve, I stop for a few seconds to try and enjoy the view. So intent on staying on my feet, I haven't really taken in the surroundings. Feeling clammy, I decide to take my bobble hat off and run my hands through my hair. My fringe needs cutting and the strands are getting in my eyes.

Brushing away tangled waves from my ears, that have got sticky and almost curly from the atmosphere, I lick my lips and it punches me in the chest that we're really high up. Much higher than I initially thought. Granite claws of drama and menace surround us.

Yes, *menace*. I'm scared actually. The jagged rocks reach up to the greying sky to grasp white, hair-like, wisps of cloud and fog; the day is getting older and getting older *fast*. "Michael! I want to go down! The sun's going home before *us*! And some iffy weather is setting in. To be honest, darling…. I'm a wee bit afraid".

I used your word there Simon. "Wee" is such a lovely Scottish word. Wee like yelling with joy, going down a play-park slide. Wee like a small black licky dog. Wee like a dram of whiskey, by a dusty stony hearth.

Oh Simon! Here I go again! It seems that I like to revert to thoughts of you mostly when I'm upset. We had such a blessed friendship; literature, art, vanilla slumber parties and deleted text conversations. It was harmless and heart-full, until we stepped into the land of lovers. But that's not for now. I need to get safely up and down this peak without a hitch!

A flash of pink and red catches my attention; It's another walker. Blonde, rangy and athletic, she grasps my right arm and skids to a stand-still up close to me. She's in her thirties, maybe a touch younger and rather bravely, has shorts on!

"Are you ok? I'd no idea The Notch would be this hard! Bloody Hell! It's incredibly steep, sugar-plum!" she says and smiles widely. The setting sun highlights her eyes and I'm dazzled by lizard green and gold flashes. "If you want, you can come down with us?" She smiles again at me; full lips and a small mole by her chin, make me want to hug her close to me. I don't know why I'm taking in all these details, but she feels important.

Michael's stood up high behind her. He has his back to the sun and is looking down at us. I can't see his expression but I can see his form. He's stiff and solid like the rocks around him. It's like he owns this place. Oddly, I wonder if he's climbed this peak before. If so, then I'm safer than I thought; he'll know how to get up and down easiest. I think I'll ask him when we reach the top. The blonde woman's talking again. "Yes, you look knackered. Come down with us!" She has a Scottish accent, but with a Yorkshire lilt. I feel a little better.

"It's ok, my Husband's just there", I point upwards and Michael slowly waves back at us. The blonde woman looks towards him and then me. I start to speak again, to say I will see her soon, but she looks down at my flimsy walking shoes and frowns. "If you're sure?".

One, two, three then four heartbeats pass between us. "Be careful in those shoes......" she lets go of my arm, salutes and slides away from me, down the path. "Good luck and God-Speed to the pub!" she cries and laughs then disappears from view. Bubbles of lava and sugar; her voice is high yet husky. It stays with me long after she leaves. With her gone and no sign of Michael, I feel alone again.

I should have gone with them. We could share a bottle of wine and talk about music and food. Maybe laugh about difficult crosswords and grumble about politics.

I don't want to be here high up, cold and damp anymore. Hang on. Did she say The *Notch?* Gasping, I slide to a sitting position with a boulder at my back. "Michael! Michael!" I call but there's no reply.

Chapter 2: To Be Fallen and Broken

Serena

Sitting on the floor of my Husband's office, I'm surrounded by the ragged flesh of wire-snakes and glittering shards of plastic, that only destroying an entire home office can create.

Screaming and grunting, I've dragged plugs from sockets, wires from plugs and kicked and stomped on anything worthy of my rage. Hurling big metal drawers out of the comfort of their desk, I briefly imagined a morgue drawer being pulled open and my own body being exposed to examination. Tearing up letters, documents and books and cutting myself several times, I eventually ended up here, in a sad looking broken-doll position.

The room's carnage; complete devastation and the only thing left intact is that fucking photograph. It sits propped up against the wheel of the office chair, which itself is lying on its side in front of me; now a grey and black plastic skeleton as if in foetal position. Yes, the chair's given up and I think this time, maybe I will too.

Killer-hands of anger and loss, press down again on my ribs, making it difficult for me to breathe evenly. Was it ever over? Has he lied to me for all the years since he said it was? My minds racing; flicking and tearing through every excuse to stay off-shore longer. Every sudden emergency call-out to the mountains. I can't stop thinking of his increasingly regular late returns from mates-dates at the village pub. Poisonous, paranoid thoughts dart here and there across the last few years of our memories. Ever since he told me it was over with Bronwyn.

Hitting my head backwards against the wall, a patch of plasterboard shatters and the dust inappropriately makes me sneeze like this is all a big joke. It *is* a joke! Leaning forwards into a crouching position I stretch long shaking fingers out to grasp at the little photo-frame.

Resting my elbows on the carpet, torn paper beneath me whispers and sighs. Turning the frame over I slide open the sensible little latch holding the picture inside. Pulling it gently out, I know I'm going to see writing before I even do.

"My Boy and Daddy October 2015". Well that's wrong! Of course, it's wrong! Dylan went on a Mountain Rescue Training course then. An update on his abseiling certificate he said. I flashback to his smiling face across the breakfast bar as he sips his coffee. "Serena, I can't cancel! If I don't get this training update asap, they'll take me off the rescue rota". Then my frown as I try to decide what I can suggest he do, to make up for missing our wedding anniversary for another boring training course.

Out of nowhere a giggle forms. It grows louder and I snort. Another one escapes. Then I laugh; my high sharp cackles explode like fireworks. Over and over I carry on. I can't smother them. Tears roll down my face and dragging my hands through my hair I bang my head back again and again until the evil barking sounds stop. So..... it was never finished?

He and Cat-Bitch just pretended, so I'd go quiet. In healing from a past affair I missed that it was actually still a present one. I was so focused on getting past it, and so convinced by Dylan's intense sorrow and shame, I simply didn't click that he seemed to end it too smoothly. Too easily. With no obvious reaction from her, I didn't question it. Face first in a wine glass, wrapped up in the silence of this house and doped up on medication, I've let them simply love each other and create a life out in the real world. With a gasp and rise of bile, I realise it's not their life that's a lie. It's mine and his.

Alice

"Michael! Where are you?! Please speak to me! Call or shout back!" Crawling up the mountainside like a wounded animal, I'm making every effort not to close my eyes; I want to shut this place out and wake up in bed more desperately than I think I've ever wanted anything in my whole life.

"Oh, hello darling! There you are!" comes his voice just inches above me. I'm being lifted upwards by the hood of my jacket and suddenly his familiar face is right in front of mine. "Wh, where....where did you go! You left me" I'm crying now, as I've given up being calm and brave.

"I didn't leave you silly billy! You got chatting to that annoying bimbo woman in the pink rain-coat and I simply went on my way. I knew you'd be fine!" He blusters in my face.

I can't speak but he has no issues waffling on at me. "Besides, all you ever do is *chatter chatter chatter* Alice". Wordless with fear, I watch as he makes little piano playing finger movements with his hands as he says this and I feel a twitch of dread. His voice has changed; it's that nasty nasally tone he uses when he's mocking my crafting or my "boring nerdy job".

Taking my hat out of my pocket and putting it on, I count to ten before speaking; I want to ask him if he's been here before. "Michael, there's something I want to ask...."

"Shut up Alice and let me talk for a change. You really must, stop messing about! We'll be there in another few minutes. Don't ruin the surprise!" I don't mention that now I think it's past 3pm. The sun's slid away, allowing hungry shadows to creep up the mountain cooling the air, fast.

Bad memories and dark secrets are marching together, snaking through the rocky crevices and wrapping themselves around us. "Ok. But please can we go down then!?" I whine to his back. He's already stepping upwards again; fast and adept, he finds and uses boulders like hopscotch squares. Although he's a big man, I really need to move faster to stick with him.

He *has* been here before; he knows the path too well. For all I know he's hidden a gift up here or maybe has plans to suggest a renewal of our vows? Now that's a nice thought! A proper new start.

A few minutes later, he stops and shouts "Yay! Here we are!". Standing hands on hips and looking away from me, Michael's almost a Peter-Pan type figure in the fog. Tugging at his jacket to steady myself, I climb up to stand at his side. He puts an arm around my waist and I feel a little better. "Look at that view darling! Just take it in! Breath-taking isn't it?!"

Turning to look fully out into the valley, my breath is indeed abruptly snatched away. Cold mist reaches into my lungs and yanks, hard. Shocked at how high we are, I'm also stunned by how striking the view is. "You chose well Michael....but....." I want to compliment him, but want to go home much more.

"Let me take a picture of you darling. Stand just.... there". Now, using both hands on my hips, he's helpfully positioning me. A bird breaks the peace; it shrieks and darts out of a small rock formation to my left. Slipping on a patch of wet moss, I cry out in surprise and Michael holds me steady again before kissing me lightly on the nose. "Whoopsie. Nearly went a cropper there Alice!" he laughs then, happy with my position, backs away smiling and begins opening his phone.

"Michael it's really dangerous up here. I want to go down right now. Just like normal, when we walk together, will you please go first? You know what I'm like and this is seriously high".

Although, I'm starting to move away from the edge, he jerks forward to plant me back in place again. "Don't turn yet. I have a clever picture idea." He does indeed start to play with the camera and holds it up a few times, choosing a good angle.

We're on a ledge with a steep, jagged drop below us. My heart starts to bang about in my chest. A ping pong game of true horror; this spot is overwhelmingly familiar. Opening my mouth to speak, he interrupts me and shouts "1 minute, darling! I want to take one of you facing out to view! It'll look wonderful for your twitter feed! Think of all the likes and followers! That's very *you,* isn't it?"

There's that tinny, nasty voice again; a mosquito trapped in a jar. As it is late in the day, we can't really see much ahead of us, only below. We're going to be chased by the evening chill all the way down. "I can't even really see the view now Michael! It's a bit too misty!"

Bracing myself to demand we turn back, more forcefully this time, I hear his sharp intake of breath as I let mine out. "You wanted to leave me Alice. So here you go. Goodbye." The words don't make sense. I turn to face him, look into his eyes and gasp. There's a shove and I'm hurtling backwards and down. Then the wave of rocks, stone and blackness hits me and I'm gone.

Serena

The pills rattle into the sink and a few bounce out and skitter across the kitchen work-top. They look like broken teeth or pearls from a torn necklace. It's been a few hours since I discovered my life was over; plenty of time for me to open more wine and make some decisions of my own.

Toasting myself in the glass of the microwave door, I yell aloud, "Why not? - let's get smashed!? Smashed like his fucking office. Smashed like my life! Those bastards....." Muttering and swaying, I'm emptying bottles of pills into the sink one after the other.

The only reason I was taking them was for him. He likes me "relaxed and happy" he says. I haven't been relaxed and happy since the 90's. Light-sticks and shell-suits. Neon lycra and crinkly perms. Boys and boy-bands. I was happy then for sure! Before Dylan decided he wanted to chain me up in this bleak, lonely, god-forsaken place.

I loved the city. I loved my friends. I loved being sociable and having money of my own from the media research job,

I liked every day but Monday. Sipping the wine, I remember I had a friend who insisted on calling me Stella. "Stella by name, *stellar* by nature", she'd giggle as she read and re-read popular articles I contributed to.

If I'd had a baby girl, I'd have called her Ella. Ella, Ella Ella. Umbrella. Ella. Some music? Great idea. Staggering to the sound system by the television, I skid a little on some escaped pills. Giggling manically and arguing with CD's, I find one sufficiently up-beat enough to accompany the fast-approaching show-down with my beloved Husband.

Alice

Red and blue lights flickering off wet stone. I can smell wet grass, moss and something meaty and irony. I think it's blood. There's a strange humming between my ears and in the distance, I hear men's voices shouting and the engine-like whir of what I think is a helicopter.

Michael once booked a helicopter ride for his own birthday with my credit card. It was early on in the relationship and I thought it was impulsive and wild. Well, until I got in the damn thing with him and screamed the full 40 minutes of the ride while he grinned and grinned like a well-fed tiger. He never once held my hand.

Grass is whipping my face but it's not painful. The damp tendrils keep catching in my lips but for some reason I can't part them to spit or lick the blades away. Stars flicker above me; millions of little lights in a busy distant city. They really do twinkle you know. I think they talk to each other in a sort of celestial Morse Code. There's a voice I recognise now. It's Michael and he's bellowing. ""Help! Help! I'm here! Help!" Over and over again.

The giant whirring machine above us hovers as though choosing a nesting site. I don't feel cold or warm or anything really, although I can hear and see everything in extreme detail. It's like being at the cinema; you're not allowed to move or talk, yet you absorb all these big images and loud sounds and it's breath-taking. But I always leave the cinema feeling shaky and tired; like it's just too much for me. It irritates Michael a lot.

"I'm here! Help me! Help me!" There's Michael again. He really is in a state! He always did panic when things got out of control. No, I stand corrected, out of *his* control.

A dragging, pulling tiredness has started at my feet and is working its way up my body like I'm sinking. A gentle voice kisses my skin just behind left ear; it's my mother. "Are you coming or not" comes her familiar upper-class demand. She always was bossy. I'm unsure why she's up here on the mountain but never mind, it's just nice to have the company. "Ally-Bee are you coming?" she's getting angry now.

"We have to go now!" comes my father's stern voice, further away. It's like he's standing behind mother and she's right here kneeling down over me. I want to reply yes, to keep her happy, but I don't want to go yet; I have too many things to do. I'm supposed to be doing that charity walk in the summer. And there's that party at work. People are relying on me.

The dragging is getting stronger. I can feel it around my waist now. Michaels voice has stopped. He was making such a fuss, they likely did help him first after all.

A stag bellows in the distance and it reminds me of my dream. The dream where I died on The Notch. Maybe that's what's happening. I don't feel panicked or afraid. After all, I know mum and dad are waiting for me wherever I'm supposed to go. I'm just not feeling the urge to go yet.

There's a presence next to me. Now it's leaning over me. It's a real person this time; I can smell their breath- something sweet, like biscuits. Aftershave catches my nostrils and I realise it's a man. I'm glad he's here. I'm not on my own after all. That's good.

"Oh shit", the man says and I want to tell him off for swearing over a dying woman. The tugging and pulling has reached my chest now. Soft, warm hands caress me, they want me to go with them; go somewhere different. A sigh escapes and drifts away on the light breeze curling around me as the hands gently envelope my head. The hands cover my eyes first, and everything goes quiet like a cloak of black velvet has been gently laid across my face.

Serena

Drum and bass pumps out into the living room; an angry heart-beat, banging a call to arms. Dancing and swaying, I try to find the familiar dance steps my school-friends and I knew so well. Big Box little Box- on the shelf. Stumbling forward because I've had my eyes closed, I realise I've danced all the way across the living room to the big, broad kitchen windows overlooking the lawn. That's silly! I tip forward and place my hands on the glass and peer out.

In the dark oily night, a woman stands looking right at me. She's on the lawn and silhouetted by the lights of our security gates behind her. She has on a winter hat and a raincoat the colour of angel-hair moss.

Screaming, I step away, tip backwards over the arm of the sofa and sprawl there; a spider fallen from its web. Scrambling up onto my hands and knees, but still on the sofa, I cup my eyes with shaking fingers, to try and see more clearly out of the windows again. The woman's gone.

Now up, and off the sofa but standing close to the glass, I've sobered up a little with the fright and am trying hard to squint into the darkness. A myopic doll with streaks of black mascara and an oversized dressing gown on, I must look ridiculous. Even more scary than her!

Snorting and taking a slurp of my drink again, I've already decided it must be a new neighbour or maybe someone renting the farm cottage down the road; the guests are always wandering up here in search of our view.

Being the furthest up the coastal path, our cliff reaches out to the sea dramatically. Our land almost waving to the other sister peninsulas, in mockery of how short and less impressive they are.

Dylan's shift usually finishes just before sunrise. Silly lost hikers and panicked sheep all safely tucked up in bed, he wanders in smelling of moss, dirt and sweat. I used to love that smell; the scent of a man who cared. His heart flickering stench of danger, risk and survival. Now, that smell just reminds me of how full his life is and how empty mine is.

The woman forgotten and taking a sniff of my cardigan, I catch stale sweat and even worse, the tang of stale wine. Closing my eyes in raw shame, I clench my jaw to stop another scream escaping. My throat hurts from my earlier roaring and I need some strength left to confront my cock-sharing baby-making fool of a Husband.

The fire's died down but it feels wrong to leave it smoking and muttering gently; it should be uncontrollable heat, licking the sides of the fireplace, all blazing and wild. Kneeling by the hearth, I shovel heaps of coal with lumps of peat, into the dying embers.

My hands grow dark with soot, but I don't stop. Crying again, I wipe my face and forget there's coal on my fingers. The fire doesn't take long to ignite again and a few minutes later, poking kindling into the now ravenous flames, I feel a curl and swell of satisfaction. Soon, I close my eyes to slump forward and put my head on my knees, in the kind of eternal tiredness only the dead or incredibly drunk can describe.

Alice

Oh! Now I'm standing in someone's garden. It's very pretty and well-tended. Yes, even in death I'm polite and complimentary, Hah!

The sun has not yet started to rise but there are lights on the gate, casting an unnatural but not unattractive, golden light across the grass. It shows up a small spider city, making little shimmery pockets on the lawn. The tiny street lights of dew and nests of moist webbing catch my attention. If I were a spider, I'd live here. But I don't have that choice right now.

For some reason the velvety, pulling whirlpool of hands left me in this unfamiliar place. Indeed, it's not like they say- the deep sing song voice beckoning you to "the light". It's a sort of strange reverse birth I suppose. Being sucked downwards, not out and then this deliverance into a different place with different things and different thoughts and sights and sounds.

The whirl-pool was warm and determined, so I just went with it and here I am. In some strange person's garden with what looks like a fancy BMW and an old gold mini in the drive.

Michael would like that Beemer. Oh! Michael! Hah! I actually forgot about him then, for a time. That's forgivable, seeing as he forgot all about me up on that damn mountain. Once he stopped shouting and the lights from the helicopter faded into the dark, I realised that he'd left me there. Yes, for sure I was already "gone" (a nice delicate way to say dead) but that's no excuse.

He always was selfish, but in all honesty yelling for help and buggering off while I lay there in the moss and bracken below him, really takes the biscuit. He didn't know I was dead, only me!

That poor lady who just yelled like a banshee in the house in front of me, must be having a fit! I didn't mean to scare her. I just sort of got plopped here on her spider city lawn and then she saw me, just as I saw her. She's disappeared from view and it's gone all quiet. Maybe I should just go and have a wander and come back when the sun fully reappears? I can test out the theory that you only see ghosts in the dark.

Serena

I hate sunrise; that cold looking sky and too-loud muttering birdsong only ever gets on my nerves. The start of a new day is all fair and well but, in my world, it's just another day to get on with that scratchy itchy pain in my soul that never seems to quite go away.

I'm a miserable creature, but today of all days, I deserve to be! As the sun comes up over the headland, I fill the kettle and watch it boil, all the while remembering what I discovered last night. I can't help but release a moan followed by a guttural sob. Ugly facial expressions and animalistic sounds, that frightening hint of my emotions growing bigger than I can cope with.

Tightly holding the empty mug, I lean forward over the worktop to feel the cool of the stainless-steel hood over the hob pressed against my forehead. The glass is smeared all over, from me doing this several times a day. For a beat I'm ashamed to be so miserable.

While the kettle rattles and spurts, promising a full shouty-boil, I catch sight of the clock on the wall above me. It's just past 7am. Dylan will be dropped off soon. He'll be expecting his usual breakfast-roll, two coffees and one quick, passionless kiss. Not today though; today I'm having the roll and he's going to explain to me, how the Hell he's managed to become a parent without his Wife not even knowing about it.

It's funny how after only a few hours with too little sleep and too much pain, I have this strangely clear view on things. A damp towel clearing streaks from a shower-door or the volume turned up on a favourite song.

"I like mine with milk". A whisper like cold mist on a lake. "With milk", the mist persists. I like mine black, my own head seems to reply. The steam in my cup swirls and turns above the black coffee that I wasn't even aware I'd poured. The Night-Voices are back again, but I'm not taking any medication to silence them. Without my Husband, I'm going to need the company.

Squatting down into the fridge, it feels like I'm on auto-pilot and without meaning to, I gently pour milk into the rippling black depths. My reflection disappears as the milk clouds the coffee and I feel like I am *inside* a whooshing sound. I tilt backwards suddenly, as though I've just been dropped from above and landed in my own kitchen. There's a movement to my right. Turning sharply, I catch the flash of a rabbit darting under the fence. Slamming the coffee cup down I run towards the window. Of course, there's nothing there. Actually, I need to take some painkillers- my head's pounding; it feels like the dance music is still on.

Sunrise hands are stroking the large peace lily I have growing in a pot on the floor by the door onto the veranda. Tracing my own finger-tips over its single white flower, and down the stem it reminds me of how Dylan used to touch me; when it was just me, he wanted. My throat tightens again and without thinking, I pinch the flower so tightly, the stem breaks. Regretting my brutality instantly, tears start to fall again and I slip to a kneeling position as if in prayer, for the now dead flower.

"I know. Yes, I know". There's that voice filling my ears again. "Mine wanted money". The intimate whisper, is harsh yet, not frightening. Maybe I shouldn't have thrown my pills away after all!

"Yeah well. Dylan only ever wanted babies, so there!" Gasping and almost laughing I put my hands over my mouth and squeeze. I'm squeezing a little too tight, making finger-marks on my jaw, but I don't care. It makes more sense to put my hands over my ears, but I never make sense these days anyway. Gravel crunching outside. Teeth on ice. Dylan's home.

Alice

Before I could go for my wander, a car pulled into the drive and nearly knocked me off my friend's gate! A man is getting out of that van, like a cow rustler leaps off a stallion. Not a care in the world yet I know, you know...we all know, he's plenty to care about and plenty to feel bad for!

I recognised his face as soon as the door creaked open and he stomped those familiar boots on the gravel. That poor woman in there! She's half mad with his nonsense.... Well maybe two thirds mad.

Ok, it was nice of him to be the first to reach me. Scaling down the rocks like a Tarantula, he was really quite impressive but that doesn't make up for what he's done to my new friend! Although new here, I know what's gone on. I've inherited it from him, somehow. This knowledge of their history.

Being dead and on the ground yet also hovering above him, I was able to watch from all angles this handsome chap. Even having a bit of a letch at one point.

If Michael was there, he'd have frowned, sucked on his teeth and not spoken to me for a week. But that's not a problem now. He can go in a huff with me forever, it's kinda how being a bloody widower works. Oh- YES! Of course, Michael's a *widower* now! Just what he's always wanted. He often joked about "living a bachelor life", and now he's managed to pop me off like a cork out of a champagne bottle. The force with which he gave me that shove?! My Husband should be in the logging trade. Timber! Over I went. *The bastard.*

These none-feelings are strange but not unpleasant. You know when you slide into the jacuzzi at a hotel spa? And there's this memory of how it felt the last time; like you never left? An enveloping, warm, fuzzy feeling that everything is ok and always will be. That's how it feels to be dead. Acceptance. Comfort. The gentle kiss of a friend. A hand stroking your hair as you drift off to sleep. It's really not that bad! What *is bad*, is knowing I'm here before my time, because a man I trusted and loved, put me here.

Perhaps this is why I'm here, sat on the Sad-Lady's gate watching her (rather dishy) philandering Husband for a reason. Seeing her make coffee this morning I felt a terrible sense of loss; she's younger than me but she feels older. Like she's lived a hundred lives and few of them were particularly nice. I felt babies' skin, saw fireworks of rage and tasted tears when I watched her.

She's thin and brittle; a lonely rowan tree on this bleak and beautiful headland. I feel an urge to help her; to encourage and comfort her. She's shined before. I get the sense she once was happy and vibrant and full. For a short time. Then the tragedies started and a couple were down to him.

Cocky Husbands, is sauntering into the house now and waving to his friends. They shout and laugh something manly, and he does a little skip of joy to be home for warmth and food. He disappears inside and a toot of the vans' horn sounds loudly. I steady myself with both hands, and hook my feet tighter inside the metal bars of the gate, as they wheelspin and zoom past me and away down the road. Dust and stones toss up like confetti at a wedding. Oh, the irony! I think he's about to get some Hell of a welcome from my new friend: His long-suffering *Wife!*

Serena

"Breakfast on?! That was bad last night! We lost one! I sat and waited with her body. She was on her way, once I reached her. We were only there a few minutes when she died. Really sad, actually". Dylan's yelling from the hall. There's a thud, then another as he throws his heavy-duty boots off. As they hit the stone floor, I wince and grip the edge of the breakfast bar. Bony jagged knuckles like snow-capped mountains remind me how much weight I've lost; how aged I feel.

"A couple went up on some sort of afternoon trip. Crap equipment. Well no equipment!......." He saunters into view, a grin wide on his face at the promise of the usual black pudding and bacon slammed between a big toasted roll.

The smile slides away; scree from a hillside. I don't move and stare expressionlessly at him, although inside my chest is warfare. I haven't showered yet and my face is most likely marked with soot and streaked with tears. I won't even consider what my hair looks like. Immediately I'm put in mind of a witch. The awful image makes me want to laugh. Dylan must be terrified that I've had some sort of breakdown, in the short time since he's been out.

Looking away from him to the fireplace, where I gently placed the photograph a few hours ago, I see the fire's dying again. Smoke gently curling upwards wrapping grey scarves around the necks of my Husband and his secret son. I almost pity Dylan in this moment. I've had several hours to get used to the shock but he's barely into 30 seconds.

My Husband's face goes deathly pale and I'm oddly drawn to his hands. Like a nervous old woman, he's jiggling his fingers almost like he's lost his knitting. Wanting to bark my cruel, evil laugh again, I gasp instead. The sharp intake of breath catches his attention. He looks at me with shock which fast turns to fear mixed with what I *think* is dismay. Perhaps he's disappointed his secret is out for a different reason. The affair over now, this means, it's just going to be another boring old relationship. These thoughts spur my mouth into action and I let loose.

"Was it a nice holiday?" Dylan winces hearing me stress, on the word *nice*. "No. But was it? Like Really? You always said you hated the idea of Disneyland". Words flow and tumble out of my mouth like a flood. Relentless, brutal and unable to stop, I reach to grasp my throat tightly. I'm trying to blockade the pointless sarcasm. "It was just the France one....." he dares to mutter. I lose the plot and start shouting; "You fucking bastard Dylan. You actual fucking bastard". Ah! There, now that's better

A movement catches my attention; the woman's back. She's sitting on my gate and waving at me. My fingers tingle as though they want me to wave at her. Closing my hands to fists, I slam both on the work-top. Dylan jumps and steps backwards. The woman can wait, I've a murder to commit.

"Sir...." My nickname; a secret joke just between us. "Yes Sir. No Sir. Three bags full Sir". The silly, giggling jokes over too many pints in the pub and too many hours in bed.

The surge of happy memories makes me want to stab him.

"My name's Serena. Serena, YOUR WIFE. Remember me?!" Marching across the room, I continue to yell in his face. "Are you happy now?! Now you've got your own kid! Does that cow even know she's basically performed a function for you?! If she's so worth it, why the Hell are you here in this house with me?! Empty, sad, fucked up me!? And for all this *time*! All these *years*!"

Spittle lands on his cheek and he closes his eyes as I rant and rave. At one point I think even his hair rustles with the force of my rage. There's something twistedly enjoyable about finally letting it all out. I've never lost it about Bronwyn and him in this way. Never like this before. Even last time he did this to me....*with* her....the extent of my pain, was bitching and crying, sat in her stupid, glamorous office.

All those years ago my life ended and here we are again. The receptionist, at the architect's office, was actually rather nice. Bronwyn must have heard me in the main reception and bolted for the safety of the disabled toilet. I now realise the main reason she hid, was to protect the baby inside her, and make sure the pregnancy remained a secret.

* * * * *

Running up the wide, winding steps in the open-plan lobby, I call her name loudly. "Bronwyn! Bronwyn Jacobs!". I trip and fall to my hands and knees. No one helps me up and no one stops me, so gritting my teeth at the new, better pain, I stand up unsteadily, re-tie my dressing gown and keep going; I'm determined to find her *no matter what*.

As I wander along the pink walled, grey carpeted corridors, muttering and crying for her, people in suits, one by one stick their noses out then disappear. Little snails poked by an errant finger, they suck their heads back into their boxy offices, as I limp past, fixated only on Bronwyn. On speaking to her and *only her*.

"Come out and face me Bronwyn! You were my friend! How could you?! You were welcomed into my home! You were paid good money to work for me! Chat shit about paint. Order panels of glass! *Not screw my Husband*!" I wail. I'm weak with blood-loss and my cervix clenches in pain.

Three days ago, we were told yet another pregnancy had failed. "Talk to me!" I whimper as a tear escapes. Emitting a growl in frustration, I stop and lean against the wall.

Beside me is the door to the disabled toilets and I feel an urge to go inside. Sliding down to sit on the floor, I start to cry heavily again. With no sign of her, my shouting is now just begging, with no anger. "Please. I just want to know *why*....".

Now I'm being gently guided to a small photocopying cubicle. "Mrs Jones......please....come with me. Let's have a seat". I don't resist.

Bronwyns chubby, dread-locked secretary (name-badge, Jenny) has appeared and hands me a tissue. She listens carefully and kindly, as I ramble on and on about empty bellies, empty beds and the terrible pain I am in.

Of course, I disclose to her far more than really is polite. Her boss's badly shaven arm-pits. Her boss's predilection for other people's Husbands and even worse, her boss's particular enjoyment of sex in the office cafeteria. Up against the grubby coffee machine no less.

Frantically and more than a little manically, I go on to show screenshot after screenshot of the Facebook messages my Husband and Bronwyn have exchanged. Grimacing, humour-lessly laughing and muttering expletives, I show the messages and even some pictures to Jenny and the small crowd of secretaries, who have gathered around us in a small flock, as if feeding from a bird-table.

* * * * *

I remember feeling oddly better, making *Jenny With The Dreads* blush, and the nosey birds giggle and flinch. Simply having someone to shout at then cry with, calmed me down

somewhat, to the point at which I even apologised for my behaviour, after. She handled me excellently and few people know how to do that! Bronwyn never showed up to defend her own honour, but of course her manager and then the police *did*.

It was late summer and it's funny how you remember the silly things. Like one of the police officers having terrible sunburn on his ears and the other whispering in my ear, "your Husband is on his way. We won't be taking you to the station this time. But be careful, next time you won't be so lucky!"

In the car home, Dylan sat white faced and simply drove. I watched him swallow over and over again, as if trying to stuff back down the poisonous truth of what had been going on. We never did talk about it properly. Over the next few days, we exchanged few words. I was waiting for the missed-miscarriage to pass and my head couldn't cope with more trauma. I just wanted to get over it and move on.

It was around then I started drinking more and my Husband started working away more.

* * * * *

Now, screaming and ranting at Dylan, all the disgust and rage hurtling into him, it feels like battering ram after battering ram. I'm not muttering or rambling or staggering or quietly seething. Yes, I'm horribly accurate and organised in the sticks and stones I hurl. He has his eyes closed throughout; like he's doing a me and clenching his eyes shut, hoping it's a nightmare. As I scream on and on, his shoulders start to sag and his neck starts to bend.

My big strong Dylan is withering right in front of my eyes. His skin seems to have wrinkled like bark and his eyes have sunk into his face; owl holes on a tree trunk, dark and empty of life. As he shrinks before me, I recognise him again.

* * * * *

White hospital sheets. Blood, sweat and tears. A nodding, grim faced doctor and cold sweet tea with a skin across the top. Terrible, cramping tearing pain in my womb, making me twist into a knot on the bed. Dylan stood in a corner, crying quietly, holding his own full cup of cold tea. My screams of hurt as a specialist asks, yet again, to take blood "to see why this keep's happening".

"I've none left!" I yell. "There's none left! Nothing inside me left!" the yells turn to sobs and I put my head under the sheet and beg for them all, to leave me alone to bleed to death and die.

"Why can't I have a baby?" I whimper once the room's gone quiet. "Why when they are so small, is the pain so bad when they come out?" But there's no one there to answer me.

* * * * *

In my own loss and hate, I'd forgotten my Husband lost our babies too. Without thinking I'm suddenly drifting across the room and reaching for the photograph. "What's his name?" I whisper. The whisper is loud enough for Dylan to flick his eyes open. And there, in the darkness of his pain, I see a light go on.

"Owen", he replies softly and his face comes alive. "Owen", I mirror him. My heart twinges in pain. It sounds like "owning" like they have each other *forever*. The hair at the nape of my neck prickles and without thinking I turn abruptly.

The woman's pale face is pressed up against the window, by the fire-place, and she's looking at me and smiling. Then she nods. I look at Dylan but he's staring at the picture in my hands. "I'm surprised you didn't destroy it", he says, more clearly now. "Wait 'til you see your office", I announce defiantly brushing past him and striding towards the stairs.

Sitting side by side on the floor in his office together, we don't touch. Exhausted, I've no more energy for shouting. "What are we going to do?" His red-rimmed eyes are sickeningly earnest. He's desperate for this to be simple and clean. An easy rescue. No casualties. Home in time for tea.

"You're going to leave. You're going to your partner. It's not me anymore and it's not been me for a while. Well, more than a while. A good few years I'd say?" The words are stiff and cold but they strengthen me; I know I'm right. "It's not what you think Sir. It's not what it looks like! Wait, *just* wait, let me try and *explain*". He sounds like he's whining and it makes me angry again.

"Shut your mouth Dylan. No more lies. No more." I look away and try to focus on the view from the little window above his desk. Dylan stands and steps back, even though my voice isn't raised. I'm clear and firm and this probably scares him more than anything.

"Let's do what we do best and ignore the truth as usual". Standing up, I wait for him to move aside so I can leave the room. Stock still, I watch as he takes a breath then closes his eyes in resignation and moves a few feet away from the doorway. I hate him for that. "I don't want her. It's never been her. Not for years", he mutters. My gut hardens in dismay at his lies. "That picture say's otherwise. Both sides of it. Anyway, I'm done. This…", I sweep my right arm in an arc around the room, "….Is not *my* problem anymore". He starts to cry again but my mind is made up.

"I don't want you. Not like this. There's a child now. It's not just us messed up grown-ups anymore". God, I sound mature. In fact, I sound like I used to, before I ended up here in this lonely dark place chasing love that I now realise was always 100 metres ahead.

It feels like he's never been mine. The thought takes my breath away but Dylan doesn't notice; he's looking at the floor. I can see tears on his bare feet.

"Get your stuff. As much as you can carry. I'll send the rest on to you in a few days once I'm organised myself. I don't want you here. I've things to do". Turning away from Dylan, I pretend to busy myself with tidying what's left of the office.

I do this because I'm breaking into pieces and don't want him here to see it. He'll use my weakness like last time and insist on staying. That can't happen. *It can't.*

I can feel his eyes are on my back; the setting sun across a desert. The room feels cold too; what's left between us is dry and empty of life. There's a whisper as my Husband of almost a decade leaves the room. His denims too baggy and his gait slow, he steps away down the corridor, to pack a bag and leave our thorny barren marriage for good.

Alice

Little pink petals from a nearby cherry tree have been gently falling and resting on my knees, balancing on my shoes and blanketing the ground pink beneath my feet. It reminds me of confetti again. It's funny how I keep thinking of wedding's!

It's not yet fully light but the sun coming up is determined and strong behind me. I wonder if I'm dramatically back-lit like a beautiful heroine from one of my books; I would like, no *love* that. Very, very much.

I'm proud of my new friend. I wonder if I'm supposed to help her before I can go to be with mum and dad. This woman, is like me but not like me.

Where I'm soft and naïve, she's hardened and salty. Neither of us have been blessed with children; my acceptance has been slow but comfortable, while hers has been a war within. Rage versus jealousy. Hate versus loss. In that war, I see she's lost herself and now, him.

The Husband's getting in his car crying softly. He doesn't look back as he slowly drives past me and out of sight. He's hoping she'll come running out of the house, bare-footed and sobbing. Shouting for him to stop the car and come back. Fix it, make up and try again. Of course, she doesn't. She's as stubborn as quick-sand; holding onto her rage tight. Sucking it down deep inside and unwilling to let it go.

When the Hot-Husband touched me as I died, something passed between us. Something unearthly. He waited in the cold and dark for a second helicopter to come and take me away but of course I wasn't *really* there, I was already on my way *here*.

I can only try to describe the connection I had with him while he was there for me as I lay there dying. He said a prayer and at one point spoke softly to me about his life and regrets; almost as though confessing to me would help him make his own way to Heaven one day.

Of course, Yes! I'm to be here for *her* now. His poor, angry lost Wife who's faced so many terrible losses herself. It's no huge surprise really, I've always been a helper.

I've been here a while now-swinging back and forth on their posh gate. It was fun the first 100 times, now, I'm definitely bored. I watch her tidy up the kitchen (again!).

She's still crying a little, perched on the sofa like a shoreside heron. All stretched, bent over and waiting. I sense she needs time, and me. Maybe at some point, I could go home for a bit and watch poor grieving Michael? Let Sad-Lady Serena sleep, and come back tomorrow when she's ready for a proper visit.

Michael

I really am rather *irked*! It's well after breakfast and last night I barely slept in that bloody cold house. Effing Alice forgot to set the heating timer in the rush to go on our trip.

And now *this*! This, whadjamacallit gloomy pit of a Police Interview Room! It's stiflingly warm and there are no windows, of course! Although I despise being untidy, I've been forced to open the collar on my shirt and loosen my tie a little.

"Thank you for coming in Michael". An officer has walked in, screeched his chair out and sat down on it, in less than five seconds. He's efficient but perhaps a little tired himself. His face is sagging with age and stress even though he is slim and well built. Below his eyes are damson-purple bags of worry but his eyes are bright and alert. This unnerves me; he's been with the police a long time but is still stimulated by a case. And this indeed, could well be a case.

"Erm, I prefer Mr Jennings if you don't mind", I smile stiffly. "Sure. No problem". The officer smiles at me but it doesn't quite feel like he means it. The mean-faced blonde female seated next to him, is also plain clothed and the I.D badge around her neck is turned inwards. Another annoyance I have to put up with! I don't like feeling wrong footed by not knowing what her name is.

My hands twitch with the desire to reach across the scratched and marked interview table and pull the I.D badge strings tight and hear her choke. My heart palpates with the image and I shift in my chair to hide what could well be the warning of an arousal in my lap.

She nods at me, although hasn't yet introduced herself. I've decided quickly, that I don't like her and that makes the images in my head worse. I wish they'd hurry up and get on with this!

"This is just a quick catch up with you since the accident yesterday, Mr Jennings. We're well aware you'll be deeply traumatised by what happened up on Triffin". He's looking at his notes and chewing the end of an old ball-point pen. Disgusting! He really should know better! The germs! *Oh god the germs*! "It's TryfAN". The letters are wrapped in a big fat sigh. He blushes, I puff up my chest and feel like I have a little more control back.

"Can you run over what happened for me, again in your own words. Then we'll get you to sign the statement and you can bob off on your way". His words please me. This is just a formality. Nothing to worry about. I flick a glance at his colleague, who still hasn't taken her flat fish eyes off me yet. She thinks she's intimidating me. Bah! Never! Never a woman with roots like *that* anyway. And that's a cheap blouse she has on. The murky peach colour isn't for her. Not at all.

The bare dangling light-bulb above us, is making my skull hurt. I haven't had anything since breakfast and perhaps am a little dehydrated too. An image of the pie, I have in the oven surprises me and my stomach loudly rumbles. The female officer looks quickly at her colleague, but he seems not to have noticed.

Glancing at my watch, I see it's almost lunch-time. I've been waiting for these two to turn up for an age! Probably deliberate. They hope that in the time I've sat and waited for them, some sort of guilt or desire to confess some assumed crime, will occur. Fat chance! If I can hurry this up, I will be home before 2pm, easily. Must get on; things to do.

"Ok. So, my Wife Alice wanted to go a hike. She likes that particular mountain range. I wasn't keen but she insisted and she really did have a temper when she didn't get what she wanted. We took her car, as again, she liked her own things. She could be quite stubborn and wasn't keen on driving my car anyway. Too quick and nippy, I think for *her*. A real *man's* car you know?" Smirking and nodding towards the male officer, I'm expecting a wink and smile back in agreement but get none. His turn to play musical statues apparently. Idiot.

The female officer lets out a small sigh. My anger at her lack of manners spurs me on. "Anyway, as I was saying, we got there in the afternoon. We hiked quite high, again at my Wife's suggestion. *For the view, she said. For her social media follower's, she said.* She wanted me to take her picture so I started setting the phone up and when I looked back to where she had chosen to stand. She was gone. Yes, sadly, she had fallen. That's pretty much it, in all honesty".

Puffing my cheeks up and folding my arms, I push the chair back to tip it on its legs a little. I needed a little light relief as my belly was a bit squashed then to be honest!

Neither officer says anything but they look at each other, make some swirls on the paper in front of them and slide it across to me. Oh! Good. All is as it should be. Nice and simple.

"You don't seem very upset, about your Wife's death Mr Jennings.....". Ah, *now she* speaks and stops the paper heading towards me, with her hand. She has a deeper voice than I expected but upper class which rather pleases me.

"It must have been horrendous up there waiting for help, knowing your Wife was inaccessible to you. Down there, in pain and most likely dying".

My fleeting pleasure dissipates and again my stomach growls. I'd better summon up some relevant emotion for these two, and fast.

"Oh, it's a tragedy! I'm devastated. She's all I have in the world. I came here to be with her you see. I left behind a good job and prospects to look after her. She needed me. She wasn't very popular and when I met her, she seemed very emotionally fragile and then later, she was....more...*unstable*". I sniff and wipe my dry eyes with the freshly pressed handkerchief I matched with my socks, before leaving the house earlier. "I really don't know how I'll cope now she's gone. She was a blessing".

Blowing my nose at the end of my impressive monologue, I tip the chair back forward, carefully fold, then tuck the handkerchief away.

Pen Chewer just coughs. Ok, seems I need to ramp it up a bit. "Her nieces and nephews! Oh lord! Her beloved nieces in particular will be bereft! How will I tell them!" This time I do manage a sob and even squeeze a tear out. Bah! I imagined her leaving all her money to that lot and that did the trick to get the water-works going.

"Well. Don't get yourself too upset Mr Jennings. You get yourself home to some food. Sounds like you need it. I'm sure you'll feel better with a full....belly"

Serena

There's a warm black treacly feeling all around my arms and face and opening my eyes is hard work. The house is quiet. No change there then. Then a sudden zooming, falling feeling. Dylan- he has a child. I'm not really his Wife. Cat-Bitch is. My eyes flick open with such force I see stars. Yesterday, oh my god, *yesterday*!

Stuffing a corner of the bed coverlet in my mouth, I yell and yell and howl and scream, until my throat is scorched again. Tears come, they take their time, but they come.

I can't hear Dylan's gentle snoring. There's no smell of his madly sweet coffee and no sound of the television down-stairs; he's done as I asked and gone for good. I never really wanted him to; be careful what you wish for.

What now? I stare up at the ceiling and beg for an answer. How does anyone get over this? Is there a handbook, website or fucking WhatsApp group? I don't have *anyone*. My best friend is Misery; there is no one else. Squirming into a ball, I pull my knees up to my chest and groan in pain. I'm preparing to wail long and hard into the bedclothes again. "I'm here".

There's a shimmery voice under the blankets. "I'm here for you", it persists. I hold my breath as the delicate, flowery voice plants itself in my skull. It's different to the last time this happened; the voices last time were bramble-bush prickly. They knew my Husband better than I did. This is something different.

This voice is like a song; sweet, soft, kind and very, very welcome." Who are you?" I ask quietly. "Alice", she whispers and my hair rustles as she breathes onto my cheek. It feels like she's lying next to me in the bed. I'm not disappointed it's not my sister. I'm used to the voices never being her.

Ceris and I would lie together in blue and green sheets, wrapped up like linen mermaids, mourning our drowned fishermen. God how I miss her.

Sometimes the excuses to lie together, were immature and silly; a rubbish boyfriend or bully at work. We lived together before I met Dylan and although in our twenties, we had this unwritten agreement, that together we felt better, even when we actually were ok in the first place. When she passed away, that's when the misery really started; not when I moved here or started losing babies or Dylan was first caught in the affair. I never really thought about that before now.

"I'm here because you need me and I need you". Alice's voice wafts over me like maypole ribbons are twisting around my head; I see light blue, green and yellow. The tones of spring freshness and hope. This strange conversation is bizarrely wonderful and the colours of thoughts and feelings are appearing in my head, with me not doing anything at all. It's different to the other times, but not so different I don't know what's happening.

"How do you need me?" my own voice now. Stronger. Clearer. "You've lost. I've been lost", she says. My chest hurts at these five simple words. "I feel our dark. I can smell it", she persists. A lump forms in my throat.

Suddenly I'm on a hill-side. Bracken tickles my neck. Earth fills my nostrils and I can see star constellations above me. They twirl across my vision and it's like time's stood still while the earth kept turning.

Looking down, I see she's lying in the grass with her eyes wide open but there is no rise and fall in her chest and her face is so pale it's almost blue. All around her are shards of rock bigger than she is; they stand fast in the ground and shadow her body. Ohmigod......this was her death.

"Help me". This time her sweet voice hitches and goes up in scale. "Not fair. Not right", again she sounds a little wild. As wild as the gorse on the mountains. Coconut and thorns. Sweet yet sharp. The smells assault my nose, and a surge of fresh grief envelopes me.

"Ok. Yes, let me help you" I whisper. Suddenly a hand over my mouth. It's mine. *Am I crazy*?! This is more intense than previous times. A lot more.

Alice smiles and for a second hides her face under a corner of the duvet. It makes *me* smile. One dark brown eye twinkles from behind the corner of the coverlet and even now, after everything, I want to laugh. There's something about her that smokes fun. Something I lost so long ago. Looks like I'm going to find out how she came to die on that cold, wet ground.

My frightening gift is back, but this time in a good way. I hear a loud sigh under the sheets. There's a lingering smell of candy-floss and ferns. She's gone but I don't mind; she'll be back.

Alice

Well, we got there in the end! I *knew* she was for me! A good match I think; not like myself and my widower Husband, that's certain!

Yes, we had an unusual union the two of us; Michael and I. I think you've worked that out. He wasn't quite.... *right*. I know I'm not exactly Marilyn Monroe but my lover Simon told me I had something special inside me; something that caught his attention and held it.

I thought Michael saw that special thing too; that's why he chose me. I always felt chosen by him. *Always*. Now the word I should use is "targeted". Yes, that's the right word. I was too soft, I know that; too easy to sigh and open my purse or smile and open the duvet.

Either way he was always in control of me. Nothing too obviously aggressive or dark in the beginning, but always this sense that little strings were wrapped around my ankles and wrists and all he had to do was *tug*.

When Simon and I met last year, I saw a way out; that sweetly dangerous, rosy light in the eye of a storm. I saw retirement together, long lazy dinners on sandy shores and laughter long into the night.

Michael simply disappeared from view, when I fell in love for the first time in my life. I lived for my meetings and intense conversations with Simon about literature, travel and psychology. I'd look into his eyes and drift away in a little bobbing boat on a sea of promises and plans. Yes, I fell blindly in love with another man and in that process, I didn't see how dangerous my Husband really was.

In the beginning, it was simply an affair between the ears. It wasn't smutty or dirty, like you would expect. Not at all. Michael's so self-absorbed and intense in his own pursuits, that my lover's arms felt like a warm shower on a frosty morning. Refreshing, comforting and invigorating.

I accepted Simon's departure for pastures new, although it devastated me. I'm used to times of sadness though. I've never fully given into it. It's why I hide in books of love and fairy-tales and romance. It's why I ended up a librarian. In many way's I lived a happy, full life because of reading about and sharing other peoples.

Chapter 3: Between Worlds

Serena

Day two of no pills and I've also decided (and you may be impressed or traumatised by this) that I'm not going crazy. I've always had "The Gift" but it's never been so.... *strong*. I don't like the word "powerful", as I am not in charge of it.

This time, something has made me more open to it. More aware of whatever messages are being conveyed. There have never been smells before, although in the past I did get images and even some voices. Well, whatever it is that's exaggerating or enhancing my Gift, it's welcome. I feel better today than I should and the urge to drink is the least it's been in a long time.

Deciding to wander over to the windows overlooking the garden, to search for a glimpse of Alice, I'm disappointed that she isn't there and feel a pang of loneliness which is unfamiliar; I haven't liked or needed a friend, not properly, for a good while now.

After Bronwyn, the first time, I deliberately closed myself off from people altogether. I even abandoned all my social media accounts. I hoped it would help, not seeing other people happy, but it didn't. Dylan encouraged me to stay off social media as he said it meant I spent more time with him and I seemed more relaxed. In the end, I simply spent more time walking on the shore or the fields behind the house; I couldn't bear his searching eyes and restless hands.

His determined efforts to warm me to him again drove me mad. I now realise, he wanted me to be closed away from the online world, in case I accidentally saw a picture of the child or him with Cat-Bitch again. This realisation is painful and humiliating; oh, how I trusted him!

Searching the lawns for Alice, I peer into the greying early afternoon and hold my breath in anticipation of her slinky re-appearance. Perhaps from behind my purple Rhododendron? Or jauntily plopping out of the Monkey Puzzle tree?. No sign of her. Nothing. Nada. Zilch. Yes, I'm definitely disappointed. Missing a *ghost*? Well, maybe I really am losing it!

Finishing my coffee and running my hands through my hair, I decide perhaps it's time for a shower! I'm disgusting. Rage and grief have run their grimy fingers all over my body and deep inside my skull for years now, and I'm suddenly ashamed at the layers of filth.

Going towards the hall almost out of the living room, I catch sight of the typical pile of paperwork Dylan always has layered up dangerously on the edge of the huge, granite fireplace. More than once I've spilled drinks on it and it's another reason he started working upstairs so often. Maybe I will have a drink after all; glugging wine to relax a swift clench of guilt is easier than facing the truth. It's always worked in the past. Why stop now?

There's a well-thumbed OS Explorer map asserting itself from the other less colourful pages of the pile. Reaching out almost without thinking, I slide it towards myself and shake it open.

I remember studying Geography at school and although bored to death by most of it, I liked the way a map, a simple flat piece of paper, told the story of something with infinite edges, ridges, climbs and drops. How a simple squiggle meant another few metres up and more of a drop to fall. Like falling in love- what goes up, must come down. My eyes blur with tears, so I step backwards to sit on the sofa. "We were there".

Wisps of words and a grass-scented breath, from nowhere in particular. My hair flutters, tickling my cheek; she's back.

"The Notch. The Notch", she starts to say over and over. The map stiffens in my hands. I have two corners, and she has the other two; it's pulled taut now between both of us. Her hissing is persistent and more than a little frightening. "Notch. Notch. Notch". The map tugs and tugs with determination.

"What do you mean?" I blurt loudly. The Map goes loose in my hands and without thinking I let it go. It flutters to the floor and rests over my feet like a paper blanket. I wiggle my toes, wanting The Map to be alive again.

There's a shattering sound and I jerk up to look towards the fireplace where a glass ornament has fallen and broken, as if pushed. "Him. Him. Him".

The words go around and round the room bouncing off sofas, shaking the dining table and rattling window latches. Lights start to swing round and round and left to right. A large bronze deer ornament, on the dining table, falls on its side, seemingly giving up in fear of whatever the Hell is in my house.

"What do you mean!?" I'm afraid now. I've never heard of "The Notch". Is it a building? A person? A place? "Him, him, him", she's still ranting. The Map suddenly takes flight across the room; a paper bird with no real journey in mind, it hits the wall and falls to the floor.

The words him, him, him over and over start to make my head buzz. It's not like a song now. It's more like a machine; rotating and humming. On and on and on.

Fighting the urge to be sick, I cover my ears and kneel to the floor childlike, as she goes on and on and on for what feels like forever. Then suddenly, she stops. "Who is The Notch?! Tell me!". My words hang in the air as though floating on water; there's a strange wave like, almost oily texture to it. "Tell me Alice", I persist because I know she's still here; I can smell soil and grass again and something bitter that makes me think of my own anger and pain. It's the scent of betrayal. "Him, Him, Him", she whispers back and the air parts, as though a hand has passed through cigarette smoke. The room feels empty all of a sudden and I know she's gone.

Alice

"My tale was heard and yet it was not told". The line of my favourite poem keeps going around and round. A little brown mouse on a wheel. "My tale was heard and yet it was not told. My tale was heard and yet it was not told".

Now, I'm standing on the headland, beyond the house, looking out to sea. Perhaps if I waited here, I could be sucked back up again and die properly; disappear and go to that warm syrupy comfort I was promised on the mountain side.

The Sad-Lady is a perhaps a bit sadder than I originally thought. I'm unsure again of why I've been put here. "My tale was heard and yet it was not told". The sea and shore are fighting viciously below me; waves crashing and rocks shouting back.

"My tale was heard and yet it was not told". If I could stomp my feet in frustration, I would! The Sad Lady did look worried for me actually. Mind you, *I'm* worried for me! Michael shoved me off that mountain and now I'm wafting around like a Charles Dickens reject with lines of old poems annoying me.

I tried and tried to tell her but it's like I don't have permission to explain properly. Desperate to shout the words "My Husbands killed me" over and over, I just ended up splitting the air and getting angry. When The Map started hurling itself about, I panicked. I didn't know I could do that and I felt her fear and then.... well.... I was here.

Then, out of the air comes the blink of an idea; "My tale was heard and yet it was not told". God knows she needs something to do; mincing around that house and wailing like a banshee isn't doing her much good either ways. New plan; I'm not going *Upstairs* until we've been to The Notch again. I know now what those rocks and waves are all about. It's not an argument, it's a dance. They need each other. I'm going to get Sad Lady to tell my tale and she's going to have purpose, whether she likes it or not.

We're going to make waves and smash some rocks. In a polite way, of course.

Serena

I loved being a media researcher. Letters, words, sentences; I could string them together like beads. Helping make stories that people would remember and comment on and want to own for themselves. "where did you get *that* idea?", I'd be asked. "How the Hell did you get *him* to talk to you?", they'd press. "You're wasted here, aim higher", they'd murmur. All the while secretly coveting my little corner office with views across the city, for themselves.

Dylan came out of nowhere. It was to be a simple interview; some basic info on a topic hot in the press around that time. Something to do with his previous job. Terrible that I can't remember now.

Having spotted his profile on a business networking site, and seeing he really was quite dishy, I changed my own profile pic to something more appealing. Gone was the be-speckled bird like selfie that my boss insisted on. The intense bun and buttoned up navy blouse. Up popped pouting, wavy haired me. My big eyes, enhanced with winged eye-liner, and a hint of cleavage. He accepted my link request within the hour and his secretary called me the next day.

And that was that. My plan was to flirt outrageously, get a great interview and sail the content past my selfish idiotic sexist bastard of a boss. Set up port with a bigger company with better pay, then go freelance. *Epic fail*; Dylan and I ended up going from coffee, to dinner, to bed.

A year later I was here. Blissfully bound up in desire and a disastrous dream of family life that quite clearly, we never quite achieved.

Has boredom sent me mad? Like literally, am I totally bonkers? I've thrown my Husband out, stopped taking my pills and started talking to a dead mountain walker. Well, mountain-faller. If she'd walked better, she wouldn't be dead. No- that's not nice. God I'm a bitch. I was never this nasty when I was working!

Agitated and disliking myself again, I'm leaning against the kitchen counter and considering the brandy, although my eyes keep finding The Map. Like a dead gull, it lies still, wings spread in the corner of the living room.

Now The Map's in my fingers and my eyes have found a cluster of lines all huddled together making what looks like the shape of an eye, getting darker towards the centre. Dylan taught me the tighter the lines, the steeper the hill. To me that sounds like betrayal; the closer you are, the more painful the loss when you let each other go. Swallowing back a yell of anger, I put my cup on the coffee table and kneel on the floor, spreading The Map out carefully and gently.

Leaning forward, I look more closely, searching for what-ever Alice wanted me to see. Tracing my fingers across the paper, there are some names I recognise. Dylan's been volun-teering with the mountain rescue around Tryfan for years now. Admittedly not all that interested, I've mumbled "uhuh" and "wow" and "oh really", while spooning gravy onto his plate or frying bacon without really taking in what exactly he did.

Don't get me wrong, yeah, his role was basically to go up hills and mountains (two very different geographical things don't you know!) and rescue people, but all the proper geography malarkey and actual saving people stuff was really over my head.

These days, I'm interested in what I'm interested in and that, really is it. Something like guilt prods me in the chest and I bat it away like it's a sleazy touch. Anyway, Alice clearly thinks this is more important; she wouldn't be here hassling me if it wasn't. I'm sure she's better things to do like waft around a grave-yard in a nightie or play a harp and gossip with cherubs or something.

A shattering sound breaks the silence. Jerking up, I see dark brown liquid streaming down the wall in front of me; a big ink-blot that *was* the cold coffee in my cup next to me a few seconds ago. In the chair to my right is Alice. Well, most of her. She's more visible and more solid than when I've seen her before. She's glaring at me but then she smiles. "Stop being mean", her voice arrives in my head. "You're supposed to help me".

The map starts to ripple and lift as though riding gentle waves. I can smell damp moss and sugary coconut again. Something touches my face and reaching up I feel bracken. Then suddenly this dark, grasping sense of terrible dread takes hold of me; it spreads up from my feet, all the way to my face which has gone numb. I feel completely alone and like everything is over. Ended. Gone. Then I feel anger, dark true-blue hatred. She's trying to tell me there's more to her death than just an accident.

The coffee has splashed further than I realised and there are a few dots of it on The Map. Walking towards the sink, with the intention of cleaning away the stains, my eye catches something scribbled on one corner. Dylan's small spidery writing is noting some nicknames for the peaks detailed on The Map. One of them says "The Notch".

Alice

That wasn't pleasant. Going over again what happened on The Notch. But it was all I had in me to try and get Serena to listen to me. I've felt her ridicule and doubt today. Watched her aimlessly plump cushions and drink coffee after coffee until she ran out of coffee and grimaced over tea after tea. Then she got her beady eyes on the drink's cabinet again, so I had to step in. God, she's a fish!

She's had purpose before and blossomed within it; inspiring awe and even jealousy at times. That Husband of hers plucked her from her place of comfort and planted her here to grow gnarly and wither. He needs a good talking to that one, *that's for sure!*

Michael was different but not good different! Worse different. Michael went to seed eagerly in my world and spread his big strong determined roots and greedy branches far and wide around me. And soon, deep, deep into my bank balance. I see that now.

Here, I'm far away from him- in a whole other realm actually! Hah! Oh how, distance creates clarity.

In the beginning, all those years ago, he was of course very charming. Witty and sharp, he cut through any awkwardness, right from the get go. I'm not outgoing, nor am I shy, but the first few dates with anyone usually are tentative are they not?

Not with Michael, they weren't. He wheeled into my life like a bracing Autumn wind; I was a little lost leaf and he carried me where he wanted. At first it was intoxicating. I've always liked being looked after- hey who *doesn't*?! But what sealed the deal, was his easy agreement not to have children. My sigh of relief was practically a weather front all of its own!

Grasping my hand tightly he skipped me down the aisle quite soon after we met, the return trip was slower now I think of it! Alongside church bells, we were celebrated by the chatter and applause of only a dozen or so guests. Each and every one smiling and frowning in equal measure at the speed of which my new Husband organised our very expensive and very intimate, special day. Oblivious to their concerns, I gazed at my new beau and watched him wave and wink and grin at everyone there; pink and proud, he was like the winner of a pub raffle.

Settling into a routine and slowly avoiding each other's hobbies, we made a comfortable existence. Perhaps, because I gave into his every whim and certainly, because I funded them.

Yes, the rot crept in slowly. So slowly I didn't notice it, until suspicion filled my nostrils and something akin to dismay, then fear, took hold. From then on, I couldn't stop the decomposition, no matter how hard I tried.

For example, I started to notice my friends' little side-ways glances; I was unaware of them before. I gurned internally and twitched with discomfort at Michaels wheedling for a new car or outfit. In the run ups to his annual blokey break away, my teeth would be on edge as I waited for the invoice. I'd grind and grind and yet smile and smile and faking expressions of nonchalance and ignorance, drove me half mad.

Then the regret seeped in. Eerily slow at first. And then fast. Like something had nibbled me, then found it's appetite. Yes, the regret at being married to Michael became almost unbearable. I started to realise why people prefer denial to reality. It was slowly, painfully, sinking in; a deathly injection to my flesh, that the calm and generous man I met, simply hadn't existed.

Looking for answers, I began hungrily reading about how and why marriages become so uneven, as ours. "Why is my Husband so controlling?" on Quora, "Why do my needs never ever come first", on Google. I hated the answers! All I wanted was for him to be like he was at the beginning!

Hunched over my laptop in the conservatory, I'd flinch at any shadow or sound behind me. Ever ready to slap the computer shut and plaster a smile on my face. Words prepared such as "I couldn't sleep! Would you like some decaffeinated tea?" or "I'm finishing some work off for that thing tomorrow". My backside hovering low, over my well-worn wicker chair. My shaking hands reaching for him, ready to take his wrist and guide him away from my awful investigations.

When Simon and I were together, I felt happy, free and accepted. And so, the light and shade of both men in my life, started to affect my rationality. Simon was swaying daisy's and whispering grass on a warm summer's day and Michael was a rain-cloud, no a *hailstorm* sweeping over a pic-nic!

I'd close my eyes and bask in everything my new lover and I, said and did together.

Reminiscing to escape the reality of the creeping fear infecting my marriage to someone I no longer liked, I became forgetful, perhaps even a little lazy. At first my colleagues noticed, then unfortunately so did my Husband, and that dreadful night last November happened.

Serena

Stuffing spare socks, The Map and a rain-coat into one of Dylan's back-packs, I'm invigorated by purpose. I'm excited but too much caffeine has me jittery and more than a little paranoid.

I'm afraid of seeing my Husband; he might try to come home today. If that happens, I might change my mind, take him back and find myself back to square one. Even worse now, I would be the side-piece. Now he has a child with Bronwyn, and clearly has been with her for years, if he and I got back together, I'd be the secret lover. Not her!

Urgh, I need to hurry and leave. I never go anywhere! I never do anything! After our battle yesterday morning, Dylan will be expecting some sort of meltdown today; perhaps me going to his parents' house or even, turning up at the volunteer station. Nah, not this time.

Is this a melt-down? Packing a kit to go up that mountain where my new dead friend seems to be saying she died? I'm not sure. Not sure at all. But it's actually quite freeing! I've smothered my instincts and my even stronger Gift with alcohol, misery and medication. It's done me no good. No good at all. The rush of giving in to it, is rather amazing!

Grabbing a beanie hat and then one of Dylan's head torches, I can't help but laugh. A true genuine if slightly crazy laugh. Looking down I take in my long bird legs encased in bobbly black leggings and I'm shot with distaste at my own clothing. An image of Bronwyn bashes me right in the chest again. She dresses beautifully; like a woman who adorns herself simply to be seen. In leggings and big cardigans, I now dress to be invisible. I don't want people to see me at the shops or in the street. Being seen means talking. It means explaining. It means having something nice to say and some news to share.

My worst nightmare, is that "Hi! Hi! How've you been Serena?!" shout from behind me in a supermarket. That shout of recognition and tumbling happy Hello, mean's I have to stop and chat and actually answer that question!

And lie, and lie, like my life depends on it.

Downstairs a door slams. I don't even jump. She's reminding me we need to move faster. "Hurry up", her whisper passes by my face. The air's colder and less sweet this time. "I am!" I reply and close the back-pack.

I'm pretty sure that Alice is the person Dylan was talking about when he came home. I am even more sure he's the "him" she was obsessing over in her scary display earlier. He was called to an accident though. That confuses me somewhat, so there's just one thing I need to do before we leave.

Alice

Now we're making progress! Sad lady, who I must start calling Serena *all* the time, is finally in on the plan. What the plan is exactly, I'm not sure…. but she's in on it! Deep inside, I know that at least, I need Serena to see where I died and feel those feelings for me. Together we can bring Michaels darkness into the light.

She's changing. Her rage and anger, those reds and blues, are melding together. Going purple and yellow; Healing like bruises. Watching her storming about with purpose and passion, is good. I've been promoted to something she needs and wants around. It feels like I'm replacing the huge grey cardigans that seem to lie draped everywhere in this house.

Those were her invisibility cloaks. Even Serena's back seems straighter; less bent and less ready to break under the pressures that grief and loss create.

She's biting her lip and muttering about a red jumper now. The wool's a scorching robin-red. The colour of my favourite bird's proud little chest. Robins are a good omen you know? Closing my eyes, I imagine her in the jumper, walking closely and holding hands with a man with no face. Now, I see she's placed the sweater in the bag. I'm getting good at this!

Serena

Dylan keeps popping in my head. It's like he's standing right in front of me with his hands clasped in front of his chest. Slightly bent over, trying to force eye contact and make me talk. Attempting to make me open up, but failing as usual.

"We loved each other once". "You are the love of my life!" "I was lonely- I needed someone". "I lost the babies too!" The most recent thud of honesty, takes my breath away so fast and harshly I have to sit down.

The back-pack between my knees, I look lost again. Like I've been hiking round this house for far too long, all alone and with no real sense of direction. In actual fact, that's *exactly* what I've been doing!

Dylan was often hunched over the computer in his office upstairs, running one hand over maps and one down the screen. The images of him blur from sharp focus as I remember this.

When I was passed out on the sofa downstairs, or out walking alone, he'd taken to getting deeply involved in online chat rooms about Tryfan and other popular areas.

On my way to bed, I'd whisper past him and peek over his shoulder to see line after line of mountaineering chatter and weather jargon. You know, all I felt was relief that it wasn't *her* he was messaging!? I never stopped to ask what he was working on. I didn't slide onto his knee or kiss his cheek.

I never showed an interest. Not once. A pinch of shame takes hold of the bridge of my nose and I can't help but wrinkle it in the sudden distaste for how selfish I've been about his interests.

Kicking the back-pack in anger, I yell "It's his fault. He chose her", although, with a little less heat than before.

Google searching for what sites I think Dylan used most on his own computer, it takes me 10 minutes to find one that looks useful and familiar. Impatiently I click and scroll through feed after feed until my eye catches something. "Tragic Death of Female Climber on Tryfan". My throat closes up in anticipation edged with alarm . It's her. It's Alice.

Pencil poised and eyes wide, I scan the half dozen newspaper articles that other walkers and mountaineering experts have eagerly shared, since the story hit. Making notes and growing more and more uneasy, it's almost distasteful how they seem to eat up the accident and spit out their own opinions and ideas on what happened.

There is mention of a Husband and I want to feel a pull of worry but strangely can't find it. Come on Serena! Poor man, he must be absolutely bereft. Broken and devastated. Another pull, no, a *wrench,* takes hold of my gut.

Deep down inside, the worry is replaced by the ringing of a bell. Church bells. Hands held tightly and a smattering of applause. One of the hands is bigger than the other and is going almost white with tension as it squeezes the smaller hand. The bells change to sirens and fear takes hold.

Almost as quickly as it arrived, the vision is gone but it's left behind a sense of suspicion I recognise. "Something funny about this", I mutter and go back to the comments on the site again.

"Why would anyone go up a mountain of that difficulty level in the afternoon? At this time of year sun-down would be well on its way before they started to descend. What was her Husband thinking? By my calculation not just the time of day but the weather forecast should have put the pair of them off!" **HikeLikes26** posted early this morning.

"I was on that hike myself, on the same day guys and gals. It was ok in the morning. A bit moody and temperamental later on. The damp air made some of the path extra slippery and with wetter weather, comes a darker sky as we all know! It says in a few of the reports he was an experienced hiker. Mind you it says she was too. It's just weird. And sad". **MountainBear1975** posted this, when the news broke yesterday.

Scottyburd777 pipes up, "It said in one report she had done a marathon recently. Yeah- a marathon's pretty different to a mountain climb! - doing that doesn't mean she's "experienced" on mountains! Just goes to show how no one really sees the different between running straight and climbing up! I think I might have seen her actually. I was coming down about 2.45/3ish and offered to take her back down with me and my boyfriend. We were going to the pub. Needed a swally after that hike, I can tell you! But this Alice lady, she wasn't having any of it. Wanted to stay with her Husband. But yeah, she looked pretty freaked out".

These people are experts by experience; they're all concerned and confused. The creeping unease is back I can feel the delicate but firm new-lovers touch of a story. I'm having to work hard not to post anything myself. Mind you.... I can use Dylan's account! His is "RescueMe33". Cheeky bastard; a smile threatens to appear but I won't let it.

Without noticing I've started to sweat; it's been forever since I didn't need at least three layers to warm my body. Shrugging off my trusty, chunky brown woollen monstrosity and dropping it on to the floor, I kick the offending cardigan below the dresser and out of view. Glancing at myself in the mirror I get a fright; flushed and glittery-eyed, I look younger. More alive. Yes, I look nice.

Is this what I was missing? A mission? A friend? Yanking aggressively on the grubby hair bobble I've relied on for far too long, I watch as my long dark red hair gives itself up and falls to settle around my shoulders. The spring sun is casting a beam through the window, across my face and through my hair and for the briefest of seconds I look like I'm on fire.

Alice

My bereaved Husband is hunched over a pile of documents. *Mine*. He's in his favourite yellow and blue striped cotton pyjama's. I remember washing and pressing them for him, the day before I died.

Watching him from the sofa (casually sitting on the arm, as Michael would hate me to sit in such an "un-ladylike way") with my knees pulled up to my chest, I'm observing the man I married and getting angrier and angrier.

He's started to aggressively hurl papers here and there, in a frantic childlike endeavour for something clearly important. I reckon he was the sort of child who'd hide his toys from friends then later, become furious at losing them. The toys not the friends, however. He's grunting and swearing to himself. It's disgusting watching him like this. I can guess what it is he's looking for, having colour coded all my papers, I am especially careful with the financials.

The mortgage papers are coded with a pale pink Dahlia sticker. The same colour as the small row of potted, pink Dahlia's along the path to our front door. The mortgage papers are sort of out of date though. I paid my mortgage off a few years before I met Michael. Ah....*that's* what he's searching for! He already has a copy of my will and testament, grasped tightly in his left hand. That one has a little green leaf sticker, and I know it well as he was keen on seeing a copy to make sure it was water-tight, in regards to the equity in the house being correctly noted. It's familiar as we last had the documents out a couple of months ago, just after Christmas I think.

A sniff and sigh of disgust escapes and I cringe. I don't want him alerted to my presence, not yet. Soon though. Very soon..... Michael hasn't heard me. He's making a right old racket; ramming the papers back in their box and whispering to himself. Most likely planning a trip to see Mr Kendal as soon as he can manage. He's too lazy to try and work out the legal stuff himself. He's taken my life, so he might as well help himself to my lovely Solicitor.

My Husband was never interested, of course, in how I like to code and order documents. That's why he's in such a mess now! Serves him right. He's just jumped up in excitement, having torn the address for my solicitor off the corner of a letter now. Taking the small, cherry shaped sticker with it. Tearing it in two.

Oh! my nieces, oh my beloved twin nieces! When they were younger, they loved stamp and sticker books for Christmas and Birthdays. Each big fat black and white book filled with promise; generous, busy outlines of gardens, cities and even plates of food. Identical books for each identical twin, so as not to trigger any bickering.

As if reminding me what I've lost, the all too familiar scents of blood and soil strike cold wet hands across my face. Then the faces of my twin teenage nieces crying, at my forthcoming funeral, sucker punch me in the gut.

* * * * *

Two little platinum blonde girls, arguing over spilled cereal and becoming tearful about mislaid rain-coats. My own face pressed close to theirs whispering "It's ok. Let Aunty Ally-bee, fix it". Wiping snotty noses and tidying messy pig-tails. Tearing open matching butterfly patterned plasters and laying them on both left elbows. "Shall we have an ice-cream or candy-floss? Get a sugar rush and be silly". Wobbly chins, watery smiles and glassy eyes looking at me with trust, love and hope.

Then a few years later, their little hands holding bouquets at my wedding. My parent's looking concerned. My mother rather pale and my father stern faced.

"She stole my boyfriend!" comes an older, more recent voice. It's Jemima. "No, I didn't! You can't steal what isn't owned!" an almost identical voice, I know to be Polly. My own reply to them "well girls....you never *did* like to share...." and them laughing hysterically, all arguments forgotten.

❊ ❊ ❊ ❊ ❊

Straightening up, it's like I've been electrocuted. He did this; that hungry, horrendous, horror of a man right there. He's sitting up straight too now and smiling. No, *he's grinning* from cheek to cheek. His hands are shaking; anticipation and glee is flooding through him. I can smell it. The scent of a new Stirling note. Bitter, acrid and almost overwhelming.

He did this for money?! Was that all he wanted? All I was to him? How long has he planned it? Or was it a just a sudden whim to simply end my life and make his life immeasurably better?

Now he has my solicitors address he'll be headed there promptly. He's so lazy, he will nag anyone he can get a hold of to help him through what is usually a messy and complicated process. Even when it really is a genuine *accident*! I'm looking forward to this.....

Serena

Strutting down the steps and along the drive, to my battered gold Mini, I feel lighter with each step. It's like the wooden beams of the house, the slates of the roof, the glass of the windows, were cloaking me and weighing me down before. As I stride forward, shards of these fall away and scatter into the wind; downy signet feathers from a newly white swan. Every step is leaving me sleeker and brighter.

Tugging open the driver's door with more effort than I expected I'd need; I swing myself in. The car's musty and cool. I feel a pang of sorrow for my old friend. I used to wheel this car enthusiastically all over the place. Meetings, interviews, story pitches. Coffee cups and crisp packets were my only passengers. Dance music blaring and menthol cigarette dangling, I owned the roads and battled parking spaces like the Queen I believed I was.

Things are going to change. They have to. In fact, I have to *change* first and foremost.

Before leaving the house, I posted up a notice on the mountaineering chat page using Dylan's login details. Choosing to simply announce my interest in visiting The Notch to pay my respects as the lady who died had been an old work colleague.

I don't know why I lied. Yeah, I do! I can't exactly put *"I've had a few mental health problems and the same day this lady passed away; I discovered my Husband had a secret love child with our architect. Oh and P. S, I've had the dead woman's ghost blethering away to me and I kind of like her, so think I might go see where she popped her clogs"*. Definitely not the sanest of posts! I wanted to post something to weed out anyone who might talk to me, when I get back.

I have more than a gut feeling, I could write a story about Alice and see if maybe I could get it published. Before now, I wouldn't have had either the ambition or the confidence. My self-loathing has dissolved my creativity and it's a bloody disgrace!

Turning the key in the engine a few times to wake the mini up, I don't panic. She won't let me down. Half a dozen tries later, my Mini sighs and groans then as if giving in to my insistence, she whirrs into life; a big cat woken from sleep by a rough but loving hand.

Flicking the radio on and tooting goodbye to my house, I wheel spin the car on the gravel easily and leave a satisfying black rainbow of disturbed dirt in the drive behind me. Music blaring and skidding a little, I'm away to see The Notch for myself.

An hour or so later, I'm zipping towards the Tryfan mountain range. Noting how challenging they must be to climb, they put me in mind of a cluster of huge grey stone and slate behemoths. All crowding together, to almost cup The Notch within them. The mountains stretch so high, it hurts my neck to look all the way to the top.

Parking at the side of the road for a quick stretch-break, I notice the back of the car slightly tipping into the flower freckled verge. The mini looks half abandoned; I never *was* a perfectionist! It's the creative in me.

Reaching into the car for The Map, I can't help but feel oddly important. Is this why people love hiking in such extremes? I've never been the outdoorsy type, but going on how good I feel in the sunshine now with the breeze on my cheeks, I could be converted!

For some reason the image of a retro 1950's postcard springs to mind. A tall, sturdy, full-bellied man in tweed knickerbockers, sporting a deer-stalker, puffing on a pipe, 1 leg positioned on a boulder, he's sternly saluting the view. The picture makes me smile until a chillier breeze catches my hair and tugs it behind me and without really meaning to, I let my eyes close.

For a brief hint of a second, I feel like I could be on one of those post-cards. It's been a long time since I felt attractive, memorable and useful. My throat tightens with the promise of tears, if I'm willing to give in to them. Which I don't. No more tears, well at least not just now. This isn't about me, it's about Alice.

"It's so high!" she whispers and my hair pulls harder and I feel it twist a little. Next, another tug accompanied by another unnaturally cool breeze. "It was too high", she hisses. The air becomes thick and buzzing as though packed full of insects and I can hear the sound of flowers growing on fast forward.

"Yes, it was", I murmur in reply. Then it all goes still and my hair flops back to my shoulders unceremoniously. "Alice?" I whisper, fearing she's gone.

A loud toot breaks the silence and almost falling into the verge, I yell in surprise; "Hey!". Half laughing and spinning on my heels, I dip down to peer into my car. I can see there's a faint outline of Alice in the passenger seat. Instead of looking at me and smiling, I'm unsettled to find her staring straight ahead. She looks deeply sad. My entire body goes cold as I feel our connection even deeper now, we are here, close to where she died. When did I start feeling responsible for her? The feeling isn't unpleasant, it's just unfamiliar.

Alice

As we enter the mountain range the smells, of water on stone and mountain-muck, become almost too intense. I'm not afraid; I'm dead. It's like touching a picture and tasting the colours combined with watching a programme and knowing what's going to happen next. A strange jumble of senses all coming from the wrong place but being correctly placed anyway.

Serena feels different again. When I caught her standing there, giving off waves of roses and gun-powder, I knew she was feeling pride. Yes, she's finding herself again but I'm losing patience. Tooting the horn was fun and when she toppled backwards and scowled at me, it felt right that we were here together.

Now we're snaking up towards The Notch, her aura's darkened again; she's feeling what I felt. That uneasy, slithering sense that all was not well with the journey on the day I died.

Deep within me, I feared Michael, but he'd been so calm and even sweet at times those few months after Christmas, that I was lulled into a sort of paralysis. I hoped my Husband had changed and I feared being alone, as Simon made his position clear. It was weak of me to stay; I know this but Michael had been my life for over a decade and he had worked so hard to be the man I had always believed he was. Albeit, only in the few months run up to him killing me!

Of course, now I realise, he was working on his plan to kill me, not working on *himself*.

Serena's bony knuckles have gone white on the wheel, so I reach out to touch her but my hand shimmers through hers pointlessly. Still she looks in my direction and smiles; the sun comes out above us. It's ok, together we can do this.

I've spent years studying literature, scientific papers and information in its many forms. Cataloguing it. Caring for it. Protecting it. Befriending wordsmiths, creatives and anyone else who shared my passion for language.

I loved my job. I loved that world. Loud, jostling coffee meets at book-clubs. Light-hearted bickering in writers' chat-rooms. The crisp autumn leaf scent of books lightly blanketing my hair and clothes. I think you know that I refuse for my ending to be fiction; Crappy Channel 5 movie cheesy fiction. I refuse for Michael to benefit from it in any way, without so much as even a tear or a sob.

A fat rain-drop then another, fortunately less generous this time, hits the windscreen and Serena presses down on the accel-erator. Tipping back slightly, we speed upwards; tail-lights dis-appearing into the mist. Red eyes closing to a waft of unwelcome cigar smoke. Yes, my tale was not told, but it *will* be heard.

Serena

Even though it's May, there's a chill in the air. With no proper rain, I still need the wipers on. My little four wheeled friend's straining up twisting roads but stubbornly pushing on. The bee-like hum of her engine buzzing up and down as I change gear and head upwards, curving round corner after corner, is comforting.

The hairs on my arms begin standing on end when we go past 1000 feet altitude. Every now and then a half-hearted sun breaks the flat greyness of the day and the light catches the fine fur on my skin. Little red and gold flashes keep taking my attention from the road and I've started to feel a little dizzy. If I stop for a few minutes, I can get some air and gather my wits a little better.

Swerving left into a lay-by, I pull up abruptly with a screech of tyres and look to see if Alice's still with me. She's gone, but she'll be back. Perhaps this is all just a bit too much for her. Do ghosts feel? I don't know.

Reaching for the backpack, I pull out the red sweater. It's soft and I get a waft of Dylan's aftershave. I'm forced to close my eyes to try to block out the fresh surge of grief that hits me out of nowhere.

* * * * *

Dylan is preparing to make a grand theatre of something; I can hear him talking to himself excitedly in the hall and the rustling of paper. I hope it's fancy wine, wrapped up, like from a good wine shop.

Now, he's walking in and beaming holding a square, none bottle-shaped parcel. My heart sinks. He proudly places the bag at my feet, steps back and looks at me. The bag is large, silver and the handles are tied with red and silver striped ribbon. Opening it up, I look at him, then explode.

"Are you actually kidding me?! Clothes? A Jumper? The baby *died* Dylan. I don't think I can wear red to its funeral! Not that we can have one, can we!?" He backs away from me;

"Serena, calm down. I just wanted to get you something nice. You look beautiful in red. You *are* beautiful". He has his hands out, palms facing me, as if trying to ward off evil spirits. "I'll take it back if that's what you want". His voice is lower now and I think it sounds thick, possibly with impending tears.

"You are stupid and useless!" I shout, kicking the bag, and watch as it skids across our wooden floor a good distance before settling, sadly, up against the foot of the sofa. Dylan, closes his eyes, sighs and walks over to pick the gift up. He doesn't see the curled ribbon, which lies like a dead flower, having fallen from the bag as he walked away. I start to cry, thinking it looks like a ribbon from a child's plaited hair. He leaves the room and I hear the office door slam, but not before I hear a sob.

* * * * *

The memory hurts. It hurts more now than oddly the event did at the time. Gently placing two hands inside the sweater, I ease open the soft stretchy neck material and almost ceremoniously place it over my head. My arms easily find the sleeves and as I pull it down over my chest and smooth it round my waist, a groan of remorse escapes. The sweater feels beautiful; like Dylan himself is hugging me. No, like the arms of a child I've just dried from a bed-time bath. That tight close fitting and cosy Thank-you-Hug that feels perfect and like you never want to let go.

Suddenly, there's a presence to my right. Letting out a yelp of alarm and pulling the door shut, I smash the lock down and rear back all double chins, gaping mouth and wide eyed. In my own crazy and rather ugly reflection, I see another person's shape. It's not Alice; it's a man. A man in army camouflage patterned trousers. Loads of pockets. I wonder what he keeps in them. Now he's tapping on the window. Broad, wide, tanned hands. Fuck- only I could end up here all alone and some psycho finds me!

"What do you want!!!". My voice is high pitched and extreme. "What do you want, please?" I try again to lower the pitch and sound calmer. It's important to be calm and polite to serial killers. I'm sure I read that somewhere.

"Can you wind your window down a bit?" His accent's English. Newcastle maybe. Its rounded but lilting. Rich and interchangeable like how the smell of coffee changes as it cools.

Tentatively, I wind the window down. My old Mini still has the old-fashioned winders, not the electric ones and there's an awkward 10 seconds of squeaking and turning giving me time to blush as red as the damn sweater!

"Thankyou. I'm a private investigator. I'm looking for a lift up, to the Notch. Hoping to meet someone there". He's stooped down to window level now. I'm taken in by light, turquoise eyes. Yes, Newcastle. Up and down the words go, almost like a see-saw. It's lovely. Did he say investigator? How weird! Mind you, it's good weird!

I tuck a strand of stray hair behind my ear to buy a little time to think. "Can I see some identification? I'm on my own and this isn't exactly my, err.... scene". Smiling awkwardly, I feel a flush of relief as he steps back a good metre and starts patting pockets like a musician pats those little drums hippies get out at hash parties.

Dylan and I once went to a terrible hash party. I remember how silly he looked playing a tambourine and grinning sheepishly. Laid back on a wet-dog scented bean-bag, I watched him and smiled indulgently at his discomfort. We made love in a disgusting door-way on the way home. I need to stop thinking about him. About us. It's the memories that are making me ill.

"Here you go. It's photographic, as well". The name beside the (not bad) photo in his passport is Dexter E. Shore. Handing it back to him, I unlock the door. An unspoken agreement that I feel safe enough now to talk more, about his presence here, on The Notch.

"I need a lift" he repeats, tucking his passport back into what I think is pocket number 57 on his trousers. "I hiked from the bus-stop in the village further down the valley. I've been on the go since first thing this morning. So yep, I'm getting a bit tired now!" he laughs and a brief, but obvious hot flush of attraction blooms on my face.

He has a deep, fulsome laugh and I smile back, remembering my manners. "Oh! yes. Sorry. I can give you one if you like?" Reaching across the passenger seat and opening the passenger door, I watch him stride purposefully around the front of the car. I'm pretty sure this isn't the smartest of ideas but then again, these days I like to do silly things, that crazy normal people do, instead of crazy-crazy people like me.

Grabbing the backpack off the seat and hurling it behind us, over my shoulder, he pretends not to notice as it embarrasses me by bouncing and landing on the floor out of sight. As he buckles himself in, I catch a whiff of citrus, ginger and something woody. He smells *delicious* and there's a pulsing and stirring deep inside. Squeezing my legs together, I cough and busy myself with starting the car and pretending to put the rear-view mirror at the right angle. It was already perfect, but he needn't know that. "Hahahaha Serena Little Star!" a tinkling sound behind my head. Alice's laughing at me; it's the sound of bells on a cat collar. She's the one who moved the bag! Urgh, she's a minx! "You're here for me not some totty!" she calls. More bells, but this time so loud I'm sure my new passenger can hear.

"Right! Let's go!" I crow loudly like an idiot. Dexter looks sharply at me. He's probably thinking I'm mad. To be honest, I think I'm mad, so we have two things in common now! We rev off into the mist before I embarrass myself any further.

30 minutes later, The Notch presents itself in all its dark glory. Jagged rock forcing itself up into sky. Now I'm closer to it and within the mountain range, the Notch's distinctive shape puts me in mind of a huge fist punching through a slate roof.

Casting a furtive glance at Dexter, I supress a smile to see he's leaning forward and staring up at it and looks more than a little unsettled; his tanned brow is furrowed and his wide neck is tense.

Actually, I think I can see his heart beating through the rather attractively tight, cream coloured hooded top that declared itself after he took off his coat and carelessly, threw it in the back of the car. I didn't care he'd dampen the back seat; I was inappropriately delighted just to get a look at him properly. This time, when I stared and blushed, Alice remained quiet.

"So, who are you here to meet?" I ask, changing gear and driving round yet, another sharp bend. "Let me check. I've forgotten. I have a terrible memory for names".

Dexter bends his head, to yet again squirrel about in his treasure trove of pockets, and I can't help but stare. He has a scar curving from the bottom of his right ear down to his jawline. It's the silvery pale pink, of a deep scar that although healed and at least a decade old, will never quite go totally smooth and white. It was deep then, and still is now. Whatever caused that was done with intention. The line smooth and purposeful. None of the gaps or waves of someone doubting drawing the slice.

"Here. Ok so, let's see......" He grandly retrieves then waggles, a crumpled scrap of paper, at me. Immediately I see it's a print off from a computer. Even in black and white I recognise a thread from the chat room I left only a few hours ago. Fear surges through me. Fuck! He's a stalker!

Oh my god! He's stalking me. He's come looking for me. Shit! I start panting in shock. Little ooft ooft ooofts in short bursts. My Gift let me down this time! I didn't see this coming! Bloody psychic abilities! They always pick and choose their moment! Missing Dylan's lies and now this, I'm a gonner! He's going to finish me off! Ohmigod, what if he killed Alice!?

"Hey! What's up with you!" he looks freaked out. So, he should be! I've rumbled him! Do I still have that torch in the glove-box? I could whack him over the head with it. Crack. Like a coconut. Then I'd be gone. Some friendly pensioner walker would find me screeching and yelling running towards them down the hill. Maybe take me to the pub for hot-chocolate with an Advocaat in. Tell me how brave I was to get away from The Mountain Murderer. That's what they'd call him! My pale face all over newspapers and my career revived by writing my own story of feminist fuelled survival and.......

"I'm here to meet a guy called Dylan. He worked with the woman who died..." What?! My brain halts. This guy's words, they don't make sense. Dylan doesn't even know I'm here!

Dizzy with confusion and suddenly fancying a hot-chocolate, it hits me and I wince. Embarrassed beyond belief I want to pull the collar of my sweater up over my face and groan in mortification, so loudly it sets off a land-slide. "I'm here to see if there's a story about that woman...."

Dexter flaps the paper again, "well there might not be one.... but it's a hunch or maybe not. I don't know!" Dammit, Dexter, quit it again with flapping that fucking paper! I feel a pique of annoyance. He's more irritating than I thought he would be! "Do you mean the woman called Alice"? The brief surge of panic's got me feeling rather woozy.

"Yes, Alice, that's her name. She died up here a few days ago and this Dylan guy worked with her apparently. I'm hoping to see him as he said he was coming up. Long shot I know, but I'm an investigative, nosey journo, kinda guy, and that's what we do; take long shots". He drops the paper on his lap and makes a gun shape with both hands and pop, pop, pops in my face. An annoying man-child playing Cow-boys and Indians.

Dexter smiles widely and I see his front tooth's chipped slightly and he has only one dimple. The other one is still missing. Sliding from his face because of whatever caused that crescent scar near his shoulder, perhaps. Stop looking, and start talking Serena! Taking a deep breath, I ready myself for him getting angry or at the very least, freaking out, but properly this time.

"Ah. Ok. I'm Dylan". My voice is small with discomfort and I stutter a little; the admittance catching between my lips. I feel ridiculous now. Not only have I had a mini panic attack in front of this ridiculously hot man, but he now thinks I like pretending to be a bloke on hill-walker chat rooms! He probably thinks I'm the serial killer. Cruising round remote hill-tops looking for vulnerable hotties, a big pink torch at the ready to batter them senseless with.

"Oh! Right. I wasn't expecting that!" he looks terrified. I watch as he glances at his coat. Then his left hand starts to sneak towards the handle of the passenger door. Suddenly I want to laugh; a big bellowing laugh. It feels good. I hear the tinkle of bells and windchimes again and have to work hard not to look behind my seat for Alice.

"Look. Let's start again. My name's Serena. I used my Husband's account to go on the site. He's called Dylan". Smiling and as pink in the face as it's possible to get, I hope he doesn't leave; I like this big guy, a lot.

"Can I see some identification?". He asks and splutters into fits of giggles. Yeah, I *do like* him. "Well, Serena.... My name still *is* Dexter. I'm still a nosey investigations type and it's *still* nice to meet you.... *Serena*".

His warm hand envelopes mine and a tingle of electricity, almost a de-ja-vous feeling, passes between us, then is gone. We both start to laugh. The car almost shakes with it. I got my landslide, just not the way I thought.

Alice

It's been a few days since I died, and Michael still hasn't shed a true tear. I'm watching him mince (yes mince) about the house. No, *my* house, and make an inventory of all we collected over the years, including the stuff collected without him and before him.

His movements remind me of one of those giant lizards in animal documentaries. You know the wide toothy ones who have big bums. The Attenborough documentary was the best; where the featured reptile waddles and yet strides forward. Snaking round tree stumps. Melting over rocks. Taking it all in. Evaluating what's possible food and what's definitely not. Little eyes darting here, there and everywhere. Tongue flicking. Ok, I've got a bit carried away now, but you get the gist.

Why didn't I see it before? The anger's starting to build. With every fat, pale darting hand towards a vase, silver picture frame or antique book, the lava inside me, bubbles and spits hotter and hotter. I can feel a darkening of the air around me.

A china tea cup and saucer on the dining table, starts to quiver then shake. The blinds he chose for the kitchen, flutter. A fork falls into the sink from the edge of the draining board and a small table lamp in the corner, by the TV, flickers. *I'm doing this*. I really am!

I thought I was gifting my other half, patience, love and a future. Now I realise he was sucking those qualities dry.

Feeding hungrily until he had his chance to discard me and move onto the next female feast.

I don't understand why he didn't just leave me? Oh, because if he left me or let me divorce him, he'd get almost nothing. He wouldn't have even put up with half the house or some sort of settlement; *he wanted it all*.

The TV spurts into life with a crackle and fizz. Michael jumps back with a strange squeaking grunt. I watch as he scrabbles about on the floor desperately trying to find the remote. He often lost it, and would get angry if I didn't find it as soon as possible.

In recent years, I'd started hiding the remote down my side of the sofa so I always knew where it was, and could minimise his muttering criticisms, if I dared take longer than 20 seconds to locate it for him.

The fringing along the bottom of my favourite armchair is dancing; like an invisible finger is gently running along the tassels left to right. Slim little dancing girls, kicking up a tiny can-can over and over again. Michael's staring agape at it and his tongue is hanging out. On his hands and knees, he's gone a strange pale blue colour. Not unlike the colour of those god-awful blinds he demanded I buy.

Snorting a laugh only I can hear, the cushion falls to the floor giving up its little black buttoned hostage for Michael to see.

"Damn remote. Alice hiding it from me!"

Stopping my antics, the house goes quiet again. "Bloody weather. Messing with my stuff". Now, he's heaving himself to his feet and I watch as he pulls his corduroys up, and tucks his shirt in over the unsightly arse crack that seems to be a permanent fixture these days. Too many rich dinners lovingly made by me and too little real work, have let my beloved fill out.

He reminds me now of a steamed pudding, pale and sweaty. The sponge pressing against the sides of the wet tea-towel, holding it while it cooks.

When did I start to see him this way? Unattractive, greedy and soulless? Why didn't I stick to my plan before?! Was I blind or was he just so good with the masks?

An overwhelming sensation of exhaustion starts to pull at me. I think I need away from him and here, just now. Even in death he drains me and makes me feel empty and small.

Chapter 4: I'm A Monster

Michael

The idea to get rid of my Wife came to me slowly. It wasn't like you'd expect; no dramatic light-bulb moment or flash of inspiration. It was more a gradual sliding darkness. But that darkness was comforting, as it always has been.

Over time, as I feared she would, Alice's tentative smiles and simpering, forced me to hold back from violence, many times. Fortunately, my own dark fantasies helped me to block out whatever artsy fartsy crap she was waffling on about *that* time.

Just like my first Wife, Alice bored me fairly soon after we married. Sooner than I expected actually! I'd hoped for a little more fight. More...zest!

When we met, I sensed the embers of a fire inside her. The potential for a romance with more burn, than my last one. By pushing her and breathing down her neck, I thought there may be that whoomph of passionate flames, lighting me up and there'd be more bravery and fight.

Yes, she had a good bash at it; don't get me wrong! In the budding, early days of our coupling, she tried to debate with me, push her own boundaries back into place and even argue back when she knew she was right. Planting her own ideas and hopes was futile however, I made sure of that. It's not my comfort zone, so it was never gonna happen for her.

I was too smart and strong for her and she loved me too much. A toxic cocktail that in the end I forced down her throat by planning our wedding, buying her dress and tucking her hand into mine at the altar. Just firm enough that she mistook the squeezing pressure of my fingers, to be fear of her changing her mind. I knew she wouldn't. She was too polite to embarrass me and often that's how I got my way. Her politeness and manners. Her fear of raised voices and silent treatments. Her desperation to make everyone happy.

Handing her a glass of champagne at the wedding reception, we locked eyes and I knew she'd succumb. Drunk on hope. Drowsy with acceptance. She sipped her drink and blushed, as I lifted a stray curl of hair escaped from the stiff French-twist I requested she have, just as the photographer's flash went off. As the strand of hair fell straight back to her jaw, I wanted to slap the delicate skin where it lay. Instead I smiled and reached over again, to tidy her up. I firmly set the stray curl neatly back behind the little silver dagger shaped pin, just above her ear. I chose the pin as a wedding gift. The sharp edge of it, kept catching my eye and making me excited. It was a good choice for a day that certainly had nothing in it, to get me sexually excited otherwise!

As an afterthought, just to make sure my point was made, I adjusted her necklace and centred it perfectly in the middle of her bust, even though it was already in the right place. A subtle hint that this was it, the agreement of who was boss and who was in control. That curl had driven me mad all through the ceremony. I hate imperfection in others. Yes, even on our Wedding Day she let me down.

Luckily Alice was easy-going and very easy to read right from the get-go. Her sweet, eagerness met my demands, usually as easy as pouring syrup from a jar. It could take time but the sweet success of "Yes. Ok darling" and her sigh of resignation, always happened in the end.

As I've got older, I've learned how to manipulate with an almost effortless ease; practice really does make perfect. I'm handsome and charming and dare I say, extremely intelligent. Women seem to like me. Men too although not so much.

I admit relationships of the "friendship" type are not my forte as they require a modicum of respect and honesty. These are the areas I don't excel in. Apart from the fact that this hinders the speed of my successes with people, it doesn't bother me one bit.

When I go away on my lad's holidays or do anything with a group of other males, it is because we share, what you would call, *special tastes*.

In terms of relationships with women, I have learned how to fake the right feelings in intimate settings so, at the very least, I can make my conquests think they are getting what they want.

For the first few years, married to Alice, I was comfortable enough but things were never quite *perfect*. Luckily for me, I have a default setting. A way to revert backwards, meet my own desires and needs, even if it is, perhaps...... not exactly..... legal. When things falter or are not ideal for me, I push the button on that setting and enjoy myself very much. Re-set, I go back to my partner, until I need to do it again. But that's not for now. It's a secret.

Anyway, inside the marriage to Alice, I had other more acceptable techniques to cope. For example, if I sensed resistance or dissatisfaction with my obvious selfishness, I'd creep into the kitchen to slide a hand around her ample hips and whisper in her ear, "Don't you love me enough, *Wife?*", and kiss her neck. She'd giggle and melt into my arms with a sigh and huskily say, "Go on then, you are a lucky man, you know that don't you?" I'd smile over the top of her head and catch my reflection in the glass of the kitchen window. My dark, glistening, true-self grinning back at me, served to confirm this was as near to perfect as I could tolerate.

It all changed drastically last year though when my life started to fall apart. Yes, *that* started when she changed jobs.

* * * * *

"I need to earn a bit more than I have been darling…. that's why the change. Keep you in the lifestyle that you, well, *we*… like". Standing in the doorway to our bedroom, dressed for her new workplace in a dark green woollen suit, Alice is hunched slightly. A frog in head-lights; she's unsure how I'm going to react. But she knows she's upset me.

Pausing for effect and staring right at her, I need a few seconds to decide if a new job, new people, new distractions, is acceptable to me.

"I'm not happy you lied to me Alice. Not happy at all. We're supposed to be a partnership and we should tell each other everything. We must, absolutely, make it a priority to ask each other about decisions that affect us both". She pales a little more and her eyes fill with tears.

We are both looking at her feet. Feet which are encased in thick wool tights and the sight repulses me. "I'm going for a shower. Finding out about this new job thing *after* you were offered it and not before the interview! It really is NOT acceptable for a Husband!" Turning abruptly away, I plan to giggle quietly in the en-suite bathroom without her ugly little eyes on me.

Having cried all night at my refusal to talk to her since the day before, she is pale and blotchy. Crying again, she's transformed and reminds me of those white rabbits that get used in magic tricks. The ones with the constantly sick looking, anxious appearance.

Grabbing a towel, I bellow laughter into it but am smart enough to turn the shower on to disguise the noise. Of course, I'm fine with this new job! More money for the household equals more money for me. Win- win as they say. I just like keeping her on her toes. Hot coals and broken glass; my weapons of choice.

* * * * *

But I was mistaken, and that's not very often I can tell you! My agreement to her new role was a vast error; indeed, it was a whopper! Within weeks of the bastarding new job, she started to give off this strange, distracted, and wistful (yuck!) air. Her interest in something not within our tiny world, misted her eyes like cataracts and she became distant and irritatingly neglectful.

Far too often I'd go on and on about my day, voice a complaint about how she'd cooked my meal or even blatantly ask for some money for some made-up trip or toy. In response, she'd nod, mutter "no problem darling" and wander away to finish the washing up, visit the bathroom or even go to bed early. Imagine such rudeness from your own Wife!

So, sensing something "off", I started to pay more attention to my Wife. More than I ever had done before. Within a few weeks of following her with my eyes, I realised her phone was never far away when she left the room for any given amount of time. I also noticed her bathing took longer, she rose earlier for work and became more needed in "after work activities".

Well, that's what she said, anyway. It took me a while to click she'd met someone else. This sort of thing had never happened to me before! Lacking in empathy and emotional understanding of such immaterial matters as love-affairs, I missed the early signs. It was only when her lack of interest in me started to affect us day to day, that I realised, something had gone wrong for me. Very wrong in fact.

My first real sense of losing critical control of my Wife was when she seemed at her happiest on a Monday morning. Like, who's *happy* to go to work?! I've avoided it most of my life! Alice was enjoying this new job so much, that I had to accept to no longer being her first priority and that, in all likelihoods, someone else was now her focus.

That plummeting feeling of being dropped from my self-made pedestal was bad. Really, really bad. A long, slow fall and silent scream, that only served to make me feel even more bitterly jealous of her books and records, and whatever else she was burrowing about in at that place.

Seething in her favourite armchair, in afternoons, I imagined Alice at work and ground my jaw in rage. Over and over, I scraped my finger nails along the soft, pale pink velvet. Making long, deep scratch marks in the skin-like material. Glaring at her picture on the mantelpiece and thinking about what she might be up to, I saw her vividly. Skimpy glasses perched on her nose, hair horrendously messy, freshly glossed lips smiling in contentment, chewing her favourite gum (which drove me crazy!) and shuffling papers here and there. A pointless little bird, making a pointless little nest. It made me feel sick in the worst moments. That nest had no space for me, even if I ever even wanted to plonk myself in it. Which I didn't!

The evening before I found out about Simon Masters, I made the decision to stalk her. She'd been singing in the kitchen as she washed up the dinner plates.

I stood in the doorway and quietly watched. She didn't feel my glare on her neck nor hear the whispers of paranoia under my breath. "What's got you so happy?" I tutted as she skipped between the sink and the cutlery drawer. "Something's afoot dear Wife, and I'm going to put a stop to it", I hissed, too quiet for her to hear.

I watched and held back a punch to her back, as she stopped to look out onto the garden with a soft smile on her lips. Alice stood there almost a whole minute until finally sensing me behind her, span round and offered me cheese and biscuits with my after-dinner sherry.

The very next day I went to her work. Having never been interested in her life away from me before, I didn't know the address of the University Library where she worked. Annoyingly, my lack of interest in Alice's life was for the first time, a hindrance but not a big one.

Cleverly, I had helped myself to her handbag while she showered. The address for the university, in satisfying neat print on the top right of a recent payslip, happened to find itself scrawled on a scrap of paper torn from one of her favourite books.

Look, *calm down*! She reads that book every year over Christmas! She'd had her value for money and it was just a book. To be honest, tearing the page felt good anyway.

* * * * *

Waving happily at the attractive retiree from number 26, I turn out of our estate and onto the main road. Well really! I didn't think going on a secret squirrel mission would be so much fun! I've obviously had cause to nosey at and watch partners before, but with Alice being so wifely and mousy, I'd not felt the need to stalk her as much as the others.

Hurtling along the motorway and spinning gayly around country roads in my new little sports car is delicious! A proper drive this time! Not just pootling round the block, showing off to the neighbours.

The red and browns of this years' Indian Summer, streak past me as though I am a time traveller. The toots of less careful, slower drivers, music to my ears!

Wind in my hair, yellow cashmere scarf whipping at my face and naughty plan in progress, I feel big, important, excited and in control. I need to know what has Alice slipping from my grasp, and then I can remedy it. Cut out the nasty little growth. Treat the problem. Get things back as they used to be. As they *should* be. All about *me*.

Every now and again a cloud of leaves whirls up in my cars wake, and knowing it was someone's carefully tidied garden, I just disturbed, really is the cherry on the cake.

Other drivers admire my skills by flashing their lights, waving and shouting loudly out of their windows. One even manages to find himself in the verge. That one there! He tooted his horn much more than the others!

Parking a few streets away from where the Library is located, I close the cream leather hood of the car gently.

Locking it flamboyantly from the pavement on the other side of the road; the pleasing loud "pip pip" and flash of her lights, draws some welcome attention to my favourite girl in the world.

Standing for a few seconds to admire her racing green shine, perfectly polished head-lights and curvaceous wheel arches, I resist the urge to blow my car a kiss.

Almost skipping the rest of the way to the Library, I feel truly alive. Today marks the start of the plan to get my life back. Perhaps it will even be better!? I can punish Alice for neglecting me and get even more time away from her and even more cash to spend while doing so...!

Pausing to take stock of my surroundings, I scan the impressive red brick buildings around me. I'm in a sort of square and it's swarming with students, most of which I note, are rather good looking.

A small, slim young woman with long bouncy black hair, is walking towards me and I stop to watch her march past. Her backside is entrancing as it sways generously left then right. Her back-pack is open and crammed full of books. Lovely Stuff! Sexy *and* smart. I consider her for an approach and make to step forward. But as if feeling my eyes on her she turns, smiles, then frowns as if my hungry expression has offended her. "Tramp", I mutter and remind myself not to stare with my mouth open next time.

Smirking, I turn around to look and see where the entrance to the library is.

My plan is to "surprise" my Wife with a brunch date but use the excuse to have a good old nosey at who she's working most closely with. What educated man works beside her, or what young student has his love-eyes in. I know for a fact, I will guess who it is immediately. *I wish I'd done this sooner*!

The sound of a door banging open and laughing nearby catches my attention. My Wife virtually falls out of the commanding double wooden doors and grasps the stupid lion head knocker to steady herself. I don't recognise the red silk scarf she has tied in a bow round her neck nor the new heeled shoes on her feet. She looks younger, slimmer and the sun catches the natural lights in her hair. My stomach hardens in rage. She's alone though, silly woman laughing on her own!

Zipping behind the nearest tree as fast as a rat, I grit my teeth and hold my chest with both hands. I need to calm down and not reveal myself yet. Something about her manner, has me determined to wait a little longer.

Where's she going all dressed up?! I close my eyes and ready myself to storm across the quad, to give her a piece of my mind. I've told her how stupid her laugh is. Far, far too loud! Embarrassing at the best of times! Slowly peeking round the tree, I see him. The man with her. Taller than me, the prick. Light grey curly hair, lighter than mine. He looks younger than I am and I hate him. Yes, he's following her out of the doors!

I watch as he comes up behind her like a shadow. She laughs again as he sweeps her hair back, looks to make sure no one is watching and kisses her quickly on the side of the neck. Agog, I watch as they join hands, once in the shadows and walk in the opposite direction to me, away from the square towards the town centre.

I can hear her giggling and the rumble of his deep, educated voice even after they disappear around the corner and away from view. Digging my fingers into the bark of the tree, I grunt then head-butt it, hard.

* * * * *

So now you understand. That day was when the plan to kill her started to form. I guess I lied to you before; thinking about it, the decision to kill her came quickly but the plan of how was slower.

My plan *always*, was to drain her money away until she retired, then slip off somewhere sunny and hot. I hadn't expected her to be the one to slip off anywhere and especially not with a new man! Someone replacing me! I never saw this coming and I was livid. Incandescent. Apoplectic.

It took all the strength and patience I had not to confront her that very night. But if there's one thing I pride myself on, it is my ability to bide my time.

Driving home, ranting and exceeding the speed-limit hoping to hit some sort of animal crossing the road, I knew then I had to be not one but three steps ahead.

It was startlingly clear she was lost to me the moment I saw her face that day. Lit up, shiny and .... disgustingly happy. Like it was in the months when we first met. So selfish of her! How dare she!? The house, my spending money, everything would be gone as soon as she ended the relationship with me to run off with him. The way she looked at up at him, eager for another kiss and held his hand so tightly, told me she would run, and run, soon.

Serena

Before setting off to find where Alice died, Dexter and I huddled over the now slightly crushed and tired looking map, to choose the correct route to travel up to The Notch. Slightly uncomfortable, I hummed and awed the best I could to show I knew what I was doing. Again, that shot of shame that I'm married to an expert in this stuff and yet know almost nothing about this place or how to navigate it.

Indeed, If Dylan were here right now, he'd ruffle my hair, give me a light kick in the ankle and say, "I warned you, you'd need these skills one day!"

Shrugging the thought aside, I reach both arms into my backpack and settle the belt into place firmly. Tugging at the straps round my waist and pulling them tight, I hope I look like I know what I'm doing.

Dexter's still looking at The Map and hasn't seen me get ready. He's taut with concentration; totally absorbed. To him, this quest is really important.

"I think we should *approach* The Notch from a different angle but *scale* it from the same one as them....". Dexter's peering closely at The Map and I'm happy for him to take control. Less chance he will realise I am a completely useless novice! Watching him I realise there's an odd feeling in my breast-bone like jealousy, so I try to interrupt his concentration with exaggerated attempts to tie my hair up.

Tugging and sighing loudly, makes him look up to see what has me in such a womanly tiz. "You ok?" He doesn't look like he's worried if I'm ok. Dick. "Yes, I'm fine. Just getting ready. This super-long hair can be such a hindrance!" Conveniently, I'm forgetting I've worn my hair scraped up and left at the top of my head like a pile of rubbish, for the last half a dozen years. "Yeah...I'll bet", he replies and looks back at The Map. What a *cold fish*!

"What I found strange, was where Alice was found...". Ok, now he's talking again so I drag my attention back to the job in hand with a barely discernible huffing-sound. "How do you mean?" I ask. Leaning to look at The Map again, I see his finger is pointing to a small v-shaped ripple on The Map, no bigger than a child's fingernail.

"So, they went up The Notch. But she was found deep down in this crevice below it. It's a long way to fall. Longer than a lot of the guys on the chat-room seemed to think was.... normal". He lets go of The Map to make fingery speech marks on the word "normal". The map slips to the ground and puddle water starts to seep into the paper. Grabbing at it quickly, I sense movement nearby.

Alice is standing on an out-crop directly above us. Strangely she's not in her walking gear anymore. She's in a wedding dress. It waves and wafts around her body like wings. Flapping at her arms and legs, the daisy patterned material is pale and immaculate. No mud. No grass. Nothing.

An overwhelming sadness sweeps over my skin as though the dress itself has touched my face. I smell the sour, lemony tang of champagne and a man's fancy aftershave. It's cinnamon heavy and mixed with some sort of herb. Gagging, I cover my mouth with my hands and stagger away from Dexter to rest my hands against a wall of cold rock and repeatedly wretch into the moss at my feet.

"Jesus! Are you ok!" Dexter has hold of my hips firmly; I think he's worried I'm going to collapse. Hell, I'm worried, I'm going to *collapse*! What is Alice doing to me!? "I'm ok. Sorry. Long story. Long, weird story actually!" trying to laugh only serves to make me wretch again. My eyes fill up and I have to gulp back a few mouthfuls of spittle before I can even think about opening them again. "Here's some water". He's pressed a bottle into my hand, and greedily, I almost finish it. "Thank you you're a life-saver". He smiles at me and I like him again.

As Dexter starts to tidy The Map up, carefully making sure it's perfectly folded in on itself, I watch him. He's so different to Dylan. Careful, quiet and almost delicate in how he focuses on things. In contrast, I'm used to Dylan (when he is around) chasing my attention quite noisily, so this is hard work! Even when he's away working my Husband calls me twice a day, not that I answer often. He still tries and I realise, I've not appreciated it anywhere near enough.

An urge to hear my Husband's voice and see his name flash up on the screen of my mobile phone, overwhelms me, so I sit on a grassy bank nearby and close my eyes for a second.

"Ready to go?" Dexter's stood in front of me, his coat around his waist and his back-pack on. "Yes. Sorry, altitude sickness!" I say, with false brevity. The last thing I want to do is talk about Dylan. I'm sick to death of feeling angry. I'm here to focus on my friend Alice. Nothing else. Something's upset her though. She felt so sad! And that *dress*! What's that all about?!

Fleetingly, I wonder where she goes when she's not with me. I haven't considered it before and that unsettles me. I'm reminded of my selfishness yet again; this no-pills and no booze malarkey has its drawbacks!

"Yeah, I've decided. I think we should take the same route that Alice and her Husband took when we get to The Notch. Dangerous yes, but no point being here unless we do it like they did. It's not proper research if we don't". He's straightening his backpack and testing the belt for a better fit. It's bigger and heavier than mine and I wonder if it has a tent in. There's that ticklish feeling down below again. Yikes!

Hoisting my denims up, I pretend to start the walk as though I know where I'm going. When suggesting the route, he'd nodded upwards and slightly right. Taking the hint, I aim for the well-worn path he looked at. A stony bread-crumb path snaking upwards to thicker, darker suspicious fog above us. "Come on then Mr Investigator! Let's go!" I call over my shoulder.

The ching and whoomph of Dexter's steps at the side of me is incredibly soothing. He has some change in his pockets, or maybe some keys and the sound is rhythmic and repetitive.

Lost in thought, neither of us talking, I let my mind drift as we hike. I wonder where he lives. What his house looks like. A vision of his bed. A big untidy domineering antique wooden headboard swings into view. White sheets and white coverlets...his big legs tangled up in the crisp snowy cotton.... argh! shut up Serena. Coming off those meds is having some interesting results!

When I first started taking them, the specialist did warn me they would "interfere with natural womanly urges". I remember looking at him and thinking "what a plonker". It was the womanly urges that messed me up in the first place. The urge to carry a child and raise another human being. To be relied upon for every possible thing. Never to be useless or un-needed.

Within days of starting the medication, I realised the owly, pudgy GP with his old-fashioned language was absolutely bang on. I felt numb, everywhere. It was strange. Yes, I stopped crying or feeling that I wanted to scream or break things, but I also lost the urge to laugh or smile and my mouth (and ahem.... everything else) went dry.

Constantly thirsty, I tried flavoured teas, fancy waters and even cans of fizzy-pop. Nothing worked so as usual, I gave up. Gave into it and drank helpful alcohol instead. I let our marriage and my own personality slide even further down the gutter.

The air's cold now. Much colder than it was when we parked up. We've walked for a good hour. Battling the steep incline, slippy stony path and my own lack of fitness, has me on the verge of grumpy. Dexter's a few feet ahead of me. He's strong, experienced and apparently much easier with the silence.

"Tell me again why you're interested in this story Serena? You just worked with Alice, yeah?" He's stopped suddenly and I almost head-butt him in the back of the knees. Skidding a little, I reach for the nearest rock. "Actually. That's not exactly true...." Dexter looks freaked out again now. The air thickens around us as his mood changes from purposeful to paranoid again.

Unsure how to explain, I look away and try to gather my thoughts as they swoop and dive. Looking up, ready to try and make some sort of story up, I stop with my mouth wide open.

Behind Dexter, stands a stag. A huge one. It's watching us carefully. Its gluey nostrils are pouting and flaring in and out, over and over, in rhythm with my rapid heartbeat. He's working out if we are friend or foe. Dexter turns to look at what has my attention. He takes a sharp breath and we both wait to see what happens next. Steam's rising from the animal's rump, shoulders and snout. The fur the same colour as the last embers of a head-land heather fire; burning away, a long time to go yet. The stag shakes its head suddenly, digs at the ground with a front hoof and snorts. Spittle and snot fire out a good 4 metres and we wince hoping none catches the wind and then us.

Dexter laughs and I join in. The awkwardness broken by this very natural and yet unnatural moment. "Can I try and explain why I'm here, but later, in a bit? It's a really weird story and I've not had the best of weeks.....months....or decades...to be honest". Putting my hands on my hips, I try to be the vision of a mysterious beautiful and...safe....none-serial killer woman.

"Sure!" one word. A darting grin and he's on his way again, stomping away from me, up into the attic of mist that is getting thicker and darker as we go.

"Keep going", the mist whispers, swirling around my knees and up to my face. Startled I fall forwards to the ground. "not far not far not far", her glassy, fractured voice hurts me. And my hands are cut a little on both palms. "You need to see the view". More distant now, her voice is deeper, almost like a man's voice. It's carried on the wind but there's no echo; no acoustics to lift her words upwards to Dexter.

My right wrist feels suddenly icy cold and I'm being lifted up. She lets go and there's a little shove on my backside that makes me laugh again. A warmer air now, on my neck. An apology kiss from my friend.

I'm absolutely going to find out what happened to her. I owe her that. Before she came to me, I was as hollow as a roofless church. I feel better now and I want Alice to feel better too.

Alice

I didn't know I was only existing until I met Simon. The connection of true love was, as they say in romance novels, immediate and stunning in its power. I'd been at the University Library for just a few weeks before we met.

Oh Simon! People spoke of you often, almost as though you were some mythical being. Whispered about, infamous even!

Initially far too busy with the glacier of paper-work my predecessor neglected to tell me was hidden in her locker, I didn't get drawn into the whisperings of your imminent arrival at the University, until almost too late. Gossip wasped over my head, and the buzz around campus was tangible, but sometimes "handsome" "vivid" or "genius" would catch my attention. I'd look up sharply, and frown impatiently at the personal assistant, or swooning student whispering too close to my desk. The offending chatter-boxes, would wander away, heads closer together, giggling and blushing. In time, I learned why.

My reading matter for pleasure has always been romance and drama; sometimes of the historical type. So, having not read your books, I felt a little left out when it seemed everyone else had.

Pink with mild panic, I finally found time to scuttle down the University corridors and visit the Psychology Library, only a few days before you were due to visit and start delivering your speaking events.

* * * *

The halls are quiet and empty of life this afternoon. My first spare one, since I started here! Wincing with each step, my sensible, black brogues clickety clacking like a cucaracha around a tomb, I look over my shoulder again for any possible witness to my intellectual neglect. The sound so loud, it only serves to make me run faster and harder!

I don't want anyone to see me looking for his most recent book. The embarrassment of being the only one in the world who hasn't read it! It's especially bad, as not only am I Head Librarian, but I've just been tasked with being the authors' point of contact for the entirety of his stay. Oh dear lord! *Run faster Alice!*

Thousands of posters and flyers of Dr Simon Masters impending visit, have been scattering around the campus as though falling from the sky, *for days*! White handkerchiefs from the wilted hands of jilted lovers. Little white flags of surrender. Magnolia petals, giving up their position on flower laden branches. Yes, Mr Masters you certainly have made a mess of the *lawns*! Every female student is desperate to meet you.

Reaching the psychology rooms, I stop and breathe a sigh of relief and push the door open, slowly. Thankfully, everyone (bar me!) has gone home for the day.

My phone buzzes but I already know who it's going to be. "Where are you? What time is dinner?", the text from my Husband reads.

Since I started this job (which I absolutely love) Michael has been even worse with his pestering about where I am at any time not specifically on the time-table.

Yes, we have a time-table. It's one he created himself. He insists I put on the kitchen notice-board and update it every few weeks.

"Finishing up at work. Home in thirty", I reply quickly. I wrote on the notice-board my work finish time so Michael has acted fast in noticing I am already 10 minutes late! In my haste I didn't put any kisses on my reply-text. That won't go unnoticed. Damn and blast it! I'm desperate to get this book and out of here, without being seen.

Running then skidding into the correct office, I give a little skip as I spot Masters' new book sitting proudly atop the big shiny and extremely tidy, lecturer's desk. In its' place, I throw down a note saying the book is replacing a lost one from the library, and the owner needs to invoice my department for it.

Once home, I will hide the book in the potting shed. Michael hates me reading anything he hasn't approved first and if he discovers the handsome chap on the back-cover, is visiting my workplace, he will make my life miserable.

The next day, I awaited my important guests' arrival. Restless, I gathered the marketing litter from the grass and benches around the University. Admittedly, getting more and more frustrated and flushed, by the strange untidy madness, that had come over my normally quiet and organised workplace.

I hadn't told Michael about the new bustling, festivities at work. Knowing him as well as I do, any mention of anyone, male or female gathering attention instead of him, would result in a stormy interrogation of why they were more important than he. As Head Librarian, I was to be Mr Masters' consort for the ten-day calendar of lecturing events he had so agreeably dedicated himself to.

Thus, I was caught up in a whirlwind of opposing feelings and contrasting thoughts that, I now realise led me to my death.

* * * * *

Dr Masters' sleek white car is curling round the corner and into the university car park, as though squirted from a cake-icing gun. My chest has just tightened with nerves, although my professional smile is ready, as always.

Dressed formally, of course, I have taken the risk of wearing 2 inch heels, which is rare for me! Plus, a new pale violet tartan wool dress, complemented by one of my teenage niece's silver necklaces. All items have been secreted in my locker away from Michaels discerning eyes. I know better, of course, than to let him know I'd "splashed out in such a silly selfish manner".

I know what to expect appearance wise, as of course each of Dr Simon Masters' books are adorned by a professionally taken head-shot. A different one for each book. Curly hair worn long in one, worn shorter in another. Bold beard in one, a meek moustache in another. Standing on the steps to the university, watching him get out of his plush car, I'm wringing my hands in worry.

I've not worked here long and don't feel prepared for this visit, *not at all*. Yes, he is very different to Michael; taller, lighter haired and slim. As he picks up his large book bag and laptop, then turns to face me and smiles, my heart skips. Now, he's walking towards me and waving. Watching him struggle with all his things but laughing at himself, he stops, breathes in as though gathering himself, then catches my eye and winks. My heart re-starts and a Hell of a lot faster than before! Oh dear, *Houston....I think we have a problem.....*

* * * * *

Men like Michael have always been my type; darker, cheesy, stockier. Slick charm and ego issues, almost always tingling my danger antennae, yet still their controlling, charming manner draws me to them. Oh, how *that* was a mistake!

Anyway, back to you. No, to you and us. Yes, Simon, we became an "us". The most wonderful word in the English Language. "Us...." even saying it slowly, creates a seductive pout of the lips and the light hissing sound of a long, slow kiss on the cheek. A gentle blow in the soft shell of a waiting ear. The word "us", when whispered makes the eyes twinkle and cheeks dimple.

I can't even stop myself being rhythmic and poetic. Even now in death, going over my favourite bedtime story. The story of Us.

Michael

Fucking bitch. All this paperwork and she can't even make a will or goddamn life insurance document easy to find. Daft little post-it notes and pointless labels. Probably because she liked the "lovely, pretty colours". Yes, I know my voice just went up a few nasally notches then. Hah! *The Notch*, now my new favourite place, *ever!*

I've thought often of those few seconds of surprise, shock then abject horror, as Alice fell backwards, cross-like over the edge. Arms wide but straight backed, she was as if in slow motion and pleasingly, never stopped looking right at me until she disappeared from sight. I know she heard what I said; My last words. Anyway, back to this draining but important document-dive.

Knee deep in what feels like a sea of paper, I'm getting nowhere fast. Ok, so let's think like my silly, but organised, Wife. How would she label, no *catalogue*, the important stuff?

Ever the Squirrel, she kept *everything* and liked to be organised with the most relevant stuff close to hand; usually at the top or front of the pile.

I've tipped all the flipping' boxes out now! Thinking I was being clever by creating a wider surface area to cast my eyes over, I now realise it's possible I have made a bit of a cock up. If she was here, she'd find the papers then tidy up while I had a bath or watched television. Oh! damn and blast it! At least I have this solicitor chap's details. He can help me sort the money stuff out, surely.

I've got over the weirdness of earlier; those wonky lights and funny noises. The weather's a bit wild outside and it's not unusual for the electrics in this big old (valuable!) house to play tricks on us. Now it's just *me* though!

At the thought of being single and rich again, I want to skip around the living room and clap my hands with glee. I won't though, that would be childish. I have however already ordered myself a new Armani suit, arranged for my football boots to be monogrammed and paid for that pretty dark blue fishing rod Alice told me *had* to wait until next month. Bah humbug! "Next month. Tomorrow. In the new year", have all now become "This month. Today. *This* year!". Ok, a squeal did just escape. It just slithered out. My bad.

I've left a voicemail for Charmaine. She wouldn't be expecting a booking from me today as I don't normally see her until the last Thursday of every month, when my Wife is usually paid.

The allowance Alice gave me covered most of my desires but more recently, having got a little greedier, I've had to be more creative with my financial requests. "It's for the next football team fundraiser thingy darling", became the best excuse I could come up with. Seeing as I do actually play 5 a side football, Alice never questioned it. Never.

I actually play football on Tuesdays when Alice is at work. I take photos and videos then show them to her on a Friday morning or during our Saturday brunch, to add that extra bit of half-truth to the lies that have enabled my little hobby of using prostitutes a tightly kept secret. That way, when I go out with a bag at 8pm on my special Thursday, Alice doesn't doubt or question where I'm skipping off too. I won't tell you what's in the bag, it's too *wicked*!

Oh! I've just realised I can see Charmaine, Victoria *and* Jade whenever I want now! No Wife, no rules! When I saw Alice with Slimy Simon last Autumn, I knew I had to come up with some way to get out of this in the best shape possible. I might be plump round the belly now, but the fattest bit is pleasingly just... about... to be my bank balance! To the right of me, a loud bang breaks the silence.

Shrieking, I fall back onto the papers. Scrabbling and half crawling across the floor, to reach the window-seat, I pull myself up onto my knees and cautiously, slide the net-curtains aside to peer out of the window. There's a small smear on the glass in front of me.

Oh! and a tiny black feather. A shudder ripples through me and I get goose-bumps. Yuck! A black-bird, I think, has just hit the glass. Stupid thing gave me a Hell of a fright! I'll need to go and scoop it up and put it in the bin now. As if I'm not busy enough.

That reminds me, I need to start to play the grieving widower and fast. Neighbours have been visiting all day; trampling the lawn like idiots. Fluffy cardiganed arms laden with soggy lasagne's, forgettable pies and dry cakes. Freshly back-combed hair and smelling of newly squirted perfume; the old biddies in the street are in full neighbourly attack mode. Swooping and squawking around each other, excited at the drama and gossip of my Wife's sudden demise.

From my side of the door, I can listen to the old birds puffed up and preening. Wittering on about "Poor Mrs Jennings. Poor Alice. Lovely lady. Gone too soon. She never had children you know". Nosey old-bags. I've listened plenty and they never say anything nice about me. Not at all!

Grabbing the door open and swinging it back harshly, earlier today, I thoroughly enjoyed making them jump! Each of the three oldies hovering on my path, nearly spilled their pathetic offerings on my recently swept front step. One by one they yelped then gasped in turn; clutching their pearls to their necks and holding onto each other for dear life. "Thank you ladies". I even managed a little bow and short smile. "Unfortunately I'm not up to visitors right now. I'm sure you understand". Before they could say another word, I shut the door in their faces and walked away down the hall, intent on putting their tasteless crap out for the foxes.

Frustratingly, those full dishes are still sitting sweating on the kitchen counter. I can only get rid of the food as soon as it's cold enough not to give off a foody scent over the fences, wafting towards the blasted nosey neighbours who made it.

I'm smart that way. Always careful. Always planning. Alice underestimated me. Shame she's dead because she might have respected me more, knowing what I was capable of.

Serena

The sun's trying to make the best of her role in the sky above us; soft grey and white clouds split by watery blue allowing her the effect of a ruined poached egg.

Dexter's ahead of me. I like watching him walk. Always with his head slightly down, he just keeps going, step after step. Emitting not a sound, unless he's telling me to hurry up or talking about The Map again.

Companionably, but separated by a few metres, we are walking across a glen, towards another steep rocky slope upwards.

I'm sweating but enjoying every step; feeling each heartbeat of my boots against the ground. I've never been here before. Before this, whatever this is, it wouldn't have crossed my mind. A city girl, more than a little selfish and often too tired, I wouldn't have accepted Dylan's idea to come here nor suggest it myself. The fresh air's clearing my head. It's the only thing about this place that's making me uncomfortable.

The land is so open ahead of us, we can actually see the rays of sun spreading across the hills and lighting them up. It's almost like a living thing; a huge swarm of yellow butterflies ascending or a cloud of golden birds carried towards us on a fast breeze. With it, moments of intense heat hit our backs and there's a warming sense of hope.

Although this feels pleasant, I keep thinking about Alice walking up to The Notch, not knowing she wasn't going to come back. Her trust in the peak and her walking partner. Her enjoyment of the scenery. Again, adrenalin spikes my knees and I need to stop and rest.

"Dex!" My voice echoes around the glen, "Can we have a break and sit somewhere?". I've already chosen a place so the stubborn bugger better listen. Reaching another incline, I realise I can't see Dexter.

A flurry of rubble from surrounding scree meets my toes. Putting my hat back a little and moving my fringe aside, I see Dexter planted there. Dylan used to have that stance; this pose of control and comfort, no matter what environment he was in. Come to think of it, at times it was like beneath his feet were roots; he'd twist when I called his name, but still stay stuck. His hips spinning round in my direction like it was a practised dance move. *Dancing the Bolero, when the matador faces the bull.* I never appreciated it before now. That sexy body twist, was I the bull? Probably, I'm stubborn and aggressive enough. Did my broken Husband love me so much he even changed how he moved around me? Did he reduce himself, to avoid unsettling me or unravelling one of my tempers again? Did she move good for him? Was there a dance between them?

The hate and disgust at my Husband and his lover flood back in. I can't stop it. That awful shaky sense of doom only the cheated on feels. *What happens*? After this? What will I do? Who will I be if I'm not a Wife or a mother or even a sister anymore?

"We need to keep moving!".. Dexter's voice comes from beyond the horizon. Almost without me noticing, the path's got steep enough that it feels like we are walking up a wall!.

"A weather front's coming!" he continues but with more volume this time. Looking up, I hate to admit, my heart flutters a little at the threatening dark cape of cloud that's opening up, fanning itself across the sky above us. It's the colour of rotten plums; an image that makes my skin crawl.

"Don't worry. It's just rain, maybe some hail. Not a big deal. But yes, we do need to take cover", he continues. "No worries though, I've a tent!".

His voice hovers on the wind but swoops away fast. Lost in the dark parts of my own head for a time, I didn't even notice the breeze had picked up. He's right, there's some serious wind now; its whipping my hair and slapping cold hands against my cheeks. As if making a point the strong air, starts pulling and tugging at the collar of my rain-coat and I almost tip back to fall down the tiny path. The sudden weather change feels like a crowd of people just arrived who want to make themselves known and get our attention. Well, it's working; I'm attentive!

I've never liked the wind; *never*. If mother nature had a temper, then this is it. My hair's getting twisted across my face and up my nose. It feels dangerous up here now. Turning to look at where we've come from, I fleetingly consider going back. Dexter reads my body-language.

"Keep going. Stop panicking Serena! There's a good tenty bit up here!".. His confidence is like when you grapple for the light after a nightmare and your fingers finally find that switch; that bloom of light. And then you lean back into your pillows, glad things are not as bad as the monsters in the darkness told you.

Chapter 5: The Storms Inside

Michael

I don't like solicitors. Too smart and too nosey. I have to use Alice's for now though. It would look suspicious to go getting my own, so soon after her death. This will be a simple, easy process and there's no point giving myself any extra work.

I'm not looking forward to this appointment, although I am interested to meet my deceased Wife's trusted advisor in such matters; it will give me a chance to read him a little and maybe even get to grips with what money may indeed be heading my way.

So boring and unglamorous, I have a great distaste for the legal profession. Nothing but trouble in my opinion. I saw it all already with the departure of Wife number one...... thank god my parachute-plan worked that time too! I'm better at getting rid of them than I thought I was.

Allow me to show off a bit and spend the time, while I walk to Alice's solicitor's office. I can tell you how I killed Wife number one.

Have you seen those flowers? The pretty ones, with freckled little cups of colour, lined all the way up the stem. Like a tall tower of little trumpets, they come in pink, purple and white. Fox-gloves, people call them. A rather striking but common flower, sadly all too often seen as weeds by people who don't know their secrets.

The Foxglove, or "Digitalis" as it is also known as, actually has the power to induce a heart attack (or treat one, depending on what your agenda is!). You weren't expecting a botany lesson, were you? Well hang tight, you'll like this.

All parts of the flower and adjoining plant are poisonous and you can make a tea with it. Then you need to get lucky. You need, a soon-to-be-dead Wife, who has a dog. God how I hated Penny's dog. Great, smelly black thing he was. Penny, called him Sooty. He was 6 years old and growly. He hated me; slinking around us constantly restless in my presence. Pressed up, sitting behind her on the sofa. Eyeing me up all the time. Refusing to let me pet him. Don't know why. Don't care why actually.

I decided to try my flower poison idea out on him first. The big daft dog loved chicken. Penny, would give him all the good bits. Never asked me if my cat was interested.

I'd sit there and watch her greasy hands eagerly tearing the meat from the roast on the table. Her silly repugnant smile as he gently pulled the meat from her hands. Stifling a gag, I'd try to eat my own meal and swallow down the nasty words and hate she was responsible for.

One day poor Sooty got carried away with a chicken carcass foolishly left on the kitchen top, on a night I carried giggling wifey to bed a little more tipsy than normal. She was devastated when the greedy dog was found dead the next morning. I on the other hand was delighted.

I'd poured a good measure of my fox-glove poison liquid (mixed with a little melted butter to help disguise any possible poison scent) on the carcass and danced off to bed, leaving Sooty sitting at the foot of the counter, salivating at the treat he planned on stealing that night. And so my plan on how to finish off Penny, was cemented.

And now here I am with a different challenge. Like so many of the others, Alice fell in love, but of course, as you well know, love is dangerous. Love leaves finger-prints. It leaves moments and memories. It leaves evidence and witnesses.

Those adoring students who watched and hankered over her ridiculous affair with that big fat writer man. The online friends who hummed and awwwed at us at first but soon became hostile and suspicious of me. Thus, I found I had a bad combination; a perfect storm. *"wealthy well-liked Wife, ready to leave her Husband for new man, dies suddenly, leaving behind a suddenly wealthy Husband no one ever really liked.* That's a news head-line, I would sell my soul to the Devil to avoid!

So, I really do need to see this solicitor pronto; in and out quick. Then, I can start planning to sell the house and move on, rent it out and move abroad? Maybe, find another Wife.... oh, so many things to consider!

"Money first. Money First", I repeat this simple, satisfying mantra over and over, stomping breathlessly up the winding stone staircase of three floors to Mr Kendal's office. Typical Alice, choosing such an awkward and tiring journey for me, over a nice simple ground floor legal advisor. Did she ever have any bloody common sense?

The impeccably clean, stained glass door greets me, but before knocking, I can't help but peer through one of the coloured glass panels to get a quick greedy look at what the girl on the desk looks like.

Pressing my face just a little too close and breaking out in an excited hot sweat leaves a mark on the glass. I don't bother to wipe it off. Much too busy; I just want in and out of here fast.

Opening the door wide and smiling gayly, I march to the pretty one's desk and announce myself. "Mr Michael Jennings for Mr Kendal". I'm rather proud of how posh and official I sound. Pretty One looks up, smiles a little uncertainly (she clearly hasn't met a man of my style before) and replies "Please take a seat in the waiting area, I'll let David know". What?! David! *David!* She's offended me somewhat with how casual she is. Blatantly unprofessional in fact!

Walking away from her, I've already forgotten she arranged this emergency appointment for me with little to no complaint.

Alice is barely cold on a steel gurney but it's important to get the ball rolling on the juicy money stuff. As they say "needs must". Still tutting in annoyance, I sit down hard on the leather topped bench in the sterile waiting area. Looking around I see ugly modern art depicting moral failures, as if to remind us why legal advice is so often needed.

The worst of the paintings is some sort of animal skull and three black horses are dragging it along behind them into what looks like flames. Damn thing makes me shudder. I suspect it's supposed to be depicting the Three Horsemen of the Apocalypse. I've no intention of any apocalypse today or any day for that matter, I thank *you*!

Shuffling on the seat and bored already, I'm forced to half-heartedly pick up yesterday's paper from the coffee-table in the centre of the room. Mr Kendal had better hurry up, I've some spending to do.

Alice

That Summer day when you first looked at me Simon, on the steps at the entrance of the University, time stopped.

At that, our first meeting, I was speechless as you took my hand and kissed it. Yes, my knees went. *I know, I know*! Ever the romantic but it was just magical! Your unexpected chivalry and old-fashioned mannerisms were quite simply, what did it! They cracked my veneer of professionalism and from that first exchange, I fell for your charms and desperately wanted you to feel the same. Put quite simply it was the *best* "Hello" I'd ever had. And now I'm dead, it's the best I ever will have.

The worst part of all of this is you and I had no true *goodbye*. That's honestly the most awful part. I think these days younger people call it "ghosting". Your messages stopped and my world turned monochrome- worse than ever before

"It's better to have loved and lost than to have never loved at all", is nonsense; a lie made up by someone who's clearly never been in true love.

Once you went away, there was nothing left to help me get through the gut-wrenching misery of every day without you.

No good morning text, poetic email or cheeky tweet. Nothing to make me take my frumpy brown tights off in the loo's before lunch. Nothing to make me tie up my newly highlighted hair and trap it with a pretty scarf to expose the neck you loved to kiss and stroke. Nothing to make me frantically squirt perfume over my cleavage as I wheeled into the university car-park at 8.50am every morning. Nothing to make each new day a wonderful opportunity to see you.

Nothing.

Dylan

Regret is an ugly, heavy, terrible thing; it serves no purpose other than to punish you for things you should never have done. Regret is the cruellest of emotions, because by the time it kicks in, it's too late to fix any damage done. The paralysing sense of desolation and spiralling self-hate both mean I'm getting nowhere, but this is all there is right now.

Regret, regret....damn regret! I wish I could go and see Owen but it's not my day to see him, and Bronwyn will suss out that something big has happened as soon as she sees me anyway.

I tried my best to juggle both lives and to not hurt anyone but clearly, I have failed miserably. It was cruel of me to not be honest with Bronwyn about my agenda for being with her and it was verging on evil of me, to not tell Serena myself.

To let her find out all these terrible things, all on her own. She is the love of my life and has been since the beginning. Oh, how Serena *lit my life up* when we met!

* * * * *

My god, who is this sweeping into my office like some goddamn celestial storm? Chunky silver chain-belt tinkling, announcing her arrival before I even saw her face. Yes! Look at her *face*! Momentarily blinded by a thrill of desire, I start spluttering something about not having an appointment for a new P.A.

"I don't need a new personal assistant. Candice is fine. Besides, aren't all secretaries supposed to be dowdy and carry big brown hand-bags! Hah! You don't even have a pen behind your ear. I like your shoes though. Nice hair. Cool belt". Why the Hell am I still talking!? Her silence is making me worse. She is sensational! *Who the Hell is she?* "Maybe you should tell me who you are so I have an excuse to shut up....".

So yeah, it took several minutes of my crap-talk until I was exhausted by my own mortification and verbal diarrhoea and finally fell silent. No woman has ever impacted me like the effervescent stranger stood a few feet away, not having yet sat down.

The next thing I notice about the woman who is to be my Wife, is her smell. By god her smell. Daisy's and ripe pears. Light yet intoxicating. Sunshine and long dark nights. It's true what they say. When you meet the one, it's like a sucker-punch to the gut and a bullet between the eyes!

"I'm not your new P.A or anyone's P.A for that matter. I'm the media researcher you agreed to meet today". Breaking her silence and now openly furious with my faux pas, she drags a chair from the corner of the room and sits down hard in it.

Finally (gladly!) speechless, I just stare at her. We've spoken mostly by email and I've forgotten how she looked in her profile on the network where we "met". Glancing at my diary, open on my desk, I see "Appointment S Reilly-Journo" scrawled under today's date, in bright red. Ever disorganised, I've forgotten who I'm meeting and why. I've assumed S Reilly is a man and the shame of it is crushing. In my industry women are sadly rare.

My ignorance was never forgotten; there then, that day, the joke of me calling her "Sir" was born.

* * * * *

The awkward combative electricity between us felt weird at the time but since that day, years and years ago, we've done the "first time we met autopsy" a thousand times. She admitted the same immediate attraction and wasn't sure how to deal with it.

We used to laugh and cringe into our pillows on our bed about that instant buzz of desire between us that is so rare to find. Now.... *now*.... I'm in a crappy Bed and Breakfast, 10 miles from my home, and not in our bed. Even worse, I have no idea how to fix the almighty fuck up that apparently is our life.

I felt her slipping within year two of us being in the village. She loved me and I took her love and assumed it was a first-class ticket to Heaven, here in my families breath-taking but extremely rural home town.

With no real idea how much, she needed the stimulus of the city, other people....and our own babies, I let her down badly. She just seemed so herself when we met. So solid. So adaptable.

I had no understanding that within her was a dark hole just waiting to be filled, ideally with children. My Wife played the game of "happy no matter what", and I played along until I realised no one was winning. She wasn't happy no matter what, not at all. Now I realise, we conned each other.

And so, right in front of my eyes she started to fade. Like when children write their names on a pavement and the rain comes; slowly the bright chalk just dribbles away. The joy of play, forgotten.

It broke my heart every day to come home, so I did the worst thing ever, I took a job that took me away for weeks on end. I left her to be sad all alone. I stopped trying.

You're angry. It's what I deserve, but let me explain a bit more. I suggest now, after thinking on it, that we left each *other* actually. Yes, I know it's not an excuse.

The neglected, silent spaces that gathered between us filled up so quickly with loss and blame, that extended periods of time together became intolerable. I hated it as much as she hated me. I felt her pause in time, and her stilted, anxious breathing, every time she got pregnant. It was like she was waiting for some sort of punishment. Yes, like she knew it was going to happen and hated herself for it. Each loss a few weeks or months after a positive result or missed period, became just a reminder we weren't supposed to mate.

When I'd come onshore for home-leave, she was ok at first- perhaps living in hope that each time I'd go *back* to work, I'd be leaving her carrying our child. But the air got darker and harder between us the longer it took and the more pregnancies we lost. Then we met Bronwyn.

Have you ever felt so lost and alone, that literally anyone or anything made you feel like you deserved to have what you wanted? Like you had a sense of *entitlement*? That hungry child stealing a cake left on a table? That nice fancy tie that some thoughtless guy left in the office; pure silk and you know you want it but shouldn't have it.... You take it just for the thrill of something wrong and pretty and stolen.... You blame the person who lost it; the justification of your seemingly vic-timless crime.

Bronwyn was just that. A forgotten tie. The last cake no one noticed. Something that represented silky risk and sugary treat wrongness. I felt alive, *darkly* alive around her.

Finally, able to look forward to something, she was like an SOS flare. But, in hindsight, I saw a "rescue" when really, she represented danger. Bronwyn was so eager and happy to see me or simply just hear my voice in a snatched, two-minute phone-call! So, with her around, I felt like I mattered.

Serena found Bronwyn first. I told her she needed a task; a project to fill her days while I was away at sea counting numbers over and over again.

My Wife decided we needed an extension on the front lawn; a large area of wooden decking topped off with a sheltered place to sit. She wanted a glass and steel awning shading us from the rain while we sat on lovingly polished wood and looked out to sea, drinking wine and planning things.

"And Dyl, I had the *best* idea yet! The children can play outside all year round. Enjoy the fresh-air, be safely attached to the house and yet not get wet!" she cried, once settled on a clever design, based on one of Bronwyn's suggestions. It was a fantasy that never came to life in the end and that thought makes me so bloody sad.

Bronwyn and my Wife became friends quickly. Hours and hours together scribbling down ideas for the designs and talking about the feasibility of something made of glass facing what is often a windy, blustery coast. They found solutions to problems together and talked over warm wine, cold gin and tepid coffee. I think it was nearly 8 years ago now; so, so long ago. Before things went from bad to worse.

I met Bronwyn for the first time having come home a day early to surprise my Wife.

Bounding into the kitchen waving a huge bunch of her favourite giant Alliums and purple Lupins, I was already un-doing my belt; enthusiastically hoping for some intimacy, before her usual three-day-tolerance of me was exceeded.

* * * * *

Stopping dead, half way across the room I drop the flowers and say "fuck". The woman, who I think is Bronwyn, is smiling at me. Her big bouncy boobs jostling for attention in that sheer black blouse and Serena's less happy, almost thunderous face, are confusing me no end. So, I just say "Fuck" again.

The moment seems to last forever then Bronwyn speaks; "I assume you're the Husband?". Serena laughs; a big booming cackle. Her old laugh. I haven't heard it in ages; I've missed it so much. Hearing it and watching her now, my chest hurts.

"Bron, this is Dylan. Yes, he's *the* Husband". Red faced I turn away to re-buckle my belt. Spinning back round, I fiddle with my jacket buttons and grin sheepishly, but yet not at my Wife; at Bronwyn. She has this cheeky sexy thing going on. The absolute opposite of my smart, cool Wife.

"Nice to meet you Dylan". Her voice is dripping with flirtation. She doesn't blink and just looks at me, smiling. Serena, hasn't noticed that the energy has changed. She's looking down at the plans on the table, between her and her friend. It's likely she doesn't think anyone else could find me attractive.

Smiling back at Bronwyn, I feel the stirring of sexual tension. I've never ever considered another woman, until now. Our marriage really has gone down-hill, fast. Far, far too fast.

* * * *

Bronwyn brought a calm, almost slick warmth, to my world. She never complained. She never moaned. Of course, like all affairs one person's feelings outweighed the other and she fell for me hook line and sinker within days of the affair starting. Ignoring her needs, I met my own.

Yes, there it is again…that anger from you. But you can't hate me more than I hate myself! And start it, we *did*! Like a bomb going off we met up to have sex the very next day.

After Bronwyn left to go home and Serena went to bed, I got unreservedly drunk on some good malt whisky. My Wife had become grumpy as soon as her friend left. A bottle of red wine down her neck, the flowers soon went in the bin and she started on me. I wasn't home early for an ear-bashing I said, but all became clear once she shouted in my face, as I leaned in to kiss her Hello properly. Her period had started, she screamed. So no conception from my *last* home trip then.

My gut clenched in disappointment, then fear of how bad she'd be now, for at least the remainder of my stay. Then, out of nowhere anger coursed through me. At myself, at *her*, at *life*, and at the conception Gods! "Fuck off Serena. For fuck sakes give me a fucking break!" She stared at me than started shouting about my surprise visit, even louder than before. "All you want is sex! You're so selfish!".

So I gave up. My refusal to engage further in the battle that night, dissipated the argument quicker than normal. Both tired, we went our separate ways. She to bed, carrying a bigger glass and a fresh bottle of wine. Me to the kitchen, where my own secret stash of better quality, less often drank, booze was always kept.

* * * * *

Sitting on one of our irritatingly creaky, kitchen chairs, looking out to sea, I fill my glass up again and again. About three spiky, peaty gulps in, my mind wanders to Bronwyn. Sunny, smiley, happy busty Bronwyn. Outlined in the darkness of the decking, I can see the shapes, of boxes of equipment, ready to start building.

Panes of glass in plastic propped up against the wall. Tins of paint to stain the wood a deep teal blue, as Serena has requested. Then, behind the burn of the whisky comes a flicker of insight; this collection, the awning not even started, means Bronwyn is going to be around longer than I originally thought. Yes, I remember now, hearing Serena saying, "we'll make those changes and meet up next week Bron", as she walked her friend to the door a few minutes after I got home. A quick shake of the head, to forget I'm looking forward to seeing Bronwyn again.

Then, a 3rd drink that still doesn't erase her boobs or ample backside in that too-tight white skirt. The 5th drink has me furtively unzipping the laptop case, firing up Serena's Facebook and searching for her friend.

As our Architects round rosy face, fills the screen and I start to scroll through her posts and pictures, something bad and bitter, inside me whispers "It'd be fun...".

* * * * *

Looking back, I wonder if that that sticky liquorice voice is what all cheaters hear. It attaches itself like glue to that bad-behaved Amygdala doesn't it? We fantasise about hot, sweaty hotel beds. We ignore the warning bells. We picture wet, giggling kisses in restaurant car-parks. We imagine the rush of desire and satisfaction that comes from lust, and getting carnal urges licked and stroked and......oh god, yes. I know, I'm a fucking idiot.

Serena

"I think we might need to pitch up here". Dexter's out of sight but his voice is so clear, I've no problem hearing him. But being up high, with less oxygen, I'm finding it hard to catch my breath. Embarrassed by my appearance, I don't call for him to come back. Then, I smell Alice's darker smell; her smell of sadness. It's not her, it's the ground beneath me and again I'm reminded how horrendously important this is. We must be closer to the place she died than I thought.

Sitting down, I take a long drink of water and close my eyes at the wave of sickness rolling over me. "Breathe in and out Sir. Breathe in and out". It's almost Dylan's voice; reminding me how to cope when the tablets didn't suit me or when I was trying to change medications. "It's just the detox", I whisper to myself. "And the smell of death". Alice's feathery voice catches my ear.

"Serena! Serena?! Are you ok?". His voice is so loud, it could part the mist. Like curls of Moses water splitting. It feels like a small miracle, when I look up to see him stood on a ledge to my right. He's waving and grinning, and lovely and handsome.

Flooded with relief, I laugh and happily wave back. "Is this where you want to pitch up?" Taking his outstretched hands, I let him hoist me up to stand beside him. Not even sure if he heard me, he's moved away- seemingly bored of me again; he's driving me nuts!

I watch Dexter as he gently places his back-pack up against a large boulder. "That's why I was glad that Dylan.... well you, erm, said you were coming today! The weather's very similar as reported the day of the accident and I deliberately brought my tent. I wanted to be here after dark to experience what they did. Hey! Let's call it method writing!".

His muscly back is dancing as he drags the tent out and starts to unwrap it with rough efficiency. I want to dance with him. This urge sweeps over me like the arms of a ballerina.

Dexter turns to me sharply. Did I say that *aloud*?!. "Can you separate the tent pegs out? They're the curved ones. Quite long. They need to be hooked through the small ground level holes in the tent". He's bossy and manly, and I want to see *his* tent peg. For goodness sakes shut up Serena! Then Alice whispers, "Not like Husband".

My neck prickles; I want to defend my Husband to her, although he doesn't deserve it. Dylan. My Dylan. He'd have loved this adventure. Right now, he'd be hankering for one of the beers Dexter's pointing at me.

The wind drops for a few heartbeats and in the distance, I hear church bells. "Not like *my* Husband", she hisses. I can't reply so just nod in the direction the sounds come from and the bells change to windchimes. She's ok now.

Taking the beer and starting to open it with my teeth, Dexter catches me doing it and wags a finger at me in false chastisement. Winking back in a cheeky retort, I then poke my tongue out at him and finish opening the beer with my right incisor, then drop it in the side pocket of my jacket. Are we *flirting*? Dexter and I? Surely not! Although it would be nice.... Dylan would be furious...or maybe not...he's busy playing at happy families with Bronwyn anyway.

Taking a long pull on the beer, I walk away from Dexter to stand with my back to him, looking up towards where the striking shape of the Notch can be seen over the headland. It does look ominous, I admit. Mostly shards of rock and with little greenery to be seen from here, it could almost be man-made; it's like a ginormous sculpture or even a ship stuck in ice. Now we are closer, I see more detail but I'm also, more uneasy.

I hope we don't get lost and have an accident like Alice and her Husband.... Dylan would know the paths and climbing points well, seeing as it's one of the most dangerous locations for climbers in this area.

"The route we've taken isn't the exact same as Alice and her Husband is it?", I ask Dexter, sitting down on a small grassy ledge, to watch him finish setting the tent up. "No. I fancied a longer hike than them. I wanted to get a feel for the place. Besides, I love being out in the wild, so any excuse to be here as long as possible!" He laughs, unrolling a sleep mat and tucking it inside the tent.

"I wasn't sure where to start, to be honest. It's not my thing all this. Deffo much more Dylan's thing, than mine", I reply, looking at his backside as he tidies the tent from within.

"It's not really the going up bit that's important. Alice fell from a particular view-point on the top, a flat bit with a ledge over a long, deep, jaggy drop. We just need to get there, really". His voice is a little muffled, from inside the tent and I'm still distracted by his bum! But I don't miss the quick flicker of worry.

"Can I ask why you're so interested in what happened? You still haven't told me". His backside stops moving and he goes still; inside the tent he's searching for the right answer.

The flicker gets more persistent, and I place the bottle on the ground beside me, ready to go and pull him out of the tent, forcibly if I have to! "There's stuff I can't tell you. Confidential information and all that, but I think he's involved in a....crime".

Dexter's crawling backwards out of the tent, and is red faced from the stuffyness inside. "Go on", I say, stood hands on hips, hopefully looking stern. "I can't Serena and it's not my style to guess at stuff. Let's wait and see how we get on tomorrow, at the site of the accident." I'm not happy at his evasiveness but he's worked with the police before.

Maybe this is more serious than I thought. A deliberate accident? would that be a *thing*? Without a map and letting her come up with the wrong clothing, The Husband could certainly be seen as in some way responsible for Alice's death. That could be what she's trying to tell me. I wait to see if she gives me some sort of sign, but there's no sound and no smell. She's gone again.

"There are quite a few ways to go up The Notch, so It's probably a good thing you bumped into me Serena". Dexter's handing me my beer. "Aye, you'd have done less hiking, but you would most likely be alone when you did!"

It's true and I'm glad. The longer I'm away from home, the better I feel. Fate has so often gone against me, but this time, it's done me a favour. A warmth in my gut that feels frighteningly like hope appears.

"Come on, let's have a bar of chocolate and get inside. Rain is coming". Dexter takes my bottle and gestures towards the tent. "Oh, I could really go a bar of chocolate right now. It's more Dylan who has the sweet tooth though, not me!" Dexter frowns at me and sighs. He's as confused about my feelings as I am. What the Hell is happening to me, out here? It's interesting. It's distracting.... perhaps it's exactly what I need.

Alice

Watching my friend appearing to sail through her trauma, I'm impressed and pleased. Perhaps, I'm here to help Serena find that horridly wonderful dangerous and treacherous island that is true love, yet again? I know, I know, it's annoyingly romantic. *I'm* annoyingly romantic! But doesn't every good story have some love in it? Just a bit. Somethings special's happening on this mountain. Something nice. Nice is ok! Nice is safe! Nice doesn't hurt!

What Michael did to me, hurt. I don't even mean the broken bones and being dead bit. I mean him slithering around, rooting through our home. Tearing through my things to choose what would become *his* things. Awful! The way he just flicked through my financial paperwork, grunted then tipped it all out! Scattering the carcass wide, like a wolf choosing which bones were worth an extra look.

It was strange perched there, watching the man I thought I loved just do his thing. He seemed, practised at it; cool and collected as though he'd done it before. The only sign of unease, was when I encouraged that dying blackbird to hit the window. My Husband barely stopped in his tracks otherwise.

Don't be angry, poor bird was passing away, anyway. I helped it. That's what we do when we're dead apparently. We do difficult things to help living things; a voice in the smoke around me guides me to it. But I don't think I'm really a part of that world or realm or whatever it's called. It's more like I'm here to do something differently important.

The guide sounds are less like voices and more like the words from songs. You know when you hear a tune the first time and you move to it without thinking? You don't know the words or the singer, but it's like you know the tune? Well, being dead's like that. The singers are giving me music and I just move to it.

Here's a thing; Simon suggested I read a book about Empaths, Super Empaths actually. I'd known him a month by this point. The book absorbed me; drew me into its soothing depths, like a warm pool. I wallowed in the whole thing; completed it in two nights reading by candle-light, so as not to wake my Husband.

As I turned the last page, closed the back cover and glanced at my Husband curled up sleeping in the duvet he insisted I buy, even though I was allergic to it, I felt something shift in me. Like a child putting its fingers between two flowers and letting a shaft of sun in; that slow gentle split between who I *thought* I was and actually who I *was*.

Reading about empathy, I realised that I had an unusually high level of it. Maybe too much! Although enlightening, it was equally dangerous for me to realise Michael didn't have these qualities or emotional connections to people. He simply did not care about anyone but himself, to pathological extremes in fact.

The book's revelations came at a time, temptation was lurking. Simon and I had only kissed on cheeks and touched through clothing in the first few weeks. Eyes to eyes. Smiles to smiles. No proper skin contact, of course not! I'm a married woman!

No, correction- I *was* a married woman; now I'm a dead married woman. Heck! I'm a widower-maker. Hah! Well Michael made it this way shoving me off the darned mountain. Yes, he's happy about it now, but not for long....

* * * * *

"Relationship-wise, a key principle in understanding how Narcissists and other *Dark Tetrad Disordered* people operate, is to appreciate that Narcs favour Empaths as a superior sort of food source. They eat up your excessive love, hope, empathy and innate instinct to help others".

I am enthralled, seated on Simons' lap, as he reads from one of his more recent books. "Doctor Masters, might I be so bold to ask something? Have you written a book, *like every year*, across your whole....*career?!*". He leans back to look at me better and grins at my false formality; a bit of a secret joke between us, especially as we haven't been intimate yet but are very, very close to it.

"Well Mrs Jennings, you make a good point, but I actually didn't mean to release so many books! There are just so few on NPD abuse. Especially written by British Authors!"

Simon kisses me lightly on the nose and settles back to continue reading. The large leather reading-chair is easily fitting us both, but I pretend to be squashed just a little and move closer to the man I am absolutely, madly in love with.

We are in his office this afternoon. In an unusually damp and sticky July. Simons' white linen shirt is sticking to his chest and I can just make out small dark curls of chest hair on what I am delighted to see, is a rather attractive chest. I cough to hide my shame at such thoughts. Simon looks up, makes eye-contact and raises an eye-brow at me, then smiles again. "May I continue Mrs Jennings?".

"You may, Mr Masters" I reply and blush even pinker. I shouldn't have worn this dress today. It's thick yellow cotton, with a layered petticoat underneath. It's far too warm for this weather, and now I'm getting myself all in a tizzy over Simon, it feels even warmer!

I've chosen this retro style frock because my hair is lighter and with walking every day at lunch with Simon, I have a tan for the first time in my adult life.

Everything is different. Everything is better. Simon is tanned too, although much darker than me. He has long arms and long fingers. The body of a swimmer.....*Oh shoot*! Simon's reading again, so I drag my attention away from indecent thoughts, although it's painful!

"It's important for you to realise that if you are in an intimate relationship or friendship with a Narcissist, that it's not your fault. They have sought you out. Spotted you from afar, so to speak. They use their cognitive empathy, to target then isolate chosen victims. People who usually, have real, true, proper *soulful empathy*...." Simons' words quieten as he lifts a rose shaped earring and kisses my neck. In the moment, I feel truly blissfully loved. In the purest and most wonderful way, anyone could ever want.

* * * * *

That afternoon was the first time we made love. Men never remember such romantic and nostalgic things as "firsts", but I suspect you do Simon. Yes, I gave in. I had to.

You showed me such kindness and respect as my friend, that allowing you to become my lover was a natural step. It didn't hurt that I found you mightily attractive either!

My note-pad slid to the floor as I turned your face to kiss me properly, the way lovers do. The way I've always read about. The way it's supposed to be. Not a soggy stamp of ownership or clumsy request for sex. Just a seal on a love-letter, promising the start of something lovely and right. I never thought about getting to know myself before; I always trusted others to label, then shape me. It just seemed easier.

Crying buckets about a sad story, hurt animal or other persons break-up. The urgent need for fresh air at least once a day and a preference for bare feet wherever possible. My love of flowers, the sea and helping people, even when it hurt or drained me to do so, suddenly made sense! I was an empath. Well, even though I'm dead, I think I still am one? Yeah, I can use present tense if I'm a ghost, can't I?

✳ ✳ ✳ ✳ ✳

Anyway, Michael always told me that I was too "intense" and "fragile". He even once, called me "needy".

As often as he could, he liked to tell me to "calm down" and to just be as quiet as possible so as not to embarrass myself. Especially irate, he'd grab my arm roughly as I readied myself to eagerly skip towards a beautiful flower bed in the park or run barefoot into the sea. My voice and laughter, shrill with joy.

Originally, I thought it was just my Husband being caring and helping me; helping me grow and be a better person and even, a better *Wife*. Now I realise he was helping himself. Indeed, Michael had no empathy and no real care for the "real me".

And so I started to plan. Perhaps I was too obvious?! Literally shrinking from our home-life together, I became smaller in my marriage. Quieter and deeply averse to Michaels' touch; even his voice made me shrivel inside my own skin.

I tried to smile. I tried to indulge him. Of course, I failed so badly, that within a month of me deciding to leave, My

Husband started staring at me, sucking on his teeth and clicking his tongue at my lack of eye contact. Sometimes even grappling at me bodily, to force a kiss or hug. It was like he was trying to drag, *yes drag*, me back into his orbit.

That word, orbit is just the best word! Michael had a whole atmosphere around us but once I decided to leave him, my own planetary course changed, but as we both know, was never quite completed.

Michael

Well, that was a bloody wasted trip! Dammit! I wish people would move out of the way.

Tempted to shove the old crone hobbling up the street, in front of me, my hands naturally ball into fists. To be honest, I have to grit my teeth to stop roaring at people to move faster and let me pass!

Sharking through the town centre and towards home, I'm livid and bubbling with frustration that Kendal wasn't quite as amenable as I had hoped.

* * * * *

"Your Wife's died in unusual circumstances Mr Jennings..." Kendal tails off as I stare back at him blankly. The silence settles between us and the seconds tick by, one by one. I shift in my chair to break the tension and hope to trigger Kendal into saying something that may actually be useful. Kendal coughs and shuffles some papers but he's uncomfortable and I like it.

Annoyingly handsome and in shape, I disliked the man as soon as I walked in. Alice always handled the boring stuff like money, paperwork and this legal fluff. It's never been my thing and even here today, I can't really be bothered but time is passing and I have plans.

I'm not stupid; I know I have to work a little to get my reward. A means to an end, this first meeting has to happen to start the process of me claiming my estate. And what an estate it should *be*!

Pushing the documents I brought with me towards Kendal roughly, I feel a bolt of anger as he frowns and pushes them back across the table towards me.

"My secretary was asked to explain this to you, when you called, Mr Jennings. She said she tried but you were rather...... *determined* to see me. Let me take you through the basics though, now you're here". Kendal takes a breath in. Crap, he must have a lot to say.

"When someone passes away in unusual circumstances, there is a process". He strokes an eye-brow and closes his eyes for a few seconds then opens them again. "And well, it was only the day before yesterday that Alice died". I tut loudly, but sit back quickly to creak the chair and disguise the sound.

This man Kendal's turned out to be a royal pain in the backside, but I need to try and appear bothered by Alice's death and not by his awkward, faffing about with my money!

Nodding grimly and patting my chest where my heart is supposed to be, I get my little note-pad out. If I look interested, he'll think I care. Kendal's brow furrows as he watches me take the lid off the pen and nod at him, in what I am sure looks like encouragement.

Oh yes, I do care! I care about my money, so I can navigate this last little hurdle. Pen in hand, lips licked, I nod again and smile. Yes, I'm ready for his advice.

"First of all, your Wife's...err.... body is currently subject to a post-mortem. Obviously in this case it's sensible to say injuries from the fall killed her".

I have to resist the urge to snort when he says "fall", but I'm doing well here and don't want to ruin it. Abruptly, Kendal flicks his eyes up and looks straight at me. Alice would have said he has "sparkly blue eyes" and I guess he does. Whoops, I must stay focused, Kendal's talking again.

"So once the post-mortem's concluded, any findings of note, may ignite the need for investigation via the relevant authorities. Coroner or Police......" He looks at me, hoping that I'm satisfied with this vague information, then Coughs nervously. I don't say anything, forcing him to carry on.

"So......As I said, because Alice was in good health, and she passed.... in an unusual way...." A sigh escapes out of my mouth before I can stop it, and Kendal shoots me another, dark, yet staggeringly handsome look. *Staggeringly Handsome?!* What?! I have an awful lot of Alice's rubbish in and about my head today!

"Well! The Police won't be interested, Mr Kendal". My words are heavy with false patience. "Well, you made quite a few errors on the trip, didn't you?" Kendal says this slowly, but isn't quite brave enough to say it directly to my face.

"It was an *accident*", I hiss through gritted teeth, but smile brightly when he looks up at me again. "Exactly my point, and had you let my secretary talk for only 1 minute, she could have told you all this and saved you the trip in".

Kendal's turn to grit his teeth. "This actually is an i*deal case* for a coroner. A *perfect accident case study*, you might call it". He smiles and places both hands, face down, on the papers in front of me. "Looks like I'll be busy Googling tonight then, doesn't it?!" I chuckle and Kendal closes his eyes as if in pain.

Shit, I wasn't expecting such a formal or....careful, process. I'm not overly keen on careful people, they make me tense up. Akin to nosey people or people with better ideas than me, they rattle my cage. Grind my gears. Cause pains in my neck. These types only bring *trouble*. I'm sure you get the idea.

"Hang on there! This is all a bit fussy and how you say, dramatic! Terrible accident and really, I just need to move on, try and....grieve...I'm sure you understand!" Now I'm babbling and panicking openly, Kendal hands me a tissue and goes a bit pink in the cheeks.

"Now, Mr Jennings, in all honesty, I think you're getting ahead of yourself a little. I'm sure it's just your.....*grief* talking and I really am trying to help you. I'm sure your Wife would want you to try and look after yourself better. Just sit back and let things take their course. *Like I said*, it's only been a couple of days since the *tragedy*". He says tragedy differently. Ending the sentence with those three, stubborn and stark, little syllables. A triple knock on a coffin lid, they seem to echo round his office.

Faking innocence as best I can, I try to tilt my head at him to look confused, but falter as a stroke of cold air chills the bare skin exposed, above the collar of my favourite blue shirt. Thus, the coy tilt of my head, becomes a flinch. At my shivered twitch, a smile flits across Kendal's nicely shaped jaw. Resisting the urge to hit him with my note-pad, I fix my collar and nod; a silent instruction for him to finish his explanation, even though I'm not happy where it's headed.

Kendal looks at his watch then, back at me. "I have a couple of minutes, so will quickly explain the basics on the Coroner related things as I wonder if this is the most likely scenario for things...."

He gets up from the desk and wanders over to the window and looks out. A small pulse in his perfectly shaven jaw, is flickering. Fidgeting with the blinds, he looks almost bored and the combination of nerves and boredom in him, unnerves me somewhat.

"At the coroners court we'd traditionally hear from the witnesses from the scene. Any emergency services staff, in this case the Ogwen mountain rescue chaps and paramedics. Any other walkers or climbers, *maybe*. Oh and also any experts in whatever, the post-mortem says, your Wife *died* from. So, it is an investigation into a *death*, rather than a *crime*. I hope that makes things clear?" He pauses to turn and look at me. He looks almost angry and low down inside, my gut tightens.

"And of course, you Mr Jennings. You will be our, shall we say, *Star* Witness?!". A flush of panic reaches long fingers up to my neck and squeezes.

Next, the muscles go tight in my face. Worst of all, my anus throbs as I try hard not to let the sudden fear escape. Blinking like an owl in torch-light, I watch as Kendal smiles an even bigger smile, picks up my mortgage documents and Alice's Will and hands them back to me. He looks pointedly at his watch. A very sexy Rolex. One I would rather like myself, actually.

Standing up unsteadily, I wince as he starts talking again. "So! All being as you hope, the coroner will find Alice's sudden death an accident and *you* can then begin the process of applying for whatever assets within the estate she's left behind!"

"Is there any chance that there won't be a coroner's investigation. I mean, it's cut and dried. Simple. She fell. End of. Finito. That's it". In my panic at this sudden turn of events, I'm not caring to be the grieving widower anymore.

This is not happening! No, no, no! The voices in my head are screaming. Then out of nowhere, "Yes…. Yes…. Yes…", a different voice snakes in. It sounds like Alice.

A flashback to her excitedly opening one of the first gifts I bought her; real, heavy duty, proper walking boots. Her exclamation of "yes, yes, yes!". Her clapping her hands and running towards me to hug me. Christmas music on the television in the background. I smell mince-pies. She made them every year.

Twisting in my chair without even thinking, I turn around to look. Oh my god! She's there! She's stood there! No! of course she's not *there*. Nothing's there! A trick of the light that had her very much there. Wearing her old Blue Jumper, the one with the Christmas Tree on, of all things!

A tall pot-plant shadowed by a blue book case are both staring back at me impassively, but Kendal's long black coat on the stand nearby, flutters slightly as if disturbed by a breeze. Turning back to face my Wife's solicitor, I can see the window is closed behind him. It's darker outside now. The large square window makes me think of the entrance to a crypt.

"You look a little out of sorts, would you like a drink of water Mr Jennings?". Kendal's already pushing his chair back and turning to the trolley to his right. He has a marvellous backside. Alice's phrasing again. She used to love saying "marvellous" and giggle stupidly at how "posh and fancy" she said it could make a sentence sound.

A memory of her crowing "What a marvellous day!". The wind is in her hair, making it flay about her head. Her eyes closed to the breeze and face upturned to the sky as we sped home from the picnic where I proposed.

She started placing her fingers on the nape of my neck that day. A way for her to touch me without distracting me from driving. I liked how it showed her insecurity and childish need to feel I belonged to her. Even though really, she belonged to me.

Her tinkling laugh needles the skin between my eyes. Then, I remember her slight confusion then thrill, as I flamboyantly presented the ring and placed it on her finger before even asking if she would say yes. Her stuttering- "yes, ok.... of course. Thank you, Michael", and me leaning forward to kiss her, but spilling my wine all over her pale blue skirt. I never liked that skirt.

We didn't complete the kiss, nor the proposal. It never mattered, not to me anyway; the wedding was the important bit.

Sitting down heavily and grabbing another paper-tissue, from the box on Kendal's desk, I quickly mop at my forehead and close my eyes in excruciating anxiety. *This is not going the way it should be.* A clatter in front of me announces the glass of water has arrived.

Kendal isn't sitting down; the meeting's over. "Now if you excuse me, I really have to get on. I've stayed late to see you and my Wife's booked dinner for us. It's my wedding anniversary. My fifth. Oh yes, I meant to say, My Wife was very fond of Alice. They shared the same reading group. She's really rather upset". He's standing at the door. How did he get there so fast? The guy even moves like an athlete. Damn him.

"I shall be in touch once the post-mortem results are in Mr Jennings. I won't be able to share much but as Alice's executor, can squeeze some info out then, I'm sure. Now, have a safe trip home. Dare I say.... sit tight?" Fuck. This bastard knows; he's read me like one of Alice 's whodunnit romancey novel books!

Nodding at him, I step out into the corridor but start to turn to say goodbye with a plan to ask how long it will be, until I can stop *sitting tight,* but the door's slammed in my face.

* * * * *

So, here I am now; angry, frightened and furious striding through town towards the solace of home and desperately trying to work out, how to manage this situation.

This shouldn't be happening! I planned and planned and planned. No one was up there with us; no one saw me push her. A perfect plan. A perfect accident. This is a nightmare?! Now I'm not the one in control, some damn *pathologist* is. Oh, *Hells Teeth*!

Chapter 6: Violent Weather

Alice

Something's happening to how much I can do. It's like the closer Michael gets to being found out, my ability to be there, well sort of there, and show myself gets stronger.

Watching him in sexy-Kendal's office stirred a venom in me. I observed, listened then sneaked up on the treacherous tosser I married, with ease.

At first, I could sense his eagerness and satisfaction. He literally quivered and tingled with greed! In response, I tightened up and felt a bigger energy from within.

Then, Kendal's smell changed and the air around him muted from deep angry red to a satisfactory burnt orange. I knew then that Kendal had control and it was confirmed when Michael started to squirm like the worm he is.

Hooked, I watched the power play and as my Husband started to lose the game, I entered his head, not easily-but I did it! When he shot round in his chair, squeaking the leather, I wanted to squeak myself! Tracing my touch across his neck, resulted in the satisfying bodily function I knew it would; he always gets gas when he is nervous. It's no surprise my little "neck-stroke" trick from the past, had him hurtling back in time to the day we (sort of!) got engaged.

Mr Kendal always was an excellent advisor and he's right, his Wife and I certainly got on well. I truly hope they have a lovely dinner together. She knew I had plans to leave my Husband; she was one of the first I told.

Michael

I should have killed her sooner; long before she joined any daft book-clubs! I knew Alice was slipping from me, before she even really started the affair with that writer guy.

I've left it so late, there are ripples of rumour now. I think that's why Kendal's desperate to rag-doll me about a court room. His Wife. She'll be the one who encouraged Alice, I'll bet.

Women! Trouble through and through like sticks of rock candy with the word written inside.

Yes, it was her manner and her movements. Alice started to go brittle and hard, like someone had covered her with hot ash. She stiffened and smiled this strange stony way. It wasn't just the affair.

Crikey, we all have affairs. I've had plenty. She'd changed mentally; like a switch had been flicked. Like she'd seen me from the inside out and was alerted to danger.

Alice looked the same, sounded the same and even smelled the same but her eyes were wary. The way she shifted in and out of my personal space was, *animalistic.* Yes, she developed to be cat-like; quick, skittish and even crafty in how she reacted.

Yes, my sneaky Wife became that pet that lives with you but doesn't like you. The instinct of things slipping out of my control had me increasingly irate. And so, my meetings with my girls, whichever one I chose, got darker and more violent; just like last time. It was all my Wife's fault. She was making me take risks again!

I tried my best to suck her back in, but she'd withdraw quickly. We have edged around each other and back and forth like this for the last few years, really.

My torment increased with the affair though, so it's no surprise at all that in November, I drank too much and told her exactly how I felt. It was my time. She was pissing me off, with all her silly pointless skirting around the issue. Her squirrel cheeks when her phone buzzed. Her longer hours at work, extra nights out and even high-lights in her hair! It was all just so repulsive. I had developed a plan of my own, one that required a show-down to kick it off. From there I could proceed with the second phase. And no, it wasn't Alice I was focusing on.

* * * * *

We've just finished dinner. I was *starving,* so have timed my attack for after the Moussaka I've watched her slave over all day. "I've been thinking about Christmas...". I say, pushing my plate away and resting my elbows on the table. Alice's skin pales a little. "Darling Alice. *My blossom!* I've decided this year we should go away for the festive season!" She goes even more pale; translucent even.

My heart speeds up with pleasure. I always did like dropping little fear bombs, but this is a cracker. How joyous, I can see through her lies and now even her skin is like tracing paper! Lovely stuff. And so I prattle on, "Yes, let's go away, just us, the *whole fortnight.* Somewhere fancy, no *classy!*" Clapping my hands when I say *"whole fortnight"* in time to their syllables; one, two, three claps and she winces at the slapping sound of each one. Fork in mid-air, the last bite of spicy steaming mince a few inches from her pathetic, slightly sweaty face, makes me almost purr with pleasure. I tilt my head and smile. Eye to eye, this is a challenge; one liar to another.

"Michael, I'm not really sure. I've a lot of work on at the library and there's that book signing. Mind, I told you? The artist woman from Israel. Then there's the staff party, I got tasked with the decorations and then there's the cake and of course, the nibbles......" Her voice disappears, as she wanders down the tunnel of deceit. It's a long dark, moist tunnel. I should know. Damn hard to find the light to come back.

Alice will be desperately fingering the slimy walls; searching for a good solid reliable excuse. Something she can strike the match of honesty on so she feels better about her filthy, dirty betrayal of our marriage. My marriage. *Mine.*

"I really do have too much on, two weeks is a long time".

Her eyes slide away and she puts the final forkful in her mouth. Looking down at the remnants of her salad for answers, she's hoping I'll give in.

"Well, all the more reason for a holiday! Just get all finished and done, then we can go away and celebrate the success of you managing it. All by yourself!" Again, I clap my hands and tip back in my chair. She flinches and the colour fills her cheeks again, as her dinner threatens to reappear. Yes, I think she just gagged a little. I know for a fact, that the Simon one, has been helping plan the Staff Christmas Party.

She doesn't know of course, that *I know,* that Mr Sex-Mad-Writer-Guy, has been employed to stay on at the University. Yes, it took a bit of fiddling about, but I've made the effort to create a fake social media account and watch his pages.

Masters announces pretty much everything he does on there. Arrogant prick. It's been almost too easy, watching him show off and with *his massive* ego, he paints a picture of where he is daily, weekly and for the next few months.

One would think, an expert in dark characters such as myself, would be more careful. Apparently not.

Yes, she has bloomed in happiness since. I can match up the date he announced it on his page with the same day these, stupid noisy dangling bell earrings, that look like wind-chimes, have magically appeared! I'm convinced he bought them for her as an *"I'm not going anywhere"* gift. Yes, she may be the *cat*, but I am the canary and I can hear her coming!

"Michael, I'm really quite serious. And the cost! Yes, *the cost*". She grasps at this excuse as if snatching a lucky white feather from the sky. Pleased, she looks at me straight faced again. Offers a tentative smile and I loathe her, even more.

She thinks she's won. It's her money and her job so ultimately, her decision.

Alice's shoulders sag in relief, at my short silence and I watch as she starts to stand up and carefully leans over to take my plate. Reaching out I snatch at her, grasping her hand tight and she stops.

"Are you *sure* it's the *money* and not that *man*". My voice is quiet. Every word carefully pronounced. Of course, I don't blink and to her credit, neither does she. Looking down I see her slim wrist is going grey. I'm grasping her hand so tight the blood's been cut off. She tugs, pointlessly.

Glaring openly now, I know my pale eyes will be virtually white with rage. She tugs again so I squeeze even tighter and press her hand down hard onto the table for traction. Her knife and fork rattle and there are tears in her eyes now. This enrages and stimulates me.

"You fucking cheating cow whore". I'm hissing and she's looking down at me in terror, her mouth slightly open. Then a big fat tear hits my hand. I recoil. "I've known for almost two months, you ridiculous creature. I saw you. I saw you with him. That great, vile, giant toad. And now, it's over".

She pulls hard suddenly with a strength, I don't recognise, so as my *"you're not going anywhere gift"*, I let her have her hand back. She's angry, but the look slides away fast, as her plate, falls then shatters on the floor. The last of the still warm food, splashes on her bare feet.

Black pottery splinters scatter everywhere. Like the claws from a long dead animal, they are sharp and bound together only by the red and brown remainders of our food. Alice is stood in the centre of the mess, head down, unsure what to do next.

"You need to tell me what you think you're playing at. All mousy, sexless and useless with me, yet...him..... he, that *thing!* He has you lit up like a Halloween Pumpkin".

She gasps and steps backwards onto the shards. Thrilled at seeing her so scared, I feel a rustle in my crotch. Not now, this really isn't the best time. "Get yourself away from me! Go to the spare room or better still, sit on your step on the stairs! Think about what you've done to me. To us! Our marriage! Our perfect marriage!".

Yes, I know I'm laying it on thick, but I'm enjoying myself. Plus, If she's out of the way for the evening, I can text my girl or maybe all 3 girls for an indulgent while. I pay an extra £50 a month to have the privilege of these extra hours of special-talk.

"Wait you! Leave that phone!"

Reaching out, palm upturned, I wait for her to do as I ask. Of course, she does. I can hear her yelping and sobbing like a kicked dog all the way to the spare room. Streaks of blood trail her where she cut her feet.

Taking the sim out of the phone I bite it, smile grimly then think again and swallow it. Why not?! No more phone for *you* Wifey. I eat up your pain and spit....it....out when I so choose.

Dylan

When Serena would lose the babies, it was all about her. I understood that; her body, her soul, her tears, her blood. But, in time, my understanding dwindled. Shamefully, I felt anger. I felt left out. I was also hers; her Husband, her best friend and the father of those little souls and yet, I was left behind in the waves of her grief.

As nurses and doctors and specialists wasped around her, great clouds of striped white and blue and green, the sounds became unbearable. The bleeping, whispering and scratching pens' on clip-boards became deafening, so I just melted away into the corners of the hospital rooms.

Watching from the edges of her pain and silent in my own emptiness and disappointment, I stopped trying to show her I was there. It's almost a cliché now, that men can cry too. Like we need permission! Oh, I cried. By god, I *wept*.

Serena thinks I like two showers a day to be extra clean. It's actually a time when I can weep with the rush of the water drowning the sounds out. I grit my teeth and gag on the words I desperately want to wail into my Wife's chest.

I imagine her stroking my hair and hear and her whispers that we'll be alright; that we'll be parents soon. But that never happens.

Yes, I sought physical, sexual, comfort elsewhere and yes, I do hate myself for it. Perhaps you can understand? Please? See somehow, that I felt selfish and greedy for reaching out to Serena? She made me feel dirty and disgusting for trying to touch her. Bronwyn made me feel like me again. It's pathetic, I know. Losing yourself and grieving are two triggers for a gun that at some point had to go off.

The affair continued fast and hard, as all good ones do. And so, I think you have guessed, I booked the hotel room before Serena even rose for the day, less than 24 hours after I met Bronwyn.

My Wife was sleeping in the spare room again. This had become a telling new ritual after an unexpected period, or worse, a miscarriage.

We'd drive home from the hospital in silence; Serenas jaw, stiff and tight. Her face cement and her skin as cold as could be.

The first few times I tried to talk to her. Rested a hand on her knee, to be met with this Hellish stare and spattering of threats of what she would do to me if I ever dared to touch her ever again.

If I turned the radio on, she turned it off. If I opened the windows, she closed them. She was happier in her rage and grief if we were surrounded by relative silence.

Occasionally a car would over-take and if children were on board, she would flinch violently as though slapped and close her eyes the rest of the journey home. Once home, Serena had a particular pattern of movements; like a dance at a wake.

By the 3rd loss, I could predict them like watching the hands of a clock. Tick-chooses a bottle of wine. Tock-reaches for a glass, wincing in pain. Tick-drinks first glass in three gulps, eyes closed. Tock- "I'm going for a bath". Tick-pours another glass and shifts to stand looking out onto the garden. Tock- "I think I hate you", she'd say not turning around.

Tick- "Go and run me a bath and shut the blinds in the spare room". Tock- I do as she asks.

By the time we met Bronwyn, Serena hadn't even dared to feel relief to get past the now almost mystical 10 week stage. Yes most people wait for 12 weeks, but we never got there; we had our own tide-mark.

Quiet and watchful, my Wife had started walking around as though carrying a precious crystal vase in the front of an apron; willing the little life to stay put, not fall and shatter our hopes and dreams yet again.

Our last loss was the worst. We didn't try again after that. I'll never forget Serenas siren wails through the bathroom door. I expected higher pitched keens and sobs but this time, 5th time unlucky, her voice blistered with rage and anger. Over and over she roared; a lioness dying. The type of empty womb roar, only a bereft childless mother could ever make.

And so, I sat there with my back against the bathroom door, listening to her and quietly crying myself.

Before, she'd scream and shout in my face. *How dare I do it to her again, she demanded,* although I never had the answer. She was always irrational and sometimes violent, so to help her get her fix of rage and release, I simply sat there, taking it. I just wanted her to feel better, quieten down, seek comfort from me. But she never did. This time, she seemed angry at herself and even, dare I say, *the baby.*

So, when Bronwyn offered up the chance for me to not be loathed, blamed or ignored, I grasped it with both hands. Literally.

I'm well aware that It's repugnant to be talking about losing our babies on one hand and go straight to the physicality of the affair on the other. You find it distasteful, I do too, but once it started, we couldn't stop.

Bronwyn fell in love with me and I fell in love with the escape. I lived for those salty, sweet afternoons in hotel rooms; almost cinematic with how traditionally affairish it all was. We didn't talk a lot, as by the time we'd get to the meet up,

I just wanted to disappear inside Bronwyn's generous body and the only sounds I wanted to hear, were my own cries of release as she clenched around me, drawing me deep into that enveloping addictive nothingness, that just never lasted long enough. Literally, I'd see stars and then we'd do it again.

The twice monthly meetings with Bronwyn went on for nearly a year until the day she gave me the worst good news of my life. She was pregnant.

Serena

The sun sank faster than expected. Slipping behind the spiked peaks, of the mountains encircling us, in what felt a like a furtive and mischievous manner. She left behind the warm smile of a sunset and 40 blazing minutes of light, to allow us time to finish setting up camp for the night. We shared another beer in thanks to her.

"It seems so odd that Alice and her Husband would be up here so close to sun-down, don't you think Dex?" Turning away, to show my back to the last ruby brushstrokes of sky and kneeling down at Dexter's side, I can't help but want to lean into him for some body warmth and maybe something else.

"Yep. Exactly why I wanted to come up here and mirror their movements in some parts. It's the best way to work out what really happened". He's not looking at me and a dart of anger jabs my ego yet again. I resist snapping at him for being so cool with me. It's embarrassing, but I'm not used to so little attention, Humph! Even Dylan tries harder than this!

Dexter's wandered away and has started putting our bags inside the tent.

"I'm no climbing expert, but anyone with any walking or hiking experience knows that as soon as the sun starts to descend, the atmosphere, especially up high, makes the air cool really fast. In addition, any swift cold up on a mountain can encourage dampness and dampness leads to much more slippy conditions. This particular peak is known for its inclines and lack of obvious paths....to safety. I don't like the story we've had so far....".

Watching him prowl around our bespoke camp-site as he talks on and on, has shut me up. Smoothing an invisible crease, wiping off barely discernible streaks of mud, and tightening guy ropes as he goes, is fascinating to see. I wonder if he has O.C.D?

Eager to impress him or at least catch a glance of his rare attention, I speak before I mean to. "Dylan had this saying "Hike after two and I'll be rescuing you, it made me laugh..." My voice trails off as I realise I haven't laughed with my Husband for months, maybe even over a year. No.... longer. *Much longer.*

"You keep talking about your Husband. I don't understand why he's not here with you. It's weird". Dexter's blunt and to the point. As zipped up and taut as the tent, I don't know what to say. "Has something happened to, well.... to your Dylan?" he probes.

"Pfffft! God no! No! It's complicated. I know everyone says that. But this time it really is. I don't want to talk about it. I wouldn't even know where to start. Put it this way I'm doing my best not to jump off this mountain myself". Now it's me, not making eye contact.

"You seem to have a lot to say when it suits you". Dexter's handsome face breaks into a smile. Then the rain starts.

The first droplets tap us gently on our foreheads, then cheeks, then chins. In under 10 seconds the rain's a lot heavier and the wind picks up again. It buffets us and curls around the tarp, tightening the guy ropes and wrenching back the opening to the tent. The Notch is telling us to stay safe and right now in this wet, dark, increasingly cold place, we need to do as we're told.

Alice

I always believed Michael would never cheat on me. In my opinion, he just wasn't the type. All his passion seemed spent on himself, rather than me.

Yes, in the early days before we married, rarely a whinge nor a whine slipped from his lips. Shiny and swollen with positivity and plans, Michael was never one for being bad tempered.

Especially in shops that suited his interests, he'd beam with pride, clasping my hands in his and virtually skipping us around whatever car show-room, DIY store or wine shop we found ourselves in. Happily chattering away, only going quiet to peer closely at a label or kiss me, I never once thought his aura would turn this vile greeny grey. Indeed, I recall a few times he was....colder or even nasty, they were usually in "Weird Women's Shops", as he called them.

The new car twice a year. The monthly allowance on the last Thursday of every month. The hand-made leather jackets for his lads' holidays. The new iPad, laptop, phone whenever a new model came out. Michael's polite requests turned to narrow-eyed demands.

Slowly, like a spoiled child training its baby-sitter, he became brazen with confidence and I grew weak with anxiety. What my Husband wanted; my Husband got. I knew saying no would ruin my week before it ruined his. Simon told me it's called "Coercive Control". I had never heard such a phrase before but on looking it up in my library, I had this awful, sickening, feeling of familiarity.

The first time I saw Michaels "Big Temper", wasn't long after our 3rd anniversary. Mind you, the word *"temper"*, hardly even covers what happened. Capital T for temper? Yes, T for Tyrannosaurus Rex. T for Terrifying. Are there any T's that would nicely describe a person losing their mind over a simple comment? T for tremendous. See, tremendous is usually a good thing. Not when it's a tremendous temper tantrum!

Hah! Indeed, I'd seen glints of my Husband's rage before. The flashes of steel in his eyes. The twist of his mouth, and the paled, pursed, skin on his lips. But nothing prepared me for when I mentioned his first Wife.

We were pottering about in the garden on one of those blurry, simmering, heavy aired days, when the best thing for it is a hat and some gardening. The cool soil and dappled shade of plants offering a distraction and relief from the heat. Gently teasing weeds out of the raised beds and dead-heading drooped, late summer blooms in companionable silence, things felt even and settled between us.

Perhaps It's not an unusual metaphor but I've always likened gardening to hair-dressing. Grooming, snipping, tidying and enhancing something already rather pretty into something even more eye-catching and gorgeous.

* * * *

Looking up through the fine wicker of the brow on my sun-hat, I can see the shape of Michael batting his hands at a cluster of angry dying wasps, who are doggedly trying to both sting and land on him. Within seconds, he's started to prance about the lawn, swearing and grunting. It's a strange high kicking dance, of pure comedy. Oh dear! A giggle catches in my throat but I stop it escaping with a small cough; feigning an errant flower petal, catching on my lips.

Any time Michael wasn't fully in control of a situation, was a situation that could turn nasty and ruin at least a whole day. "Fucking buzzing bastardy bastards" he's ranting over and over and twirling in circles.

Readying myself to help him, I see he's even taken his cream trilby off and started to bat at the insects! I close my eyes and hold my breath, desperate to not giggle again.

There's a drum-like thudding of his bare feet on the slightly damp lawn so I count to ten before being composed enough to look again. Nope, he's still at it. Twirling, batting and swearing. Redder and redder in the face with each swipe and stomp.

Sliding my gardening gloves off, to get ready to help him, the light catches my wedding ring. A breeze passes by my cheek and a waft of yellow roses fills my nostrils, taking me back to our wedding day. *Such a special, sparkling, day it was.* "Darling. I wish we could get married all over again! It was a wonderful day for us. You're lucky, you got to do it twice!".

Still kneeling on the little gardening cushion, I twist and turn to face him with a smile on my face, waiting for him to return the same. In the silence between us I get a prickle of unease and take my hat off and smile wider, hoping he's just not heard me.

He's stock still and staring right through me. I'm turned to glass. My smile falls away and I stare back. Slow motion blends the seconds together and they stretch and blur between us.

"What did you say?" I'm not even sure if his lips moved. He streaks the air launching himself towards me; all mustard yellow jumper and Mediterranean blue shorts. The strike hits me on the side of my head and I fall back into the thorny rose bushes, legs up in the air like a beetle shocked by the forceful flick of a stranger's finger.

"Don't you ever, ever, ever talk about my Wife again, you ridiculous woman". He spits in my ear, bending close and low over me. There's no eye-contact now but I don't think I'd want to look him in the eye anyway. "She ruined our marriage. I told you! She left me for some French-man then went and *died*! She broke me!". He's yelling now. I hope the neighbours can't hear; I would be so embarrassed and ashamed.

Rigid with surprise with my eyes tightly shut, I just lie there until he sighs, takes a deep breath in and steps away from where I'm laid. Opening one then both eyes, I watch my Husband smooth his hair and pat his pockets as if searching for the temper he's lost, here in the garden, quite so spectacularly.

"Now, now! Less of your silly nonsense now darling, we still have some mulch to make and the rest of that pruning to do". Light and airy as if nothing happened, he walks away with the basket of trimmings and bends over a fat row of bruise coloured irises.

* * * *

We never spoke of it again. Michael had reacted so viciously and then so detached, I knew better than to refer to Wife number one in any other way than within the safer corners of my own secret thoughts.

Whatever areas he didn't want to discuss, were made clear by these child-like fits of irrational rage. Then, later, he would exaggerate the stress or trauma of my "nosiness" and "rudeness", to such a point I feared he would either have a heart-attack or give *me* one.

After these outbursts, I was given the silent treatment or he demanded extra money to "cheer him up". Gone were the days where he wanted sexual favours for that purpose and dear lord, I was glad of that! Simple peace from his moods was priceless by the time we hit our 5th wedding anniversary. Like a cheap celebration balloon, I understood that what went up, certainly came down.

Michael

I've decided to treat myself-there's plenty of cash in the joint account, so I've just texted one of my girls for an appointment; *asap please*! Then on my way back home after that horrendous solicitor attempted to ruin my week, I stopped off to buy some brandy and half a dozen of my favourite cigars.

Yes, Kendal got under my skin, but it didn't take long for my usual confidence to return, once I went over and over again how organised and careful, I've been. The secret to getting away with anything, is to plan, plan, plan. *Oh how I planned*!

Between the show-down confrontation dinner and the day I ended Alice's life, I visited the Notch 3 times. I pressured her to update her life-insurance and more carefully observed her behaviours than ever before.

My Wife had no idea I was monitoring her calls and plotting her death because I started the process of wooing her all over again. Reducing my intensity of before, I went in for the kill much more gently.

Making cups of tea, buying her new books and smiling gently as she began sharing stories from her work again. Laying my large hands across her slightly shaking ones, I'd look in her eyes and do an incredible job of pretending I cared. I even bought her a new phone which benefited me, once a special recording app was installed.

Mulling over the day's events with a quick sandwich and espresso in the garden helped my mood a little this evening, but stepping back inside the kitchen, I realise it really is rather chilly in the house today. I can't seem to get comfortably warm.

It must be the shock of that idiot lawyer and his daft ideas about court cases and what-not. Putting on the heating was always Alice's job. She just seemed to know the right time of day to do it. She was so controlling!! To be frank, having to do everything myself is stretching my patience but I'll get used to it once I'm rich! I think I'll run myself a bath before making dinner.

I've a few hours to relax, before my 11pm appointment with Charmaine, the girl I chose for tonight. She was very amenable, *squeezing* me in. Now, there's a *thought*....

Chuckling to myself and stomping up the stairs, freshly decanted brandy in hand, I stumble at the top but don't fully trip. Bloody carpet all wrinkled up where she used to sit and wait while I made my way slowly out of a huff.

Banging the bathroom door open a little too roughly, I let out a cackle and stumble forward to slam my brandy on the top of the toilet cistern.

Bending to turn the taps on the bath, I briefly think about Charmaine. Yes, she'll warm me up. Unzipping my flies, I let loose and tilt my head back in pleasure at the release of urine. At my age you can't hold it in for long! No need to wipe the toilet-seat; I'm a widower now and have no pointless female to nag at me and peck my head in my own house!

10 minutes later, I'm lying back in the water with a frothy mountain range of snowy bubbles resting on my shoulders. Yes, this was a *grand* idea.

I've used Alice's special bath foam liberally and am rather enjoying it. This is why women spend so long in here! It's a revelation! Getting into the spirit of things; the lights are off and I've even lit some candles too.

A screech startles me up and out of the water fast and I sit up a little to peer out of the window. Sounded like a fox or cats mating. Be still my beating heart! Hah!

Slurping at my brandy and sitting back again, I can't help but purse my lips in frustration. If wifey was here, I could yell for her to bring the bottle up. Stupid Alice, never here when you need her. Sliding down into the water, I let it flow over my head and lay there under the surface for a few seconds, enjoying the watery silence.

Then a bang downstairs has me shooting up out of the water and spluttering again, but worse this time.

I move so fast, my brandy glass skids away from me, falls and shatters on the floor. Cursing, I watch the brown oily shards shoot across the pristine, light blue tiles. Little iridescent boats heading for deeper sea. Oh, I'm a little drunk after-all!

The candles flicker madly; dancing with each other and casting shadows of nothing at all across the walls. Bang! Bang! There it is *again*! It sounded closer; something in the house, this time.

One of the candles goes out with a hiss, as though pinched by wet fingers. But both of my hands are either side of me, clenched tightly round the rails on the side of the bath. In front of me, a hillock of bath-bubbles starts to split apart....

Deadly silent now, with the orange candle glow all around me, I watch as the water freezes and starts to crystalize. The ice forms, then cracks. I can't move. It's all happening in slow motion. Freezing frosty veins reaching out across the water begin to creep towards my knees. Another candle hisses out.

It's almost completely dark in the bathroom now. My breaths are coming in tiny grey puffs, lit amber by the last lonely candle I pray doesn't flicker to nothing like she did, when I pushed her off that mountain. "Are you ready to die yet?" her whisper comes out of nowhere.

It sounds like Alice, but that's not possible! The plastic rings of the shower curtain jangle slightly above me and I recoil in fright.

I half expect her to be stood there in that mangy old bath robe. The star patterned, bobbly one that I liked to tug, push and criticise. "Make an effort. Stop being such a frump". Now that, yes that, sounds like me, but I haven't opened my mouth! The echo seems to make a shadow of my own voice, as it booms against the porcelain my Wife so fastidiously kept clean.

A dog barks twice in the garden and a squeal escapes me. I've drunk too much brandy. No! It's the stress of that fucking solicitor. The initial worry of being on my own. None of this is real. She's gone. Dead! I made sure! I stood and watched her body go still! Yes, I'm just a bit creeped out and tipsy. Probably even rather uptight with sexual tension! I should have made the appointment for earlier. I'm being silly, there's nothing here. "Oh, I'm here Michael. I'm really very, *very* here".

The shower-curtain twitches as though poked. Then, holding my breath, I watch as a shadow slides between the creases or maybe it doesn't. Rearing up with a roar and grabbing at the curtain to expose who's stood there, I almost slip but grasping at the fabric, I hold tight and start to screech, "I'm calling the Police! Go away!". The last candle fizzles out. I think I hear Alice's tinkling wind-chimes of laughter out in the hall, then everything goes black.

Serena

I feel a total idiot sat in this tent. Crushed together like fat kids on a church pew, Dexter and I are awkwardly waiting for the time to pass. He's not chatty and I'm not open; it's a bad combination.

The air has become thick with our mutual shyness. He was right, the rain swept in fast. The sudden tirade of water sounded not unlike clapping! Both thinking the same thing, we smiled at the applause for our timing; our almost perfect readying of the camp-site for the night. The rain drops grew bigger so in unison we dove for the tent scrabbling for cover, as though it was acid, not water attacking us from above.

Sneaking a glance, I'm a little relieved that Dexter doesn't seem quite as uncomfortable as me. He's crossed legged and appears to be listening to the rain; almost counting the drops and unaware I'm even here. I need to say something; anything!

"How long have you been doing this sort of stuff, for work then?". Yes, it's pathetic but it's a start. I close my eyes in embarrassment. "A few years now". Dexter replies and the simplicity only adds to my frustration. "I loved it. I really, really miss it. Working in the media". The words tumble out and uncomfortable at my own rare openness, I pretend to be busy taking my coat off and tying my hair back up. The tarp beneath us crackles and I feel like it's laughing at me. In fact, I bet this tent has seen some action.

"Why did you stop working Serena?" He's looking at me now. "I met a guy. Long story. Old story", urgh, now I can't stop talking! "I was doing well career-wise but then I met Dylan. Fell in love. Moved to where he was brought up. About an hour or so from here". Dexter's listening carefully and it spurs me on. "I just thought things would fall into place instead they just fell apart". The lump in my throat from earlier today returns in a flash and I want to cry.

"These things happen I suppose", he replies and turns away to start to unravel what looks like a well-used, slightly shabby sleeping bag.

"I can see her ghost". My words fill the tent and Dexter stiffens with the pressure of them. And still, I babble on. "I'm not crazy. Honestly. Alice has been with me on and off this whole time". The relief at saying it is intense.

A breath of citrussy yellow-rose scented air, tickles the fine hair at the nape of my neck and I wonder if she's here again.

Outside the wind's stopped and there's a heavy silence wrapped all around us. I wish Dexter would bloody well turn around. I can only imagine what he's thinking now. Probably planning how to get me out of the tent and lob himself down the mountain at warp speed. Far, far away from Crazy Lady!

Turning round and shifting his frame to sit cross-legged again, Dexter wrests his right arm casually across the back of his back-pack as though it were a person, and replies "That's cool. Could make a good story even better".

A gust of wind tears the opening to the tent open and a sheet of icy air and rain whips our faces. I hear a tinkling laughter flying away into the dark and smile. "Any more beers?" I ask and Dexter nods with a grin. "I've got something better....." with a flourish, he lifts a half-finished bottle of Johnny Walker Black Label out. "Cheers".

Alice

Once Serena met Dexter on the road below the mountain and that shimmer of belief in my story passed between them, I felt a glow of strength. That feeling when you see a rainbow and you can't help but feel hope and even smile. Something magical happened, and this time it was nothing to do with me.

Wanting to keep an eye on Michael, I've tried to use all the strength I have to be around him as much as possible, but this last short while, he's been sapping me like a vampire. His toxicity feels like teeth. I feel them puncturing me, tearing, tasting and sucking all I have, which being dead really isn't much.

Simon used to say that the dark, pathologically seductive people he studied and wrote about, the Casanova Psychopaths I think he called them, were feeders on hope. That they lied like breathing and sometimes just for fun. It made so much darn sense! A lot of this actually is starting to make sense!

The exchange between Michael and Kendal, in his office, filled me up somewhat so when my Husband ran that bath, I decided to have a little fun. I didn't expect he would be so receptive!

Michael's giving off a sexual air tonight. He's all wound tight and swaying between excited and anxious; I wonder if he's been having an affair. I hope he treats her better than me! It's reminded me of when Simon and I agreed to be together.

* * * * *

I am dreading leaving for our Christmas break away tomorrow. Almost two full weeks alone, just Michael and I. Twenty-four hours a day for him to monopolise my time. Nip nip nip at my patience. Poke poke poke at my silence. Going *on and on* about his new favourite topic; our fresh start.

Don't get me wrong, he's not been aggressive or even nasty since he confronted me about my "filthy mistake". Thrusting a huge bunch of flowers at me and leaving slobbering dog-breath kisses on the corner of my mouth several times, since our confrontation several weeks ago, has made my stomach harden more than is healthy. This cannot go on. Once home from the trip, I'm moving out and filing for Divorce.

"We need to talk. I want to leave him sooner, than I originally planned", I whisper and choke on a sob. I'm leaving a voicemail for Simon from the solace of the toilet upstairs. Michael has returned from his drive out, absolutely full of beans. Sitting on the toilet seat and panicking a little, I am willing my lover to call me or text me back, so we can simply agree once I'm home from my break away, we can be together properly.

"I'm going to pick you out some clothes to take Alice!" Michael gayly shouts from the bedroom. "It'll be cold in the North. Blustery, chilly and very very Christmassy!" he sings. I close my eyes and press my knees together in fear. He's excited and I think he wants us to get physical again. The thought forces me to try calling Simon a third time, but again, straight to voicemail.

Michael has started doing this weird whistling, and he's really good at it. Opera Whistling, one of my nieces once called it, when she heard it on the T.V. Yes, he puts me in mind of a small song-bird, announcing its intentions to mate. Yikes!

My phone buzzes and grabbing at it, I almost fall to the ground in relief. "Yes, agreed, don't call me or text me while you're away though. Too close for comfort and he will catch you xx".

Simon's reply is all I need, to get me through this next fortnight. "I'm going down to the car to put my bag in! Back in a jiffy!" Michaels high pitched voice tails off, as he heads out of the bedroom and towards the stairs. "Okay! With you in a minute!", I call back. Hoping I sound as content and positive as he does.

* * * * *

In the month since the horrid dinner, I hadn't told Simon that Michael knew about us and had demanded we finish. I didn't have the words in me (for a change!) to explain to my lover, how my Husband had found out and what his reaction was. Even worse, how could I tell him that I planned on staying for a good while, before finally physically leaving him? I also feared that he would leave me, if I didn't leave Michael, on his terms.

I watched Michael go in and out of the house, with our travel-bags.

From my spot, at the spare bedroom window, he looked like a nice person and genuinely happily helping his Wife pack for a lovely trip away.

I felt a pang of guilt, then another one, as he waved up at me from the drive, and carefully closed the boot on his car, with a tenderness my skin had missed for years. If he hadn't already been so....nice.....that last few weeks, I would have thought all his hard work and keenness to help, was unusual for him. But he had been much more helpful in general, since I pretended to end things with Simon.

And surprisingly, our Christmas trip away was actually rather pleasant. He let me have my own room and he was, dare I say, attentive and kind. He was the man I'd met all those years before.

Michael

The emergency waiting room stinks; all these sick people are making me feel sick! There's a faint scent of urine emanating from the man to my right, so I shuffle to the side slightly and cross my legs to twist myself out of the waft. Not very successfully mind you.

Sniffing and sighing, I catch the eye of a young dark-haired woman seated opposite me. The round bump of her pregnant belly makes her chest look even more ample. Smiling widely, I wink at her but she doesn't smile back and quickly looks away back to her magazine. Simple creature, not my type anyway. Glancing at the clock, I feel a little better.

I still have time to get ready for my appointment with Charmaine later. What happened in the bathroom really is no big deal; waking up on the tiled floor, I realised I must have just slipped after having too much of that fine brandy. Don't know how long I was out for, but left with a tender big egg, at the back of my skull, and ever conscious of my health, I've taken myself for a check-up.

I have far too much to lose if I pop my clogs suddenly! Thank goodness for the NHS; there's even time for a pub visit before I race over to Charmaine's flat. Admittedly my head's a little tender, but I'm not re-scheduling with her! An A and E confirmation all is well, a couple of painkillers and a pint and I'll be fit as a fiddle. I hope she's ready, I have a lot of anxiety and frustration to get out.

A throb makes me close my eyes. Well, two throbs. One in my head and the other much further south. Ruining my day dream, a loud robotic voice startles me.

"Mr Michael Jennings to consulting room Seven please", the tannoy announces. Resisting the urge to bow to the adoring glances of the two elderly ladies across from me, I re-button my blazer, straighten my chinos and march purposefully (and rather handsomely) across the room to my appointment.

I've always loved talking about myself; doctors' appointments, job interviews, first dates...all excellent opportunities to display how wonderful I am. This is no exception. I'm told this is a new doctor I haven't met before, so I get 8 minutes to impress him.

Nattering away quite happily about my career in football coaching (well, I play in 5 a side on a Tuesday as you well know) and collection of vintage cars (ok- I only have one but the Alice-Money can soon fix that). I relax onto the seat, and wince dramatically, as the doctor parts my hair and starts to gently press the big bump on my head. "So, as I was saying, I'm thinking Sardinia next Spring.... perhaps hire a boat, certainly a good hotel...all-inclusive is a must".

"Sorry to interrupt Mr Jennings but can you tell me again how this happened?". A spurt of annoyance, at being halted in my story, makes me frown.

"Ok, well, I was having a bath and then a little noise from downstairs startled me. My Wife recently died and I'm rather unhappy living alone. Uncomfortable you could say. Even lonely". I cast my eyes down to my lap and fiddle with my hands in what I hope looks like abject grief.

"I'm very sorry to hear that Mr Jennings. Do go *on*. How did you find yourself when this bump occurred? As in, where exactly *were* you?" His eyes show concern but I'm ready to show him I'm fine. I can't have him keeping me in hospital for the night! Good lord, *no!*

"I was on the floor of the bathroom. Bloody cold too!", I laugh loudly and the doctor flinches at my sudden upward change in demeanour. I shut up fast, before letting myself get too carried away. I rearrange my face, look away out of the window then back at him and nod, making a show of swallowing down invisible tears. Nodding quickly, I'm permitting him to carry on his diagnosis.

"I'm going to run a few other tests..... as it's rather odd for someone to just suddenly lose consciousness and fall like this. In fact, not just odd but a touch.....concerning".

Unease prickles my chest and immediately I feel angry. For goodness sakes what now?! As if I don't have enough to bloody worry about. "If you're insisting, then that's fine", I say through barely parted lips. The doctor, smiles and pats my hand like I'm some sort of old idiot.

"Nothing to concern yourself with just now. I'll take a little blood and urine and get you back in if we need to, another day. With your recent.... stresses, your age and ....err, large.... stature. We need to rule out any possible pre-existing or even hidden health issues that might have triggered the fainting episode, ok?"

He doesn't wait for me to agree, and I bite back a cheeky retort and try again to reassure him so I can escape quicker. "I had a little to drink and the water was mighty hot Doctor... Could it be that do you think?" My voice goes up an octave.

"Hmmmmmm......*maybe*". He's turned away now and is tapping away on his computer with his back to me. Rude little man! My usual doctor would never be so ignorant. He always asks about my holiday plans or comments how I look so fantastic for my age! "Look at that hair Mr Jennings. Its magnificent!" he exclaims as soon as I enter the room. *That usual Doctor better come back from his training course soon, that's for sure!*

This one's talking again, does he ever sit quiet? "So, after taking those samples, I'm going to weigh you, check your blood pressure and book you in for a further check-up, in about a week...ok?". Pfffft! Typical youngster. Hardly out of nappies this one. Over-dramatic and pernicious. I'm going to need Charmaine to be extra good, after all this nonsense!

Dylan

I've tried calling serena 6 times since she made me leave the house. I'm not surprised she won't talk to me. She always was a master of the silent treatment. Jedi warrior of huffs. Queen of evil looks. I'm a talker. It's just my way.

It's me who breaks the silences with an apology or affectionate squeeze of her shoulders. Me who buys the sorry-flowers, me who cooks the make-up dinner or books the Fresh-Start-Restaurant. Picking up the shards of our relationship and gluing them back together over and over again has worn me down though. But I would have done it for the rest of our lives; I love her so much.

Bronwyn's pregnancy announcement just blew my mind 7 years ago, and not in a good way. A huge mirror falling. A car hitting a tree. An empty building exploding. That noisy shocking breaking of a fragile, high risk reality.

＊＊＊＊＊

Dear God! Bronwyn's just stood there smiling inanely like this is a good thing. A lovely birthday surprise like a cake with my face on it or some expensive aftershave. Her blouse is still slightly undone and her shoes are on the floor, by the door, where we left them 26 minutes ago.

This was just supposed to be fun! An outlet. A relief. An escape from my own selfish misery! Now look what's happened. How has this happened? I don't understand.

"I thought you had that.... implant thingy", my voice is weak and bizarrely I'm embarrassed talking about such a personal, private thing with the woman I've bedded perhaps fifty times; in pretty much every way possible.

"It's due to be replaced and well, what with work and.... you.... I've just got a bit distracted and I guess, the strength.... potency.... of it wears off towards the end...." She's looking out of the window and has the indecency to blush. The familiar print of a sunset painting above the bed we just fucked in is blurring and twisting and I want to be sick.

As the silence stretches between us, she starts to babble. It's hitting home that I'm not overjoyed that my side-piece is up the duff while my Wife, is still grieving the loss of every child I ever wanted. "It's not like I planned it", she whimpers; she's lying. "But we can work it out! Be together like a proper family. Your unhappy at home with her. This is your chance to be a daddy. It's a shock I know but a good one surely?". Jesus on a bike! Bronwyn's done this on purpose. She knows I want a child more than I want her.

The child's a gift to me. It's better than a wedding ring. This is a life between us now. A commitment. Something I can't avoid. Someone I can't break up with. Damn her!

My Wife's face, tear stained and blotchy. Her lips all puffed up with hate and loss. Unable to get my thoughts in order, all I can think of is Serena and how this will kill her. Putting my head in my hands and grasping my hair I pull, until the pain makes me scream in rage at Bronwyn. It's not even words. Just a yell of anger and fear.

She flinches then her face folds in on itself. She sits down heavily on the bed, making a huffing sound. There's no smile now. "Don't you understand! I can't be with you. I don't even want to! I love serena. I love her! I just hate our life and how she is!".

The last word sticks in my throat, so I yell again and then the tears start. Bronwyn and I are both crying now. She because I don't want her. Me because I want someone who seems to spend every day hating me.

* * * * *

So here I am. A full day into my Bed and Breakfast lifestyle and thoroughly miserable going over and over how it came to this. Punishing myself. Maybe I should have just told Serena right from the get go? We might have got through it. Back then, I just didn't know *how* to tell her. Like, how do you tell your Wife, who seemingly can't have children, that your scheming lover and her best friend, is due your child in 8 months?

What words could I have chosen? Whatever way I had framed it, my biggest fear wasn't her leaving me, it was her killing herself. Yes, fear clammed my mouth shut like a vice. My only, tiny, saving grace, is that the day that Bronwyn told me she was pregnant, we finished. I couldn't go on with the affair, knowing she deliberately set out to sabotage my marriage like that.

Seeing past the generous cleavage, bouncy hair and constant positivity, I saw a sneakiness. It was right there, lurking behind her big, heavily made up eyes and slippery lip gloss smile. Her sexy clothes held inside them not a warm, sweet body, but a cold determination to get what she wanted by any means possible.

So my attraction to her, the fun and lust, all went as fast as I did; storming unsteadily, drunk on shock, out of that hotel room, past the staring receptionist and straight to my car.

Head on the steering wheel, I sat there and cried for almost two hours before going home to my Wife to watch and wait for the right moment to tell her about the affair but not the baby, never the baby.

Serena

The whisky's going down a treat. It's really warmed the cockles! I'm watching Dexter as he talks- he's really opened up now we both know we're crackers and I'm seeing ghosts.

The pair of us relative strangers, hiking up a mountain, playing super sleuths and looking for clues, has had us in giggles more than once. Although we are well aware our reasons for being here are dark; as sad and dark as the weather outside. Alice would want us to be up-beat. That's her nature. Having her around, has made me more self-aware and certainly, more reflective.

"Yeah, so she was waving at me from the gate while I confronted my Husband!". I can barely get the words out for laughing. Plus, the slurring isn't helping either! "What were you arguing about?" Dexter splutters, and tips back, eyes closed. He's shaking with the force of his own laughter and hasn't noticed I've gone quiet.

The reality of my situation is painful and no amount of good whiskey will change that. "Oh, it doesn't matter", I mutter. "Can I ask how you got your scar? The one on your face?". There, that'll distract him.

"I got attacked in the street when I was 19. Three, older guys went for me. Apparently, I'd said or done something that they didn't like, so there was a fight and a glass bottle found its way into it, somehow".

Dexter says this so matter of fact I'm struck dumb by how cool he is but venture on. "Why? I don't get it? Why would anyone *do* that?" I want to cry for his younger self. Taking another sip, I close my eyes in hurt. If he were my son or brother, I most likely would have hunted his attackers down and killed them myself! Resisting this slightly scary declaration, I shut up and let him talk. I've always been a terrible listener. Again, Dylan's voice, "I wish you'd listen to me Sir! I need a chance to talk too. Get it all out!"

Forcing myself to open my eyes, I swallow and press my lips together, in an effort to look at Dexter and not cry as he talks. "I don't get along with everyone. You might have noticed that I'm a bit different to most guys? Well, I have something called Asperger's. It attracts idiots. I'm too trusting but also, too honest!"

A warmth not just from the whisky spreads through me. Now it all makes sense! His direct stare but occasional pickiness with eye-contact. The simple way he plans things out and the careful yet correct way of talking. His skilled ability to read me and failure to give me the attention that I've childishly sought from him. Now I *am* embarrassed! I once helped research an article on Autism. As usual, I should've known better.

Dexter's talking again and I'm fascinated. "They never found the guys although to be honest, they didn't really work hard to! Back in those days there was a lot of ignorance around people like me. Very cool, smart people, I may add!" He laughs and takes another sip. "It was even suggested by one paper, that I *asked for it*. The lads were known to the cops and the families were involved in some heavy shit; Informants. Drugs. Smuggling. All sorts. So I left it well alone and headed off to join The Forces. *But* it piqued my interest for investigative journalism. Not to mention, it's still rare for anything we read in the papers to be the truth!"

I smile when he says this and nod, feeling no betrayal to my ex-colleagues. Dexter's right.

"I've a real thing for crossing the T's and dotting the I's..." He says a little more quietly then looks away. I think there's something he's not telling me. Not about his attack, it's something about his reason for being here. I'm not going to press him; I don't want to ruin the growing friendship. "Yeah...I've noticed", I blurt and it takes a few seconds till he laughs.

"It's quite handy actually because I like things to be ordered.... labelled and correct, so once I have one of my obsessions, such as a story, that's me. I'm off on one. A dog with a bone. I've been all over the world and here I am now in a tent with you getting sloshed and rained on".

My turn to laugh. "Well, I think you are brill! *And brave* to be doing your own thing and earning a living off it. I wish I had your brains and balls!" Dexter chuckles into the bottle and coughs until his eyes fill with tears. "Well, maybe you should pull your finger out Serena, you can do whatever you want now". His voice is raspy from the whisky burn. An idea has started to form. I'm absolutely amazed by this man. Dylan would love him.

Fuck, there it is again, thoughts of my Dylan.

"Look. I've been a bit of a cow. I know, I've been all over the place with you. I'm really embarrassed. I'm coming off some tablets and there's a lot going on at home and Alice barely shuts up! Can you accept my apology for being a bit weird? And by the way, I never apologise or talk about stuff like this!".

"No problem. Come on, Cheers to me!", he says lifting the whisky bottle to his lips again.

We settle into companionable silence, as the wind and rain batter the tent and we wait for the sun to come up over us.

Alice

The Doctor's appointment was interesting. Although tempted by some ideas for mischief, I made sure I behaved this time. Fascinated by this new turn of events and wondering if there was an angle I could use, I sat on the examination table at the other side of the room, and listened closely. Admittedly, when Michael put on his "sad hubby act", I had to summon all my energy to not take the GPs' biro and ram my Husband right in the eye with it.

My patience was rewarded somewhat as after the check-up, Michael was visibly less cocky. The curvature of his shoulders

suggested the half-news in the surgery had knocked some
wind out of his sails. Sure, it wouldn't do him any harm!

Michael enjoyed stressing me out and panicking me a
plenty when we were together!

Pretending to lose his passport when we were hours from
going abroad. Emptying the savings and not telling me, just
before a night away with my friends that I'd looked forward to
for months. Disappearing and turning his phone off after football and laughing at my panic when he finally returned home in
the small hours of the morning. But, none of those nasty, frightening episodes compared to how I felt when Simon left.

* * * * *

Gagging and almost choking on tears and snot, I'm carelessly
running to the lady's toilets. I can't breathe. I don't understand!
Why has he done this!?

Drawing a few looks from students as I stagger past, I'm
fixated on reaching the loo without being stopped and forced
to explain why I'm in such a mess. Banging the door open, I
crouch down sobbing, and check to make sure the cubicles are
empty. I can't bear sharing this with anyone and I'm in such a
state, questions are unavoidable.

I untie my scarf from my neck, carefully chosen this
morning, while I was thinking about places we could run
away to.

Choosing the one furthest from the entrance, I slide down
the cubicle wall, to crumple like a child with my hands over
my ears and sob. My head against the cold porcelain of the
toilet seat, I cry and cry in despair. I'm grieving for the wonderful life I had planned in my head for us.

The moonlit walks on the beach somewhere tropical and
warm. Big glasses of cheap, white wine in our hands as we
kissed under low hanging pink flowers on a balcony. Lying
together in bed talking about books and books and more
books!

"Yeah Boss, Dr Masters sent a letter to HR saying he got a placement in America. Better money than we had offered". Saffron's voice is going round and round my head and I want to hit myself.

"Why? Why? Why?" I whisper, trying to pull my phone out of my dress pocket. I get up onto my knees and successfully manage to tug the phone free. "Please pick up, please *pick up*", I pray into the phone. It's slippy from my tears and I drop it.

Uttering a cry of panic but picking it up again, I hold my breath to listen closely but am met only with a dead tone. He's changed his number. He really has abandoned me. Gone. Given up on us. I think I might die from the pain in my heart.

*****

Knowing I would never have a life with Simon, I sat on the toilet floor and cried and cried....and cried. I hated myself for letting him down.

Stuck again with Michael I did the best I could for as long as I could. Wherever Simon is now, I hope he is happy and found someone nice. Goodness knows I won't meet anyone! Unless Heaven has a Tinder or Dating Site....oh, mind you....I bet the men are lovely looking!

Michael

I'm rather pissed off about that bloody GP poking his nose in and ruining my mood. I've had a pint and some crisps, yet I still feel rattled. It feels like everyone is out to annoy me at the moment. If Alice were here, she'd most likely annoy me too, so at least I dealt with that one good and proper.

There's a man with his back to me at the bar. He looks like that writer idiot she was messing about with last year. I know it can't be him. He's dead as a door knob, all wrapped up neat and tight in cling-film and bin bags, rotting away in a shallow grave up the Northumbrian Coast. The chap at the bar, kinda does look like him though.

When Alice and I drove out there for our Christmas Break, she had no idea his body was in the boot! I loved that part of my plan the most.

"Thank you for packing us up to go", she meekly whispered, as we started the car engine the next day. I wanted to laugh my head off and tell her then, but held back, of course!

Once we arrived at the cottage for Christmas and Alice started the dinner, I declared a need to go and buy some brandy and cigars at the local shop. It gave me almost an hour to get rid of Smarmy Simon's body then. Genius timing, I thought!

Silly woman thought my excitement at going away was to reignite our physical relationship. Nope, I brimmed with glee at solving my marital problems a very different, more permanent, way.

When Alice was calling, to tell him she was leaving me after our break, I was a few feet away, whistling to hide the sound of the phone buzzing. I texted her, as Simon, to keep her sweet and make her disappointment and pain at his "sudden departure" to America, even more agonizing.

True, I could have had Simon dump her by text, while his body cooled in my boot, but I liked the America Story better. According to his Facebook page, he had a lot of state-side friends and colleagues, so it was believable and usefully, created a few thousand miles between her broken heart and his dead one. *So to speak*!

Throwing back the last of the beer, I slap my hands on the table announcing an ambition to head home. Standing up, the ground moves a little beneath my feet so I feel the need to steady myself on something solid, and reach for the person next to me a little clumsily. They treat me to a look of pure disgust and I want to punch them.

Looking up, I see the lookalike Simon Man at the bar has gone and I'm oddly relieved. Reckon it's his fault I feel a bit iffy again. The memory of that daft writers squashed face in the plastic bag, as I rolled him into the cold sandy soil, is getting me all upset. He was even uglier dead than alive!

Chortling at my own joke, and feeling a bit better, I pat my neighbour on the back and wait expectantly for him to turn to me in mutual manliness. I'm also rather keen for an apology for his rather rude look a few seconds ago. As he turns and looks up at me a surge of horror swipes the air from my throat and my feet go out from under me. It's the man from the bar. No! it's bloody Simon. The last thing I see is his smile, then the ground smacks me in the face.

"Are you ok Mister, err, Mister whatever. Are you ok?! Nasty fall that one!". The voice is young. Yes, it's a young woman. Am I at Charmain's flat? Did she come and get me from my house? That'll cost me a fortune. Her time isn't cheap! A squirt of stomach acid burns the roof of my mouth. I can smell stale booze and realise I'm on the floor of the pub. Bugger, I've had another one of those dizzy spells.

"Mister? Are you alright? Should I call an ambulance?" Opening my eyes, a series of big pale blobs greet me. I try to focus and their faces start to form more definition. Eyes then mouths then shoulders and arms appear.

Flushed from alcohol and stunned by whatever just happened, they are crowding round me and staring in awe, like I'm some sort of freakish exhibit in a jar. "Get off me. Get away!", I shout without thinking. Pipe down Mikey! I must not draw too much attention to myself. Not this kind anyway. At least last time this happened it was at home! "Someone, help him up", a hole in the closest, still rather blurred face says. "Yes. That's all I need, thank you. Just help me up and let me sit down. I'm fine. I'm fine".

Sitting in a booth on my own and feeling steadier now, I'm still glad to be handed a small brandy. "On the house. You look like you need it", the bar-man whispers in my ear before walking away. He probably doesn't want me making a fuss as it's not a good look, having mature chaps like me fainting on his premises. Throwing it back in one gulp without a nod or wave of thanks, I close my eyes and sink into the seat for a minute to try and work out why this keeps happening.

Scanning the bar nervously, I'm glad that there's no sign of the lookalike any-more. Relief flushes my cheeks and I can't help but clutch at my chest and let a long slow breath out. It's been a funny old day, so my time for home. Certainly!

A few minutes later and I'm out in the fresh air. It's colder now that it's late evening and leaves chase my feet as I weave up the town cobbles, towards home. I'm forced to turn the collar up on my coat against the evening chill and putting my head down, I walk faster.

Purposeful and bad tempered, it's of no matter to me that I'm cutting a strange figure all alone and wafting booze at every turn. Paranoia is following me, tugging my eyes here and there and trying to get in my head.

As I walk, unseen arms place pressure on my back and shoulders, forcing me to almost jog the last of cobbles before the bridge. I don't know what's happening! All the stress of the last few days, the silly tumbles and that Doctor freaking me out can't be good for my health! A man of my age should be reclining on a sun-lounger somewhere with a pretty blonde in a string bikini stretched out next to him; bronzed and glistening with tanning oil.

Humph... this is all Alice's fault. Why did she have to go and meet that decaying corpse of a writer and have a bloody affair?! Why ruin things! It was all going so *well*! That stupid text message did this. Her whimpering lusty desperation to get away from me and run off with him!

Once she started telling him details about me, it became inevitable that, he had to go. She started looking for where he was working, quite quickly after he (in her mind) dumped her! Silly woman! I still had the recording app on her phone and in one conversation with her assistant, she was asking her to go to HR and find out where Simon had gone in America.

"Surely we have some sort of record of where he went? So we could forward any mail or a reference or have a need to contact him, to book him in here, again?"

I could almost hear Saffron shrugging with disinterest, but then, rather shockingly, she agreed she would help Alice find him! So, then I knew, I had to get rid of Alice faster than I had previously planned.

A gust of wind steals my hat. It bumps along the ground then flies away from me, much too fast to catch it. That's my hair all messed up now! And it's at least another mile or so before the cosy warmth of the fire and a soothing shower.

Women are nothing but trouble! Just like my first Wife, Alice wanted it all her own way. Her own money. Her own car. Her own space. Even her own fancy job! *Ridiculous.*

Wife Number One was called Penelope, but she went by Penny most of the time. A bloody bad luck penny more like! She sent me half-crazy with her tight purse strings and even tighter work schedule in the end. Just like Alice she cooled and drifted from me; a swan on a Winters day.

I knew Penelope was pretending to be fine but beneath that icy rippled water, her little mind was frantically paddling and splashing away trying to get traction and away from me.

When I saw her that first time in the campus canteen, I knew she was an ideal target. It didn't matter I already had a girlfriend- I was 21 for goodness sakes! Young men are supposed to play the field especially away from home with so many options. Eager young women, desperate to stretch their boundaries and open their legs.

It was a feast I didn't resist, even when so-called friends told me I was getting a bit of a reputation for being a heart-breaker. They were just jealous and boring; all settled down with steady partners and study books. Undeterred, I carried on regardless; like most smart men, I went to Uni to avoid my parents and hit on females.

* * * * *

Transfixed on the girl's mop of blonde curls, I glide through the bustling, noisy, fried food scented crowd with ease. As I get closer, I can see her mouth moving slightly as she reads and chews at the same time. She's seated alone in the far corner and I like that.

I stopped choosing the popular girls a while back, too much trouble; too visual and angry when I humped and dumped. Last thing I need is another gang of supportive harpies, all banging on my door to scream and shout what a nasty/abusive/violent/cheat I am. Blah, blah, blah.

The girl doesn't even look up when I slide into the seat opposite like a ghost. I slowly reach across the table to gently place my left index finger on the page she's reading. She jerks her head up so fast, that her Heavenly hair whips back and forth. I smile as it bounces several times and I watch it; fantasising about wrapping it tightly in my hands and pulling hard, while kissing her roughly.

"Yes. What is it? Do I know you?". Her voice is higher pitched than I expected, but with an upper-class lilt. 10 extra points! I like them wealthy. Her eyes are an interesting light blue- almost grey, like mine. Admittedly, I'm a little disappointed in that; I prefer dark eyes on women usually. They look better when they are puffy and bruised.

"I haven't seen you before. I definitely would've noticed you. Where have you been hiding?". I smile my most winning smile and cross my arms and legs in perfect synchronicity. I'm letting her know I'm settled here in my seat for a while. "What's your name? I bet it's something glamourous. To go with your glamourous face and your glamorous hair". She sits back in her seat, smiles a crocodile smile and crosses her legs too. Then pushes the books aside, "Penelope", she replies holding out her hand for me to shake it.

*****

I took Penny to bed a week later and met her family within the month. Once I'd seen the large family home, three cars in the drive and met her Company Director Parents, I knew she was the one for me. For then, at least.

Oh Yuck! Bird pooh? For good luck? No, it's rain. I'm not sure when it started to spit with rain. I've been too busy going over old dead history. That was stupid of me. Plus, rather irritatingly, I haven't got my glasses with me so this isn't the smoothest of journeys home.

Stumbling on a loose cobble, I swear loudly and even manage to bite my lip hard enough that it bleeds. Nauseous suddenly, I stop and lean against the wall of the tow-path I'm on.

The path along the river turns to continue below a bridge, across which trains hurtle regularly. Their deafening screeching yelps of steel announcing themselves twice every half hour.

A small bedraggled fox skitters across the path, stops, stares at me and walks on more slowly. As though showing off how comfortable it is here in the dank gloom.

Pushing both hands deep into my pockets, I put my head down again and force myself forward. Trying to calm my nerves, I remind myself that in ten minutes time, I'm going to be taking my coat off and clinking ice into Alices' mothers Wedding Crystal.

The trees on the bank are creaking left and right with the pressure of a fresh new wind. They whistle and scarce of leaves, do look rather sinister, I have to admit.

An errant branch scratches my cheek and grunting in anger, I snap it off in my hands and throw it into the bushes. "Bloody thing". My voice echoes and I'm reminded that not another living soul is either in front of me or behind me. Everything's a deep navy-blue, bar the yellow streaked stone at my feet. The strange light is caused by a lonely street lamp, blinking its light on and off. My anxiety is jarred by it.

Once under the bridge and back into the relatively better lit walkway, I'll feel better. From there I can make out the roof of my house poking nosily up above the apple trees at the foot of the garden.

Alice up a ladder, laughing. She's in a green flowered sun-dress and white woollen cardigan. She's giggling and stretch-ing for the highest, biggest apples at the top of the tallest of the two trees. Her long slender fingers are trembling with the effort. Shards of late October sunlight. Glistening strands of her hair catching in the leaves. My own bigger hands holding the ladder still, as she squeals and laughs again at almost falling.

The images are old, years old and I feel tired suddenly. Actually, I think I can smell apples now? That sweet cidery tang.

Alice's familiar laugh tinkles and bounces around the tunnel. Spinning to face the sound, I expect to see her there waving at me and smiling. Loaded with Sainsburys shopping bags. Long purple scarf around her neck. That old burgundy wool coat she wore every winter. Of course, she's not there.

The laughter echoes again and I fall back against the wet stone of the tunnel wall, almost slipping on thick slimy moss and something else unpleasant at my feet. It's just some kids. Or some daft woman on the phone in a garden nearby. I really need to pull *myself together*.

Sniffing and wiping my mouth with some tissue I hadn't realised I was gripping tightly in my pocket, I take a few deep breaths and count to five.

A flash of something moving sharply just outside my eye-line makes me gasp. Without a beat, but *with* a squeal, I push myself off the wall and start to run.

Chapter 7: Haunted

Dylan

You're going to hate me even more now; I didn't even tell Serena about the affair. You hoped I was going to tell you I did, didn't you? Nope, gutless through and through that's me. She found out herself and I hate even thinking about it.

I imagine she goes over and over it, fuelling her rage, strengthening herself with it. Serena's always fuelled herself with negative thoughts and behaviours, it's just the way she is and strangely I love her all the more for it.

She's built a whole new, protective shell around herself, simply to survive day to day. Instead of lying around crying or even doing that thing I dread her doing.

I'm old enough and unwise enough to know that people in pain, can go one way or the other. They wither away and let more and more pain in and become a victim or they fight life. They fight it viciously and anyone who tries to reach them, ends up as hurt as they are.

Serena swithers between the two occasionally and I worry the most when she acts like a victim instead of a fighter. I hate the phrase "opposites attract"; it's so contrived, over used and often makes peoples eye's roll in boredom.

But, let's face it, that label should be stamped all over our life in neon. That bold, bright flashing at the scene of an accident. Yes, the warning sign that you're coming up to a car-crash on the motorway.

I really need to stop thinking about Serena and I; she's only going to be sitting at home planning what weapon to murder Bronwyn and I with, or fast asleep passed out on the sofa.

This hotel room's vile. There's a strange musty feety smell and the no smoking signs aren't deterring someone partial to puffing on something illegal, but poor quality, next door. I've had to go for the cheap accommodation option, knowing I'm here for the foreseeable.

My marriage is dead in the water; I need to accept that we bobbed along in a ruined boat and now the inevitable tsunami just capsized what was left.

I'm not due back at work again for 5 days so these four walls and I better get to know each other better. Although I'm rather familiar as it is.

The Africa shaped damp patch in the corner next to the cobweb, that quite possibly once had tarantula in it- the size of it! The rough towels- both of which have given me a facial, with exfoliation as an extra none-benefit. The telly works but there's something wrong with the sound.

Sick of laying in the bed, I'm sat on the rooms only chair, like someone's taken me hostage and forgotten to put my hood on and tie me back up.

Misery likes company but there's no way I'm calling Bronwyn. She'll get all the wrong ideas and try to come onto me again. She's done that regularly since we split and yes, we've stayed split the whole time, ever since that day she told me she was expecting Owen. Even on the Disneyland holiday, I shared a room with my son and she slept alone. Albeit, with a lot of complaint!

My son and I have a relationship, Bronwyn and I do *not*. Ah, surprised, are you? Good. Could you perhaps let my Wife know? At least then she might divorce me without killing me. The lesser of two evils. Although right now, I feel so wretched I think I might top myself. If I could summon the energy to leave this room to go and buy some rope, but I can't.

I've greasy patchy stubble, hair that sticks up if I run my hands through it *and* smell quite badly. If Serena saw me, even she might be worried and she stopped caring about me a long time ago.

There's a film reel of disasters going around and round in my head. These weird heart palpitations started earlier and I think I've aged 10 years.

Out of the shadows comes that night when Serena found out about Bronwyn and I. There's a stretching, tearing pain in my chest whenever I dare think about it.

* * * * *

Serena's taken to social media voraciously this year. I think she must have joined over 20 chat-room things! She sits there for hours and hours in an evening, sometimes through the night. She's seeking answers. Any comfort at all.

That birdlike tap tap tap tapping on her laptop, as she rants and raves and sometimes breaks down in cyber-land, makes my nerves twitch. To her left is a bottle of wine, to her right is a glass of wine and as the bottle empties, the tapping gets faster but I can hear the tell-tale sound of the delete key more often.

Once Bronwyn finished the sun-deck, she and my Wife remained Facebook friends. There was no way I was going to put my head on the chopping block and suggest it was odd to continue the friendship now they really had nothing in common. Not even *me*, now I've ended the affair.

Angry at my blunt rejection, Bronwyn rather frustratingly also refuses to delete and block my Wife citing that it would look suspicious. Thus, followed a big long text argument between us where she got more and more determined to say in our lives even though it was mainly via the woman, she happily betrayed with me.

I feel physically sick when Serena wanders into the living room carrying her laptop. Sliding past me, missing my out-stretched hand, she's fixated on getting to the kitchen island. All ready to settle down and chat with my ex-lover and the other 100 or so strangers online, whom she prefers to spend her evenings with.

"Come and sit with *me* babe. I'm away back to work soon and I feel like I've hardly seen you Serena. I don't think you've even made eye-contact this weekend!" I try to laugh but it catches, although of course, she doesn't notice. She has this glassy-eyed look and strange wistful air thing going on. I think they upped her meds last month. Diazepam, almost certainly.

"Hmmmmmm?" She's already bending down at the wine-rack and choosing a companion for the evening. "Sir, please.... sit with me instead tonight. I'm worried about you. *I miss you*".

I've dared to approach her from behind and start to massage the nape of her neck. Resisting the urge to kiss it, right where her tiny bird tattoo sits, I remain stiff and stand at the sort of distance I know signals affection, not sex. I gently close the lap-top in front of her and she tightens up in my hands.

"There's a new chat group I want to try. It's all about different foods and natural therapy things rumoured to help with sustaining pregnancy. Somewhere in Australia I think". She's shrugged me off, patted my hand and is flipping the computer back open. The screen lights up and she's cast in a pale blue glow and for a second looks a little scary.

Serena unscrews the wine bottle without even looking at it. She does this with an almost magician-like flair. The screen floods with images and text and she's lost to me again.

"Ok- well, I'm going to have a shower and get to bed. There's some big jobs need doing in the garden before I head back off-shore. Make a list for me, will you?". I've walked to the doorway but stop before the hall; I'm hopefully looking back, but my stiff smile just hangs there. I wish she would at least look up and smile to wave me off to bed, but she doesn't.

* * * * *

Then of course, thanks to Bronwyn, my Wife found out about the affair anyway.

Bronwyn was clever enough to not post about her pregnancy, mainly as that secret suited her. However, she was nasty enough to choose to be careless with her social media posts, once it sunk in that I wasn't going to go back to her.

Serena

There's a strange thudding and snapping sound and I'm freezing. Reaching for the bedside lamp, I touch Dylans' stubble. No! it's a shaved head. *Jesus Christ!* Stifling a scream, I jerk backwards and begin to get out of bed, then remember I'm in a sleeping bag, in a tent, on a mountain with a guy I met yesterday. My heart has lost all rhythm but at least I'm alive. Heart-attack stuff *that* was!

I've not woken Dexter with the commotion and I'm relieved; I don't think I could talk any-more. It was good to open up a bit, but when we talked about Dylan and some of what happened.... I got upset. It wasn't even the whisky; I always get upset when I think about him and Cat-Bitch. My problem, I think, is not talking about it properly before. Silently stewing and raging over and over internally, has got in the way of everything. It's ruined *everything.*

The sleeping bag whispers softly, as I tuck myself back in, and lift the thick, silky hood up over my head. Cocooned again, I'm warmer but wide awake.

It's not raining but it is still really windy. It sounds as though the rocks are moaning and groaning to each other, complaining about being pushed about and battered by the weather. Every now and then the sounds vary and there's this long drawn out "wooooooooh", like a crowd at a football match.

I used to love going to watch football when I lived in the city. Dylan hated it. He said the crowds gave him the willies. I used to howl with laughter when he used that old-fashioned expression of discomfort.

Promised some fresh tears suddenly, I realise it's not Dylan's fault I was lonely and sad; I could have tried harder to do freelance work, teach in the village or even tutor bad tempered, hormonal students.

I lost my motivation a lot more each time, when I lost the opportunity to be a mother each time. Yes, failure in that area just fed failure in others. My throat squeezes and a sob escapes- albeit a quiet one.

A hot tear slides out and runs down my cheek, to settle in the curve of my ear; it's gone as fast as a baby's first smile. Yes, unfortunately, the booze has worn off to leave me nostalgic and sad.

He didn't have to cheat though! There, red hot anger again. Good, that usually puts me back in place. Glaring up at the roof of the tent as though I could bore holes into it, I deliberately revisit the night I found out about him and Cat-Bitch the first time. It's a sort of self-harming habit or cruel exposure therapy. I've let these intrusive thoughts in a hundred times and a hundred times more.

* * * * *

Woops! Finished that bottle fast! It's a good job Dylan decided to go to bed, he's not happy with my night-time habits these days. *Not at all.*

Glancing at the wine rack, then turning to look at the spirits' trolley, I wobble a bit on the stool that I favour at the kitchen island. One of six, it's the only one really used much. The only one that's faded and has deep wrinkles of age. Sad but clear evidence we never have anyone to dinner and rarely even sit here together. Rubbing the soft, cracked leather, I realise this stool is as used up and tired as I feel. Ok, dark-rum it is!

Trying to hop off the stool but stumbling to an almost full-fall, I steady myself on the back of it and it spins round taking me with it. Giggling, I pull some escaped hair from my dressing-gown collar and tuck it back up into my bun. The spirits trolly is only three metres away but with my tipsy-ness, the unsteady journey there takes longer than it should.

Ice tumbles into the big bauble shaped glass with pretty festivity, and I watch as the molten bronze liquid fills up right to the brim.

One glass equals one drink- well, it's true for me anyway. Back up on the stool, I take a slurp and crunch an ice-cube satisfyingly. The meds I'm on at the moment have a strange way of numbing physical pain. Very odd and I'm sure there's a reason for it, but right now my focus is on finding the right cyber-friend to hear my story and answer my questions about fertility. Last-nights cyber friends are already forgotten and the one's before, also, are now just a blur. I'm selfish in my dark quest for relevant company and deep in my misery, I don't care one iota.

Scrolling through the chat-rooms, I like or comment on the posts that seem most relevant to me, make some notes and send friend requests to women who I feel sound most like me. Wincing at the good news posts where IVF has worked or a rainbow baby has been born, I scroll a bit faster and drink. Like some sort of twisted drinking game, I take a big gulp of alcohol when I see one of those.

A chime in the hall signals midnight; my parents old grand-father clock. Dylan polishes it with proper bees-wax every New Year's Eve. He says its good luck, seeing as my parents had two beautiful perfect babies in myself and my sister. I used to love him saying that, now his optimism grates on me.

A tiredness has creeped in; unseen fingers pressing my eye-lids down and putting pressure on my shoulders, so I rest my head on the counter and catch my hands in my hair for a minute. Eyes closed, I let out a long sigh and steam the laptop screen up. Wiping it with my dressing gown cord, I decide one last quick scroll through Facebook. Maybe Bronwyn's page will cheer me up. Cat pictures, her selfies, memes about "bastard men", are pretty much the entirety of Bronwyn's contribution to the world of social-media.

Oh, a picture of her dinner this evening! She's made a sterling effort with something that could be lasagne *or* Shepherd's Pie!

I'm a good cook and it slightly annoys Bronwyn that she can burn salad and forget to boil the potatoes to make mash! Giggling at her ineptitude in the kitchen, I tap like and write, "Urgh Bron! Food crime of the century!", and laugh knowing she will jokingly tell me off and try to get her own back on my page, if she's still awake. She likes mocking how uptight and nippy I am, and often remarks about "Poor Dylan", whenever she gets the chance.

Idly scrolling down to see what she's been up to the last few days; I realise I'm genuinely interested. I haven't heard from her since last week when we had a long phone conversation about her considering using a dating site in the New Year. I think it's a pretty good idea! She's been single for an age! Yeah, I must try and get a girls-date with her, it's been months since we got together.

A shock of bright yellow catches my attention and squinting from both booze and tiredness, I lean in closer.

Past the bright yellow rain-coat which really suits her, I see something that shoots a red-hot poker into my back and out through my chest. She's wearing a scarf I recognise. Its grey and black tartan with little purple flecks in it- a sort of scratchy tweedy material. I know it's scratchy because I've worn it. It's my Husband's scarf. A scarf I bought him when we had a dirty weekend away in the Scottish Highlands a few years ago.

Looking more closely, I can see she's cropped the picture at some point. Cropped another person out. A man. Yes, I can just make out a sliver of stubble and the edge of a smile. A smile I know well, but haven't seen in a while. The selfie is of Bronwyn and my Husband. It's dated last year.

I shoot back in shock, moving so fast that I fall to the floor, taking the stool with me. Sitting there on the floor with my hands over my mouth staring straight ahead, I have a panic attack and vomit rum, red wine and 6pm cheese and biscuits everywhere. It goes all over my pyjama trousers and up the front of the cabinets, set neatly into the kitchen island.

* * * * *

Lying here now in this tent, all these years later, the horror and pain is still as harsh as it was then. I've held onto the humiliation and rage like it were a child. It's filled my belly and made me swollen with nastiness and paranoia. I've been sick with jealousy all that time, thinking it was over but furious it had even happened. And yet, he went and did it again....and *created* a life with her.

"Are you ok?", comes a deep, sleep-muffled voice next to me. Dexter's pulled his blanket down to just nose level and is peering out, owl-like at me.

Having given me the sleeping bag, he was left with his own clothes and the two blankets he also lugged up the mountain, all rolled up tight inside his Mary Poppins-esque back-pack. The thought creates a bubble of laughter and half crying, half laughing, I try to tell him why I'm more tense than the guy ropes outside.

The only thing I left out last night was about Owen. My *Husband's child*. As my wheezing and sobbing turns to breathless whimpers and the tears dry up, Dexter watches me quietly.

At some point he's sat up and wrapped his jumper round his head like some reject from Lawrence Of Arabia. I don't think I've laughed this much in maybe 2 or 3 years. I've even forgotten what my own laughter sounded like.... that probably means Dylan has too. My heart squeezes again.

"You still love your guy, Serena. People don't cry and keep pulling funny faces whenever they are reminded of a person if they don't still have feelings for them". Yet again I'm glad Dexter's here.

"I do keep thinking about him but I'm pretty sure it's just because he's a horrible Husband and I'm broken hearted. Besides there's no telly or radio up here to silence my thoughts. You're not the most conversational of people". His turn to smile.

With a nod, Dexter leans forward and opens the tent entrance to peer out. I'm reminded again what a great physique he has, but now, it's not attraction I feel, its admiration.

Alice

It's getting easier and easier this haunting stuff. Unsurprisingly, also more fun. As Michael loses his confidence and sense of safety, I regain more of my strength. I'm not coming back from the grave any time soon. Fine, but I might as well send him to *his* or make him wish for it, while I get the chance!

As I linger in the doorway to the kitchen. Oh! My *beautiful kitchen*! I watch my Husband sweat. Little silvery beads of panic and anxiety are sliding down his face almost like tears. In his hands the glass is trembling enough for him to struggle to put it to his lips. His shirt's escaping from his waistband and yet again I see more than I want to, exposed above his waist-line.

Indeed, I fed him far too well, in more ways than one. He's breathing quite heavily. Mind you, he was never into fitness. "I'm blessed with a great physique and looks without even trying my darling!" he said a few dates in.

Watching him across the restaurant table, as he tore open and buttered a third bread roll, I swooned at his charisma and confidence and yet again thanked my lucky stars to have found him.

What a fool I was. Early on in our courting he made a real effort to inspire confidence in my ability to be the right sort of partner for him. "Penelope never appreciated me. She was neglectful" he said a few more dates later as we drove out of the city towards the coast.

"You're different to anyone else. So attentive and kind Alice. The one for me", he murmured in my ear, as we checked into yet another, expensive hotel.

I felt so sorry for Michael, having lost his Wife twice; her death shortly after they separated, taunted him. He seemed much happier when we were having little trips away, so we did that quite a lot, until I met Simon.

* * * * *

Lying together on the chaise lounge in his study, dappled with Autumn sun, Simon's running his fingers around my ear as though tracing the exact shape and repeating the process again and again. Gently pinching my ear lobe, each time he completes the cycle, to make me smile. Eyes closed, I'm listening to his rich caramel voice, as he reads from the open book in his left hand. I open one eye, to sneak a peek at my lover, and see that the sun has crystallised his hair to a halo of opals. To me, he is an angel.

It's a passage from one of his own books. "The Dark Triad of disordered personalities is a three-point formation, representing three dangerous personality types. Each type has slightly different unpleasant characteristics and yet there is almost always some overlap. The Narcissistic type. The Machiavellian Type and of course the Psychopath".

The last word makes my spine tingle and I can't help but shiver. Simon reaches to pull the throw out from beneath us and wraps it over my shoulders. I purr and smile, eyes closed, as he pulls me in closer to his body.

As he talks, describing the traits of these dangerous people, the hairs at the nape of my neck stand on end, as if one by one. Both eyes open now, I'm reading the book while he talks. "Simon, with Michael, how do you think he will take it... for...example....if I left him?".

I haven't told Simon much about my home life regarding my Husband; it's never felt like appropriate dinner-table chat and I've wanted to reserve my time with him as pleasant. Not ruin it with talk of such unpleasantness as Michael. All Simon knows is that my Husband more or less lives off me, has a rather active and plush social life and can be bad tempered when he doesn't get what he wants.

An unwelcome thought butterflies into my mind. It hovers and flutters there making my mouth twitch. The words are out before I can stop them. "He was married before, you know. She left him. He's never got over it.". There the words have escaped from the jar and are soaring round the room.

Simon stops reading and slowly lays the open book face down on our laps. One side his, one side mine. We are wedded by his genius; joined together now.

"Was he?....",he mutters, then reaches up to gently tug on his generous light brown beard. I know this means he has an idea, having watched him often enough. I'm resisting the urge to tug his beard myself. It's one of my favourite ways to touch him quickly, without sexuality, when we pass each other in the corridors at work.

"Does he talk about his Wife at all?" His voice is slightly higher pitched. He's definitely got something twitching up there in that incredible mind.

"He told me she left him for another man. Moved away to France but died shortly after. It was about a year before he met me.

He told me it sounds terribly sad! Some sort of heart thing. Worst of it is, she took everything and left him high and dry just before she popped her clogs".

"Anything else. Anything at all?" Simon looks worried, so now *I'm worried*. We were having such a lovely afternoon. The room feels cooler and I realise my hands are icy, so I tuck them under Simons arm-pit and snuggle closer. He smells of hay and books, and something citrussy. It's probably the beard oil I bought him last week.

"Well, there is something...." My voice grows smaller and smaller, as mouse-like, I tentatively explore what happened in the garden. I skitter and skirt around how viciously Michael reacted that day, to my bland reference to his first wedding.

By the time I've finished the story, Simon's gently eased himself off the chaise, wrapped me inside the blanket and started to build the fire. He hasn't spoken once. Ever the conversationalist, his quietness means something is not sitting well for him. "If you don't mind, I'm going to have a little dig about", he says turning to look at me. He's pale and his eyes are red rimmed.

Startled at his change in appearance, I gasp. Is my lover afraid? "Darling, are you worried? Don't be! Michael's selfish yes and can be....*tempestuous and mercurial....* But, really, that's it". I cross the room to crouch behind him and put my hands on his shoulders. But he doesn't react. He's on his knees, staring into the fire-place, lost in whatever thoughts have him so out of sorts.

The fire starts quickly, aided by the new addition of today's newspapers. We read them together, over breakfast.

Michael thinks I'm on a meditation retreat in North Wales. Of course, I'm here, the only place I *ever* want to be. Simons' cottage with its small stables, old thatched roof, drafty kitchen and, best of all, his huge book lined study.

The kindling licks into life but the slightly damp logs start to spit. The quick sharp bangs make me jump. "Well, I don't suppose it'll do any harm...."

Simon relaxes a little at my agreement, offers me a small smile and stands up. As he leans down to kiss me gently, I can feel he's shaking a little. I hope it's from the draft coming through the old shuttered windows beside us.

"Just to appease me Alice, let me have a friend look through some bits and bobs. Maybe some local authority records, and see if he's telling the truth. A man who reacts so strongly to such a minor thing, is a man with secrets and a man with secrets is a man to be wary of. I'm not madly keen on his....*sob story* about a Wife who took everything and ran away to leave him destitute. His moods. His tantrums. His ability to gain pity but be cruel......it sounds rather narcissistic to me". He takes my chin in one hand, strokes my hair with the other and looks deeply into my eyes. His smile is long gone. "I have the strangest feeling of.... *foreboding*, Alice"

I'm already wary of what my Husband's reaction will be, if I ever have the courage to leave him, but I don't tell Simon this. I fear he will be doubly bitter and angry at my departure because of how awful he feels about his first Wife. It is also likely I will lose my job. Ruin my career. The shame of it all, on my family will be terrible. The only way I'm leaving my Husband is if Simon can take me with him. We can move abroad. I'd go anywhere but it has to be far away. I'm not strong enough or brave enough to do it alone.

Thinking about these sad facts, I follow Simon into the kitchen, where we turn the radio on and start to cook dinner in a newly uneasy silence. As I peel carrots and watch Simon sear the meat for a casserole, my mind keeps going back to my Husband's blisteringly angry face, as he stood over me in the garden, that time he hit me.

* * * * *

Now, remembering that lovely weekend and Simon's instinct to try and protect me, I'm losing substance and it's like I'm fading. I can't let that happen. I'm getting somewhere now with Michael. He's unravelling. Serena and Dexter are almost where they need to be. So, for now I need to stay here; watch and learn from My Murderer. Gain energy to see this through.

Michael's sitting in his favourite armchair now but this time he's stabbing away at his phone with intensity. He seems to have forgotten about the earlier shock I treated myself to on the underpass. The air around him has changed though. Its familiar. Bitter, acrid and almost sweet. The scent of plotting something evil. I think it's a woman he's messaging. He stops tapping and waits, fixated on the screen. If I had a heart-beat it would be frantic right now.

A few minutes later his phone ignites and in the green glow, he smiles like a gargoyle. She, whoever she is, has made him happy. Whatever that is, in his twisted dirty little mind.

Michael

I feel much better now. I've had a shower (I don't think another bath is a good idea) and have my favourite mustard jumper and green corduroys on. Indeed, I'm all set for my date with Charmaine.

I'm running late, but she says it's ok. She even offered me the chance to cancel, but that's not on the cards! She really is a true lady. Well, if prostitutes can be ladies.

She's not my favourite of the three, but she's the cheapest and until Alice's money comes through, I'm reluctantly working to a budget. It sits rather uncomfortably but I know it won't be for long. I am however, treating myself to a taxi tonight; I could walk to Charmaine's flat but after today's silliness I'm a bit uptight. Plus, it's now after 10pm! Oh, what a day it's been!

Smelling of cinnamon after-shave and the slight body odour of eagerness that crept in, while I sweltered in the far too warm cab, I take my time going up the twisting stairs to Charmaine's first floor flat.

She's worked at this for years. An old hand, you might say. She's in her late 40s and has invested her time, body and earnings in a nice flat in a part of town you wish you could afford a flat in. It's not a patch on my lovely big house, but it's smart and clean enough.

I've been seeing Charmaine for 6 years now, the other two for a little less. Every miserable Husband does it; It's just one of those things people don't talk about. Porn, cam-girls, sexting complete strangers. This is the life-blood of society now. It's where we, the *neglected*, get our kicks. In the majority of my cyber-land, it's free, *harmful* and satisfying. And best of all, if one is clever, there's no paper trail. My arrangements with my girls, is full blown, delicious cheating but without the strings. No one loves each other- we just love the exchange. The women the money and me, the kinky kink kink!

Approaching the familiar dark grey painted door with the pristine, rust free letter-box, I get a twitch in my trousers.

Enjoying the anticipation, I crick my neck from side to side. Patting my coat, to feel the swelling of my full wallet, I'm in control and I'm excited. I can smell incense. Charmaine knows I adore it. There's something mystical and sensual about smoky Sandalwood. It reminds me of the 70's when I first discovered my desire for women's trust, bodies and money.

She has music on and I can't resist listening at the door, without first knocking to let her know I'm here. I like being here but not being here; a silent watcher not in her space and yet, *about* to be.

Licking my lips, I close my eyes and sway just slightly to the beat of a song she knows I like. Hunger gets the better of me, so I tap the door knocker. "rat-a-tat-tat (wait a second) tat tat"; Our code. Her code. Whatever.

Inhaling deeply through my nose, I open the belt on my coat, re-centre my tie and step back a metre, so she has to step across her own threshold to bring me in. I like to be invited in formally. Details to you, *critical* to me. As the door opens widely, I'm reminded again why she's indeed one of my three.

"Good evening Mr Jennings'. Lovely to see you. Let's get you in out of the cold". A breeze catches my damp fringe, but eager to continue the formality as long as possible, I sweep it back into place and offer a wide smile, all teeth and flaring nostrils. Taking her hand, she pulls me into her apartment.

"Drink? Your usual?", she says as she sashays (yes, she *sashays*) ahead of me. She's curvy. The curviest of all three and not particularly tall. It makes it easier for me.

I watch as she takes off her black, dragon patterned, robe and places it on a chair; I'm pricked with disappointment by her attire. Charmaine *knows* I prefer white lingerie above all else.

Now, in burgundy studded satin, with her mane of curly black hair crowning her head, I can *almost* forgive her- but not totally. Frowning I step around the sofa to face her as she bends over the coffee table, where she always sets the drinks out. She's not making eye-contact but that's not unusual, especially at the start of an appointment. After several years of this, she will sense I'm angry that she's not ready for me, *the proper way*.

The freshly crimped curtain of hair falls low to cover her face, but knowing I despair of untidiness, she tucks a generous bunch of the dark waves back behind her ear, all the while dropping circular ice-cubes into a glass. I watch silently as she spins the lid on my favourite brandy.

The top spins and spins, almost hypnotically like a roulette wheel. Keen to not let her get too comfortable, I speak. "I like the white. You know that". My voice is colder than a few minutes ago; abrupt, even. My happiness at being here is tainted somewhat, by her lack of attentiveness to my very specific needs. She flinches, then smiles so quickly that the two movements meet in the middle.

"I know Mr Jennings. I had to rearrange some appointments for you. You are a pleasant surprise tonight. You're two weeks early! Yes, I keep the white just for you but I wasn't expecting you. And, well, after last time, some of the......stitching needed fixed".

At the mention of my last visit and how I hurt her, my smile returns. She returns the gesture with a wide, glossy magenta smile herself. "I like the lipstick. It's a good choice". I allow her this minor compliment, as I'm pleased to see her acting has improved. The smile isn't mirrored in her dark, brown eyes. I respect her for how hard she tries for me.

Yes, she's good. Worth every penny. Hah! Penny, she had no idea that I enjoyed my hobby while I was married to her too! I really am fantastically bad. Pleasure tickles my buttocks, but I need to stick to our routine. "Well you need to put the stockings on. Yes, the fishnets. That'll cheer me up. I brought a new pair for you. A little present".

Leaning forward over the coffee table, I plant a wet, fish-like kiss, full onto her mouth. She doesn't part her lips or make my tongue welcome and I feel her go stiff. But when I pull away, she smiles widely again. Wonderful! This is even better than our usual dance.

Charmaine's eyes flick to the bag in my hands and her pretty, highly rouged face, loses colour a little. I watch as she spins the lid again; a decision to make herself a drink. It's twice the size of mine and I know why.

Dropping the bag to the floor and sitting down on the sofa, I don't take my eyes off her. My pulse quickens. I like watching her grow in fear at this, *the beginning bit*.

I pay her good money. I know she needs it and the power play always turns me on. Laying my brandy down on a coaster on the table, I notice that her hands are trembling. She finishes her drink in one, sees me looking at her, noticing her fear, and leans forward and cups my face. "Come on then Mr Jennings, shall we get started?"

An hour later, I'm counting out several fifty-pound notes. As a last flourish, I can't resist fanning the pile of cash out and adding an extra twenty on top, right in the middle. The display looks like a flower. She'll like that, I'm sure.

Zipping up my bag and checking my hair in the mirror by the door, I shout a cheery "bye-bye, my beauty!", unlatch the lock and step out into the stairwell. Trotting down the stairs and whistling, I'm delightfully invigorated. Money well spent!

Alice often commented on how much perkier I was at the end of the month. She thought it was the fresh air and too many drinks with the lads after football. Stupid woman had no idea it was because I got most, but sadly not all, of my frustrations out on one or sometimes two, of my very special hookers.

When I was married to Penny, I got a bit carried away occasionally; sailed close to the wind, a bit. It was one of the reason's I had to press the eject button and disappear.

Married to Alice, well, apart from tonight, I have been a good boy and not gone too far. I won't be able to see Charmaine again but I still have two of my girls left......mind you, I am thinking about relocating so I might as well get my moneys' worth from them before I leave. Perhaps in a few days?

It's almost midnight now and the ground has turned frosty, so before stepping onto the street, I stop to button my coat up and re-tie the belt.

Looking left then right I'm gauging which way to go. I opt for the better lit walk, which threads through town, with a short stroll through a busy estate. Its longer, but that tow path and bloody underpass, has given me the jitters. The train hurtling by and the weird row of trees, are not on my agenda again tonight, that's for sure!

Nothing shall ruin my mood. Nothing at all. Walking purposefully into the night, my Burberry camel rain-coat and grey hair are momentary lit up, as I pass beneath the street light and disappear into the gold tinted gloom.

Alice

I don't even want to know what just happened inside that apartment. I heard Michaels grunts and a woman crying at one point and some certain slapping sounds, some thuds and then even louder crying. Waiting in the shadow of the stair-well staring straight ahead, I couldn't leave and disappear into the night even if I wanted to, in some way, it felt like being there was the very least I owed her.

Wondering what's happened in her life to mean this was her chosen option for earning a living, I sat hunched and angry. Head in my hands, slightly rocking until I heard my Husband making his exit.

As he appeared at that poor womans doorway and did his favourite coat back up, I wanted to send him straight to Hell, there and then. But I knew the woman inside, would be blamed or at the very least arrested and interviewed if anything happened to him there. Her business exposed and life inevitably over, it would be my fault. So, all I could do was watch as he virtually skipped home. If I could feel sick, I would, but I feel heavy and dark and weak and lost instead.

Simon would know what to do; he was always so organised and in control. The brightest man I ever met. His ideas and plans were like a healthy human body; everything in the right place, working the right way for the right reasons. We had such synergy and were so in love, that my biggest fear was us breaking up. So, when he texted me at work, a month or so after our weekend at his cottage, the urgency in his messages made my blood run cold.

* * * * *

"Alice. I need to see you. We must talk today. Now! xx". Normally when his number comes up on the screen on my phone, my heart soars! A dove on the wind bursting up and out of a cloud, gliding on thermal air, travelling somewhere wonderful. This time, though it's bad news! We're over! He's ill! Michael's found out about us not breaking up! He's confronted him! Simon's met someone else! The images and thoughts crawl over each other, trying to take hold and I freeze, gripping the phone in severe panic.

I can sense Saffron behind me, hovering, trying to decide if she should ask if I am ok. She won't; she's incredibly polite. She knows I need her to keep working, even if I am not. I hear her walk away, down a row of book-shelves and once she starts singing along to the music, playing through her little pink head-phones, I know I am safe to react.

Weak with worry and staring at the offending phone, I crumple into the seat at my desk, to stare stupidly at the papers I'm supposed to be filing, and put my head in my hands.

190

Willing myself desperately not to cry, I gasp in relief as the top lines of another message light the screen up. "I'm coming your way now. Leave your desk and walk down the corridor towards me". Frantic, I ram the papers into my desk drawer without even shutting it properly. Saffron is staring but I don't care.

Pushing my glasses back up my now, rather sweaty nose and smoothing my blouse, I grab my neck scarf and run out of the library, while still trying to wrap the silk around my neck. "Going for lunch Saffron", I shout loud enough for her to hear. The words are left in the air behind me. "It's only 10.am!" she calls after me weakly.

Clickety clacking down the stone corridor past marble pillar, after pillar, I'm alone and thankful for it. My scarf waving behind me; pink, patterned with black-birds, I'm flying.

As Simon rounds the corner ahead of me, I almost cry out to him. He's walking briskly but puts his finger to his lips to silence what he knows will be me babbling and crying in panic, as soon as we get near each other. He puts both his hands up; a red stop-sign to my running. Doing as he wants, I halt abruptly.

My steps echo around us, then the corridor falls quiet. Jerking his head sharply, he gestures we cross the grass square to the other side of the quad. We often meet in the shadows there just to whisper and more recently, emboldened by the solitude, we've dared to kiss.

Several metres apart, we walk in unison across the grass. The smell of Mid-Winter is with us. Smokey and peaty. Roasted, almost. Somewhere in the campus one of the gardener's is burning leaves before the Christmas holidays allows them to be neglected and grow rotten. I'm desperate to speak but Simon's gait is stiff and he's not looking at me. My fear grows with every step. The frosted grass beneath our feet crunches and there's a hint of snow in the air.

Reaching the most shadowy part of the wall at the same time, Simon then embraces me. It's not an embrace of love or lust. It's a tight, breathless embrace of fear. Actually, I'm sensing relief too. What on earth? The squeezing's too tight and I tense up mute with confusion, not returning the embrace.

"You need to get out of that house Alice. He's been lying to you". Simon's broad, freckled temple, is glistening with sweat. A cold breeze snaps my scarf up to my face and I pull it away roughly, hating to miss my lovers face, for even a second.

"What do you mean? I don't know who you mean? What he?" I'm staring at Simon in confusion.

"Michael, Alice! He's been lying to you. It's not what you *think*. It never has been. France was a lie". These are words for other people. For on the television. From the pages of books.

"Of course, he hasn't lied, you *silly*!", for some reason I laugh. My lover recoils. His face is a sinister stone colour and is badly mottled with worry.

"I've a friend in the records department at the council. He helps me with research when I'm writing my fictional stuff and what not. Anyway.....". Simon flaps his hands, annoyed at himself for not getting to the point quick enough. "He found a death certificate for the first Wife. Penny Jennings? She didn't die in France. She died in the same district that she lived with Michael in..... and later than he told you, too! Almost six months before he met you, not two years, like he said! Alice are you listening to me?! Oh, for all Hell's *sakes!!*".

Simon's voice catches and my heart stops, as I realise he's going to cry. My chest has relaxed but it has left a shadow of worry. Simon's still flapping his hands madly, so I reach out to hold them still. "It'll just be a mistake Darling. Please calm down". Utterly relieved that this meeting wasn't for him to end things between us, I'm missing the point. "It's of no matter now, I'm leaving him". Simon sags and embraces me again.

"Good. Let's go and get your stuff now. You can come to mine". He's pulling me towards the library, but I pull back.

"No. Not today. There's too much to sort out! He's adamant we are going away for Christmas. It's just a few days away. It's all booked and paid for! Me as usual.... I need to sort out the house. Tell my family. Prepare to lose my job....". My voice tails off, as Simon's face hardens in anger and disappointment. He drops my hands and steps backwards, away from me.

"Simon, please listen....". I'm pleading with him and have the most awful feeling that he's going to leave me, as I always feared. All because I have to leave Michael *my way*. The way I'm planning. The only way it can be done. Slowly, carefully and quietly.

"I've waited long enough Alice! It's been six months! That bastard *Michael*, is *not* the man you think he is and I'm worried for you. *For us*, actually. These types don't let go easily, especially once rejected, before they have their chance to abandon or ruin you. Why lie about his Wife's' time and place of death? Why?!". Simon's voice has got louder and I frown in a mixture of impatience and shame. Trying to calm Simon down, I reach for him again "Shhhhhh. Someone will hear you. Calm down!".

He makes a guttural sound, like a growl then moves away from the wall to stand in the bright sun-light. In clear view of the quad lawns. "If you go away with him, next week, I won't be here when you get back". The cold breeze, has messed his lovely hair up and he looks a little crazy. "I mean it Alice! I will be gone!", he yells in my face. Struck dumb with shock and hurt I stand and watch him march across the quad, gathering eyes from a cluster of student's sitting on the grass by the entrance to the Library.

Stumbling and weaving across the impeccable, university lawns, it's taking all my strength not to run after Simon, but I can't give him what he wants; not yet. He stops walking and half turns as if to come back towards me. I watch as he drops his head, shakes it as though annoyed at himself and turns fully, to face me. We are a few metres apart. He is crying and very pale and I want to cry too. I hold my palms up in a subtle but clear sign of resignation and shrug; offering the silent question, "what else can I do?". He nods and makes a phone sign with his hand and offers a tentative smile.

I nod and walk back to the Library, ready to pretend my life is, as usual, absolutely fine.

Miserable for the rest of the day, the only thing that stopped me screaming with worry, was knowing I would see Simon again, in the New Year. The new year that I would start my new life, with him.

* * * * *

I've never been good at confrontations so, with being already controlled by Michaels weather-like moods, I didn't mention what Simon told me and for a while, simply carried on as if his strange lies had not been uncovered. Of course, I never saw Simon again.

Serena

A sun-beam on my left cheek is the first thing I feel before opening my eyes. It's like the warm caress of a lover and for the smallest half second, I think it's Dylan.

He used to cup my face and just lay his hands there, until I woke up in a morning. He'd watch my fluttering eye-lids, as I tried to pretend to still be asleep. I loved the feeling so much, I wanted it to last as long as possible, so I'd pretend to still be in slumber, until one of us laughed aloud first.

Then I hear the papery rustling of something familiar yet not. A strange smell is wafting up my nostrils. It's grass. Yep, it's grass and stale alcohol. Yuck! Have I got pissed and fallen asleep on the decking again? Dylan will be *furious*.

"Urgh", a strange noise to the side of me. I open one eye and it all rushes in. "Hey", I croak. "Hey", Dexter replies with the same roughness of a hangover. We must have fallen back asleep.

The brightness of the tent signals full daylight outside, and blessedly, it isn't windy, or even raining, anymore. Dexter's got a tremendous cow's lick on the thick, wavy part of his trendy Mohawk hair style. It's pointing up to the sky; a sort of hairy aerial. Smirking, I quip that I half expect a radio to splutter into life. In his ruffled state, he looks younger. Again, I feel a stab of hate for anyone, who would want to touch a hair on his head. I feel absurdly parental towards him, although he's perhaps similar in age to me.

"It's after 10 now. We still have a bit of a hike to go and it's going to be a good hour to get some coffee on, make some eggs and get the site all tidy. It's only right we make it like we were never here". Dexter's rolling the blankets up neatly and firmly pressing them deep down, to the bottom of his bag.

"My job's breakfast, if you pack up everything in here then?". I'm already wriggling out of the sleeping bag; a determined, hatching butterfly, not waiting about. It's important he sees I'm not as grumpy and bad-tempered as I was yesterday. I have an idea for when we get home.

"Here you are take this, you can get on with making brekkie yourself". Grinning, he hands me a thick black woollen jumper scrunched up in a bundle. For a second, I'm confused and he smiles as he senses me catch on. Ah! He's put the eggs inside it to protect them all the way up the mountain. "Smart arse", I pretend to grumble. "Now, now!", he chastises and we chuckle together, before going about our separate tasks.

Opening the tent flaps wide, bright sun-beams cast us blind with a giants' torch. We both wince; more the whisky after-effects, than the sudden light. Crouching down and crabbing out into the fresh air, I feel oddly capable; I have eggs, we can eat and I'm going to be the one to make it happen.

Standing up and stretching, eyes closed tight, the morning's warmth reaches across my whole body. Widening my arms further, I smile back at the sun. Eggs in one hand (Dexter actually brought them *still* in the box) and his sweater in the other, I'm an odd-looking scarecrow but really don't care. This just feels amazing!

Once adjusted to the brightness, I absorb the mountains and valleys below us and I salute the view. This is why artists use watercolour paint! There's no actual set series of colours out here. The greens and blues and oranges and yellows and greys and blacks just sweep and meld together. The rain last night's left tiny diamonds on every little blade of grass. Every little frond of moss and every finger of slate has a glint of its own. Far, far down the valley I can just about make out a small colourful village. It's strikingly, startlingly, memorably.... *beautiful* out here.

It's like being in a jewellery shop! I don't understand why this place hasn't been a part of my life before. Then, it hits me again. Regret and shame; This is what Dylan *wanted* for us. He wanted me to be a part of this beautiful country. He's volunteered here and saved lives (and sheep) to just experience it, as often as possible.

Falling to my knees, a sudden howl of self-hate and shame escapes. My knees get wet and muddy immediately, but I don't care. My Husband didn't bring me here to trap me or make me his, he brought me here because he knew eventually, I would fall in love with Wales, as he fell in love with me.

What have I done? I pushed him away. I hurt and abused him. I chipped away at his love, then his confidence and worst of all, I hated him for loving me! For *wanting* me. For making *babies* with me. Jesus Christ. I'm evil! I hate myself. Falling back into a sitting position, I utter a low, deep, howl of grief and pain.

Big arms envelop me from behind and Dexter murmurs into my hair, "Its ok. We can sort things with you and him. For now though, I'm hungry and we've still got a bit of investigating to do".

Michael

One is definitely feeling rather off today; It's all the stress being put on me! Seeing Charmaine last night shifted the weight but not for long. Mind you.... now I don't have Alice restricting my money, I can arrange to see one of the others soon anyway! I think a more regular arrangement is in order whatever decision I make. Whatever town I end up in! Yes, a good regular timetable for my hobby will sort me out, for sure!

Hitting the boiled egg on my plate, hard, I smile grimly as the pristine, skin-like shell shatters, with a smart little crack. Bitter steam is rising off Alice's favourite coffee cup and inhaling the caffeine before taking a tentative sip, I feel a tad better. There should be news today from the post-mortem and I can feel more at ease then. They won't find anything. I know *that*.

There won't be bruises around her throat- little finger-print kisses goodbye. No bloody, smiling cuts from a knife. No poison in her body. *Nothing*. It was a genius plan, practised over and over again. The weighted back-pack shoved over the edge of the mountain right at The Notch's summit; weighing exactly the same as she did. Very clever indeed.

Standing there, icy wind lifting the hood of my water-proof and running its cold hands down my spine, I'd lean slightly forward and watch as the bag tumbled and landed further and further. Bouncing from jagged rock to jagged rock until eventually slowing its roll and stopping, rocking and then going still. The resting place, far away from normal, human accessibility.

My plan was Alice had to "fall" too far for me to climb down to her aid. Fall, far enough into the Notch's infamous ravine. So far that it would take a good while for rescue to come and certainly too far for anyone to save her life. The fall was to cause her injuries, serious ones, but the long wait for help, was to be my perfect nail in the coffin.

One practise run, I even shouted "Help! Help us please!" and hearing my echo, I laughed and laughed and that too echoed. I had to stop my guffawing, just in case a freshly successful climber came upon me. This large laughing man, no bag, no climbing partner and flushed, rosy cheeks, budding with plans of murder.

My chucky eggs have cooled now, just enough for me to slather cold butter onto the toast starting to smoke under the grill. I always liked my toast blackened a bit. Bitter and worthless to anyone else. Not sure why. Yes, true to form, Alice complained in the beginning about it.

* * * * *

"Your toast's burning, darling!" she's calling with her back to me, hands in the kitchen sink, washing up our plates from the full cooked breakfast, she makes me every day. She soon stops her whingeing when I pour her own coffee on to her perfectly golden toast. "I think that coffee was burnt darling. Can you smell it?". She flushes, blinks, licks her top lip and considers a retort. Closing her eyes and scraping back her chair, she thinks better of it and quietly cleans up the mess.

"I like things the way I like them Alice. Don't try to change me. I advise that strongly. Besides, you married me, so I must be perfect!", I crow, mouth full of food, and wait for her agreement.

"Absolutely correct, Michael. As always". I'm annoyed by her fake smile and dark eyes of anger. She needs more training, I think to myself.

* * * * *

She never complained about the way I liked my toast ever again.

Grinning at the memory and enjoying how clever I always am at controlling the women in my life, I sloppily chomp and slurp my way through four slices of mashed boiled egg on toast and scribble down questions I need to ask Kendal later today.

He pissed me off at our first meeting, but I mustn't let my annoyance way lay me. Strategy is at the very heart of success.

Serena

I miss Dylan and have finally accepted it. It's become a constant lump in my throat. Now, I have to carry that burden like the bloody back-pack Dexter brought.

"I'm going first Serena!", he call's cheerfully. "I'll carry the bag now, you made breakfast".

I smile at his sensitivity. I think he's seen me struggling this last few minutes. There's a sort of valley ahead, a wide expanse of green. Shortened grass, interrupted by clumps of bushes and reeds. It's wet and boggy in parts but there's no chance I'll lose Dexter. I can hear the gentle ticking sound of crickets, almost as though we are somewhere hot. It's a clear way and actually, rather pretty.

But as we get higher, the air starts to feel heavy and thick again. Cold and wintry even. Dexter's scrambling and skidding down a path ahead, using his arms, aeroplane style to keep his balance. As he makes his way for us, checking the safety of the path as he goes, Dylan's face swims into view again. He'd do the same. Go ahead. Keep looking back to see if I'm ok. My heart pinches and I lose my footing, feeling dizzy.

"Dex! Dex! The Husband made Alice go ahead for some of the hike, didn't he? Creepily clever of him as he was the more seasoned walker!" I've sat on a boulder for a breather. Dexter's stopped and stiffened. He could be one of the big rocks, from around us, he's so still! "I was waiting for you to notice that...". He's walking back towards me.

"Yes, he was more experienced, that much seems true", Dexter's looking away from me, towards The Notch, as he says this. Something like fear, grumbles in my bowels. I've the most strange, strong, urge to just run back down the mountain and away from this.

"Do you think he actually, planned this, like *properly*?! Surely not! Sounds like he's a proper killer!".

Dexter's gone still and is looking at his feet, "Let's just keep going. Stay focused on the job in hand just now. It's what Alice deserves". He smiles shortly at me, then starts stomping away.

Now he's weeping bracken left and right like a Giant destroying a forest. Then, as if by magic, the sun's rays cast stripes across the ridge ahead of us and for a few seconds it's so bright I have to close my eyes and count to five, breathing in deeply again. Dexter's disappeared from view, around the ridge and I stomp a foot in frustration.

There's more to this. Of that, I'm now positive. Next time we stop, I'm going to ask Dexter out-right. I might have, "The Gift", but it comes and goes and right now, all that I'm getting is a gut instinct and no more. In Alice's absence, I'm all alone.

Michael

Kendal better bloody hurry up. It's a different girl on reception today. Chubby, short haired and pale; she's not the eye candy of yesterday. She's eyeing me suspiciously and eating what looks like a large tuna salad baguette. I can't help but wrinkle my nose up.

Without losing eye contact, she smiles a big smile at my distaste and I see something green is stuck in her teeth. I want to ram the entire remaining five inches of calorific Hell, all the way down her roast pork neck. The thought makes my pulse race, so I look away, toss my head and cross my legs.

I'm bad tempered today, even after my lovely breakfast. My trousers aren't pressed. Alice knew I liked all my favourites ready at least 10 days in advance. Damn inconvenient all this dead Wife malarkey.

In the background, a local radio station is on low, and a familiar melody starts. It's the wedding dance that Alice and

I had; Phil Collins, "every move you make, every step you take, I'll be watching you", croons smoothly out of the retro speakers, mounted on the wall, high above me.

A vision of her in her wedding dress. The daisy patterned train caught up by a small yellow ribbon tied round her left hand. The disco lights of pink, blue and green chasing each other across her bust. There's a small crowd watching us, some smiling, some simply watching or quietly talking, as we dance. I can feel her cheek move along my neck and she murmurs something into my ear. "I'm so glad you found me. I love you Michael".

A sickness fills my throat and a sharp pain spreads over my shoulders. Twitching a look at the fat girl at her desk- I see that she's watching me expressionlessly, but of course, she's still chewing. Closing my eyes, I uncross and straighten my legs to wipe my alarmingly sweaty hands on my thighs. My chinos are a dark green today so the streaks of sweat stand out on the material which makes my temper flare.

Where the heck is Kendal?! "You never *loved me* though, did you". The words have changed. What? That's not the words! The radio crackles and the lights above me start to sway in a circle a little. They could be disco-lights. The girl at the desk now has head-phones on, and is typing frantically. She's not noticed what's happening to me. Dear God, she's useless.

The music has stopped but the radio voices haven't. A rotten smelling mist has gathered at my feet and I'm put in mind of The Notch. I can smell damp moss, grass and oil. The oil from the helicopter. "You do know that you're not getting away with this don't you Michael".

The last letters skitter and rattlesnake around my head as the mist gathers higher, now up to my knees. I can't see my feet and it feels like I'm rooted, yes rooted to the spot, by *actual roots*, deep into the ground. Oh, my lord! Now, I can't move or speak! I must be imagining this. I'm having a heart attack! No, *a stroke!* Hallucinating with the trauma of all this paper-work pressure. Not to mention, the new agony in my back and shoulders!

My throat feels tight and I see a pale shadow flitting past the reception doorway. That blasted girl is still not even noticing any of this! I want to catch her attention but find I can't move even my arms. Yes, it's a stroke!

The proper radio boosts back into life. The song's finished and the presenters are talking; something banal and normal, about the price of fish.

"Mr Jennings. Ready now?". Jumping at the sudden human presence, I put my hands together, in a prayer position and raise my eyes to the ceiling in thanks.

Kendal's poking his head round the corner and looking at me in confusion. "I've been calling your name for a half a minute or so. Are you alright?".

"Yes, absolutely. Certainly. I'm just coming!", I stutter. Before I get a chance to smile at him in reassurance, he's gone; having walked back down the corridor and left me alone again! I don't want to be here alone.

Grabbing my coat and not bothering to sweep my sweaty fringe from my forehead, I stagger after him, almost tripping over shoe-laces that I didn't even know were undone. As I walk behind Kendal, I hear a tinkling and something crunches under my feet. The tinkling is wind-chimes, like Alice's laughter.

The crunching is what looks like the contents of a kitchen bin. Shaking my shoes free of it as I step, I have to trot after Kendal as fast as I can to get away from it. No matter how hard I try to avoid them, I crunch carpet all the way to his office. I am literally walking on egg-shells.

Chapter 8: Bad Baggage

Dylan

I'm restless and the lack of daylight and washing, has my skin papery and itchy. I've woken up, head on the desk in the hotel room. The only table in here and it's not even clean. Bottles and glasses cover the other surfaces around me.

Slapping my face hard, I grunt and in desperation, then bang my head off the television table; once then twice. Crying in self-pity and pain, I come to rest it on the cold plastic or glass or whatever the Hell the table's made of. I cry for our babies and for each year we've lost together, while stubbornly, grieving separately. Why didn't I try harder? Did I try *too* hard? Try in the wrong ways?

Why didn't she just leave me years ago. Yes, abandon me, after Bronwyn? How did I sit back and watch the grief tear us in two? No, not two! more than two....to *three*!

All alone now, I realise how alone my Wife's been too. She never cheated. She never would. It's not her way. "Urgh, Idiot!" I slap my face and lay my head on the table again.

The last time I saw Serena with that sunny smile and spectacular shiny hair, was when I walked in that day to find her beautiful face pressed up close to the woman, I went on to sleep with. No, to fuck. We never actually *slept* together. I know that's what Bronwyn wanted. A whole night. That closeness. That warmth. She never got it.

A surge of nausea at a waft of stale beer and cold coffee, sends me running to the shower room. Tripping over a towel on the floor, I miss the toilet and vomit into the sink. It's like I can't stop remembering.

* * * * *

"You need to tell her. Serena, just knowing about me and you isn't good enough. This baby's coming whether you like it or not. *Our baby!*" Bronwyn's shouting down the phone. Grimacing in fear and with my teeth bared in anger, I creak open the door to the new veranda, to get away from the bats-ears of my Wife, seated a few metres away, at her laptop.

"Let me just go outside. My Wife's here and I know I can't talk about this in much detail around her". I say in an overly formal voice.

Pretending to be on the phone with a HR colleague at work, Bronwyn gets the hint. She tuts and goes silent, until she hears the familiar click of the glass door and the breezy sounds of the garden, through the phone.

It's been several months since Serena found out about the affair. Things have calmed down although the air between us is colder than it ever was.

Once we got home from Bronwyn's office that day, Serena just shrank further into herself and we haven't spoken of it since. In fact, we've never discussed it and I fear deep inside, that we never will. There was no chance Serena would find out about the baby, unless someone told her. I've thanked The Gods she was isolated before she met Bronwyn so there's no friends or colleagues queueing up to spill the beans.

Bronwyn was blocked from Serena's page and when she slept, I deleted and blocked Bronwyn's number from my Wife's phone. In my own phone, I changed her name to a work colleague's so Serena couldn't even get it from me.

Bronwyn wouldn't come to the house, she's gutless and afraid of my Wife's temper. I've told her enough, between the sheets, to know if Serena got anywhere near her, Bronwyn would end up disfigured for life and certainly lose a favourite outfit as Serena tore it from her body in rage. The images make my eyes well up, in terror.

"Ohhhhh Calm down. I've told you why I'm not telling her. She's not strong enough and I'm NOT going to be responsible for her actions". Hissing into the phone and turning to look inside to make sure Serena's not closer than I thought.

For the first few months, after she found out about the affair, Serena shadowed me everywhere. She checked my phone and I was only permitted to go to work as long as I showed her my shift time-table and let her double check it randomly with the HR managers' number, which rather cleverly, she had taken. I deserved her paranoia and watchful ways. But, recently, she's lost interest and I'm grateful.

I can see now, that my Wife's left the room. Probably to go and have a bath. "Bron. Look, we've got a good thing here. You have the baby coming. I am going to see you alright with money and I'm pretty sure you don't fancy seeing the inside of a grave any-time soon?". I try to laugh at my sarcasm and hope she will too. Instead, she tuts and sighs again; not good.

"What about if I make it possible to see the baby twice a month. I will stay at yours. I can maybe even swing a holiday once a year?" Bronwyn's gone quiet; she's thinking about it. She probably thinks if she takes her time, she'll get me in the end and we can all be one big happy family. No chance.

"If you were to tell Serena, none of that could happen. I wouldn't be able to visit at all. Nothing". I can almost hear Bronwyn's gassy head bubbling with ideas for how she can press me for a relationship in the times we are together. Her head is filled with Prosecco; her brain is all fizzing and bubbly....and sour. "Ok. Deal". She breaks her silence and my knees buckle with relief. "Thank you. *Thank you*", I whisper into the phone and start to turn the handle to go back inside the house again.

Opening the door, a crack and closing my eyes at the screech of the hinges, I can smell eucalyptus and jojoba. Even downstairs the bath-oils spread through the house like Serena's there at my side. I'm suddenly tempted to turn around and go to her and be with her. Wash her hair like I used to. I loved washing her hair, we almost always ended up in the bath together ….Bronwyn ruins the moment.

"But, if you don't arrange regular contact and make an effort with our son when he arrives, I'm going to tell her". Bronwyn repeats her favourite threat. She's nasty and persistent, like a stain I can't clean off. I regret every touch of her calculating, needy body! My throat burns with stomach acid. I need an indigestion tablet. No, I need a miracle.

"She can't handle the idea of anyone else having a baby Bron. If she finds out about you, she will die". I'm still using my persuasive voice. Manipulating her name. Creating a softness between us. The promise of intimacy hurts because I have no intention, ever, of fulfilling it. That would be my second worst nightmare; being in a proper relationship with Bronwyn.

"And, by the way, I can't have her coming to the office again. The drama isn't good for me or our child". The word *child* smacks me in the face. Child, not baby. Child. "That was ages ago!" I cry, then put a hand over my mouth. Bronwyn tuts again and takes a breath in to shout back at me. "Ok. Ok. Ok. Will call soon with plans". I stop her in her tracks and hang up gladly.

"You ok?" Serena's stood behind me. Flushed with wine and bath steam. She sways a little and leans against the veranda door. She's had more to drink upstairs. Her neck is blotchy and her eyes are large and dark with medication. Wrapping her bathrobe around herself more tightly, I see that she still has a slightly rounded tummy. The thought of why, makes me want to scream. *Scream and scream.*

"Let's go to bed Sir. I'm exhausted. Lots on at work. Redundancies. That's why I can't talk about it in front of you. Data protection and all that". I'm guiding her back upstairs and holding her hips to keep her steady. Touching her hurts, a lot. A waft of her favourite shampoo catches my nose, so I close my eyes. I'm stifling the urge to lift her up and Fire-Man carry her to bed. I did that almost every night, before it all rotted away to lies and loss. Stopping, she slurs "Don't try and carry me. I'm fat", and turns away from me. She can't quite focus on my face but I just want to hold hers in my hands. Yet still, I don't. It's been a while since I did that.

* * * * *

Something's woken me. Having got back into bed, I'd nodded off again. There it is again, a rattling sound.

The Tv's timed out and the bedside lamp's flickering. My head hurts now worse than ever. My mouth's dry and now there's a weird battery licked taste.

Reaching for my phone with one eye shut, the screen blooms into life, shocking my already fragile retinas. "Please let it be Serena. *Please* let it be her", I whisper to myself holding the phone to my chest before opening the message.

My heart sinks as I see it's just an email that has made the phone come to life. "Crap", I grunt and throw it into the corner of the room. The bedside light goes out, turning the room completely pitch black. They are bloody good blackout blinds!

"Fucksakes. Give me a break!". I'm grasping at the lamp and even though we've been friends for nearly three days now, I've forgotten where the switch is.

Swinging both legs out of bed, and deciding two hands and two eyes are better than none at all, I take a deep breath in and wait a few beats before trying again. Fingering up and around the lamp, I find a warm space where the bulb was. That makes no sense. Bloody lamp was on!!

A bang makes me jump, so I toss the lamp away from me, like it's exploded, and squeal like a girl. Serena would screech with laughter at me.

She always loved taking the mickey out of my fear of stupid things. "Get a grip, Strip!", she'd shout at my refusal to remove a spider from the bath or moth from a corner of the bedroom wall. She would dive back under the duvet, to laugh uproariously at me but refuse to do the job herself.

At first, I'd scowl, faking that my fragile ego was dented, making a huffing sound and crossing my arms. But watching the bedding twist and curl and hear her laughing, long strands of her fiery hair snaking and wriggling with her, I couldn't pretend for long.

I always ended up tearing the duvet back to expose her naked, curled up and giggling. The way she'd look straight at me, dimples, freckles and all, made me kiss her and the rest would be history until later when we said good night. "Good-Night sir" I'd whisper. "G'night Strip" she'd say and cackle again into the pillow. We often fell asleep that way. Pillows absorbing our love and joy ready for the morning.

Now I'm here with one lumpy pillow, in the dark, and the room smells of death. Actually, when *did* that *stench* start? Oooft, It's gotten cold too. Not sure how or why as I haven't even been outside.

Something touches my face, but I stifle the Strip-squeal this time. A movement. Christ! There might be someone in the room. They've seen my nice car, saw I paid cash up front, from a big roll of money that's in my bag! Places like this are always a risk. The only other reasonable hotel in the vicinity is the one I used to book for the affair. There's no way I'm staying *there*! So, I'm stuck here, in this place.

"Just go away!" I yell and cringe at how scared I sound. "She loves you". It's barely there. But its words on the air. No, *in* the air. Like an echo but you never heard the first sound that set it off. Actually, I'm not even sure I heard anything.

The door clatters again and then the lamp comes to life. It's on the floor and facing away from me casting a triangle of light towards the door-way. Below the door handle is hanging the Do Not Disturb Sign. Crawling across the floor and fixated on it, I can see that something is written on it. "Wife"

Serena

A snort disturbs the air and I want to snort back. I'm not remotely fearful. This stag has stalked us for miles and just seems to mock us.

Up here, the bruise coloured sky is easily throwing the punches; its shifting and changing, constantly. Sunny one minute, cloudy the next. The best, most polite way to describe it now, is "atmospheric".

The temperature is skipping up and down too. The stag blinks, tosses his head and canters away. I watch him stride confidently up and over a small, heathered hill, towards a smaller deer. Likely a female by the size and shape of her. Dexter's yelling breaks the sweet moment.

"It's here. This is the place". His voice carried on the wind changes like a Chinese whisper. It sounds like, "The deer. I liked his face", and I laugh. It's actually the shrill excitement in his voice and not the words that tells me we've arrived.

Half sliding and half slipping towards him, I'm barely smothering the relief, fear and thrill. This is it.

The clouds part as he steps away from the edge and the sudden, sharp light blinds him. He holds his hand up for shade. The wet mountain slate is reflecting the sun momentarily, so he can't see. I run faster desperate to reach him and pull him back. "Dex, stand still. Don't move at all. Stop dead!" My voice cracks and turns pitchy with it.

Reaching him a second later and tightly holding his big daft arms, is the *best* feeling! We fall to the ground together, laughing hysterically. "Just you wait a minute. I'm going to *edge* over *the edge*". Dexter laughs into his hood at the silly joke and starts crawling, on his belly, towards where the rock stops. I tug him back, to face me. "No Dex. I mean it. You just wait. Your balance is crap. Almost crapper than my eggs!".

Standing up and twisting sideways but keeping an eye on Dexter, I slowly turn 360 degrees and breathe in long and deep.

The view really is breath-taking. The sun is at its height now and it has become oddly warm. Small dragon-flies and what look like midges are clouding together in puffs. I can hear crickets again. Where sunlight catches it, the bracken and moss glow a luminescent green, like something from that old Wizard Of Oz movie.

Slowly inching towards a pouting lip of rock I fancy, I've my arms out to balance like Dexter did earlier; aeroplane style. Leaning forward, I venture to a point where I see down the huge rocky scar, scored into the mountainside that resulted in this, The Tryfan Notch.

The weather's glorious and not remotely like it was yesterday or the day Alice died. I'm disappointed, somehow the difference matters and it feels like I'm detached from her.

Suddenly, out of nowhere I want to cry. I like it here but it's where someone, no quite a few people, have died. This was a mistake. We can't help her. She's dead anyway now. This was all a stupid arrogant, crazy mistake.

My throat closes up and the urge to sob intensifies but I stop. Something is happening. Alice is here or something else is....

Sparks and hummingbirds. A hand deep in a bunch of white-blonde curls. The smell of wild-flowers. A woman crying leaning over a black dog laying on a kitchen floor. A buzzing sound and then coins falling to the floor.

Putting my hands to my head, I close my eyes in extreme pain. My heart hurts like I'm having some sort of attack.

Foxgloves. The sound of police-car sirens. Fat crackling and spitting. The smell of roasting meat. Chicken. A voice whispering, *"The penny drops"*.

"Wait. Wait Serena. It's ok...." Dexter's behind me. He's crept up to avoid startling me. "Hang on Dex. Let me speak. I have an idea. See, your backpack? It weighs pretty much the same as a small woman". Dexter's mouth is hanging open. I think he knows what I'm going to say. "Let's push it off the ledge. See how far it goes". He either thinks I'm a total genius or a wierdo.

"Did Alice suggest that? Is she here now?". Dexter spins round to see if he can see my ghost-friend. I start laughing at how funny he's being.

"No. Cool it! It's more that..... the *idea* just bloomed inside my head. Could be my gift or my massive brain! Who care's!? Are you in or are you out?!". I shift on my feet to try and look more authoritative and this only serves to make Dexter grin. "Go on then. Let's have a go", he says and starts taking out stuff we *don't* want lost away down in the gully.

Dexter's quickly taking out both our mobile phones, his wallet, a set of keys and putting them in his pockets. "Now, look at the weather Serena. Like emotions, it changes really quickly and is supremely unpredictable. Rain, sun, mist, whatever. They all take their turn and affect the terrain and people's ability to stay safe up here and going down". He's now placing the back-pack upright and quick as a flash before it topples of its own accord, he pushes it. Hard.

We watch, mesmerised as it flies off the edge and soars away from us through a few meters of sky, then down. It hits the ground, many metres away from us. It rolls a few times, rests in a spot and rocks side to side slightly, then stills. From here the bag looks alarmingly like a fallen hill-walker.

Dexter slips to my side and holding tightly onto my shoulders, he leans over to see where the bag landed. "He pushed her. Alice. Really *hard*". Dexter's looking at me and backs away from the edge, as if in disgust. His skin is grey. "That murdering bastard, definitely fucking pushed her".

As he whispers this harshly, the sound of the sea blocks my hearing. From my feet a strange white buzzing begins to spread up through my body. My face prickles with cold sweat, so I try licking my lips but my tongue won't work. Before

I know it, I'm tipping forward, off the edge, and then there's only blackness.

Michael

"So, Mr Jennings, the results of the post-mortem were as you expected. No signs of anything......how you say.... *particularly sinister*". Kendal's looking down at the documents on the desk in front of him. My heart relaxes and I reward myself with a tip back in my chair, just a little though. Kendal is still focused on the paperwork, so I sneak a quick look up at the ceiling and roll my eyes back in relief. "Thank you, God", I whisper under my breath. *Oh, the irony!*

"Ah....However...here's a side note towards the end....". Kendal's interrupted my plan's for dinner; I was just forming thoughts around a nice curry from the take-away down the road. Now, it's sinking in that my relief may be a little premature; his *"However"*, has just made me go cold from the belly up. What now!? My chair clatters forward and my knees crack painfully off the edge of Kendal's desk.

Kendal coughs, steeples his fingers under his chin and pauses for effect. "Ah, glad I have your attention again Mr Jennings. By sheer, wondrous coincidence, the post-mortem was conducted by a friend of mine!" He's rather cheerful, and that scares me somewhat. Staring at Kendal, I'm surprised the rotter doesn't clap his hands.

Two feet away from me, across the desk, he's close enough for an assault. I want to reach out, snatch the results from him and run. Tear them up as I fly down the stairs and into the street. Little pieces of white scattering like the annoying, untidy confetti that I loathed on both darned wedding days.

"It looks as though, you won't be able to action a claim on The Will and insurance for your Wife.....yet". The blood runs from my face, down to my feet and away. Far, far away. In a split second I see my plans for retirement go up in flames. The house on fire. Me, destitute on a street corner.....

Kendal's found his stride; "Yes! Dr Milton is himself a walker! Well, *mountaineer* actually. Can you imagine the coincidence!" Kendal daren't look at me and I see his slim, muscular neck, is flushed with what I take as excitement.

Of course! *He's out to get me! They all are. Ruin my plans. Ruin my life! Take my money!* Curling my hands into fists, I push them tightly under my thighs, like a child, bitterly waiting for the cane at the head-teachers office. "Yes. Go on". These are my first few words since entering the office, now what feels like an age ago. I didn't even say hello as I arrived- I saw no point; I just wanted in and out with the news that I could set about starting my claims. Now this!!

Kendal's mouth is moving and I recapture the sounds, as though falling to earth with a thud.

"Dr Milton has scribed personally, that he felt it was rather odd, that your Wife seemed to have a large amount of spinal damage and bruising across her back and shoulders. As executor of her will, I am privy to more detail of the situation she died in, than is usual for a victim's solicitor you see". He looks at me and raises his eye-brows. I don't reply as the word "victim" has me a bit stumped. He emits a small sigh, and carries on.

"So.......It is my understanding, Alice was found a good few metres away from the cliff face and not directly below it. I can't say much more but, it is a bit *odd*, considering what you told the police and myself. I believe you said she slipped as she was facing away from you?.......she wanted some sort of special artistic photo?"

An image of Alice stood in front of me, takes my breath away as it zooms into focus. The wind in her hair. Long mousy tendrils either side of her face. Her flushed cheeks, runny nose and pale mouth. Her uncertain, wide eyes and tense stature. She was afraid before I pushed her; hearing what I said, and turning to look at me, she knew what was coming. Her instincts were right. *Her nightmare came true.* She gave me the idea and I ran with it.

A strong draft, of cold air, lifts and rustles the papers on Kendal's desk. He slams his palm down hard and fast, to stop them flying about the room. The loud bang makes me jump. He looks up sharply, frowns, then smiles again. He has excellent teeth and I see dimples, I never noticed before.

"So, Dr Milton's referred the case on to the relevant authorities, and it *is* a *case* now. There will be a deeper investigation and a thorough look at every.... single.... aspect of what happened to your lovely Wife".

My mouth's gone dry at some point in the last few seconds. Gulping and blinking like a stranded fish, I want to speak, but find I can't. Kendal just won't shut up.

"I wonder perhaps, Mr Jennings..... if you made a mistake? You know, in the police interview. It's absolutely standard all this enquiry lark, I'm sure, you have nothing to worry about"

"But I don't understand! She fell. *She fell.* It was *terrible.* I called for help as soon as it happened. One minute she was there, looking out at the view, the next she was gone! It's traumatised me. All of it. I called for help! A lot!" The image of a squealing pig crosses my mind. This can't be happening!

Sweat itches my arm-pits. Leaning forward, I'm desperate to convince this man it was all just an accident. "I called for the emergency services people! I did all I could. It was all her idea, that walk! She drove!......" my voice tails off, as Kendal appears unaffected by my desperate begging to be believed.

He matches my movement and leans towards me. "Yes Mr Jennings. I'm aware of what you said at the time. It's all in the report.

A waft of his fabulous aftershave tickles my nose, as he leans back in his chair and slowly crosses his ankles under the table.

As if changing his mind at the distance he's created, he leans forward again, puts one elbow on the desk, rests his chin in his hand and looks at me smiling. Then starts talking again.

"Even my *Wife* knows that Alice was rather short sighted and wasn't a hiker. She was at best, a *walker*, Mr Jennings". He stares at me for a second then sits back and takes a drink of his coffee. As he swallows, his mouth on the edge of the cup, curls in a smile. The slurping sound makes me grit my teeth.

"What is also quite interesting, Mr Jennings, is that Alice had told my Wife she planned on leaving you. She also left a message for me here at this office, asking about divorce proceedings. All of this, coming together, is reason to have a more....... *robust,* enquiry. For Alice's sake. You understand this, of course".

He knows! He's made it his business to go meddling in my life. This is a set up! He's decided, to make sure this is as Hellish as possible for me! My eyes glitter with hate as I attempt to stare him out. It's a rarity but I don't know what to say.

Kendal simply takes my water glass, stands up and wanders over to the almost human shaped pot plant in the corner and slowly empties it.

The sound of pouring water onto the soil takes me back to The Notch. To the small rivulets of water running down the rocks in the garden-feature Alice built, just after we married. To the pouring of champagne on our wedding day. To the tiny mountain streams trickling between our feet, as we ascended the place I chose for her death.

There's a creak and I open my eyes. I didn't even know they were shut. I'm disorientated and sense a movement by the door. No, that's not a plant. It's a person. It's my Wife. I think my blood is curdling with terror.

I whip back round to alert Kendal, but see he is seated again comfortably opposite me. Looking back, the corner is as it was. Just a plant and coat stand and shelf, as usual. "Kendal, I......." My chair squeaks as I return yet again, to face the man who is clearly, my undoing. His rich, dark hair is freshly combed. He smells excellent.

I jump, as the phone on his desk rings and he answers it quickly, almost as though he knew the call was coming. "Yes Melanie? Oh? Are they? Excellent. Tell them I'll call back in, say....one minute". He gently places the phone back on its cradle and again, smiles at me. He's prepared carefully for this meeting and the thought makes me want to slam my hands on the table and stamp my feet. I need my medication! I need a drink and I need away from here, fast.

Kendal pushes his chair back, smooths his dazzlingly well pressed grey suit trousers and re-adjusts the matching waistcoat. He's like a musician preparing to walk on stage.

If you'll excuse me, I have an important call waiting and then, straight after, a late lunch date with my Wife. We like to treat each other once a month and today, it's my turn. We are going to Alice's nephew's favourite restaurant. You must know it..." He's walking towards the door but not bothering to make sure I'm following.

He spins back to face me as if an idea has come to him and I clench my backside tight, trying not to release the gasses of fear. "Oh, before you go, may I ask if you would like me to contact her family, what few she has left? Let them know that an investigation is starting?"

Pale faced and shaking a little, I'm being gently but firmly guided towards the door. Clutching my brief case to my chest, like a shield, I'm now clumsily tripping out into the hall.

"Yes. Yes. Of course. I don't think I could call the family Mr Kendal. All far far, *far* too upsetting you see. In fact, I feel rather unwell. Have done for a couple of days now.....". Patting my breast pocket and searching for a handkerchief, I flick a basic smile of sadness in his direction, but it has no obvious impact.

No wonder Alice liked him. He's smart and cool. He is every part the man I want to be. *Next time,* I shall fashion myself on him.

First things first, I must get away from here super fast. Kendal nudges me towards the reception, but keeps talking. "Yes. Yes. I'm sure Mr Jennings. All the stress of losing your lovely, *lovely* Wife, will take its toll. Last thing.... please do get yourself some advice from *The Dark Side* Mr Jennings. You know, those chaps in *Criminal Defence*. I think there's a legal aid one based across the street in fact. Handy for you!". Kendal lets go of my arm and briskly starts to walk away, down the hall.

I start to open the door out onto the stairs to leave, but Kendal shouts after me, "Oh and The Police will want to speak to you Jennings. That's them on the phone for me now! No rest for the wicked, as they say!" He calls this from around the corner. It's a high pitched almost song-like ending, to what has only been a ten-minute meeting.

Inside his office, behind the now closed door, the window bangs shut and I think I can hear wind-chimes.

Dylan

My phone's buzzing over and over. It's just going to be Bronwyn. She sees this as an opportunity. For sure, I'm gonna ignore it! Fact is, even if it's not Bronwyn, it won't be Serena; she never calls when we've had a fight and this is *way* beyond a fight.

Grunting in self-disgust and wrapping my body up tighter in the stale smelling duvet, I childishly cover my head with it and moan in self-pity.

Too sad and tired, to even try and work out the scribbled message from earlier, I just want my Sir. For all I know Bronwyn's found out I'm here via the small-town-grapevine and thinks it's a funny joke to freak me out with daft notes. Sir will kill her! That's if I don't do it myself.

I told her NO PHOTOGRAPHS, but of course she ignored me! I think she planned for me to end up alone, so she could swoop in like a big vulture and snaffle me. All her moves are adding up to that.

Oh, my lovely, wild, sad Sir! It's a cliché, but right now I'd rather be with her hating me, than without her at all.

Something touches my ankle. Jerking it back I'm expecting a big fat hairy spider. Not surprising in this hotel from Hell. Then something strokes, yes strokes my hip. "Whatthemuthafuuuuck!"

Yelping and pressing myself backwards into the headboard, my entire body still under the duvet, I'm too creeped out to move much more. I don't have it in me to dare peek out of the relative safety of my home-made cave. My coward-o-meter just leaped from eight out of ten to a solid eleven.

A short but strong, puff of cold air hits me full in the face, and a strange crackling sound deep in my ear canals makes me want to slap myself in the side of the head again. Weird! it sounds like ice forming?

In the gloom of the bed-cave (which I realise is more of a tent), a face starts to appear in the cold cloud of my warm breaths. Shivering, I realise I'm not shaking from shock; it's from bitter, deep, middle of the night on a mountain, cold.

My heart stops then freezes with the rest of me. "Hello again", the face in the frozen air, in front of me, says. Now I really am shocked but, for sure, this is a hallucination?!.... No food, too much drink, the stress of all stresses and zero contact with the outside world, has me loop-the-loop!

Ok, it took 3 days, but here we are; I'm certifiably insane. "Your phone", it... no *she*! hisses. Stiff with horror I can't speak or move. There's a whooshing sound and then the she-thing is gone. The duvet abruptly drops, but there's a lingering smell of moss and dirt. A barrage to the senses triggering thoughts of Mountain Rescue sucks me into the darkness.

Men's deep voices talking urgently. Some laughter echoing and bouncing off the rocks as we hike. The repetitive thunderous whir of helicopter rotors. Intense wind tugging at our waxy jackets. The scent of coffee first then out of the dark comes a waft of Serena's old perfume. Her cries of pain echo, then eerily fall silent. Oh God the memories are so real.

Reaching out my fingers tentatively, I am expecting to touch my Wife. "Help me" I whisper. I think I'm going mad with grief. "Help *her!*", the air whispers again.

Scrabbling and clawing the bedding off my face, I sit bolt upright, pressed flat against the headboard. I'm unashamedly panting in fear. Jesus, I've avoided this manky stained thing all week, and now it's my best friend! The sweat stains and suspicious brown streaks across the fabric of the head-board, have made me gag more than once, and now I couldn't be closer to them.

I try to quieten my breathing and listen to the room. I'm scanning every inch of these four walls, for an answer to what's going on.

There's something small and black on the sheet to my left. It's a phone. Mine. The same one that was across the room, on the floor a few minutes ago. "Mountain Rescue Office", is flashing on the screen as the phone buzzes with the call, over and over.

Alice

Torn in two, paper thin and weak, I don't know what to do next. It took all my effort to try to get that useless, whingeing lump Dylan, to go to his Wife and now I'm horrendously low on whatever it is that gives my dead self, energy.

I didn't expect Serena to fall; it was never in the whispery, hissing voices that circle me. They never told me that this was what was supposed to happen. If it was indeed supposed to happen? Have we interrupted the natural order of events? Have I meddled too much?! In that case I might as well get packed for Hell.

Talking of Hell, I'm watching Michael again. Sickeningly, I'm getting some energy back by being here. My Husband is even more hunched than before. Like some sort of lumbering troll-like beast, he's stomping head down through the town centre. Forcing his way through the crowds, not caring who he shoves or what toes he stands on.

A few moments ago, he harshly nudged a girl pushing a pram aside. So hard she stumbled and drove it off the pavement and into the busy road. Luckily a person, walking past, grabbed the pair of them and pulled them back, out of the path of a double-decker bus, before it was too late. That *cretin*, Michael, just forged on without even turning around.

I really need to pull myself together. Make a decision of what next. Dylan will be on his way to Serena and Dexter's with her in the meantime. The baby will be fine. Baby?! *What baby?* That thought just fluttered into my head. A little pale dragonfly; all trembling wings and bobbing tail. Well, Serena's pregnant! How wonderful!

Pale pink, blue and lilac rays of happiness surge through me and momentarily I lift up, above the crowds, feeling a warmth unlike anything I've ever felt before. Now that's better; the *right* kind of energy!

Yes, I feel stronger now; purposeful. Below me, the swathes of people are parting slightly as the dark grey head of my Husband signals him storming through them, like a bullet through flesh.

Glaring at him, and drifting low again, my darker colours bloom and glisten; ink on wet paper; blood on damp stone. He's going to get what's coming to him. I've arranged him a first class ticket, straight.....to Hell.

Serena

My leg hurts, although my arm is worse. That hurts a lot. The red-hot barbed wire wrapped around it is getting tighter by the minute. I can't see anything, so stretching out what I think are my fingers, I force open one eye to see blurry green hair. No, not hair... grass. Opening a second eye, I see that my hand has got something smudged on it and my nails are finished in black.

Have I fallen over drunk in the garden again? Above a screeching sound, there's someone yelling my name. It's not Dylan. Perhaps a neighbour. Then that agonising poker in my shoulder again, makes me scream, pure and clear, like a person being slowly stabbed. Fuck! It's me making the screeching noise, not someone else.

My tummy has started to throb and it feels strangely tight and full. It's those breakfast *eggs*! Reaching down I cross my hands to steeple my fingers churchlike and hold my belly, as though there really is something in there to protect. It's oddly comforting, this position of pretence.

"Serena! I can see you moving but don't! You've not fallen far! I'm gonna scale down to be with you. Don't move anymore! Stay still!" Dexter, yes that's his name, sounds cross. I better do as he tells me. First time for everything I suppose.

It's damp and I can smell sheep shit. Tangy and earthy, the air is telling me, I haven't fallen too far from the cliff, Yeah, I fell straight down, like a weighted corpse in a Sopranos' movie!

That clever little thought reminds me of Dylan. He used to love sharing those little mountainy tips with me. "If there are signs of animals, for example sheep, then it is possible for a human to get there, even on foot".

As he proudly announced these facts, I'd smile weakly, look away, spin the lid on the wine and pour another glass without replying. His chatter would tail off and by the time we were half way through our meal, no one spoke at all.

My gut clenches, so I curl up in pain of all types. Whimpering my Husbands name, I want him here, desperately.

"I've called Mountain rescue! I've said to ask for some guy called Dylan. I don't know your second name! Embarrassed much?! Yes! Hah!" Dexter's voice is nearer and clearer now. Eyes closed and still in desperate pain, I can't help but smile.

Michael

I'm going to get the Hell out of here; I never liked this town anyway. It was Alice's home not mine. She just assumed that with my football friends, regular spending, breaks away and an attractive decent sized home, all was well. Well clearly it wasn't! Otherwise I wouldn't have bloody killed her! Not once did she ask if I was happy! Not *once*.

Even so, this was never the plan; not *at all*. It's all got a bit, how you say...*intense*?

Sweat is trickling down my back into my trousers, even though its cold today. My breath is coming in fast little pops of rage, as I'm forced to storm home, stressed, yet again! All because of that meddlesome Solicitor. I can't bear being surprised. I loathe any shocks to my system. Any last-minute changes to plans. Yes, I'm way past *manners!*

"Move it!", I grunt at a couple holding hands and taking their time to cross the road. The young man looks at me and frowns. The girl pulls him away from me, as though she almost expects a fight. I must look particularly furious. Good!

Get a Defence Lawyer?! Get a *Defence Lawyer!?* Hah! Not on your life Mister!! Look, *calm down* Michael, killing him won't help. Don't give yourself ideas.

The streets are less busy as I round the corner, up and away from the more popular shops. I feel I can breathe again with less people around. Even so, my heart's palpating at a rate of knots and I keep getting white flashes and spots before my eyes.

The irony of me dying of a heart attack, on the eve of my escape, forces me to consider stopping and resting for a few minutes, even though I'm desperate to get home.

Armed with a plan to take some time to rest against the nice cool mossy wall outside the corner shop nearest the house, I'm annoyed on approach to see the owner's inconveniently right there sitting outside.

Perched like a hungry Puffin, on his stupid tatty little stool, he's watching my approach intently. "Is *nothing* bloody going my way today?!" I huff, under my breath. Who, over the age of 21 wears a tracksuit with red, yellow and white stripes down the arms? Honestly!

Rude chap! He's openly staring at me, sucking on his pipe! Not a blink nor a wink! Maybe I should kick the seat right out from under him...enjoy his yelp of pain as his black track-suited ample arse bounces, on the chewing gum freckled pavement, right at the entrance to his common little shop! As I reach him, he starts to open his mouth to speak. "Fuck off!" I spit.

A rapid blush of shock, colours his expression and I feel a little better. Leaning heavily against the wall, I start to mop my brow with a handkerchief. Satisfyingly, the shop keeper stands up and drags his stool inside. Smiling at his incoherent muttering and lack of guts to say anything directly to me, I fold the hanker-chief up and neatly place it in my blazer pocket again.

Now, one must make a plan! A *new* plan. With The Police soon more heavily involved and Kendal clearly onto me, I'm well aware selling the house will take weeks, maybe months. It's not the end of the world. I've some cash aside and can easily travel heavy with a few bags of her valuables! It's better than the next 25 years in prison sharing a cell, with someone called Bruno who likes it rough with well-spoken silver-foxes like me! Oh yes! For sure, I've no choice other than to cut my losses and run, *tonight*.

The word "cut" wakes a pulse in my buttocks. Dammit, I can't see any of my girls before I leave and that saddens me, hugely.

Oh well, I can get new girls wherever I decide to settle next. Just like last time, I'll fade away into a new town or city, find a new fuel source and *nestle in*. Safe and well and ready for new adventures. It'll be easy enough to let some new wealthy female look after me while I indulge myself in my hobbies! This time will probably be my last, or maybe second last? There's a few more years in this old dog yet....

Chuckling, and confident in what to do next, I feel good. There's plenty of time, maybe 8 to 12 hours at most, to get packed up and be gone. Slip into the misty rise of tomorrow's morn.

I imagine myself as a little dandelion seed caught on the air, ready to embed itself in someone else's life like a weed. It's amazing how destructive they are; they seem fun and even harmless at first. You grasp at the round, fluffy cotton-headed stem and *blow*. Then watch dozens of the same little fairy-like seeds scatter on the breeze. Children chase them to make a selfish wish. Couples giggle and try to grasp them for the same reason. Up, up and away we go! I'm enjoying this fantasy and close my eyes.

There's something about being so apparently harmless; a tiny feather-like pod of harm, floating far then catching on the lapel of a coat or an insects wings. One seed spreading, then going on to entirely ruin an impeccable lawn. Settled and destructive. Stubborn and difficult to get rid of. That's me; The Dandelion.

Right. A breath in then out and off we go again! Pushing myself off the wall and surging forwards, a thought strikes me. I reckon just like with Wife number one; the pigs will arrive; snuffling and shuffling their grubby hooves at my front door, of course in early morning. Interrupting my breakfast and leaving mud streaks on my carpet as they demand the pleasure of my company at the local station again. Acid scratches my throat; dammed indigestion.

In all the drama and stress, I've neglected myself. Typical! Food first then a plan, yes.... a nice simple escape plan and definitely some swift packing.

"Bastard", the whisper slices my ear like a surgeon's knife. Whipping my right hand up to rub the skin at my neck and bringing it back down, I half expect to see blood on my fingers. Nope; nothing.

Turning sharply and catching my elbow on the wall, I curse again. Likely to be that creepy idiot of a stool-dwelling shop keeper getting his own back. Yes, it'll be him, shouting like a coward behind his door most likely. Irrelevant now. I need to hurry up and get home. Hanging about here like a fool, isn't packing the parachute!

Dylan

I've never felt fear like this and that *stupid* 80's song *"Time After Time"*, is playing; Serena's favourite dancing song. "Tom, can you turn that thing off?!". My friend turns the car-radio off. But still, I don't relax. I don't think I ever will, again.

With my face pressed up against the cold, passenger seat window, I whisper a prayer. Am I going to collect her body? Did she go there to kill herself, because of what I've done? My throat closes up as I imagine myself at my Wife's funeral. I'll hurl myself into the grave after her, if it comes to it. "Drive faster Tom. Please. We need to be faster".

My words tail off and catch on the jagged edges of my shame; the shame of leaving my Wife when she told me to. It's almost an hour till we reach the car-park closest to The Notch. Each minute the longest of long sighing breaths. Breaths I wish I was hearing, with Sir in bed next to me.

So many nights I lay there angry at her deep, snuffling alcohol-rich slumber. What a bastard I was! At least she was sleeping! Why wasn't I thankful?!

Right now, I'd give anything for her to be shouting at me alive and well and pissed as a fart. "Apparently the bloke on the phone, who called it in, said something about some other walker that died. Some Anna or Alice or something". Tom's focused on the road and waffling on. I wish he'd drive faster and talk less.

"Dylan, are you listening to me? That's what they went up for". A spear of jealousy jabs my throat. "They?!"

"Let's just get there Dyl, ok? Deal with any other stuff later". Blessedly, Tom puts his foot down and we speed faster into the clotted cream mist. "The boss sayss the chopper will be at the helipad by the car-park, and all we need to do, is be there on time".

Again, a vision of Serena in our warmer, rosy days. Chicago was playing. It's another old favourite of ours.

The cheesy chequer-board dance floor is grubby, but bright pretty lights are circling my Wife. She is mesmerising and it's like she has a sequinned dress on, but she doesn't. Just jeans and a skimpy black top. Twirling and spinning herself round and round, she always was the last off the dance floor.

Yes, in the beginning, Serena was alight; a disco-ball herself. The music stops and changes to a different number. Something with a fast, hillbilly type beat. My Wife stops and looks at me with her familiar, drunken, half smile. I watch, as she tosses her hair, lifts an invisible dress hem, exaggeratedly bows at me, winks, then starts to Irish dance- fast and skilfully.

I loved her in that moment more than I ever have. That feels like a life-time ago now. A lifetime wasted.

The engine revs up as we hit the foot of Tryfan mountain range. I stifle a sob as cold rain starts to hit the windscreen, *hard*.

* * * * *

It's raining. Great buckets of cats and dogs. Pelting it down, hour after hour. Not fazed by it one bit, Serena has laughed and smiled all day. Her sister keeps wiping her face for her; the expensive wedding make-up hasn't lasted in the almost tropical barrage of elements.

The sun came out at one point sending beams of multi-coloured light across the pews. The stained-glass washed clean by the weather, now gleaming in its full glory.

As this happened and all our guests cheered, Serena shook her head and whispered in my ear, "it's going to rain again, for the rest of the day, just you wait". And reared back to cackle uproariously.

The old church roof isn't quite equipped to stop the rain getting in and a few of the guests, with fancy hat's on, keep wincing as drops hit the big feathers and flowers on them, making loud tapping sounds that ensure fresh giggles from the little brides-maids close by.

"Photographs!", Someone shouts as we lean in together to seal the deal as Husband and Wife. I think we are all eager to hurry things along now; go and get warm and dry. But at least I got my kiss.

We're outside now. It's raining again. Someone smart and organised has started getting umbrellas out.

Waiting for the photographer to leave the bar, in the hall next door, we are all crowded together in the doorway of the church and laughing hysterically, as we try to take cover under random umbrellas, stolen from a big basket in the doorway. Pop, pop, pop each brolly unfurls. Flowers fast-forwarded, paisley patterns, spots and stripes.

Serena has this little children's frog one. The frogs' big googly eyes are on the top of the brolly, staring out as if this is all in a days work. Ceris is bent over laughing, but Serena is pretending not to notice, to make her laugh even harder.

My new Wife's hair is wet against her face and a little mascara has smudged near her left eye. I kiss her and wipe it with a licked thumb, just as the photographer stumbles out to meet us, lifts his camera and yells; "Now *cheese* everyone! *Wet cheese!*".

* * * * *

Waking up with a start to thunder and lightning, I realise we're at the helipad. The beautiful giant insect is there, right there waiting for us, just like it always is. After today, I'm never ever going anywhere near it again. Near to this, means far from her. If she lives, I'm resigning from both jobs; she will have my full attention. For once.

Michael

Rattling open drawers and slamming closed wardrobes, I'm hurling pile after pile of clothes onto our bedroom floor.

Roughly wiping sweat away with the sleeve of a pale pink sweater Alice bought herself, I almost spit on it in distaste at the memory.

*****

"Do you like it?" her whining, mousy voice pressed up against my ear. Resisting the urge to grab her cheek and push her bodily away into the mannequin next to us, I close my eyes and count to three.

"Nah. It'll wash you out. Your hair's too fine and your skin's too pale". I've never been so harsh, but it's time I was. Its past 2 pm and the lunch she suggested, was a little too heavy. Because of her, I feel grumpy and tired.

Alice's neck blooms with shame yet she glances at the shop assistant hovering nearby.

I watch as the nosey bitch tenses at my comment, and narrows her eyes at my new fiancée. What's that? A shy smile of empathy?! Not on my watch!

"Go find the same in navy blue, you. Yes, you!" My bark makes the shop assistant jump. I watch her scurry away, clutching the offending pink sweater like a rejected child.

"Michael. Don't be so…. harsh". Alice searches for the right word to partially scold me and partially keep the afternoon atmosphere light. "She's just doing her job. I actually quite like that colour".

Her small hand grasps my wrist but I tug it away, like she burns me.

The ring on her finger is small and modest but it'll do. The wedding can't come soon enough. Stage two, my new life as a wealthy Husband can start then. It's all that keeps me going, in the stifling pressure of yet again being trapped with someone, just not right for what I want….*and need.*

Alice's slipped away and is bending over a rail of coats. Her profile in false concentration, as she fingers a large tulip shaped button at the collar of one. She's desperate for me to join her and help choose; take control, make the decision and flatter her with my opinion. Instead a woman a few feet away catches my eye.

Thick shining, fake dyed, black dark hair far down her back towards generous hips. Her ears are dripping dangly gold earrings the shape of whips... My buttocks twitch in need.

"I'm off to the loo darling. You choose just what you want. Swiping a kiss on her upturned face, I'm already fixated on the woman's swaying backside, disappearing too fast towards the escalators. If I can just watch her step onto the first set of metal teeth upwards, the day will become infinitesimally better. Alice can have whatever blasted pink jumper she wants.

* * * * *

A waft of my dead Wife's perfume drags me from that sharp point in the past. Startled, I drop the sweater at my feet. I didn't even know I'd stood up. *It feels like she's in the room.*

A faint squeaking to my left has me turning slowly, towards the mirror Alice used for the measly amount of make-up she *did* wear. The glass has a light covering of dust.

In dreadful slow motion, a small, perfect tulip shape forms itself. Each petal a curve in the ash-like skin of dust, the same width of a finger.

The room blurs and a strange whiteness pulses behind my eyes. I slump to the floor clutching my throat, desperate to catch a breath. She's here! I knew it. Now, she's strangling me. She wants me to die. I need to leave- *now.*

Scrambling across the floor through the discarded clothing my Wife loved and I hated, I'm whimpering and snorting trying to breathe evenly.

Perspiration stinging my eyes and grabbing a small carved box, I know has some of her mother's jewellery in, I reach the door and scoot out on my backside, staring back at the mirror, that now, has nothing but pristine, dust-free glass. Indeed, there's not a mark on it.

Alice

When you're in love, no one tells you the truth. It's an unwritten rule that close friends become fence sitters and family members become enablers. These people you love and trust, watch from the side-lines as you slowly lose the game and they wait for the inevitable own goal that is, *absolute trust* in a total dick-head.

Watching my Husband from another plane might be weird, creepy and unsettling but it is also really rather useful. Everyone should have a chance to go all ghostly Big Brother on the person they chose to share their life or.... hah! Share their *death* with.

Yeah, I know it was a bit naughty, the mirror thing, but you know he deserves it. In fact, he deserves worse. Much worse. For every little bruising dig, scratchy criticism or thump to my confidence. For every sickening lie, every pound he took....

He doesn't deserve to get away with this. This is my redemption. This is his comeuppance.

Following my scavenging, sweating scumbag of a Husband out onto the dimly lit landing, I don't even flinch as flicking a wrist behind myself, the newly clean, dressing table mirror, falls to the floor and shatters. Tiny specks of glass glisten on the carpet; scattered like dew drops in amongst the mess he left. He won't have time for his 7 years of bad-luck; I have my own idea crystallising.

Chapter 9: Waking Up

Serena

"Let me tug your hair out from under your neck Serena". His voice is familiar but I can't place it.

The smell of stale coffee and the salty, thick smell of panic touches my nose. I want to tell this person it's all fine but I can't move my lips. Someone's turning the lights on and off; it's really annoying. No, they aren't. It's actually my eyes stuck on a strange flickering as if my controlled by someone overly nervous with a dimmer switch.

Sparks of heat are nipping at my midriff. I remember being at home. Kneeling in front of the fire. Crying. Angry. Broken and wanting to break something else. I don't remember why now. I don't think it really matters now, does it?

"Don't try and open your eyes. Just try and relax". He's still talking. The man. His name's Dexter. Yes, I do know him! Flashes of army camo material, the smell of frying eggs and the tap dance sound of rain on plastic. Our laughter and my tears.

He's still blabbering on; "I called the mountain rescue. Dylan's coming. It's going to be ok".

More pictures; my Husband's hands holding mine. A gentle kiss on the lips. Umbrella's. Mickey Mouse. A yellow rain-coat. Blood. My screams of rage and his back hunched as he leaves the house, walking fast into the black, rainy night. The images don't make sense. None of this make sense.

"They won't be long. Twenty minutes tops". Dexter's voice slides away and I can hear bird-song. No, it's the music from a child's toy.

A mobile hanging over a cot. Little sheep, ducks and flowers dancing up and down, round and round above us. Pale blue, yellow and green. Strong, light haired downy arms wrapped around my waist and a small round pink face looking up at me from its bed.

A soft, happy feeling cocoons me. Dylan's here and so is a baby. A blurry golden light where the window should be, starts to widen and open up, like sunrise coloured ripples in a puddle. I wonder if I can pick the baby up and take her with me. The arms are gone from my waist now and it's gone cold in the room. The light hasn't gone though and I wonder what will happen if I move towards it. The baby might be inside, waiting for me. *Needing me.*

"Serena! Serena! Stay awake for me. You need to stay awake!" that annoying idiot Dexter just ruined everything; I was happy then. I want to tell him off but instead a long moan escapes. It's bloody freezing and someone's put the washing machine on spin.

"That's them here! God, longest wait for anything in my life!"

Dexter's fingers are cold and I want to tell him to let go of my hand so I can roll over and wrap the duvet over me. Trying to squirm away is agony as knives dipped in red hot lava streak the skin on my arms and legs. The sharpness and persistence in the pains in my tummy, remind me of The Losses.

The nausea at the car-park. Dexter opening The Map. The dizzy spells. The fall. The stirring in my breasts and groin. I'm pregnant and this one's leaving me just like the others did.

"I can see the helicopter, Serena. They're here. Wait a bit longer. Just wait. Don't go to sleep". He's so bossy but I think he knows what I know now. "I've told them you fainted and fell. That you've been dizzy and sick. I wonder if maybe you're up the duff".

I want to laugh but I can't. Then I want to cry and realise, I can. The warm rain of tears moistens my face and somewhere, in the distance, an animal is howling.

Dylan

Have you ever been so afraid that your brain simply doesn't work? Like all these thoughts, are a huge crowd of people all pushing each other and shouting and getting nowhere. A stampede, but you are rooted to the spot right in the middle. Frozen and silent, with your eyes closed? It's Hellish, absolutely Hellish.

Straining to look out of the helicopter window, desperate to see anyone or anything that might mean we're nearly there, all I want to do is yell with frustration.

It's only the afternoon but dank and grey, like someone forgot to turn all the lights on. A familiar, fine mist blurs the skyline but some pretty pink and pale blue is on the way. Better weather is creeping over the horizon, but what if it's too late?!

A pressure on my knee signals Tom, silently offering what manly comfort he can. I can't even bear to look at him. He knows what I've done. He knows this is all my fault.

The last time he saw Serena and I as a couple, was months ago, at the village Valentine party. Forced to go, as it raises money for the rescue fund, my Wife came with me.

* * * * *

Serena's ridiculously drunk. Beside the fire, next to the DJ booth, I watch her talking to one person after another. She's talking manically, high on anxiety, her medication and alcohol.

Waving her arms around, and talking too loudly, she occasionally catches her one remaining earring in the sleeve of her velvet dress. A dress that used to fit her beautifully, but tonight just hangs there. It's now, just a deep wine-red curtain, across a stage long empty. I can see how slender she's become, as even her wrists look child-like and brittle, mirroring her personality of the last few months. She's given up.

Every now and then she stumbles, offers a smudged smile to whoever saw her, and rights herself against the grey stone of the fireplace. Each time she does this, I flinch, but don't go to help her. My discomfort openly on display, means our friends are watching her, but Tom's watching me. He's furious. I recognise the flush of his cheeks and his repetitive habit of rubbing the bridge of his nose. I've known him forever but even this time, I have no interest in doing the right thing and appeasing him. I'm too tired and rather drunk myself.

"Mate, you need to get this sorted. She's a bloody mess and she belongs to you". He's right but no one here's been right for a long time, especially not me.

Making a "cheers" gesture to him I tip the last of my pint back in one. Setting the greasy glass back down hard, I watch as my best-friend stands up, and goes to my Wife. Gently, grasping both her hands to guide her back to the table where his own Wife is seated nursing their second child; a massively well-fed boy, called Beau.

Resentment spikes at their fortune, and tears fill up behind my eyes, so I look away, searching for another drink on the table I've barely left all night. The same table my Wife has barely sat at.

Then Serena and I are stumbling out to the car-park. Someone called us a taxi, someone else said. Trying to hold both my Wife, her coat, her bag *and* shoe's, isn't easy but I'm past caring. I just want to go home. It's my day to visit my son tomorrow. Serena thinks I've been called back to work on an emergency, this time. Owen's beautiful brightness gets me through times like this. My lighthouse in a storm.

"I hate you", she's saying over and over again. "I really, really hate you". I just want her to stop talking so I kiss her.

A few minutes later we are behind the pub, up against the wall, fucking like we want to hurt each other. Fast breaths of rage. Thrusts of anger. Hands scratching and pulling. Smart, expensive clothes tearing. It's a fight but it's not.

* * * * *

A thud and tilt of the chopper, brings me back; we've landed. "She's down there to the right. About 20 yards down and slightly away from the rock-face. She fell straight off the top. Sounds like a faint or something. Flat landing almost directly below the edge". Tom's shrugging his jacket on and looking at me; willing me to speak, but I can't.

The Paramedic is shouting efficiently over the slicing, thunderous whir of rotors. "Base just told me that she's been drifting in and out since she fell. The guy with her has done a good job keeping her conscious. He's called 999 to chase us, four times. Bloke must be frantic!"

Guy with her? what *guy*?! What? Why's some guy bothered?! I'm too late. *She's met someone else.* That's it. It all makes sense now. How long? Oh my god how *long*! She's up here having some sort of broke-back mountain camp out with a guy. A guy who isn't me and never will be me again.

My mouth goes dry and I feel the blood run from my face in panic. "He's not gonna be with her *that* way Dyl." Tom's nudged me. I'm aghast to see he's half smiling. "Shut the fuck up. Let's just do our job and get the fuck home". My best friend, rears back at my nastiness, sighs and closes his eyes in impatience. I don't bother to apologise.

Fuelled by self-hatred, I yank the helicopter door open to jump out into a wind-tunnel of freezing, shocking weather.

Slithering ropes between my legs, up and around my shoulders, tightening knots and strapping myself into my kit, each manoeuvre just makes me angrier and angrier. Not at *him*, whoever he is down there. Not at her either. Only at myself.

The others are all busying themselves with their own tasks and are as efficient as ever. Another group of our rescuers climbed up on foot, and were there to meet us as we landed with the paramedics. They have readied the stretcher and are moving towards the edge. It takes eight of us to carry it. Leaving a scene with an injured person or......fatality, is always the most physically demanding part.

Turning away from my team-mates, I cover my mouth with my hands and close my eyes in abject terror. I imagine Serenas's body on the stretcher and swallow stomach acid.

Spinning back round and walking towards the edge again, I start shouting in sheer panic. I don't know what else to do. "We need to hurry the *Hell up*!" Each rescuer turns to look at me sharply and Tom shakes his head in exasperation. I hear him stage-whisper "Dyl thinks Serena's down there with a new bloke. He'll calm down soon enough".

The urge to punch him is stifling. Closing my eyes to shut out the anger, I see Serena passionately kissing another man. Holding hands with him while they hiked up here. Writhing naked and sweaty, in a sleeping bag with him.

"Argh!" the growl escapes and giving in to my rage, I start to walk towards Tom with both fists raised. Robotic and seeing red, I'm all done with this crap-storm now.

A crackling, metallic shout stops me mid-stride, fists raised and Tom's face inches from mine. To his credit, he hasn't flinched. He knows Serena almost as well as me and a black-eye won't change it. The Pilot is talking on the radio then I see him stiffen. Adrenalin spurts through my limbs so fast it hurts.

"It's just come through. Some news everyone. It's something important. The guy down there thinks she, er, your Serena might be up the duff".

My Wife's hair in my fist, as I turn her roughly to face me. I let the tendrils go and fall to my knees to tug her knickers down, pushing them to the gravel with my left foot. My recently shined dress shoe catching the light of the neon bar sign and Serena's voice. "Do it. Just do it. Get it over with. I still hate you", and her pulling me up to kiss her again.

We've not had sex since that time. It was months ago and the first time in almost a year. Looking down at my hands I start counting the weeks on my fingers and once I run out of digits, start to get excited.

"Twelve, thirteen, maybe even fourteen weeks", I mutter, then realisation makes me yell again; "We need to get down there! He's bloody right! Move, move.... *move*!" My colleagues were statues a second ago; the low set sun behind them, casting them to stone. Then, play button pressed, they launch into action.

Our group moves together towards the edge. The sun comes out from behind a cloud and the earth below us lights up. "Let's do this", Tom says and we begin the descent into the gulley.

Michael

"Yes. That's correct. A taxi for the early hours. 5am please. I've a seat booked on the 5.30am train, to the airport. Quick break away in Sardinia. I'm treating myself". Using my special, calm voice, I lie easily. In actual fact, I'm going to get off the train a few stops early, then jump on another and head to Portsmouth.

I fancy the South of France or perhaps even Portugal. It doesn't do any harm to throw a cheeky red herring in at this stage. I'm being extra careful, just in case the police do track down my cab, once they've checked the house-phone records.

"Oh! And I assure a nice fat tip for the driver, if you can make sure they're slightly early or on time. They cannot be late. Bye for now!" Before the cab office operator has the chance to do it herself, I cut her off. It makes me chuckle doing that. Such small pleasures!

The faster I'm out of here the better. Darn house is starting to spook me. I'm not even a believer in such things. Got my knickers in a knot upstairs over that mirror palaver, but on reflection, hah! I'm sure it was just a trick of the light. It's that time of day now, and that room always was *dusty*.

If I had a conscience, I'd think that guilt was sending me crazy. It's more likely to be a combination of worry about my getaway and the heart pills the GP put me on the other day.

However, it's doing me no favours being creeped out and I'm eager to get finished packing. Might book myself a hotel for tonight, maybe even try and get to see one of my girls. Now there's a plan I can look *forward* to!

Rushing around the house and getting more and more excited, I'm headed for the under-stair cupboard.

Whistling lightly, I dig about roughly in my Burberry Coat pocket for the keys to the pad-lock, that's kept my snooping Wife out of my private business for the last few years. Far, far too nosey for her own good that one. I like to keep my special bag there, some cash, my passport and a few other items of need

"Ahah! There you are! With a flourish, I toss the keys in the air from one hand to the other and celebrate by kissing them. "Well on our way now! Nearly done!" my voice echo's a little in the gloomy hall.

But my glee is short lived. Both hands are sweaty, so the key and lock aren't meeting as they should.

I shouldn't even need a bloody lock in my own home! "Fuckety fuck fucking fuck", I hiss. The effort has started to make my hands tremble somewhat; low blood-sugar I reckon. "Must eat something" I mutter, and a breeze tickles my neck. I think I can smell burnt toast and turn around automatically, to lean back and look into the kitchen.

Of course, it's empty but a flicker of something passing the oven catches my eye. "Cat from next-door's got in. I'll bloody lock it in the house and it can die slowly. "Little rat-cat!" I say loudly, almost as though reassuring myself I'm completely alone.

"Focus Mikey. Focus!" Trying the key again and managing this time to slide it into the lock, I realise the idea of a hotel for tonight, is actually growing on me rather fast.

Kneeling down to be level with the cupboard door and bracing myself to lean inside, I wince at the discomfort of my belt digging into my belly.

An image of my expensive little Nicola, crying with a hand-mark across her face, as I undo my belt behind her, takes me by surprise. So, decision made about plans for tonight, I turn the key aggressively. "Hey presto!"

Pushing the stubborn, warped old door open, I'm met with a draft of stale air. The cupboard runs long and narrow beneath the stairs, but I've made sure my things are closer to the entrance, so I need not delve too deep.

Never a fan of the dark, especially cobwebs, I'm thankful to the pad-lock again. No need to be too clever with the hiding place, if she couldn't get in here anyway.

"Why do you need to lock it Darling", I whine, mimicking Alice. "No need for secrets between us Darling", I continue, rather pleased with my impression skills. Giggling, I lean into the dark.

A scratching sound deep inside makes my neck tingle. "What the...?" There it goes again. And, that musty breeze *again*! It's an internal cupboard! The nearest window is two walls away, in the kitchen, and the front door is one wall away to my left, a good 10 yards distance. "Dirty old man...." the voice hisses.

An icy, stinking, whisper of air lifts the collar of my shirt to touch my jaw fleetingly, like a finger. Yelping I almost fall forward, into the cupboard with fright.

Holding onto the door frame, I pull back, hitting my head on the bare hanging light bulb, which swings dramatically left then right. As I reach up to stop it, the bulb swiftly goes out with a ping and pop and the slight electric shock takes me by surprise. "Effing house!"

Determined to get my bag, I drop to my knees and trying not to look into the darkness, I reach out both hands.

Eyes closed, I stretch my fingers to search for the familiar rough Velcro handles. "Dirty old man", the hiss says again then something touches my hand. Crying out and rearing back I fall to a sitting position but move back, fast, to sit with my back against the telephone table.

The familiar black and blue handle of my bag, is now poking tantalisingly out of the cupboard as if mocking me.

Swallowing fear but tasting anger, I start to lean forward desperate to reach the only thing I really need. The door slams hard, whipping towards my face, lifting my hair and almost flattening my nose like a pancake.

I can't leave the bag behind; it has some things I've collected over the years. Important things. Personal things... *incriminating* things.

"Alice? Is that you?" my voice wobbles but I'm pleased I sound more angry than afraid. "Leave me alone!" the door rattles as though she were inside the cupboard locking it. But there is no lock on the inside. "Alice! I mean it!" now I do sound freaked.

Sitting back and lifting my legs, I kick out kangaroo style with extreme force. Desperate to loosen the door or maybe even shatter the wood and break it. The door is shut tight but I try again and then again.

I'm not sure if it's the bulb shattering inside the cupboard or the echoing, spikes of laughter within, but I don't care about how I look or sound now, maybe for the first time in my whole life.

I emit a scream full of rage and frustration into the empty, yet hateful house.

Serena

It's raining gently. No, it's not rain, my eye-lids have a bright orange glow of sunset against them and the wetness on my face is warm and salty. The pain in my tummy has stopped and even Dexter's shut up.

The ground is grumbling, rumbling and moving. There's some sort of stampede of animals circling now. Maybe more deer, or stags. Whispering, crackling and beeps all around me. It's all so confusing. The only thing that I know, is I can smell lemon and bergamot- Dylan's shower smell.

"Sir. Sir", he's whispering in my ear. "Sir. It's ok. It's going to be ok". As usual he's wrong. He always said that before and the babies still slid away. They never listened to him either. Must be a family trait.

Reaching to the waist band of my jeans feels like the biggest effort of my life. I know I'm muddy and grassy and my arm is killing me. When did I open my eyes? Looking down, I can see my fingers shaking then Dylan's enveloping them. His are warm, dry and clean- they always are.

"Hang tough Serena. We're going to get you checked out. Your, erm…. *Friend,* Dexter…. told us that you might be…… pregnant again". Dylan sounds sharper than before; more fragile, like glass. It's different. He's afraid. I don't like it. This is his land; his place of strength and smarts and power.

Why's he afraid? I need him to be as solid as the bloody cliff I just toppled off. "mmmmmfffff", I have a go at speaking, to tell him off, but fail. "bbbbmmmmmmmff". I want to tell him about the light-baby and the mobile, and the birds I heard. It's too late now anyway. I know when the pain stops, the baby's gone. The hurt is just my body telling me to say goodbye; the language of loss.

Alice

It doesn't matter that I'm starting to show myself and give the game away to Murderous Michael (I know not very original, but I'm a bit busy to think up a better name just now) I've decided what to do to him. He's trying to get away with what he did to me, his first Wife and that poor hooker woman and perhaps many others.

Ever slow on the catch-up, I realise now, that my Husbands first Wife died by his hands. Sadly, I was too late to save myself but it's not too late to avenge us both.

When I slammed that door, I desperately wanted to break his nose, at least for a start off. He was always so vain and often referred to his "intelligent nose". I can imagine his face squashed in, badly. A burst of fresh red blood, then his cheeks turning pink, then blue. Big black eyes, like the bruises he enjoys inflicting wherever he can.

My Husband is skittering room to room, hunched and podgy. He reminds me of a James Bond villain.

His arms are laden with small, expensive trinkets. A little silver tea-pot we got in Morocco. Some of my jewellery. A few of my first edition books. He's hung my mother's heavy, gold necklace around his neck for convenience and is reaching for an antique pen and ink-well on my desk.

Argh! I want to run at him and smash the items out of his hands! Without the cash in the bag, he's gathering what he can, before being eaten up into the night and disappearing forever. He's been clever thus far, if he's quick he will indeed get *away!* Oh! *Think, think, think Alice!*

A few of my little occasional lamps highlight the corners of furniture. The yellow beams tail the shadow of him, as he busies himself here and there, left to right, and up and down the stairs.

He's muttering, swearing and shaking like a leaf; occasionally shooting looks sharply down the hall to where I stand in the corner by the coats. He knows I'm here so I need to move fast, faster than him this time. *I want him dead.*

Dylan

Wiping stubborn, sticky, damp hair from my Wife's face is harder than I expected. The dull red strands cling to her skin, like I want to hold her to myself; stubborn and desperate.

She's coloured grey but mottled with pink. Oddly her complexion mirrors the sky above us and it unnerves me. I've seen her ill, oh so very ill before but never, ever has she been the colour of putty. Never.

Resisting the urge to yell in her face, just to startle her and get some sort of reaction, I close my eyes and start to pray. I pray to her, not God or whoever it is up there in charge of the mess we call life, but to my Wife. She is my goddess.

"Please, Sir, *Pleasepleaseplease,* don't leave me. I'm sorry. *Properly sorry.* Not *take me back sorry.* Sorry, *never take me back and punish me forever* sorry. I'm so sorry that I don't want another chance. I want *you* to have another chance. Find a nice guy. A *good* guy. Someone better than me. Take this baby and be happy". Her eyes flicker then roll up and away under her eye-lids.

Serena's throat twitches and my heart seizes painfully, as she makes a strange gargling noise. "Sir, sir, please wake up!" she makes the strange gargling sound again but longer this time and I want to scream. I think she's dying. I've heard that gargle a few times up on these mountains. It's so familiar to me, the sound of something taking its last breath and giving itself up to the elements.

I'm fighting for my own life here; she *is* my life. Every single part of me is taut with fear and I know for a fact, if she doesn't survive this, I'm coming up here tomorrow and throwing myself off the edge. I know it like I know the freckles on her face.

Leaning forward I rest my forehead on hers and start to sob and mumble incoherently to anyone nearby. They don't know I'm muttering baby-names and hoping it triggers her heart to beat stronger. "Leon. Poppy. Ruby. David. Nathaniel. Yes! that's a nice one. Coby. Milly. Alice......" I list name after name even though she's colder now. She's gone.

There's only silence as chaos descends and all around are legs, boots, hands and blurred faces. Their mouths are moving but I've gone deaf in fear. My ears are ringing and I can't move my tongue to speak. I fall backwards as someone roughly pulls me away from my dead Wife.

Closing my eyes and starting to wail in grief, I see her casket being lowered into the ground on the sunniest of sunny days. I see lilies being dropped on the lid and hear the murmuring of our minister reading a section from the bible.

Someone hits me in the face. Once, then twice. The noise floods in; an explosion of yells and shouts and instruction.

In my shock, all I can focus on is a small blade of grass trembling on Serena's forehead with the force of all the movement on and around her. Someone leaning over her shouts "Can you hear me Serena?", then blows into her mouth.

I'm rooted to the spot and time slows as the blade lifts and twisting slightly, tilts, waits, then spins off her jaw and disappears on the wind.

She's gone; my Wife is dead. I retch stomach bile and spit into the grass next to me, and everything goes black.

Dexter

I don't advocate hitting anyone, especially a bereft Husband in the worst few moments of his life. The silly idiot was so messed up I had to move him so the paramedics could do their job. Half mad with grief and fully mad with the guilt of what he has done to my new friend, he was in no fit state to see how the team just needed to get to her properly.

When he leant over her and started to cry, I admit that got to me. Didn't do him any harm to get the fright of his life though did it?

"Dylan. Dylan. Let's have you. Wake up mate. Serena is going to be ok. "You need to pull yourself together mate". He smells of sheep poop and fresh sweat. "It's a wonder she didn't come around *without* the CPR. You're like human smelling salts".

Serena's Husband is a changed man from only a few minutes ago. He arrived tense with urgency, prickling with anger and smelling freshly washed. I watch as he wipes drool from the side of his mouth and looks towards where the stretcher is now being carefully taken up towards the helicopter.

"I don't understand what happened. What's happening. She's gone. It's all my fault". Dylan covers his face with his hands and starts to weep again.

"No mate. She was out…for a little bit but they got here in time. She was breathing when they strapped her in. Touch and go *yes*, but it's looking ok for her actually".

"Dylan looks at me again; his face is inflamed with hatred, as though I'm lying. Then as the news seeps in, his eyes close and he wobbles as though getting ready to pass out". "Thank you God", he whispers and looks up at the sky. "Thank you". His face goes even more pale with relief and I feel a little sorry for him but give myself a shake. I've something to say to him that he needs to hear, bad timing or not.

"Serena told me enough for me to have a bit of a word with you though. I'm not even going to ask if it's ok". Hoisting the reason for Serena's broken heart up, by his collar and dragging him to a cluster of large boulders, I sit down first and gesture for him to join me. He's a hailstorm-sky colour and trembling more than a little.

"I prayed. I prayed", he's saying over and over with his head in his hands. "I prayed to her. I prayed to Serena. I prayed and prayed and....."

I'm getting exasperated with him. I don't believe in god. "Be quiet a second. I need to speak. *So*, one of the crew said that I can tell you that the suspicion is her arm is broken in at least two places, and there is a really bad gash but not a break on one of her legs. She's bashed up but landed, on soft ground, literally inches from one of the shards of rock. They look kinda cool from up there, true, but not so great when you're up close and personal with them".

Dylan takes his head out of his hands and looks up at me. He's still hunched over and puts me in mind of a big garden gnome sans his fishing rod. I don't tell him this; it's not the best time.

"I'm sure you know that no one will know anything about the, erm, pregnancy until they can do more tests. I have my fingers crossed for you both..."

Dylan, still isn't talking but his body-language hints that he's listening. He's in shock but won't die of it. "She didn't know. No one did", he mutters "we gave up a long time ago".

His voice catches on the word time and without thinking I put my arm around him. He's not such a bad guy, he clearly loves her. If this is his Karma, it's done its job spectacularly. He'll never hurt her again. That's *if* he gets the chance.

"Now Dylan, here's the important bit. You're going to listen to me and listen properly". He nods. It's satisfying. People always do listen to the big tall muscly guy with Asperger's. I talk too much sense to be ignored.

"That woman loves you and hates *herself*. She needs you to get a grip of something other than a chubby blonde or whatever's inside those baggy denims you're wearing. She needs you to LISTEN to her and WATCH her and HEAR her. Above all she needs you to grow some honesty to go along with those balls, you've been so proud of flinging about. She's going to be ok it seems, and my guess is this is your last chance to prove she's not crazy, but you *certainly* are".

The man next to me is dried out and wrinkled with stress and fear. Maybe time to give him a bit of sugar with the sour. "I think you know what you've done wrong. Every line on your face tells me you know the script of what needs to be said when she wakes up".

He looks at me and for some reason, I hug him. He reminds me of my father, John; he was always up to no good too and only ever regretted it on his death bed as my mother sobbed into his cooling, blanket wrapped lap. "Well...too late to be sorry now", I said (all 20 years old and cocky) but instantly regretted it, as it was the last words he ever heard.

A fresh shower of rain hits us and we hunch together in unison, to throw over our hoods and run for the ropes that scale the cliff.

I'm certainly ready to leave this place. But I don't like flying. It makes no sense to me. It *terrifies* me actually. If humans were to fly, we'd have wings. But, today, I'll make an exception and get inside the damn thing without yelling my head off.

My fiancée Laura, always says I make too much of a fuss going on flights. She's going to laugh her slippers off, when I tell her about this last, few days. I could do with seeing her radiant smile, stroking her lovely soft hair and definitely, a cuddle in bed. A big plate of her Lasagne wouldn't go amiss, either.

Alice

Michael looks different; he's shrunk a little. Stubble's formed in patches on his face. In places that I've never seen it sprout before. He's bent over by the weight of fear. It's pressing his shoulders down and close together.

I can almost see long, oily, black wings, drooped and glistening behind him. Hear, dragging, sliding sound of them, as he slinks from room to room. The horrible sound, is echoing round my home and I'm glad I'm dead.

Its fully dark outside now. The baby-blue early evening sky, has slid away to leave the house in almost complete darkness. Serena doesn't need me just now and there are things to finish here. I know Michael well enough to grasp he's not just packing to leave; he's cleaning the house of evidence.

The laptop he seemed so in love with, is just visible under the dining table on the chair he favoured. It had a view of both the kitchen and living room, plus the bottom of the stairs. He liked being able to keep an eye on me when I was at home. I realise that now.

If I could race towards my Husband and kill him with my own living hands, I would. I've a different, *better idea,* though. I've read enough books, to have a decent catalogue of clever murder plans *myself,* Dear Husband!

Michael

Easy to set up shop again soon enough. Cash rich, freedom intact and a little more experience this time, it's certainly best to get out of here lickety-split. Far too messy, with *two* dead Wives now.

No more weddings for me! The tiresome paper trail, meddling solicitors and cumbersome friends and children, just ruin the beauty of my plans. I see that now.

Online Dating is all the rage these days, I hear. Fast track the seduction. Fast track the win. Move onto the next sex-mad, love-sick fool! Shorter sharper hits, quicker recovery times and less, *far less*, mess. That's the way, to do it!

Pockets of the house feel cold, every now and then. More than once, what sounds like a sigh, reaches my ears. The house settling as it cools perhaps, or a distant scratch of a falling leaf against a window. Yes, that's what it is, although it is making me very uncomfortable, even though I don't like to admit it. My fear at being caught by police far outweighs my fear of some sort of ghost or spirit or whatever!

The house always did feel cluttered and tonight, the chairs, sofas and irritating little tables feel like they are judging me. They gather around the many rooms of the house as if paused, watching and waiting for something to prevent me from leaving.

Pesky paranoia keeps creeping in and it's getting badly on my nerves. Greener grass and pastures new, beckon me!

"Don't get drawn in Mikey. Don't let her get to you", I mumble bending down to look under the sofa for my computer. "Damn laptop!", hissing and grunting, I hear my knees creak as I stand up to straighten my trousers and re-tuck in my shirt. "where can you be?!" Slowly turning, my eyes linger on the dining table where I think I last sat with the computer.

A small blue flickering light catches my eye, and yelping with satisfaction, I almost leap in the air. Yes! the laptop is almost hidden from sight, on my usual chair a few feet away. "Boom! Out of here in a Jiffy!", I yell and march forwards towards the table, which sits at the entrance to the conservatory. I'm already mentally flicking through a list of favourite hotels near the train station.

I won't bother cancelling the taxi. That's a good plan within a plan, having that little red herring and annoyed taxi-driver to rant at Police about my fake plans to go to the airport.

The keys in the glass doors rattle and I stop. I'm too far away to have caught them with my sleeve. They rattle again and I blink in confusion.

Cold air wraps itself around my neck and I realise the doors aren't quite shut fast. Stupid woman must not have locked the doors properly, when we left for the mountain the other day. She couldn't even do one last useful thing right.

Stepping forwards I reach for the handles, but they seem to bend out of the way. Frowning, I try again and they bend the other way. Grunting and not yet quite panicking, I reach out slowly with both hands to grasp at them. The handles fall to the floor as if broken. Now the door can't be shut tight and locked! "Bloody wind".

Hoisting my trousers up, I crouch to lift the handles off the floor. "Damn nuisance! Girls to do. Places to be". The handles are both ice cold. Frosted, even. Which is odd as it has been a warm day.

The glass has steamed up, in the short time I've been breathing on it. Wiping the condensation away, a streak of something pale and lithe darting across the lawn catches my attention.

It'll be those kids from next-door. Always getting into our garden. Whingeing and whining about lost footballs or trying to steal the cakes, Alice almost always had cooling on the kitchen window-ledge.

She'd laugh and say she left them there on purpose, because she liked to hear the children giggling about who had more icing or who dropped a cherry. She'd stand there waiting for all of the cakes to be eaten, before watching the children skip back over the wall.

The cake-game irritated me no end. More than once, I deliberately tipped them onto the decking and blamed it on the other neighbour's cat. Icing and sprinkles and chocolate chips, satisfyingly splattered on mossy wood; treats irretrievable and a good half hour to clean up.

Sweeping my sleeve across the glass again, I'm already looking away and back at the laptop. I really need to hurry up if I'm to catch a dinner in the hotel bar. I start to put the handles back into place, with no intention of screwing them in properly; no time and no point.

Two eyes are staring back at me. Two black eyes. Familiar eyes. My Wife's eyes but not my Wife's eyes. Alice is here! She's on the other side of the glass. No, she's *in* the glass!

Screaming and stepping backwards, I hit the table and the laptop falls to the floor. But I can't stop yelling. In the distance I hear her talking as though she's stood in the kitchen nearby and making conversation as she prepares my dinner; "Where are you off to darling? You're a busy chap!".

Chairs are knocked to the ground as I try and run backwards, still staring at my Wife in the glass. I trip and hit the floor backside-first. Turning, to crawl away, I catch my head painfully on a table leg.

The wind knocked out of me, I lie there with my belly up in the air. My shirt is untucked again and a shoe's fallen off. I'm panting and sobbing for the sanity, I think I've finally lost. She's finally done it. She's sent me crackers!

Twisting to a crawling position, I'm out of the kitchen on all fours and heading down the hall fast. The laptop can stay. I can't. I'd rather leave here empty handed and sane, than rich and dead!

Reaching up to the first rung of bannister, I hoist myself up onto my feet. I'm swearing and begging to be left alone, to get out of here in one piece.

The conservatory doors bang shut even though they were never open. I can hear foot-steps behind me. Dragging, sliding, slow footsteps! I kick my other shoe off to make it easier and start to run up the stairs. Stuff the house. Stuff her! "No no no no". I'm muttering in terror. "No no no. Leave me be! Leave me be Alice!"

Reaching the top step where Alice would sit, a pair of bare feet greet me. Dirty, grassy, muddy feet. Bluish white and almost translucent. My hair feels like it's being pulled to yank my head up. I can't turn away. A marionette, I'm forced to look up to my Wife as she looms above me.

There's a suffocating smell of mountain mud and I go cold all over. It's all in slow motion. Of course, it is. Just like you imagine it to be, when it all catches up with you.

I see Penny's face on the pillow next to mine. Smiling and reaching up to kiss me. I see Alice's face filled with joy, as I let her drive my sports-car for the first time. Her wedding-ring catching the sun, as she waves out of the window and disappears around the corner at the end of our road. I hear crying, moans of pain and begging. Faceless women from over the years. My *secret women*.

"Good bye Michael. We won't forget you". She doesn't speak, but the words appear in my head. Then a force like nothing I've ever felt, strikes my throat as she kicks me there, breaking my neck. Down I go hitting bannisters, steps and skirting over and over again, I don't even try to stop the fall; there's no point.

She's standing over me. I can feel the chill of her death. There's a wavelike crashing between my ears and I taste blood. My mouth is filled with it. The scent of bracken and wet grass fills the space between my eyes and a terrible sweeping black tar-like blanket of fear, starts to creep over me.

I can hear whispering. Harsh, eager, hungry voices. They twist and curl together like poison ivy on fast forward. I hear the crackling and snapping of invisible twigs and leaves and a brushing sound as the voices arrive together and surround me.

Then they start to touch me, gently probing then pulling and tugging then scratching and dragging. Their whispering is deafening. But I know Alice is still here, watching and waiting to make sure I'm really gone; all the way to Hell and never coming back.

The now broiling, sweltering air moves and turns as she steps over me. The whispering has stopped; they're waiting to take me. Their choice is now made.

I hear Alice's feet slide away to the unimaginable distance of the front door. The last sound I ever hear is her chiming laugh and then the door slamming.

Serena

Someone with cold hands is pulling at my clothes. A harsh light is pressing onto my face, almost burning my eyelids. Beeping and pipping and low voices, all clammering with each other- jostling to take control.

A man's crying. Sobbing and begging. It's annoying. He woke me up. Bloody inconsiderate. If it's him touching my leg right now, I'll remove his arm from the elbow socket before he can blink. Talking of blinking, I think I might have a go. I wish someone would turn the lights off.

"Mmmmmghhhhhhuuuurtsssss", is all I can manage but all the movement around me, stops. "huuuuurgghhhhhttssss", I try again and stretch what I think are my hands, towards where I think my belly is. It's all so confusing and awkward and bloody sore!

"She's waking up! She's waking up! Quick quick. Look look!" the man is yelling now. I think I know him. "Sir! Sir! Oh my god Sir! Can you open your eyes!" I do know the man, its.... whatsisname.... Darren, no I dated him when I was 12, I don't think I'm 12. Declan....no......Dylan!"

Jerking with satisfaction, in an attempt to congratulate myself, I bring about a whole new tidal wave of agony and buck. The urge to be sick sends me into a panic.

There's a mask thing on my face- I need it off. I'm going to be sick. I can taste the acid, feel the sweat of impending retching, and the burning in my gullet makes me want to cry.

Magically, a hand cups my forehead, a gently lifts the mask from my face. It makes an unpleasant sucking sound as it releases from my jaw and cheeks, but the fresher air is beautiful. Then he kisses me. The rise and fall of memories takes my breath away.

Dylan's shining eyes slowly closing as he kisses me at the church altar. Sun beams blinding me as he leans forward and frees the light from the stained glass hidden behind his shoulders. Sand and salt and something icy, as our lips meet on a beach holiday, we took too many years ago. The musk of sweat and my own sweet taste as we meet each other again under pale blue sheets and greedily tug ourselves together. Sticking like Velcro- never to be separated.

"Serena. You need to wake up. They need to ask you some questions about the pain. Can you talk?" My Husband's voice is high, scratched and broken. He's being a bit formal too. I wonder if he's been yelling more than crying. He sounds broken and only held together by strands woven of desperation.

Then I remember the pain. The burning, drilling, stretching pain down there makes sense now. I should have remembered that's exactly what it feels like. To lose a baby is so familiar now, it's just another secret family recipe, except we don't have any family.

"Let her sleep. She's still experiencing a lot of pain. I'm going to give her some morphine. We don't need her to be awake just now. Not if it hurts her. I can do a blood test to check for a pregnancy, as fast as ya like". A chirpy womans voice this time.

She has a soft, Welsh accent. I like her voice; she sounds happy and organised. I bet she's a good singer. Yes, she's in a choir. A big one like you see on TV. The Singer-Lady's fades away.

Here comes the blackness again. I drift away on a warm, calm sea towards a quiet place, without so many noises and voices and cruel lights.

Dexter

I'm not one for interfering. I like to stay in my own lane for sure. Serena didn't know I'd done a little research, well more research than I let on, before we met at the foot of The Notch.

My main motives for being unusually secretive (not a natural trait for me- I get anxious) was to protect Dylan, then when I realised it was his Wife not him, I was extra cautious about making sure she knew only what she needed to. I knew Michael Jennings was rotten. Stinking, rancid, rotten.

When Michael was interviewed the day after Alice died, he set off some red flags. They in turn alerted *me*.

The 2nd name *Jennings* had me straight away. I knew him as the main suspect in "The Beater Case". A cold case, I've never really let go. Both officers felt something "off", about Michaels lack of empathy and appropriate emotion when he spoke with them, so they did a bit of digging.

Luckily, my name was mentioned a few times in the files and Laura is still with the police, so knowing I never really let the case go, she asked permission then texted me as soon as she heard the rumours; The Beater was back.

Michael Jennings first came up on my radar as part of a crime writing project I was on, many years ago. Eager to establish some experience, I took an assignment from a local paper, to observe officers in vice. There had been rumours of a spate of violent attacks during "Escort-Client Meets". One woman, the most recent, had a broken nose and wrist from the brutality, and had been violently raped.

It shocked us that even though she had engaged in consensual sex with her attacker in the past as part of her work, he chose to violate her this time. So far, no actual murders had taken place. Little did we know, how huge the whole thing was going to get.

The working girls involved were understandably keen to avoid too much time with Police, as they didn't want to appear to be "grasses". Nor miss out on any income by making enemies of clients, who were typically keen to remain private. Any sniff of a cop and the earnings dried up. Plus, one of the women was a mother and knowing "The System", she knew any attention on her own work and safety, would drag her back into the risk assessment process with Children's Services.

This was the worst nightmare for any prostitute, irrelevant of her status or income. "Kids over Cash" was a saying I heard more than enough times-sad but oddly comforting.

With my ex-special forces experience, and new blood-thirst for writing about the darker crevices of society, I was tentatively welcomed in to the project- cleverly called "Operation Echo".

Anyone with a little Greek Lit or Psych knowledge knows Echo was the adoring, addicted, Nymph who gave her love then life to the arrogant, neglectful womaniser, Narcissus. I also rather liked the Echo concept, as it mirrored these women and their repeated whispers of warning to each other. For once, gossip was *good*.

For weeks then months we checked car registrations, appearance descriptions and circumstances between the beaten women. Leads sparked hot then fell cold and the officer numbers rose and fell like wasted breaths against a windscreen, then we got lucky.

We noted shocking and important commonalities; the bastards taste of giving out beatings particularly focused on the victims' faces and backs. A bag he carried. The preference for white or cream coloured lingerie. The "old fashioned medium blue car".

It tickled my antennae that the rape was a change in M.O and I wondered if this meant something had changed. The Beater had even given this latest victim a tip. An extra £20 note on the pile of money, that looked strangely like a flower. To me it seemed almost a gentlemanly act. A thank you. But what had triggered him and made him more violent and braver?

Cornering the local forensic psychologist on her way back to her car, as she was leaving to go home, annoyed her. But she gave me enough of her time, to change the course of the investigation abruptly.

* * * *

Dr Corinne Baker has short dark hair, cut boyishly. She has a dramatically attractive face, is tall and to be honest, could be a model. Alongside her looks, she is smart and grave. All of this adds up to her having every heterosexual guy in the entire station, *all worked up*. Her smile is rare but worth the wait.

She gives me the time of day because she gets none of that vibe from me. I met a brilliant girl called Laura recently and rarely stop talking about her.

"Corinne! One, maybe two, maybe three minutes!? Please?!" I'm running after her through the station car-park. Those damn long legs! She should be a runner, not a forensic psychologist. "Go on then. But I have a not-so-hot date and it won't microwave itself", she says turning around to face me.

"It's a good job there's no cops around as the stampede would have me on my arse", I joke, more than a little out of breath. She laughs and I know I've just bought myself some of her precious time.

"I'm guessing it's about the vice case? The one with the prostitutes?". She leans against her car but jumps away when the metal scalds her bare wrists. "Bloody sore!" she exclaims but the irony isn't lost on us both. She starts to talk without me even asking her to.

"The Beater is a sadist with high-level narcissistic personality disorder traits. As a sexually disordered individual, he plans his attacks and chooses his victims with both arousal and care. He feels no remorse before or after his appointments with the women and sees no purpose in killing them as they provide a function to him. This to him is pure power and pleasure. He is over confident but single-minded, which may make him sloppy soon enough. With this escalation of violence, seemingly out of nowhere, I would predict something has set his anxiety, and therefore rage, off. Something has going or has gone wrong for him in an otherwise very ordered life".

Corinne's eyes are lit up in excitement but she keeps glancing at the food-shopping bag at her feet. She's hungry and I'm running out of time.

"One more minute, please Corinne?" I clasp my hands in front of my chest and she smiles again and nods. "Right, so it's how he rationalises the brutality- by paying for it?" My eyes wander to the windows of the office we've borrowed from a different team. Pressure is on for us to get results or they shut us down. My new best friend is talking again.

"Is he married? Yes, most likely. I heard that the victims describe a forty-something, well-spoken chap? Well these Narcy types get through life with an outward show of respectability and charm. So, a partner *and or* job is essential cover for them".

She's getting in her car now and I watch as she throws her bags onto the passenger seat. As she puts the key in the ignition, a last thought comes to me. "Ok. So, something's happened at home or work?"

Writing notes frantically, I'm already considering new search parameters for The Beater that I can suggest to the few police officers, who do listen to my theories. "Go on. Please. Keep going", I urge her.

My first plan is to get the extremely bored cops working around me, to look for medium blue cars owned by women. "one more minute! You are really helping!" I smile winningly at her.

She sighs but doesn't turn the engine on. "The hate he uses to target his brutality is built on a need for control and punishment. He vents his anger this way. Irrational anger, mind you. To him he is owed what he does, and is entitled to do as he likes, to feel less weak or maybe, less *imprisoned*. Yes, look there, look what has changed at *home*! Now I am starving and I start early tomorrow! So good bye Mr Shore!". I can hear her laughing as she drives out of the car-park and do a little skip of happiness; now I have a few good ideas!

* * * * *

My colleagues were irritated and slightly baffled, by my annoying habit of looking for tiny details, rather than evidence, so agreed to let me try a method they weren't keen on. The deal was they got me the list of female car drivers I wanted and I got to go mad on social media.

A few hours later they presented me with a list of 23 women who owned a mid-blue car and lived near enough to the areas, where most of the beatings took place. As they worked their way, I worked mine.

I started a simple but methodical, social media search on each woman. I had no idea what exactly I was looking for, but instinct told me to keep this going.

Several hours later with a sore back and a sugar-low and getting rather fed up of with dog pictures, dinner pics and new-haircut-selfies, I almost missed it. Crossing each car owner off as just not *feeling right*, the lightning struck.

"My Sister, Mrs Penelope (Penny) Jennings, tragically passed away last week. Her workplace will be less bright, her home less happy and all our lives less bountiful with her passing. Penny leaves her Husband Martin, myself and my son all absolutely broken. Her work in pharmaceuticals will be carried on with the team she also leaves, totally devastated. May she rest in peace. I'm closing this account the day after her funeral, as looking at it, is absolutely driving me crazy. The funeral is tomorrow......" My eye's blurred in excitement and I didn't need to read any more.

This was it! His Wife! Either he's bereft at her passing and has escalated his beatings during his crimes or he popped her off! Oh my god!

The investigation lit up like a surprise party all at once. Two token coppers jerking out of post lunch carb comas, the dozen phones ringing like a kicked hive of bees and a new plan to gain a search warrant for The Beaters home, created a dizzying whirlwind, lifting us all up and spinning us back into direction. Our hope was to find at least his abuse-kit (described as a black and blue bag) and ideally also him.

No matter how fast we moved, we weren't fast enough. The next day we attempted a dawn raid on the home where Penny died and where we were convinced The Beater would be.

We were too late. He'd packed up and gone. With no Wife to hold him back and the distress at her sudden heart attack combined in scribbled letters on his note in the kitchen, The Beater had fled. He had apparently moved abroad; to France.

The last one to leave the empty, echoey house, I readied myself to trail after the hunched almost tearful tribe of officers trudging their way back to the half a dozen cars clustered on the lane, at the end of the long, grand, driveway.

Before leaving, I snatched a photograph of Penny and her Husband, off the television stand. Her pretty, beaming face and his stubbled, smug, well fed grin, have remained folded up inside my wallet for the last dozen years. Mr Martin Michael Jennings had been cleverer than the Police for a long time indeed.

Serena

There's sand everywhere. Around my feet, up to my ankles. Little bags of it pressing down on my eyes, granules catching and sticking my eye-lashes together. It's even in my throat and trying to open my mouth to speak feels impossible.

Perhaps I'm on the beach, from before again. I've fallen asleep there and the sun's bouncing off the sand, blinding me and scorching the air around me. It's warm and bright but I feel stuck. I can't be on a beach...maybe I'm dead?!

Trying to wiggle my fingers is a little more successful than the other movements I tried, and I can hear paper rustling.

"Sir! Sir! Can you hear me? Look she's moving her hands! She's waking up!" It's that idiot Dylan with his stupid, new, high-pitched voice again.

"Hhhhhhhhhmmmf". No matter how hard I try, it's not coming out right. Who decided that "idiot" should have so many syllables in!?

"Sir don't move too much. Stop bloody trying to speak! The meds are still making you really groggy! You've been asleep for a few days. Well, in a coma type thing, not asleep. When they found out you were definitely pregnant, they helped you have a proper long rest so they could check you out fully. We had to look at your brain, spine, and all sorts!" His voice has gone up even more, he sounds a bit nuts! "and apparently, it also helps your body start to recover too"

Typical of Dylan to ruin the surprise and shout it all over the place and not wait for me to wake up and enjoy it properly. I'm so cross, mind you….these drugs are goooooood. A shock of light startles me and makes me do what I think is a wince.

My mouth suddenly feels cool and wet. Dylan's gently touching my face with a beautifully cold, damp cloth. I might forgive him after all, just because he did *that*. The rustling sound again has me more interested now. Probably a doctor or someone scribbling on my notes.

"Sir if you can try and move your good arm, or at least turn your head, there's a surprise for you". My goodness! He's persistent. Doesn't he know I fell off a fucking mountain?!

Moving isn't as painful as I expected this time. Bless the medical profession and their magic beans!

It's blurry then comes into focus. A little black and white drawing. That's confusing. Blinking once, twice, the little drawing gets finer and blooms into an image. It's not a drawing, it's a baby. A scan of a baby. My baby?!

The tubes around my wrist are catching on the bed-clothes and confusing my coordination. In frustration I shake them and try to make it easier to lift the picture closer. I can hear Dylan crying yet again, but I'm not angry anymore.

The ghostly image is bigger than the last few times. Bigger than the others. I can see eyes, the tiny outline of hands and even skinny folded up legs. This one's made it to…… 13 weeks nearly 14?! It's made it? No, it can't have done. I fell. I felt dead. I was dead. The cold, blackness and then those lights.

He's given me a scan of another baby we lost. How cruel. "Hhhhmmffdead"

"No. No. Sir. Please stop crying. Stop! The baby isn't dead. It's right there. Still with you. With us. We're just past 13 weeks. A record for us!" He wipes my face of hot salty snotty tears, with his sleeve. I'm trying to work out how this happened. My brain won't sort itself in to order but Dylan is helping.

"Do you remember the Valentines fundraiser party thing we went to? The one where you got pissed, and danced like a plastered-plonker and talked to everyone, like twice!? And then you told me loads you hated me......and then.... well.... *you know*...." For goodness sakes! My Husband's embarrassed, but I can hear the grin.

"Idiot", I manage. Muscle memory rather than skill. He laughs and kisses me on both cheeks, cupping my mouth shut and kisses me there. "Idiot", I manage again but he swallows it with his lips and interrupts me.

"Yes, I'm an idiot. Can we be idiots together and do our best to avoid making another mess of things....there's things you don't know about the....situation....with Owen, Serena. It's not what you think. We really need to talk.....properly".

Closing my fist around the picture of the little none-ghost-baby, I squeeze so tight it hurts. I fall asleep with it in my hand and wake up, what feels like a few hours later.

My mouth isn't as dry and I feel less foggy. Dylan's nowhere to be seen and I feel relieved. I like the peace and quiet. I can lie here and think about my baby.

"You look a lot better!" the singer-lady's back. Of course, she's a Nurse but she likes singing better.

Secretly she wants to be a pop-star. The idea blossoms in my head and makes me smile. "More cheerful too", she whispers as she lifts me to a sitting position and gently makes sure my arm cast is resting on a pillow in front of me. Someone has drawn flowers on it. A Take-That logo and a smiley face too.

"You like singing", I say clearly, even though my voice is hoarse. Startled, she pulls away from me, frowns then grins.

"Ah. It's true then?" she chuckles. Dylan's been blabbing. Dexter too, most likely. Those two are going to be trouble together.

"Now I know why it's been so intense. So.... easy", I croak, as she sits on the bed. Her name badge says "Robin". "Yes. I've heard psychic energy gets stronger with surges in hormones. All baby Jones's fault!" she laughs again, louder.

I want to smile widely, properly, show teeth, but my lips are a bit cracked. She hands me a cup of water and I drink greedily.

"It's pretty cool having "The Gift", and you have some real fans as a result!" Nurse Robin, stands up and walks over to open the door to a row of faces I recognise. All of which I love, whether I like it or not.

<u>2 weeks since I died.</u>

Alice

I know, It's not exactly angelic to have killed off my Rotten-Tomato-Husband, but let's face it, I didn't apply for the job of perfect dead Wife or really, *any roles* as dead Wife, thanks!

Clearly, I was left here or shall we suggest, "gently encouraged" to hang about, for a purpose.

The urge to look after Serena's gone for now- the feeling she's in safe hands and on a new journey without me, is lovely. Like lying in a field amongst wild-flowers and listening to music while the sun warms my skin.

You know? I think I can hear a baby laughing too. The most beautiful sound in the world. If I could, I'd squirm with delight. Serena's finally got what she wanted. No, what she *needed*. And at the right time too. I don't think we will be apart for long, there's something special between Serena and I.

Was my purpose here, to dissolve my Husband's mental capacity by means of a rather extreme haunting over a few days? Was it ok to then launch his big fat arse down the stairs? It's up to you. All I know is the world around me feels lighter, brighter and a touch softer now he's gone. So much happened and now it's all neat and tidy and as it should be.

Even the main door to the building that Charmaine lives in, is a happier shade. It's gone from dark grey to a bright fuchsia pink. There are hanging baskets there now too. Some bright red Dahlia's and fat yellow tulips and, I think I can even see a little purple snap-dragon bravely peeking out.

Simon is holding my hand and looking towards the door too. He came to me once I left the house.

"So, you finally left him then", he said, sat on the garden wall, bathed in sunlight but transparent all the same. I smiled and leaning down to kiss him, whispered, "You could say that".

So, we are together again and this time *forever*. "We're going to be dead happy", he whispered into my hair, kissed my neck and took my hand. We laughed together all the way down the road away from my house and Michaels fast cooling corpse.

Oh, and what of the contents of the bag? The one Michael was so desperate for? The police took that, but not before we took the cash out. Michael won't need money where he's gone. Charmaine however, should have the money he stole from me over the years. A good twenty grand he managed to hide away. *The rodent he was!*

Simon and I arranged for Serena to put the money in a wee paper-bag and come here. She left the paper-bag on Charmaine's door-mat a few minutes ago. Serena waved to us and turned away, waddling slightly although barely showing.

She's enjoying the feeling of being pregnant more than most. The cast on her arm will be off long before the baby's born and yes, it is a little girl.

"Oh, look!" I nudge Simon and he squeezes my waist and stretches his neck to see what I'm looking at.

From our bench, across the street, we can see Charmaine opening her door a crack. We watch as she peers out, bends down, wincing in pain, and carefully opens the paper-bag as though it were a bomb! She closes it fast, crushing the bag. Then opens it again and looks inside exactly the same as before, but deeper. Her face almost disappears inside! Simon chuckles and I nudge him again. "Wait for it. She might not take it!"

Simon and I drift upwards and raise our faces to the sun in relief, as The Beaters last victim, smiles the biggest smile on Earth and holds the bag close to her chest then disappears inside.

Chapter 10: Comeuppance

Excerpt from The Cardiff Voice: May 2017

Alice Marie Jennings died in tragic and unusual circumstances, on the infamous Tryfan Notch but the news story did not.

Various reports at the time described her as a skilled mountain-walker and regular to the area, along with her Husband Michael.

Alice, loved her work as Head Librarian at Saint Barnabus University, and loved books and the outdoors, "almost more than anything", according to her beloved nieces and nephew.

On closer inspection, the team here at *Star and Shore News Agency*, felt something wasn't quite "right" with how a pleasant hike in the mountains ended so terribly.

Our own tentative research then deeper, investigations threw up that Alice preferred walking to hiking, had poor eyesight and actually planned to leave her Husband at one point. Michael, Alice's play-boy, happy go lucky Husband was not what he seemed. But then again, neither was Alice.

Our sources claim that Alice had an intense and passionate love affair with master of words himself, Psychologist and Best-Selling Author, Dr Simon Masters. We can't say much right now, regarding Mr Master's own death as police investigations are continuing.

His remains were found by a dog-walker, at a beauty spot, in a location a short drive from a village in Northumbria, that Alice and Michael had stayed in, the Christmas before her death.

Although Michael himself passed away a few days after his Wife, the police were already tipped off by an unnamed source that there would be evidence in the house that linked, and eventually identified him, as the person responsible for the many attacks on women in cold case, Operation Echo.

The case where a man, had badly beaten and occasionally violently raped women he booked as Escorts.

Investigation's also are now linking him to the death of his first Wife, Penelope Jennings who died around the same time the Beaters crimes against women in her local area, stopped. Police are currently seeking more attack victims, who believe they were booked by The Beater, here in Wales.

Mr Jennings had suffered from ill health for a short time and had even presented to A and E with what appeared to be fainting spells, shortly after his Wife passed away. Neighbours and a local shop owner also disclosed he seemed "out of sorts". Mr Kendal the couple's solicitor, also advised police that he noted Mr Jennings seemed anxious, stressed and often sweated profusely, and once acted as though in pain. We spoke with the local pub land-lord, who described Jennings as a "greedy drinker", "ladies' man" and apparently had recently had a bad fall in the pub.

Michael Jennings untimely death was recently deemed to be caused by a fall down the stairs in his late Wife's home. Police reports and ambulance staff said from the look of the scene, it appears he had been frantically rushing around and tripped in his haste to leave the city and start again. Start what? We can only surmise. Jennings' body lay for some time as neighbours had been told to stay away and not visit. He was identified by dental records.

We would like to thank Alice's and Simon's friends and family for supporting our investigations. Stay tuned for more of our stories and work unearthing mysterious deaths.

Dexter Shore and Serena Jones: *Star and Shore News Agency, Cardiff.*

Authors' Note

Thank you for buying *The Notch*! I hope you enjoyed reading it as much as I enjoyed writing it. It is VERY different to my 1st book (a mini memoir) about domestic abuse and Casanova Psychopaths, that's for sure! That 1st book is my diary of domestic and narcissistic abuse spanning 2013 to 2016.

Alongside my story of what happened to me, are nearly 100 red flag sections that explain the abuse behaviours and the reasons for them. That book "Dangerous Normal People. Understanding Casanova Psychopaths and The Narcissistic Virus" is still on sale.

After reading The Notch you may now have an interest in how people like "Murderous Michael" behave in more detail. If so, then please do buy and review it!

I like the idea of taking the "Star and Shore News/Investigations Agency" forward into a series.

I'm still playing with the name of the type of agency though! This lovely, random, group of Serena, Alice, Dexter, Ceris, Robin, Saffron, Simon, (and maybe a few others!) all working together on cases of death's that remain unsolved and of course were *cruel and unusual*, really has the creative juices flowing!

Tell me who your favourite characters are so far!? Oh, and I think a Stags Head could be a fab logo concept for their company!

While the ideas come quick and fast, I aim to write a book every 9 months. Here's a taster of the some on the way!

I am madly in love with "The Forgivers Club", my next book about media witch hunts, stalking, trolling and small-town vigilantes.

The Forgivers Club features a new character of mine, Lola. She escapes an abusive partner and his crazy side-piece, to move to Bridgefell, a fictional coastal village, in Cornwall, where she settles in relative peace but not for long!

Lola has many (many!) flaws and struggles to manage her Demon's. She makes friends but are they all to be trusted? She commits a crime, but should she die for it? She attracts plenty of male attention, but is any of it decent? She is stalked and harassed by a woman she helped, but when will it stop?

So many choices, so many consequences and in the end, someone has to die but who will it be? Who will confess all, at *The Forgivers Club*?

Hopefully this will be released (as a sort of follow on from my 1st book) on or around the 1st November 2020.

2021 will have at least one publication, maybe two. To start off, I have a story sketched out, about a sexy, ambitious Grifter called Ruby.

She finds a whole new lease of (naughty!) life when the spirit of the Greek nymph Echo, takes over her body after a gang rape and near-death experience. Ruby had been travelling with her (useless) boyfriend, in the Greek islands, before she completely changes her personality and life.

Yes, possessed by Echos' spirit, Ruby changes from a shy, needy and mousy girl, to a seductive, smart and vengeful professional.

She's a fantastic character to write! She has the makings of a very likeable female protagonist for sure! This book "Echos' Revenge" (title may change) should be out in Summer 2021.

If you enjoyed this book and have genuine authentic feedback as a reader, please do leave me a proper written review on Amazon or any other site you purchased the book from. You can get in touch with me, via my website

www.thenarcissisthunter.co.uk.

The End- perhaps.

About The Author: L.W. Hawksby

The Boring Bit;

Hello book lovers! My name is Lucy Haughey and I write as L.W Hawksby for now. I am a Scottish author based in Glasgow.

Raised on The Island of Mull by my eco-entrepreneur parents, I came to live in Glasgow in my late teens for a wider choice of careers.

Attracted to the idea of helping people via educational endeavours such as training and public speaking, I worked and volunteered during the day and studied at night, to gain 3 Diploma's in Mental Health and Social Care. What followed was a varied career in The Charity Sector.

But I made some poor relationship choices with partners and friends. So by 2016 I was mentally ill and unemployable due to three criminal convictions.

I followed a gut instinct to write my story down and caught the writing bug! I now focus on writing books that explore criminal behaviour in who I call, "Dangerous Normal People" (the title of my first book about Narcissistic Abuse). I want to help people understand and avoid similar bad paths to mine. There's plenty of those I can tell you!

The Nosey Bit;

When I'm not writing (which isn't often!) I am found in my kitchen on the window seat reading a book or sketching and sipping horrendously strong black coffee. I can also be spotted pottering in my garden enjoying the sunshine (yes folks it does happen in Scotland!) with a gin and lychee cocktail. I am a serious foodie and have won a few cookery and recipe competitions. I am blessed to have three lovely children and three brilliant Staffordshire Bull Terriers.

The Spooky Bit;

As an Empath, Cancerian Decan 2, "1980 Golden Monkey", with rare A neg blood, I can't help but be fascinated by The Paranormal and associated theology. I am unashamedly a weird wild and wistful creature who reads Tarot Cards and far too often, have little spikes in psychic ability. I thoroughly enjoy being a writer and mother.

A percentage of income from my books, is donated to charity every year on the 31st of October, the favourite festival of my youngest son Rufus, who has Asperger's. For more info on me as an author and my projects, go to www.thenarcissis thunter.co.uk